MEMORY'S LEGION

By James S. A. Corey

THE EXPANSE
Leviathan Wakes
Caliban's War
Abaddon's Gate
Cibola Burn
Nemesis Games
Babylon's Ashes
Persepolis Rising
Tiamat's Wrath
Leviathan Falls

Memory's Legion:
The Complete Expanse Story Collection

THE EXPANSE SHORT FICTION
Drive
The Butcher of Anderson Station
Gods of Risk
The Churn
The Vital Abyss
Strange Dogs
Auberon
The Sins of Our Fathers

MEMORY'S LEGION

THE COMPLETE EXPANSE STORY COLLECTION

JAMES S. A. COREY

orbit

orbitbooks.net

Copyright © 2022 by Daniel Abraham and Ty Franck
"Drive" copyright © 2012 by Daniel Abraham and Ty Frank; first published in
   Edge of Infinity, ed. by Jonathan Strahan © 2012
The Butcher of Anderson Station copyright © 2011 by James S. A. Corey
Gods of Risk copyright © 2012 by James S. A. Corey
The Churn copyright © 2014 by James S. A. Corey
The Vital Abyss copyright © 2015 by Daniel Abraham and Ty Franck
Strange Dogs copyright © 2017 by Daniel Abraham and Ty Franck
Auberon copyright © 2019 by Daniel Abraham and Ty Franck
"The Sins of Our Fathers" copyright © 2022 by Daniel Abraham and Ty Franck

Cover design by Lauren Panepinto and Kirk Benshoff
Cover illustration by Daniel Dociu
Cover copyright © 2022 by Hachette Book Group, Inc.

Orbit
Hachette Book Group
1290 Avenue of the Americas
New York, NY 10104
orbitbooks.net

First Edition: March 2022
Simultaneously published in Great Britain by Orbit

Orbit is an imprint of Hachette Book Group.
The Orbit name and logo are trademarks of Little, Brown Book Group Limited.

The Hachette Speakers Bureau provides a wide range of authors for speaking events. To find out more, go to www.hachettespeakersbureau.com or call (866) 376-6591.

Library of Congress Control Number: 2021949465

ISBNs: 9780316669191 (hardcover), 9780316426619 (BarnesAndNoble.com signed edition), 9780316669146 (ebook)

Printed in the United States of America

LSC-C

Printing 1, 2021

To the next generation of science fiction writers, and the one after them, and the one after them.
Keep it going, folks.

Contents

MEMORY'S LEGION

Drive

Acceleration throws Solomon back into the captain's chair, then presses his chest like a weight. His right hand lands on his belly, his left falls onto the upholstery beside his ear. His ankles press back against the leg rests. The shock is a blow, an assault. His brain is the product of millions of years of primate evolution, and it isn't prepared for this. It decides that he's being attacked, and then that he's falling, and then that he's had some kind of terrible dream. The yacht isn't the product of evolution. Its alarms trigger in a strictly informational way. By the way, we're accelerating at four gravities. Five. Six. Seven. More than seven. In the exterior camera feed, Phobos darts past, and then there is only the star field, as seemingly unchanging as a still image.

It takes almost a full minute to understand what's happened, then he tries to grin. His laboring heart labors a little harder with elation.

The interior of the yacht is cream and orange. The control panel is a simple touchscreen model, old enough that the surface has started going gray at the corners. It's not pretty, but it is functional. Solid. An alert pops up that the water recycler has gone off-line. Solomon's not surprised—he's outside the design specs—and he starts guessing where exactly the system failed. His guess, given that all the thrust is along the primary axis of the ship, is the reservoir back-flow valve, but he's looking forward to checking it when the run is finished. He tries to move his hand, but the weight of it astounds him. A human hand weighs something like three hundred grams. At seven g, that's still only a little over two thousand. He should still be able to move it. He pushes his arm toward the control panel, muscles trembling. He wonders how much above seven he's going. Since the sensors are pegged, he'll have to figure it out when the run is over. How long the burn lasted and whatever his final velocity winds up being. Simple math. Kids could do it. He's not worried. He reaches for the control panel, really pushing it this time, and something wet and painful happens in his elbow.

Oops, he thinks. He wants to grit his teeth, but that's no more effective than grinning had been. This is going to be embarrassing. If he can't shut off the drive, he'll have to wait until the fuel runs out and then call for help. That might be problematic. Depending on how fast he's accelerating, the rescue ship's burn will have to be a very long one compared with his own. Maybe twice as long. They may need some sort of long-range craft to come get him. The fuel supply readout is a small number on the lower left side of the panel, green against black. It's hard to focus on it. Acceleration is pressing his eyeballs out of their right shape. High tech astigmatism. He squints. The yacht is built for long burns, and he started with the ejection tanks at ninety percent. The readout now shows the burn at ten minutes. The fuel supply ticks down to eighty-nine point six. That can't be right.

Two minutes later, it drops to point five. Two and a half minutes later, point four. That puts the burn at over thirty-seven hours and the final velocity at something just under five percent of c.

Solomon starts getting nervous.

He met her ten years before. The research center at Dhanbad Nova was one of the largest on Mars. Three generations after the first colonists dug into the rock and soil of humanity's second home, progress had pushed the envelope of human science, understanding, and culture so far that the underground city could support five bars, even if one of them was the alcohol-free honky-tonk where the Jainists and born-again Christians hung out. The other four sold alcohol and food that was exactly the same as the stuff they sold at the commissary, only with piped-in music and a wall monitor with an entertainment feed from Earth playing on it all hours of the day and night. Solomon and his cadre met up at this one two or three times a week when the work load at the center wasn't too heavy.

Usually the group was some assortment of the same dozen people. Today it was Tori and Raj from the water reclamation project. Voltaire whose real name was Edith. Julio and Carl and Malik who all worked together on anti-cancer therapies. And Solomon. Mars, they said, was the biggest small town in the solar system. There was almost never anyone new.

There was someone new. She sat beside Malik, had dark hair and a patient expression. Her face was a little too sharp to be classically beautiful, and the hair on her forearms was dark. She had the kind of genetics that developed a little mustache problem when she hit about thirty-five. Solomon didn't believe in love at first sight, but as soon as he sat down at the table, he was profoundly aware that he hadn't brushed his hair very effectively that morning and he was wearing the shirt with the sleeves a little too long.

"Mars *is* America," Tori said, waving his beer expansively. "It's exactly the same."

"It's not America," Malik said.

"Not like it was at the end. Like the beginning. Look at how long it took to travel from Europe to North America in the 1500s. Two months. How long to get here from Earth? Four. Longer if the orbits are right."

"Which is the first way in which it's not like America," Malik said, dryly.

"It's within an order of magnitude," Tori said. "My point is that politically speaking, distance is measured in time. We're months away from Earth. They're still thinking about us like we're some kind of lost colony. Like we answer to them. How many people here, just at this table have had directives from someone who's never been outside a gravity well but still felt like they should tell us where our research should go?"

Tori raised his own hand, and Raj followed suit. Voltaire. Carl. Reluctantly, Malik. Tori's grin was smug.

"Who's doing the real science in the system?" Tori said. "That's us. Our ships are newer and better. Our environmental science is at least a decade ahead of anything they've got on Earth. Last year, we hit self-sustaining."

"I don't believe that," Voltaire said. The new one still hadn't spoken, but Solomon watched her attention shift to each new speaker. He watched her listen.

"Even if there are a few things we still need from Earth, we can trade for them. Shit, give us a few years and we'll be mining them out of the Belt," Tori said, backing away from his last point and making a new, equally unlikely assertion at the same time. "It's not like I'm saying we should cut off all diplomatic relations."

"No," Malik said. "You're saying we should declare political independence."

"Damn skippy, I am," Tori said. "Because distance is measured in time."

"And coherence is measured in beer," Voltaire said, the cadence of her voice matching Tori's perfectly. The new woman smiled at the mimicry.

"Even if we decided that all we had to lose was our chains," Malik said, "why would we bother? We are already *de facto* our own government. Pointing out the fact is only going to stir up trouble."

"Do you really think Earth hasn't noticed?" Tori said. "You think the kids back at the labs on Luna and Sao Paulo aren't looking up at the sky and saying *That little red dot is kicking our asses*? They're jealous and they're scared and they should be. It's all I'm saying. If we do our own thing, the earliest they could do something about it still gives us months of lead time. England lost its colonies because you can't maintain control with a sixty-day latency, much less a hundred and twenty."

"Well," said Voltaire drily, "that and the French."

"And good damn thing, too," Tori said as if she hadn't spoken. "Because who was it that came in when the Nazis started knocking on England's door? Am I right?"

"Um," Solomon said, "no, actually. You just made the other point. We're really the Germans."

And because he spoke, the new woman's gaze turned to him. He felt his throat go tight and sipped his beer to try to loosen up. If he spoke now, his voice would crack like he was fourteen again. Voltaire put her elbows on the table, cradled her chin in her dark hands, and hoisted her eyebrows. Her expression could have had *This should be good* as the caption.

"Okay," Malik said, abandoning his disagreement with Tori. "I'll bite. In what ways are we like a murderous bunch of fascists?"

"By-by how we'd fight," Solomon said. "Germany had all the best science, just like us. They had the best tech. They had rockets. No one had rockets, but they did. Nazi tanks could destroy allied tanks at something like five to one. They had the best attack submarines, drone missiles, early jet aircraft. They were just that much better. Better designed, better manufactured. They were elegant and they were smart."

"Apart from the whole racial cleansing genocide thing," Julio said.

"Apart from that," Solomon agreed. "But they lost. They had all the best tech, just like we do. And they lost."

"Because they were psychopathic and insane," Julio said.

"No," Solomon said. "I mean, they were, but there have been a lot of fascist psychopaths that *didn't* lose wars. They lost because even though one of their tanks was worth five of the other guy's, America could build ten. The industrial base was huge, and if the design wasn't as good, who cared? Earth has that industrial base. They have people. It could take them months, maybe years, to get here, but when they did, it would be in numbers we couldn't handle. Being technically advanced is great, but we're still just building better ones of the stuff that came before. If you want to overcome the kind of demographic advantage Earth has, you'll need something paradigm-shiftingly new."

Voltaire raised her hand. "I nominate *paradigm-shiftingly* as the adverb of the night."

"Seconded," Julio said. Solomon felt the blush creeping up his neck.

"All in favor?" There was a small chorus. "The ayes have it," Voltaire said. "Someone buy this man another drink."

The conversation moved on, the way it always did. Politics and history gave way to art and fine-structure engineering. The great debate of the night was over whether artificial muscles worked better with the nanotubules in sheets or bundles, with both sides descending in the end to name-calling. Most of it was good-natured, and what wasn't pretended to be, which was almost the same. The wall monitor switched over to an all-music feed out of a little community on Syria Planum, the wailing and brass of rai juxtaposed with classical European strings. It was some of Solomon's favorite music because it was dense and intellectually complicated and he wasn't expected to dance to it. He wound up spending half the night sitting beside Carl talking about ejection efficiency systems and trying not to stare at the new woman. When she moved from Malik's side to sit next to Voltaire, his heart leaped—maybe she wasn't here with Malik—and then sank—maybe she was a lesbian. He felt like he'd dropped a decade off his life and was suddenly stuck in the hormonal torture chamber of the lower university. He made up his mind to forget that the new woman existed. If she was new to the research center, there would be time to find out who she was and plan a way to speak with her that didn't make him look desperate and lonely. And if she wasn't, then she wouldn't be here. And even so, he kept looking for her, just to keep track.

Raj was the first one to leave, the same as always. He was on development, which meant he had all the same burden of technical work plus steering committee meetings. If, someday, the terraforming project actually took hold, it would have Raj's intellectual DNA. Julio and Carl left next, arm in arm with Carl resting his head on Julio's shoulder the way he did when they were both a little drunk and amorous. With only Malik, Voltaire, and Tori left, avoiding the new woman was harder. Solomon got up to leave once, but then stopped at the head and wandered back in without entirely meaning to. As soon as the new woman left, he told himself. When she was gone, he could go. But if he saw who she left with, then he'd know who to ask about her. Or, if she left with Voltaire, not to ask. It was just data collection. That was all. When the monitor changed to the early morning newsfeed, he had to admit he was bullshitting. He waved his goodnights for real this time, pushed his hands into his pockets, and headed out to the main corridor.

Between the engineering problems in building a robust dome and Mars' absolute lack of a functioning magnetosphere, all the habitats were deep underground. The main corridor's hallways had ceilings four meters high and LEDs that changed their warmth and intensity with the time of day, but Solomon still had the occasional atavistic longing for sky. For a sense of openness and possibility, and maybe for not living his whole life buried.

Her voice came from behind him. "So, hey."

She walked with a comfortable rolling gait. Her smile looked warm and maybe a little tentative. Outside of the dimness of the bar, he could see the lighter streaks in her hair.

"Ah. Hey."

"We never really got around to meeting in there," she said, holding out her hand. "Caitlin Esquibel."

Solomon took her hand, shaking it once like they were at the center. "Solomon Epstein."

"Solomon Epstein?" she said, walking forward. Somehow they were walking side by side now. Together. "So what's a nice Jewish boy like you doing on a planet like this?"

If he hadn't still been a little drunk, he'd just have laughed it off.

"Trying to get the courage to meet you, mostly," he said.

"Sort of noticed that."

"Hope it was adorable."

"It was better than your friend Malik always finding reasons to touch my arm. Anyway. I'm working resource management for Kwikowski Mutual Interest Group. Just came in from Luna a month ago. That thing you were saying about Mars and Earth and America. That was interesting."

"Thank you," Solomon said. "I'm an engine engineer for Masstech."

"Engine engineer," she said. "Seems like it ought to be redundant."

"I always thought thrust specialist sounded dirty," he said. "How long are you staying on Mars?"

"Until I leave. Open contract. You?"

"Oh, I was born here," he said. "I expect I'll die here too."

She glanced up his long, thin frame once, her smile mocking. Of course she'd known he was born there. No way to hide it. His words felt like a weak brag now.

"A company man," she said, letting it be a joke between them.

"A Martian."

The cart kiosk had half a dozen of the cramped electric devices ready to rent. Solomon pulled out his card and waved it in a figure eight until the reader got good signal and the first cart in line clicked from amber to green. He pulled it out before he realized he really didn't want to get in.

"Do you—" Solomon began, then cleared his throat and tried again. "Would you like to come home with me?"

He could see the *Sure, why not* forming in her brain stem. He could follow it along the short arcing path to her lips. It was close enough to pull at his blood like a moon. And he watched it turn aside at the last moment. When she shook her head, it wasn't a refusal so much as her trying to clear her mind. But she smiled. She did smile.

"Moving a little fast there, Sol."

Speed isn't the problem. Unless he runs into something, velocity is just velocity; he could be weightless going almost the speed of light. It's the delta vee that's hurting him. The acceleration. The change. Every second, he's going sixty-eight meters per second faster than he was the second before. Or more. Maybe more.

Only the acceleration isn't the problem either. Ships have had the power to burn at fifteen or even twenty g since the early chemical rockets. The power is always there. It's the efficiency necessary to maintain a burn that was missing. Thrust to weight when most of your weight is propellant to give you thrust. And bodies can accelerate at over twenty g for a fraction of a second. It's the sustain that's killing him. It's going for hours.

There are emergency shutoffs. If the reactor starts to overheat or the magnetic bottle gets unstable, the drive will shut down. There are all kinds of shutoffs for all kinds of emergencies, but nothing's going wrong. Everything's running perfectly. That's the problem. That's what's killing him.

There is also a manual cutoff on the control panel. The icon is a big red button. A panic button. If he could touch it, he'd be fine. But he can't. All the joy is gone now. Instead of elation, there's only panic and the growing, grinding pain. If he can just reach the controls. Or if something, anything, could just go *wrong*.

Nothing is going wrong. He is struggling to breathe, gasping the way the safety instructors taught him to. He tenses his legs and arms, trying to force the blood through his arteries and veins. If he passes out, he won't come back, and there is darkness growing at the edges of his vision. If he can't find a way out, he will die here. In this chair with his hands pinned against him and his hair pulling back his scalp. His hand terminal in his pocket feels like someone driving a dull knife into his hip. He tries to remember how much mass a hand terminal has. He can't. He fights to breathe.

His hand terminal. If he can reach it, if he can pull it out, maybe he can signal to Caitlin. Maybe she can make a remote connection and shut the engines down. The hand laying across his belly presses hard into his viscera, but it's only centimeters from his pocket. He pushes until his bones creak, and his wrists shift. The friction of skin against skin tears a little hole in his belly and the blood that comes out races back toward the seat like it was afraid of something, but he does move.

He pushes again. A little closer. The blood is a lubricant. The friction is less. His hand moves farther. It takes minutes. His fingernails touch the hardened plastic. He can do this.

Power and efficiency, he thinks, and a moment's pleasure passes through him despite everything. He's done it. The magic pair.

The tendons in his fingers ache, but he pulls the cloth of his pocket aside. He can feel the hand terminal begin to slip free of his pocket, but he can't lift his head to see it.

Three years after he met her, Caitlin showed up at the door to his hole at three in the morning, crying, frightened, and sober. It wasn't the sort of thing Solomon expected from her, and he'd spent a fair amount of time in her company. They'd become lovers almost seven months after they'd met. He called it that. *Becoming lovers* wasn't the kind of thing Caitlin said. With her, it was always something crude and a little raunchy. That was who she was. He thought it was a kind of emotional protection that she was never exactly sincere. It was a way to control fear and deny anxieties. And really as long as she still wanted to come share his bed some nights, he was fine with that. And if she hadn't wanted to anymore, he'd have been disappointed, but he still would have been fine with it. He liked the way she smirked at the world. The confidence she carried herself with, especially when she was faking it. He liked, all in all, who she was. That made everything easier.

Twice, her contract had ticked past its automatic renewal dates without her exercising the option to leave. When he'd taken a position with the functional magnetics workgroup, one of the issues he'd considered was whether the extra time he took with it would alienate her. Neither of them had made any sexual or romantic connections with other people at the center. Everyone treated them as if they were each other's tacit property, and so even though they'd never made any explicit promises, Solomon would have called them *de facto* monogamists. Certainly he would have felt hurt and betrayed if she'd been sleeping with someone else, and assumed she'd feel the same about him.

But sex and companionship, as pleasant as they were, didn't mean a great deal of vulnerability. So he was surprised.

"Did you hear?" she asked. Her voice was ragged and low. Fresh tears ran down her cheeks, and her mouth pulled in and down at the corners.

"I don't think so," Solomon said, standing back to let her past. His hole was a standard design: a small multipurpose room at the front with enough resources to cook simple meals, a quarter-sized wall monitor, and space for three or four people to sit. Behind it was the bedroom. Behind that, a storage closet and a bathroom. On Mars, the joke went, a man's hole was his castle where values of castle approached dorm room. She sat heavily on one of the benches, and wrapped her arms around herself. Solomon closed the door. He didn't know whether to talk to her or hold her or both. He started with holding her. Her tears had a smell to them; salt and damp and skin. She wept into his shoulder until curiosity and distress drove him past the consolation of being her soft monkey. "So. Did I hear what, exactly?"

She coughed out a phlegmy laugh.

"The United Nations," she said. "They invoked the breakaway province rule. Their ships have already done their acceleration burns. Forty of them. They're already ballistic."

"Oh," he said, and she started weeping again.

"It's those fucking secessionists. Ever since they published their manifesto, people have been acting like they're serious. Like they aren't a bunch of short-sighted assholes who're in it for the attention. Now they've started a war. They're really going to do it, Sol. They're going to drop rocks on us until we're just a carbon layer ten atoms thick."

"They won't do that. They won't do that," he said, and

immediately regretted repeating himself. It made him sound like he was trying to talk himself into it. "Every time the breakaway province rule's been invoked, it's been because the UN wanted to grab resources. If they break all our infrastructure, they can't get the resources. They're just trying to scare us."

Caitlin raised one hand like a schoolgirl asking to be recognized. "Working. Scared now."

"And it isn't about the secessionists, even if that's what they're claiming," Solomon said. He felt himself warming up now. He wasn't repeating sentences. "It's about Earth running out of lithium and molybdenum. Even with the landfill mines, they need more than they've got. We have access to raw ore. That's all it is. It's all about money, Cait. They aren't going to start dropping rocks. Besides, if they do that to us, we'll do that to them. We've got better ships."

"Eighteen of them," she said. "They've got forty coasting toward us right now, and just as many playing defense."

"But if they miss one," he said, and didn't finish the thought.

She swallowed, wiped her cheeks with the palm of her hands. He leaned across the room and plucked a towel out of the dispenser for her.

"Do you actually know any of that?" she said. "Or are you just talking a good game to calm me down?"

"Do I have to answer that?"

She sighed, collapsing into him.

"It'll be weeks," he said. "Minimum. Probably months."

"So. If you had four months to live, what would you do?"

"Crawl into bed with you and not come out."

She reached over and kissed him. There was a violence in her that unnerved him. No, that wasn't right. Not violence. Sincerity.

"C'mon," she said.

He woke with his hand terminal buzzing in alarm and only vaguely aware he'd been hearing the sound for a while. Caitlin was curled up against him, her eyes still closed, her mouth open and calm. She looked young like that. Relaxed. He shut off the alarm as he checked the time. On one hand, he was egregiously late for his shift. On the other, another hour wouldn't be particularly more egregious. There were two messages from his team lead queued. Caitlin muttered and stretched. The motion pulled the sheet away from her body. He put the hand terminal down, pushed his hand under his pillow and went back to sleep.

The next time he woke, she was sitting up, looking at him. The softness had left her face again, but she was still beautiful. He smiled up at her and reached out to weave his fingers with hers.

"Will you marry me?" he asked.

"Oh, please."

"No, really. Will you marry me?"

"Why? Because we're about to get into a war that'll kill us and everyone we know and there's nothing we can do to affect it one way or the other? Quick, let's do something permanent before the permanence is all mined out."

"Sure. Will you marry me?"

"Of course I will, Sol."

The ceremony was a small one. Voltaire was Caitlin's maid of honor. Raj was Solomon's best man. The priest was a Methodist whose childhood had been spent in the Punjab, but now spoke with the faux-Texan drawl of the Mariner Valley. There were several chapels in the research center, and this one was actually quite lovely. Everything, even the altar, had been carved from the native stone and then covered with a clear sealant that left it looking wet and rich and vibrant. Lines of white and black ran through the red stone, and flecks of crystalline brightness. The air was thick with the scent of lilacs that Voltaire had bought by the armful from the greenhouses.

As they stood together, exchanging the formulaic vows, Solomon thought Caitlin's face had the same calm that it did when she was sleeping. Or maybe he was just projecting. When he put the ring on her finger, he felt something shift in his breast and he was utterly and irrationally happy in a way he didn't remember ever having been before. The UN fleet was still three weeks away. Even at the worst, they wouldn't die for almost a month. It made him wish they'd done it all earlier. The first night he'd seen her, for instance. Or that they'd met when they were younger. In the pictures they sent to her parents, he looked like he was about to burst into song. He hated the images, but Caitlin loved them, so he loved them too. They took their honeymoon in the hotel right there in Dhanbad Nova, drying themselves with towels and washing with soaps that had been made in the image of luxury on Earth. He'd bathed twice as much while they were there, almost feeling the heat of the water and the softness of his robe as magic, as if by being decadent he could pass for a Terran.

And, by coincidence, it worked. Whatever negotiations had been going on behind the scenes paid off. The UN ships flipped for their deceleration burn early and burned twice as long. They were on their way home. He was watching the announcer on the newsfeed tracking the orbital mechanics of the voyage out and back. He tried to imagine what it was like for the marines in those ships. Out almost all the way to the new world, and then back without ever having seen it. Over half a year of their lives gone in an act of political theater. Caitlin sat on the edge of the bed, leaning in toward the monitor, not taking her eyes from it. Drinking it in.

Sitting behind her, his back pressing against the headboard, Solomon felt a ghost of unease pass through him, cold and unwelcome.

"I guess permanent just got a lot longer," he said, trying to make a joke out of it.

"Mm-hm," she agreed.

"Sort of changes things."

"Mm-hm."

He scratched at the back of his hand even though it didn't itch. The dry sound of fingernails against skin was drowned in the announcer's voice so that he felt it more than heard it. Caitlin ran a hand through her hair, her fingers disappearing in the black and then re-emerging.

"So," he said. "Do you want a divorce?"

"No."

"Because I know you were thinking that the rest of your life was going to be kind of a short run. And if…if this wasn't what you would have picked. Anyway, I'd understand it."

Caitlin looked at him over her shoulder. The light of the monitor shone on her cheek, her eye, her hair like she was made of colored glass.

"You are adorable, and you are my husband, and I love you and trust you like I never have anyone in my life. I wouldn't trade this for anything but more of this. Why? Do you want out?"

"No. Just being polite. No, not that. Insecure all of a sudden."

"Stop it. And anyway, it hasn't changed. Earth is still running out of lithium and molybdenum and all sorts of industrial minerals. We still have them. They turned back this time, but they're still coming, and they'll keep on coming."

"Unless they find some way to do what they need to do with other metals. Or find another source. Things change all the time. Something could make the whole question irrelevant."

"Could," she agreed. "That's what peace is, right? Postponing the conflict until the thing you were fighting over doesn't matter."

On the screen, the UN ships burned, arcs of flame flaring behind them as they went back where they came from.

The hand terminal eases a little farther out of his pocket, and he's fairly sure it's going to leave a track of bruise as wide as the case. He doesn't care. He tries to remember if he left the voice activation on, and either he didn't or his throat is too deformed by the thrust gravity for his voice to be recognizable. It has to be done by hand. He can't relax or he'll lose consciousness, but it's getting harder and harder to remember that. Intellectually he knows that the blood is being pressed to the back of his body, pooling in the back part of his cerebellum and flooding his kidneys. He hasn't done enough medical work to know what that means, but it can't be good. The hand terminal comes almost all the way out. It's in his hand now.

The ship shudders once, and a notification pops up on the screen. It's amber-colored, and there's some text with it, but he can't make it out. His eyes won't focus. If it were red, it would have triggered a shut down. He waits for a few seconds, hoping that whatever it is gets worse, but it doesn't. The yacht's solid. Well-designed and well-built. He turns his attention back to the hand terminal.

Caitlin will be at the hole now. She'll be starting dinner and listening to the newsfeed for information about the shipyards crisis. If he can put in a connection request, she'll get it. He has the sudden, powerful fear that she'll think he sat on his terminal. That she'll say his name a few times, then laugh it off and drop the connection. He'll have to make noise when she accepts. Even if actual speech is too hard, he has to let her know there's something wrong. He's thumbed in connection requests without looking at his terminal thousands of times, but everything feels different now, and his muscle memory isn't helping him. The weight of the terminal is overwhelming. Everything in his hand aches like he's been hit with a hammer. His belly hurts. The worst headache he can imagine blooms. Nothing about this experience is fun except the knowledge that he's succeeded. Even as he struggles to make the terminal respond, he's also thinking what the drive means practically. With efficiency like this, ships can be under thrust all through a voyage. Acceleration thrust to the halfway point, then cut the engines, flip, and decelerate the rest of the trip. Even a relatively gentle one third g will mean not only getting wherever they are headed much faster, but there won't be any of the problems of long-term weightlessness. He tries to figure how long the transit to Earth will take, but he can't. He has to pay attention to the terminal.

Something in the topology of his gut shifts, changing the angle the terminal is sitting. It starts to slip, and he doesn't have strength or speed to catch it. It reaches his side, falls the centimeters to the chair. He tries to move his left arm from where it's pinned beside his ear, but it won't move.

It won't move at all. It won't even tense up with effort.

Oh, he thinks, I'm having a stroke.

They had been married for six years when Solomon took the money he'd saved from his performances and efficiency bonuses and bought himself a yacht. It wasn't a large ship; the living space in it was smaller than his first hole. It was almost five years old, and was going to require a month in the orbital shipyard docks before very much longer. The interior color scheme—cream and orange—wasn't to his tastes. It had been sitting in dry dock for eight and a half months since its previous owner—a junior vice president of a Luna-based conglomerate—had died. His family on Luna didn't have any plans to come to Mars, and the bother of retrieving it across the months-deep void made it easier for them to price it low and sell. For most people on Mars, a boat like that was an ostentatious status symbol and nothing more. There was no settled moon or inhabited L5 station to travel between. The trip to Earth in it would have been neither comfortable nor par-ticularly safe. It could go around in orbit. It could run out into the vacuum near Mars, and then come back. That was about it, and the pointlessness of the exercise helped drive down the price ever farther. As a statement of wealth, it said its owner had had too much. As a means of transport, it was like having a race car that could never leave its track.

For Solomon, it was the perfect test vehicle.

The yacht had been designed around an engine he knew, and the build code was one he'd helped to write. When he looked at the technical and maintenance history, he could see every control array, every air recycling vent and cover. Before he'd even set foot on it, he knew it as well as he knew anything. Some parts of the exhaust sys-tem were things he'd designed himself a decade before. And, since he held the title to it, half a year's worth of red tape would simply go away if he wanted to use it to test some new refinements to the engines. That idea alone could make him cackle with delight.

No more permissions committees. No more hard capital liability reports. Just the boat, its reactor, a couple EVA suits and a set of industrial waldoes he'd had since he was in school. In previous eras, a scientist might have a garage PCR machine or a shed in the back of the house with beehives or disassembled engines or half-built prototypes of inventions that would change the world if they could just be made to work. Solomon had his yacht, and getting it was the most self-indulgent, delightful, important thing he'd done since the day he'd asked Caitlin to marry him.

And yet, even as the fertile garden of his mind sent up a thousand different green shoots of ideas and projects, tests and tweaks and adjustments, he found himself dreading the part where he told his wife what he'd done. And when the time came, his unease was justified.

"Oh, Sol. Oh, baby."

"I didn't spend my salary on it," he said. "It was all bonus money. And it was only mine. I didn't use ours."

Caitlin was sitting on the bench in their multipurpose room, tapping her mouth with the tips of her fingers the way she did when she was thinking hard. The system was playing a gentle ambient music that was all soft percussion and strings loud enough to cover the hiss of the air recyclers but not so much as to overwhelm the conversation. As with almost all the new buildings on Mars, it was larger, better appointed, and deeper underground.

"So what I just heard you say is you can spend as much money out of the account as you want without talking to me if the total you pull is less than whatever you've made in bonuses. Is that what you meant?"

"No," he said, though it was pretty close. "I'm saying that it wasn't money we were counting on. All our obligations are covered. We're not going to try to buy food and have the accounts come up empty. We're not going to have to work extra hours or take on side jobs."

"All right."

"And this is important work. The design I have for the magnetic coil exhaust can really increase drive efficiency, if I can get—"

"All *right*," she said.

He leaned against the door frame. The strings rose in a delicate arpeggio.

"You're angry."

"No, sweetie. I'm not angry," she said gently. "Angry is yelling. This is resentful, and it's because you're cutting me out from the fun parts. Really, I look at you, and see the happiness and the excitement, and I want to be part of that. I want to jump up and down and wave my arms and talk about how great it all is. But that money was our safety net. You're ignoring the fact that you spent our safety net, and if we *both* ignore it, the first time something unexpected comes up, we're screwed. I love our life, so now I have to be the one who cares and disapproves and doesn't get to be excited. You're making me the grown-up. I don't want to be the grown-up. I want us both to be grown-ups, so that when we do something like this, we both get to be kids."

She looked up at him and shrugged. Her face was harder than it was when they met. There were threads of white in the darkness of her hair. When she smiled, he felt the hardness in his chest erode away.

"I may…have gotten a little carried away. I saw it was there and we could afford it."

"And you zoomed ahead without thinking about all of what it would mean. Because you're Solomon Epstein, and you are the smartest, most rigorous and methodical man who ever made every single important choice in his life by impulse." If there hadn't been warmth and laughter in her voice, it would have sounded like a condemnation. Instead it sounded like love.

"I'm cute, though," he said.

"You're adorable. And I want to hear all about your new whatever it is you're going to try. Only first tell me that you'll try to think about the future next time?"

"I will."

They spent the evening with him talking about power and efficiency, ejection mass and velocity multipliers. And when that was done, they talked about building a responsible retirement plan and making sure their wills were up to date. It felt like an apology, and he hoped that they'd be able to do it again when she understood how much maintenance on the yacht was going to cost. It was a fight for another day.

The days, he spent working as usual with the team at the propulsion group. The nights, he sat on the monitors back at their hole and designed his own things. Caitlin started a program over the network with a group in Londres Nova discussing how companies like Kwikowski could intervene in the destabilizing spiral of threat and avoidance that Earth and Mars seemed locked in. Whenever he heard her talking to the others—about propaganda and divergent moral codes and any number of other plausible-sounding vaguenesses—she brought up lithium, molybdenum. Now tungsten too. All the other things were interesting, important, informative, and profound. But unless they could figure out the ore rights issues, they could address everything else and still not solve the problem. He was always proud of her when she said that. A liberal arts background was a hard thing to overcome, but she was doing great.

Eventually, the time came to test his idea and plans. He made the long journey to the shipyards on the new public transport system: evacuated tubes drilled through the rock and lined with electromagnetic rails like a slow, underpowered gauss gun. It was cramped and uncomfortable, but it was fast. He got to his yacht an hour before the sun set at the nearby Martian horizon. He finished the last-minute tweaks to the prototype he'd fabricated, ran the diagnostic sequences twice, and took the ship up beyond the thin atmosphere. Once he reached high orbit, he floated for a while, enjoying the novelty of null g. He brewed himself a bulb of fresh tea, strapped himself into the captain's chair, and ran his fingertip across the old touchscreen monitor.

If he was right, the additions he'd made would increase efficiency by almost sixteen percent above baseline. When the numbers came back, he hadn't been right. Efficiency had *dropped* by four and a half. He landed back at the shipyards and rode the transit tube home, muttering darkly to himself the whole way.

The United Nations issued a statement that all future Martian ships would be contracted through the Bush shipyards on Earth. The local government didn't even comment on it; they just kept on with the scheduled builds and negotiated for new ones after that. The United Nations ordered that all shipyards on Mars shut down until an inspection team could be sent out there. Seven months to get the team together, and almost six months in transit because of the relative distances of the two planets in their orbits around the sun. Sol was a little nervous when he heard that. If they closed the shipyards, it might mean grounding his test yacht. He didn't need to concern himself. The shipyards all stayed open. The rumors of war started up again, and Solomon tried to ignore them. Tried to tell himself that this time would be no different than the one before or the one before that.

Raj, to everyone's surprise, resigned from development, rented a cheap hole up near the surface, and started selling hand-made ceramic art. He said he'd never been happier. Voltaire got a divorce and wanted all the old crew to come out to the bars with her. There were eight of them now, but pretty much nobody went. Julio and Carl had a baby together and stopped socializing with anyone. Tori went in on a little chemical safety consultancy that pretended to serve any business with a Martian charter, but actually got all their business from the terraforming projects. Malik died from an unresponsive spinal cancer. Life struggled on, winning and failing. Solomon's experimental drives got to where they were almost as good as the unmodified ship. Then a little bit better.

A year almost to the day after he'd bought it, Solomon rode out to the yacht with a new design. If he was right, it would increase efficiency by almost four and a half percent above baseline. He was in the engine room installing it when his hand terminal chimed. It was Caitlin. He accepted the request.

"What's up?" he asked.

"Did we decide to take that long weekend next month?" she asked. "I know we talked about it, but I don't think we made a decision."

"We didn't, but I'd better not. The team's a little behind."

"Overtime behind?"

"No. Just keep-showing-up behind."

"All right. Then I may plan something with Maggie Chu."

"You have my blessing. I'll be home as soon as this is done."

"All right," she said, and dropped the connection. He tested the housings, did an extra weld where the coil would suffer the most stress, and headed back up for the captain's chair. The yacht rose through the thin atmosphere and into high orbit. Solomon ran the diagnostics again, making sure before he started that everything looked good. For almost half an hour, he floated in his chair, held in place by his straps.

As he started the burn sequence, he remembered that the team was going to be in Londres Nova the weekend he'd been thinking about taking off with Caitlin. He wondered whether she'd put her plans with Maggie Chu in place, or if there was still time to change things. He started the burn.

Acceleration threw Solomon back into the captain's chair, then pressed his chest like a weight. His right hand landed on his belly, his left fell onto the upholstery beside his ear. His ankles pressed back against the leg rests.

The ship sings a low dirge, throaty and passionate and sad like the songs his father used to sing at temple. He understands now that he's going to die here. He's going too fast and too far for help to reach him. For a while—months or years—his little yacht will mark the farthest out of Earth's gravity well a manned ship has ever gone. They'll find the design specs at the hole. Caitlin is smart. She'll know to sell the design. She'll have enough money to eat beef every meal for the rest of her life. He's taken good care of her, anyway, if not himself.

If he had control, he could reach the asteroid belt. He could go to the Jovian system and be the first person to walk on Europa and Ganymede. He isn't going to, though. That's going to be someone else. But when they get there, they will be carried by his drive.

And the war! If distance is measured in time, Mars just got very, very close to Earth while Earth is still very distant from Mars. That kind of asymmetry changes everything. He wonders how they'll negotiate that. What they'll do. All the lithium and molybdenum and tungsten anyone could want is within reach of mining companies now. They can go to the asteroid belt and the moons of Saturn and Jupiter. The thing that kept Earth and Mars from ever reaching a lasting peace isn't going to matter anymore.

The pain in his head and his spine is getting worse. It's hard to remember to tense his legs and arms, to help his failing heart move the blood. He almost blacks out again, but he's not sure if it's the stroke or the thrust gravity. He's pretty sure driving blood pressure higher while having a stroke is considered poor form.

The ship's dirge shifts a little, and now it's literally singing in his father's voice, Hebrew syllables whose meaning Solomon has forgotten if he ever knew. Aural hallucinations, then. That's interesting.

He's sorry that he won't be able to see Caitlin one more time. To tell her goodbye and that he loves her. He's sorry he won't get to see the consequences of his drive. Even through the screaming pain, a calmness and euphoria start to wash over him. It's always been like this, he thinks. From when Moses saw the promised land that he could never enter, people have been on their deathbeds just wanting to see what happens next. He wonders if that's what makes the promised land holy: that you can see it but you can't quite reach it. The grass is always greener on the other side of personal extinction. It sounds like something Malik would say. Something Caitlin would laugh at.

The next few years—decades even—are going to be fascinating, and it will be because of him. He closes his eyes. He wishes he could be there to see it all happen.

Solomon relaxes, and the expanse folds itself around him like a lover.

Drive
Author's Note

*M*oving *a little fast there, Sol.*

Puns may be the lowest form of humor, but that's still one of our favorite lines in the project.

One of the things that comes up a few times in the course of The Expanse is the idea that the prophet can lead people to the Holy Land, but cannot enter it himself. Solomon Epstein is that guy: the one who ushers in a whole new era but won't live to see the effect of what he's done. It's a story that has power because it's something we all experience, especially as we get older: that sense of momentous things coming just after we're already gone. Existential FOMO.

The story was written originally for Jonathan Strahan's *Edge of Infinity* anthology, got repurposed as a San Diego Comic-Con-exclusive chapbook by SYFY, and put up for free online for a while. Of all the short fiction in the Expanse universe, this is probably the one that was read the most and for which we were paid the least. Sometimes the business is funny that way.

Someone asked once if the Voltaire who went drinking with Sol way back then was connected to the militant OPA faction the Voltaire Collective that figured in the later books. It seems like there probably was a connection, but we never looked into what that was.

The Butcher of Anderson Station

When Fred was a kid back on Earth, maybe five or six years old, he'd seen a weed growing in the darkness of his uncle's cellar. The plant had been pale and thin but twice as tall as the ones out in the side yard, deformed by reaching for the sunlight. The man behind the bar looked just like that: too tall, too pale, too hungry for something he'd never had and never would. Belters were all like that.

The music in the bar mixed Punjabi rhythms with a high-voiced woman rapping in the polyglot mess of languages that made up Belter Creole. The battered pachinko machine in the back rang and skittered. Hashish smoke sweetened the air. Fred leaned back on a bar stool meant for someone ten centimeters taller than he was and smiled gently.

"Is there a fucking problem?" he asked.

The bartender could have been Chinese or Korean or a mix of

the two. Which meant his family had probably come up in one of the first waves. Five generations of grubbing for air, packing extended families into surveying ships with seven bunks, looking back at a sun that was hardly more than the brightest star. It was hard to think of any of them as human anymore.

"No problems, *jefe*," the bartender said, but didn't move. In the mirror behind the bar, Fred saw the door slide open. Four Belters slouched in. One had an armband with the split circle of the Outer Planets Alliance. Fred saw them see him. He saw one of them recognize him. The little trickle of adrenaline in his blood was automatic and pleasant.

"Then how about you serve me my drink?"

The barkeep didn't move for a time, and then he did. Whiskey poured differently in spin gravity, but not so much that Fred could tell quite what was wrong about it. The Coriolis of Ceres Station shouldn't have been enough to change the angle, not this close to the asteroid surface. Maybe it was just that it fell slowly. The bartender slid the glass across to him.

"On the house," the man said, then a half beat of silence. "Colonel."

Fred met his gaze. Neither spoke. Fred drank the liquor neat. It burned and left a taste at the back of his tongue like old mushrooms and bread mold.

"You have anything that isn't fermented fungus?" Fred asked.

"*Als u aprecie no, koai sa sa?*" a voice said from behind him. *If you don't like it, why are you here?*

Fred twisted in his seat. One of the four-pack who had just come in was glaring at him. He was broad-shouldered for a Belter. Mech driver, maybe. Or maybe he just spent a lot of time in the gym. Some of them did that, using machines and weights and expensive drug cocktails to give them what gravity never would.

Why are you here? Decent question.

"I like whiskey that used to be some kind of grain. You want to suck fungus, don't let me stop you."

The mech driver shifted in his seat. Fred thought he was going to get up, but instead the man shrugged and looked aside. His friends glanced at each other. The one with the armband had his hand terminal out and was tapping on the screen rapidly.

"I've got some bourbon came from Ganymede," the bartender said. "Cost you."

"Not enough to stop me," Fred said, turning back. "Bring the bottle."

The bartender bent down. His hand shuffled under the bar. There was probably a gun down there. Fred could almost picture it. Something designed to first intimidate, and if that failed, to put a man down. A shotgun, maybe, hack-sawed down for close range. Fred waited, but the man's hand came up with a bottle. He put it on the bar. Fred felt a quick rush of relief and disappointment.

"Clean glass," Fred said.

"So I think to myself," the bartender said, reaching back toward the glassware by the mirror, "you're here for something. The Butcher of Anderson Station in a Belter bar."

"I just want a drink," Fred said.

"No one just wants a drink," the bartender replied.

"I'm exceptional."

The bartender grinned.

"You are," he said, then bent low, his head almost level with Fred's. "Look at me, Colonel."

Fred unscrewed the cap from the bottle and poured two fingers into the new glass. He put the cap back. The bartender didn't move. Fred met the pale brown eyes. He was about to say something, not even sure what it was besides cutting, belittling, and mean. In the mirror, something moved. Men, behind him.

Fred had a moment to brace himself for the knife or the bullet or the blow that didn't come before a black bag dropped over his head.

Three years before, everything had been different.

"*Dagmar* in the pipe, ninety seconds to contact, all green."

"Roger that, *Dagmar*. I show you go for breach in ninety—"

Fred chinned down the volume on the pilot's band, reducing their exchanges to faint background music with lyrics about positionals and vectors. Ninety seconds before the breaching team went in.

An eternity to wait.

Fred let out a long exhale that fogged the inside of his helmet for a second before it cleared. He tried to stretch, but the crash couch wouldn't let him extend his limbs fully in any direction. The command console showed eighty-three seconds to contact with Anderson Station. Breathing and stretching had burned only seven seconds.

He switched his display to the *Dagmar's* forward airlock. She was a Marine landing craft, built to lock on to a ship or station and cut a hole, and the display showed two hundred marines strapped to vertical crash cages, weapons locked into quick release clamps next to them. The airlock was designed to iris open once the breaching charges had made an opening and the exterior seals were latched on.

It was hard to tell when they were all in vacuum-rated combat armor, but the marines looked calm. They'd been trained on Luna until maneuvering in light or null gravity and vacuum was second nature. They were put in cramped ships until advancing down claustrophobic metal corridors with blind corners at every intersection didn't scare them. They were told that marines doing a full breaching action assault could expect as high as 60 percent casualties until that number stopped meaning anything.

Fred looked over his people in their cages and imagined six out of ten of them not coming back.

The readout said thirty seconds.

Fred switched his console to radar. Two large blips flanking the *Dagmar*. Her sister ships, each with two hundred marines of their own. Beyond them, the small, fast-moving escort ships. Ahead, growing closer by the second, the massive rotating ring of Anderson Station.

Everyone was in place, his troops were ready to go, diplomacy had failed and it was time to do his job. He opened the command channel to his squad leaders, ten variations on background static suddenly piping into his helmet.

"All squads, ten seconds to breach. Sound off."

Ten voices responded with the affirmative.

"Good hunting," Fred said, then pulled up his tactical display. The layout of Anderson Station appeared in a misleadingly crisp 2-D floor plan. No way to know how much fortifying the Belters might have done when they took over the station.

His soldiers showed up as six hundred green dots, hovering just outside the station.

"Breach, now! Now! Now!" the *Dagmar's* pilot yelled into the comms. The ship shuddered as the airlock claws sank into the metal of the station itself, a metallic shriek that Fred felt right through his padded chair. Gravity returned in a sideways lurch as the station began carrying the breaching ships along on its 0.3 g rotation. A series of high-pitched bangs sounded as the breaching charges went off.

Above his tactical display, ten smaller screens flickered on, his squad leaders activating their suits' helmet cameras. The marines poured through the three new holes in Anderson's skin. Fred flipped to the tactical floor plan, his fingers tapping against it.

"All squads establish beachhead and fallback position in Corridor L, from Junction 34 to Junction 38," Fred said into the comm, surprised as always by how calm his voice sounded during a battle.

Green dots moved through the corridors marked on his display. Sometimes new red dots appeared when a marine's HUD detected return fire and marked the individual as a threat. The red dots never lasted long. Every now and then a green dot shifted to yellow. A soldier down, their armored suits detecting the injuries or death that rendered them combat ineffective.

Combat ineffective. Such a nice euphemism for one of his kids bleeding out on a piece-of-shit station at the ass end of the Belt.

Sixty percent expected casualties. Four green dots for every six yellow, and each one of them his.

He watched the assault play out like a high-tech game, moving his pieces, reacting to threats with new orders, keeping score by tracking how many green dots stayed green.

Three red dots appeared. Four green dots stopped advancing and took cover. Fred sent four more green dots into a side passage, moving them into a flanking position. The red dots disappeared. The green dots moved again. It was tempting to get lost in the flow of it, to forget what all the glowing symbols on the screen actually meant.

The squad leader for his point team broke his reverie by calling him on the command channel.

"Overwatch, this is squad one actual."

Fred shifted his attention to the helmetcam view from squad one's leader. A makeshift barricade squatted at the other end of a long, gently sloping corridor. His tactical display marked a dozen or more hostiles defending it. As Fred watched, a small object hurtled over the barricade and detonated like a grenade just a few yards from his squad leader's position.

"Overwatch here, I read you, squad one actual," Fred replied.

"Heavily fortified position blocking access to the main corridor. Could clear it with heavy weapons, but there would be significant structural damage, and possible loss of life support in this section."

Fred glanced at the tactical map, noting the proximity of several key life support and power nodes to the barricade's position. *That's why they set up there. Because they think we won't.*

"Roger that, squad one," Fred replied, looking for an alternate route. There didn't seem to be one. The Belters were smart.

"Overwatch, interrogative. Use heavy weapons to clear the barricade, or clear by advancing?"

Blow up a big chunk of the station's life support, killing who knows how many civilians hiding in their rooms, or send his men in and let them soak up their 60 percent casualties to take the position.

Fuck that. The Belters had made their decision. Let them live with the consequences.

"Squad one actual, you are authorized for heavy weapons use to clear this obstruction. Overwatch out."

A few seconds later, the barricade vanished in a flash of light and a cloud of smoke. Seconds after that, his people were on the move again.

Three hours and twenty-three yellow dots later, the call came. "Overwatch, this is squad one actual. The command center is taken. The station is ours. Repeat, the station is ours."

His arms, tied behind him, ached. Bound at the ankles, he could either lay on his side or lever himself up to his knees. He couldn't straighten his legs to stand. He chose kneeling.

The darkness of the sack over his head was absolute, but judging from the spin gravity, he was somewhere near the station's outer skin. An airlock, then. He'd hear the hiss and pop as the inner door sealed. Then either the slow exhalation of evacuated air or, if they were looking to blow him out into space, the cough of the security override. He ran his feet across the floor, trying to find the seams. Would it slide open, or was it one of the old hinged designs?

The sound that came wasn't mechanical. Somewhere to his left, a woman cleared her throat. A few seconds later, a door opened, then closed. It had the soft sound of a pressure seal, but that didn't mean much on station. Most doors were airtight. Footsteps approached him. Five people. Maybe six. The woman with the tickle in her throat wasn't one of them.

"Colonel? I'm going to take that sack off now."

Fred nodded.

Light returned to the world.

The room was cheap flooring and raw stone. Conduits and ducts ran across the ceiling and walls, and a squat metal desk sat unused in one corner. A service tunnel. The lights were harsh. He recognized the four men from the bar. Another man had joined them. Thin, young, with a case of acne that deserved medical attention. Fred craned his neck to see the woman. She stood at attention, a fifty-year-old fléchette rifle in her hands, and the split-circle armband of the OPA on her bicep.

None of them were wearing masks. When the new man spoke, his voice wasn't modified. They didn't care whether Fred could identify them.

"Colonel Frederick Lucius Johnson. I've been looking forward to meeting you. My name is Anderson Dawes. I work for the OPA."

"Anderson, eh?" Fred said, and the man shrugged.

"My parents named me after the Anderson-Hyosung Cooperative Industries Group. I think I got off pretty light, all things considered."

"So what? Anderson Station was like a brother to you?"

"Namesake. Call me Dawes, if it's more comfortable."

"Fuck yourself, Dawes."

Dawes nodded, knelt down facing Fred.

"*Chi-chey au?*" one of the men from the bar asked.

"*Etchyeh,*" Dawes said, and the men walked away. Dawes waited until the door closed behind them before he went on. "You've been spending a lot of time in Belter bars, Colonel. Someone might think you were looking for something."

"Dawes?"

"Fred?"

"I've been through better interrogation training than you'll ever see. You want to build rapport? Go for it. Talk for a while, take my shackles off, start telling me that you can save me if I just tell you what I know. And then I'll rip your eyes out and skull-fuck you. You understand?"

"I do," Dawes said, not missing a beat. "So tell me, Fred. What happened to you on Anderson Station?"

Once the skirmishers had finished sweeping the corridors for stragglers, a detachment of marines escorted Fred into the conquered station. He paused at the fallback position they'd set up just outside the airlock doors. Marines were beginning to return there from other assignments. They were hopped-up on adrenaline and twitchy with post-combat fear. Fred let them see him. He put his hands on their shoulders and told them they'd done a good job.

Some of them came back on stretchers. Yellow dots made flesh. The corpsmen hurried among them, plugging their hand terminals into ports in the downed soldiers' combat armor, reading the diagnostics, then assigning their place in line for surgery based on the severity of their wounds. Sometimes they tapped a button on their terminal and one of Fred's yellow dots shifted to black. His command software flagged the fatality and sent a message to the appropriate squad leader and company commander to write a letter to the family. His own task list received a matching entry.

It was all very clean, very organized. Centuries of warfare in the electronic age had distilled it to this. Fred put his hand on the arm of a young woman whose suit was reporting severe spinal injuries, and squeezed. She gave him a thumbs-up that felt like a punch to the solar plexus.

"Sir?"

Fred looked up and found his first lieutenant standing at attention. "Are we ready?"

"Yes, sir. Might be a straggler or two, but we control the corridors from here to Ops."

"Take me there," Fred said.

They covered the ground it had taken his marines hours to win in just a few minutes. The post-combat cleanup teams were still in the breaching ships, waiting for the all clear. Scattered along the corridors lay the bodies of the fallen enemy. Fred looked them over. Other than a noticeable lack of OPA insignias, they were pretty much what he would have expected. Long, thin men and women blasted open by explosives, or repeatedly punctured by small-arms fire. Most were armed, but a few weren't.

They rounded a corner into the main corridor and then came to the barricade he'd ordered destroyed. Over a dozen bodies lay around it. Some wore makeshift armor, but most were in simple environment suits. The concussion rocket his marines had used to clear the corridor had burst them like overripe grapes. Fred's vacuum-rated armor protected him from the smell of viscera, but it reported it to him as a slight increase in atmospheric methane levels. The stench of death reduced to a data point.

A small pile of weapons and makeshift explosives lay nearby.

"That's what they were armed with?" Fred asked.

His escort nodded.

"Pretty light stuff, sir. Civilian grade. Most of it wouldn't even make a dent in our armor."

Fred bent over and picked up a homemade grenade.

"They threw bombs at you to keep you from getting close enough to realize their guns wouldn't work."

The lieutenant laughed. "And made us frag the lot of them. If we'd known they were packing peashooters, we could have just walked up and tased them."

Fred shook his head and put the grenade back down.

"Get a demolitions team to come clear these explosives before this homemade shit goes off and kills someone."

He looked at the nearby life support node that had been wrecked by their concussion rocket. *Enough bystanders have died today.* Fred called up the station status report his cyberops team was updating by the minute. It showed a total loss of life support in the section he was in, and in two neighboring sections. Just over eleven hundred people with no air and no power. Every door he could see might have a family behind it who'd gasped out their last breaths banging to get out because a bunch of idiot Belters had built their barricades where they did. And because he'd chosen to destroy it.

While his lieutenant called for a bomb-disposal unit, Fred

walked toward the command center. Along the way he saw a few more Belter corpses. They'd tried to hold the corridor even after his people had blown up the first barricade, hiding behind makeshift barriers and throwing their bathtub-brewed explosives. Buying time, but for what? The final result had never been in doubt. They'd been undermanned and grossly underequipped. The only reason his soldiers had taken three hours was that Fred had insisted on moving cautiously. Looking at the unarmored bodies on the floor, he realized they could have had men in the command center in half that time.

They had to have known it too, these people spread across the floor around him. *The idiots made us kill them.*

His lieutenant caught up with him just as he was entering the command center. Corpses filled the room, easily twenty of them. While most of them wore some form of environment suit or another, one man in the center of the room wore only a cheap blue jumpsuit with a mining company logo on the shoulder. He'd been shot dozens of times. A small-caliber pistol was glued to one hand with his own blood.

"The leader, we think," his escort said. "He was doing some kind of broadcast. The others fought to the last man to buy him time. We tried to take him alive, but he pulled that little gun out of his pocket, and…"

Fred looked at the carnage around him and felt a disquieting sensation in his belly. It lasted only a moment, and then was replaced by a white-hot anger. If he'd been alone, he would have gone to the dead man in the cheap blue jumpsuit and kicked him. Instead, Fred gritted his teeth.

"What the fuck was wrong with you people?" he demanded of the dead.

"Sir?" his lieutenant said, looking at the comms station. "Looks like he was trying to broadcast right up to the last minute."

"Let me see it," Fred said.

"What happened on Anderson Station was that I did my duty," Fred said.

"Your duty," Dawes echoed. He didn't make it a question. He didn't mock it. He just repeated the words.

"Yes."

"Following orders, then," Dawes said.

"Don't even try it, asshole. That Nuremberg crap won't work on me. I followed orders in that I was instructed by my superior officers to retake the station from the terrorist forces occupying it. I judged that order to be legal and appropriate, and everything that came after was my responsibility. I took the station, and I did so while trying to minimize, first, loss of life to my people and, second, damage to the station."

Dawes looked at him. Tiny frown lines competed with his acne. Something in the ductwork clacked, hissed, then clacked again, and stopped.

"You were told to do something. You did it," Dawes said. "How is that not following orders?"

"I gave the orders," Fred said. "And I did what I did because I judged it to be right."

"Okay."

"You're trying to give me wiggle room. Let me say that the Belters who died on Anderson died because the guy above me made a call. That's shit."

"And why would I be doing that?" Dawes asked. He was good. He seemed genuinely curious.

"Build rapport."

Dawes nodded, then frowned and looked pained.

"And then we're back to the skull-fucking?" Dawes asked with a grimace. Before he could stop himself, Fred laughed.

"This isn't what I'm here for, Colonel," Dawes went on, "and I don't want to get sidetracked, but doesn't that go the other way too? You didn't fire a shot. You didn't touch a trigger or key in a launch code. You gave orders, but your soldiers judged them to be just and legal."

"Because they were," Fred said. "My people did the right thing."

"Because you told them to," Dawes said. "They were following your orders."

"Yes."

"Your responsibility."

"Yes."

The woman with the antique rifle coughed again. Dawes lowered himself to the cheap flooring, sitting with legs crossed. Even then, he was half a head taller than Fred. His skin was pale where it wasn't red. Between the zits and the gawky-elongated build, Dawes looked like a teenager. Except around the eyes.

"And the terrorists," Dawes said.

"What?"

"The men who took the station. You think it was their responsibility too, yes?"

"Yes," Fred said.

Dawes took a long breath, letting the air curl out slowly from between his teeth.

"You're aware, Colonel, that the assault on Anderson is one of the best-documented military actions in history. The security cameras broadcast everything. I've spent months playing those streams. I can tell you things about the assault you don't even know."

"If you say so."

"When the barricade blew, eleven people died in the blast. Three more stopped breathing in the next two minutes, and the last two survived until your people came."

"We didn't kill the injured."

"You killed one when he tried to bring his pistol up. The other one had a collapsed lung and choked on her own blood before your medics looked at her."

"You want an apology?"

Dawes's smile was cooler now.

"I want you to understand that I know every action that was

taken on the station. Every order. Every shot fired, and from what gun. I know everything about that assault, and so does half the Belt. You're famous out here."

"You're the one who asked what happened," Fred said, shrugging as best he could with bound, numb arms.

"No, Colonel. I asked what happened to *you*."

General Jasira's private office was decorated like somebody's idea of a British gentleman's club. The furniture was all dark oak and darker leather. The heavy desk smelled like lemons and tung oil. The pen set and globe of Earth on top of it were both made of brass. The bookshelves were filled with real paper books and other souvenirs from a long lifetime of constant travel. There wasn't an electronic device more complex than a lamp anywhere in sight. If it weren't for the 0.17 lunar gravity, there would be no way to know it wasn't an office in London in the early twentieth century.

The general was waiting for him to speak first, so Fred swirled the scotch in his glass instead, enjoying the sound the ice made and the harsh smell of the liquor. He drained it in one swallow, then set it back on the desktop in front of him, an invitation to be refilled.

As Jasira put another two fingers into it, he finally gave up on waiting. He said, "I imagine you've had some time to review the video the terrorists transmitted from Anderson."

Fred nodded. He'd guessed this was the reason for the after-hours invitation. He tried another sip of scotch, but it had taken on a sour taste, and he put it back down.

"Yes, sir, I have. We were jamming radio all the way in, as per protocol, but we didn't detect that little tightbeam relay they'd left—"

"Fred," Jasira interjected with a laugh. "This isn't an inquisition. You aren't here to apologize. You did *good*, Colonel."

Fred frowned, picked his glass up, then put it back down without taking a drink.

"Then to be frank, sir, I wonder what I *am* here for."

Jasira leaned back in his chair.

"A couple of little things. I saw your request for an investigation into the negotiation team's work. The declassification of the negotiation transcripts. That surprised me."

As he spoke, Jasira rolled his shoulders, though in the moon's fractional gravity they could hardly be tense. He must have spent a lot of time dirtside, and the habits died slow.

"Sir," Fred said, speaking slowly and picking his words carefully, "because of the relay, the public has already seen the battle footage. We can't put that genie back in the bottle. But no one seems to want to talk about the tightbeam they sent to us at the end there. We—"

"And how will this information change anything? You did your job, soldier. The negotiation team did theirs. End of story."

"As it stands, sir, the people who took Anderson look like they're insane, and we look like executioners," Fred said, then stopped when he realized his voice was getting loud. Quieting down, he said, "There was some kind of mistake. That second message makes it clear that they thought they'd surrendered. A lot of people died over that miscommunication."

Jasira smiled, but there was no humor in it.

"Don't be so hard on yourself. You barely lost anybody," the general said. "Anyway, the request's denied. We have no reason to do any investigation on this matter. The battle footage is out, and as it stands that works in our favor. The simpler the message is, the more people will understand it: Take one of our stations, and we take it back. Hard. We can only confuse the issue by turning it political."

"Sir," Fred said, all warmth gone from his voice. "I killed 173 armed insurgents and over a thousand civilians in this action. You owe it to those people—you owe it to *me*—to show we did the right thing. What if we can avoid this happening next time?"

"There isn't going to be a next time," the general said. "You're the one who saw to that."

"Sir, you're making it seem very much like this wasn't a mistake at all. Who gave the order to ignore their surrender and send me in? Was it you?"

Jasira shrugged. "It doesn't matter. You did what we needed you to do. We won't forget that."

Fred looked at his hands. He rose to his feet, a little too quickly, bouncing in the low g, and snapped a sharp salute. Jasira poured himself another glass of scotch and drank it off, leaving Fred standing as he did.

"Will there be anything else, sir?"

Jasira gave him a long, resigned look.

"They're giving you the Medal of Freedom."

Fred's arm turned limp, and his salute collapsed under its own weight.

"What?" was all he could manage to say.

"I'm going back down the well. I'm too old to suck vacuum anymore. They'll pin you with the UN Marines' highest honor, then shortly thereafter give you your first star. You'll have a seat here at OPCOM before the year is out. Try to look happy about it."

The silence stretched. Fred focused hard on nothing about ten feet in front of him. Dawes watched him for almost a full minute, then gave up.

"All right. Why don't I start, then?" Dawes said. "Here's what happened. You were sleeping with one of the marines. Keeping it quiet because you were the commander, and that's a no-no, right? So you're very careful taking the station. You keep your casualties low, but you don't get lucky and your lover dies."

Fred kept his face stony and still. Dawes leaned back, resting on one long, thin arm like he was lounging under a tree in some sunlit park.

"You can't get the usual psychological support," Dawes went on, "because that would mean exposing the relationship, and you're still ashamed of it. You have a little breakdown. You end up knocking around OPA bars hoping someone'll kill you."

Fred didn't respond. His legs were past numb now and starting to hurt. Dawes grinned. He seemed to be enjoying this.

"No?" the OPA man said. "Don't like that one? All right. How about this? Before you joined up with the Marines, you were a troubled kid. Did all kinds of bad things. Wild. Joining up is what straightened you out. Made you into the staunch, upright, legal, and appropriate guy you are today. But then the Anderson Station broadcast comes out. A bunch of people from your past see the feed and someone recognizes you. You come back a hero, but there's a sting in it. You're being blackmailed for…mmm. How about rape? Or, no. Drug trafficking. You used to cook tabs of grace in your dorm room, sell it at the clubs. Now it's come back to haunt you, and you have a little breakdown. And you end up knocking around OPA bars hoping someone'll kill you."

Dawes waved a hand in front of Fred's eyes.

"Still with me, Colonel? Don't like that one either? All right. Maybe you've got a sister who came up the well, and you lost track of her—"

"Why don't you save your fucking air," Fred growled. "Whatever you're here for, do it and be done."

"Because *why* matters, Colonel. *Why* always matters. Whatever your story is, I know how it ends. It ends with you, here, talking to me. That's the easy part, and I think you're here looking for easy."

"What the fuck is that supposed to mean?"

The woman with the rifle said something. Either her Belter patois was too accented and fast or it was some OPA verbal code because Fred couldn't even cut the flow of syllables into individual words. Dawes nodded, took his hand terminal out of a pocket and keyed something in. Fred leaned forward, trying to get the blood flow back into his legs. Dawes put the hand terminal away.

"You changed, Colonel. The way you behave changed after

Anderson Station. Before that, you were just another inner planets asshole who didn't give a shit whether the Belt lived or died. You stuck to your bases and your stage-managed outreach programs and the station levels where the security gets paid by Earth taxes. And now, you're not.

"I've lived in the Belt my whole life. I've known a lot of men who wanted to die. They act just like you. Women don't. I haven't figured that out yet, but the men? Even if they do take a walk outside or swallow a gun, there's always this part before. Taking risks. Hoping the universe will do it for them. Make it easy. And the Belt's an unforgiving environment. You want to die, getting sloppy's usually enough."

"I don't give a shit what you think," Fred said. "I don't give a shit what you want, or who you know. And your popular psychology horseshit? Yeah, you can drink it with milk. I have nothing to justify to you. I did my job, and I'm not ashamed of any decision I made. With the same information, I'd do the same thing again."

"*With the same information,*" Dawes said, latching on to the phrase hard. "You found something out, then?"

"Fuck off, Dawes."

"What was it, Colonel? What kind of information turns the Butcher of Anderson Station into a suicide? What makes him into a coward?"

The hundred and seventy Belters occupying Anderson Station hadn't taken offensive action yet. Fred watched the station in false-color IR.

"Priority flash traffic from OPCOM, sir, cross-checked and verified," the intel officer on his monitor said. "Eyes only. Sending it to you now."

There was only one line of text.

AUTHORIZATION TO RETAKE STATION GRANTED.

And that was that. Thirty-seven hours of negotiation was over.

Outer Planets Command was tired of waiting, and they were unleashing the dogs.

Fred called up the company major and said, "Put them in their racks. We're go for assault. Set the countdown timer to one hour."

"Roger that, sir," the major said with more glee than Fred was comfortable seeing.

One hour until they went into the station. Fred called up the negotiation team on the command ship.

"Psych Ops here," said Captain Santiago, the team commander.

"Captain, this is Colonel Johnson. We've been given authorization to retake the station. My people go in in an hour. Do we have anything left to try? A Hail Mary pass? Have you warned them about the assault?"

There was no reason for secrecy. There would be no way to hide three Marine assault craft on breaching maneuvers.

The silence from the other end stretched out, and Fred was almost at the point of checking to see if the line was still open when the reply came.

"Colonel, are you double-checking my work here, sir?"

Fred counted to ten slowly.

"No, Captain. But I'm about to send six hundred marines into the station. In addition to the 170 hostiles, there are over ten thousand civilians. Many or all of them could die before the day's out. I just want to make sure we've exhausted every other possibility before we commit to—"

"Sir, I've got my orders just like you do. We did what we could, but Psych Ops is standing down now. Your turn."

"Am I the only one that sees that this doesn't make any sense?" Fred said. "They claim they took the station because of a three percent cargo transfer fee? I mean, they already threw the administrator who implemented it out the damned airlock. There is literally nothing left for them to win by forcing a fight."

The only answer was static.

"Let me talk to them," Fred said. "Maybe if they hear it from a different voice, they'll understand—"

"Sir," Santiago cut in. "I am not authorized to do that. You want to argue about it? Call General Jasira back at OPCOM. Santiago out."

Fred launched himself at Dawes, pushing out with numbed legs, and Dawes scuttled back. Fred landed on the deck hard. The world grayed out for a second, and he tasted blood. He struggled forward, trying to get at Dawes's feet with his teeth if that was the best he could manage. He saw the Belter up to the knees, stepping back. Fred twisted. Something in his left shoulder made a sick crunching sound, and a sharp pain shot up his neck. Then the woman stepped forward.

He looked up into the triangular barrel of the fléchette rifle, and then past it to the woman's eyes. They were the blue of oceans seen from orbit. There was no pity in them. Her thumb was on the safety. Her finger on the trigger. A little pressure, and the rifle would send a hundred spikes of steel thinner than needles through his brain. And she wanted to. It was in the set of her shoulders and the angles of her face how much she wanted to end him.

"The problem with you," Dawes said, his voice calm and conversational as if they were sitting in a bar somewhere sharing a beer, "and I don't mean this as a criticism of you in particular. It's true of anybody who didn't grow up in the Belt. The problem with you is that you are wasteful."

"I'm not a fucking coward," Fred said through his rapidly swelling lip.

"Of course you are. You're smart, you're healthy. Maybe a few hundred people out of forty billion have your combination of talent and training. And you're trying to waste that very valuable resource. You're like the guy who delays replacing his airlock seals when they start to leak. You think it's just a little bit. It doesn't matter. You're one guy. You get killed, no big loss."

He heard Dawes walking behind him, but his gaze was still

on the rifle. Dawes grabbed Fred's collar and hauled him back to kneeling.

"When I was growing up, my dad used to beat the crap out of me if I spat someplace other than the reclamation duct because we needed the water. We don't waste things out here, Colonel. We can't afford to. You understand that, though. Don't you?"

Slowly, Fred nodded. Blood was seeping down his chin even though Dawes and the woman hadn't laid an angry hand on him. He'd done this to himself.

"When I was about fifteen, I killed my sister," Dawes said. "I didn't mean to. We were on this rock about a week from Eros Station. We were going out of the ship to get some survey probes that got stuck in the slurry. I was supposed to check her suit seals, but I was in a mood. I was fifteen, you know? So I did a half-assed job of it. We went outside, and everything seemed fine until she twisted sideways to pull up a rock spur. I heard it on the comm link, and it just sounded like a pop. We had the old Ukrainian-style suits. Solid as stone unless something broke, and then it all failed at once."

Dawes shrugged.

"You're a fucking piece of shit, then, aren't you?" Fred said, and Dawes grinned.

"Felt like that, yeah. Still do sometimes. I understand why someone could want to die after a thing like that."

"So why not kill yourself?" Fred asked, then spat a dark red clot on the deck at his feet.

"I've got three more sisters," Dawes said. "Someone's got to check their seals."

Fred shook his head. His shoulder vibrated with sudden pain.

"Why are you telling me this?"

"Builds rapport," Dawes said. "How's it working?"

Fred laughed before he knew he was going to. Dawes gestured, and the woman put up the rifle, walking back to her doorway.

"So. Colonel," Dawes said. "What information did you get on Anderson Station that you ended up here talking to a sad sack of shit like me?"

Fred took a long breath.

"There was a message sent to us as we went in," he said. "A message I didn't see until it was too late."

"Let me see it," Fred said.

"There are a couple things here," the lieutenant said. "Got a partial that was never sent. And one that looks like it's being sent to the command ship on infinite repeat. Also, a running feed that looks like a straight dump of the security cameras."

"Do the unsent partial first."

The video started, and the man in the mining jumpsuit stared out of the screen. For Fred, there was a surreal quality to watching a man alive and speaking while his corpse lay cooling on the floor behind him.

I could have told him this would happen.

The dead man said, "Citizens of the solar system, my name is Marama Brown. I'm a freelance mining technician for Anderson-Hyosung Cooperative Industries Group. I, and some like-minded individuals, have taken control of the company resupply station."

Fred hit pause and turned to his lieutenant. He had a sinking feeling in his gut. The dead man had expected this to get out. Even though he had to know they were jamming, he'd expected the message to be heard.

"Where was that security camera feed going?" Fred asked.

"I'll check on that right now, sir," the lieutenant replied, and called up the electronic warfare people back on the *Dagmar*. Fred tuned their conversation out, and hit play again.

"I believe—we all believe that this action is justified by what has been done here. A man named Gustav Marconi, the station administrator, recently implemented a three percent surcharge on supply transfers. I know that doesn't sound like much to some of you, but most of us are living on the ragged edge out here. Prospectors, wildcat miners…you strike it rich or you starve. That's the game. But now a bunch of us are going to have to buy three percent less supplies because it just got that much more expensive. You can eat a bit less food. You can drink a little less water. You can fly a little slower and stretch your fuel, maybe. You run life support at bare minimums. But—"

"Sir?" said the lieutenant, and Fred paused the playback. "Sir, the transmission, at least some of it, got out. They'd left a tight-beam receiver and broadcast transmitter anchored to a rock just outside our jamming range. We missed it. But the e-war geeks have triangulated its location and are sending a Phantom to frag it."

Too late, Fred thought, and hit the play button again.

"—what if you're already running at the bare minimum? How about every year, you just don't breathe for three days? That would about cover it. Or you don't drink any water for three days. Or you don't eat for three days when you're already on the brink of starvation. When there's nothing left to cut back on, how do you make it up then?"

Marama turned away from the camera for a second, and when he turned back he was holding his hand terminal. He held it up to the screen. It was displaying the picture of a little girl. She was wearing a powder-blue jumpsuit that had "Hinekiri" hand stitched on the breast, and grinning with small crooked teeth.

"This is my little girl, my Kiri. She's four. She has what the medics call 'hypoxic brain injury.' She was born a little prematurely, and instead of the high oxygen environment she should have had, she was in my prospecting ship where the air is a little thinner than the Everest base camps back on Earth. We didn't even know anything was wrong until we realized she wasn't developing normally."

He turned away from the camera and put the terminal down.

"And she's not the only one. Developmental problems arising from low oxygen and malnutrition are becoming more and more common. When this was explained to Mr. Marconi, his reply was, 'Work harder and you can afford the increase.' We complained to the Anderson-Hyosung head offices, but no one listened. We complained to the Outer Planets Governing Board on Luna.

"This isn't...We didn't start out intending to take over the station. It all just sort of happened," the man said. For a moment, his voice seemed to waver. As Fred watched, the man forced himself back into calm. "We want everyone to know that, other than Mr. Marconi, whose crimes would have led directly to the deaths of thousands of Belters, no one has been harmed in our taking of the station. We don't want anyone else to get hurt. We're not violent people, but we have been pushed so far that there is nowhere left to retreat to. We've been in discussions with a UN military negotiator for almost two days now. In a short time, we will be surrendering the station to them. We'll send this message out prior to handing the station over to make sure our story is heard. I hope no one ever feels like they have to do something like this again. I hope, after all of this, that people can begin talking about what's happening out here."

The video ended. Fred queued up the tightbeam that had been sent to the negotiation team during the assault.

Marama Brown again, this time holding a pistol, his face twisted with fear.

"Why are the Marines attacking?" he said in a panicked screech. "We just needed some time! We're surrendering!"

The message immediately repeated. Fred stopped it and turned it off.

"Sir."

Fred took a long breath to fight back the vague nausea he suddenly felt.

"Go ahead, Lieutenant."

"Phantom reports a clean hit. The relay is toast. But, uh..."

"Spit it out, soldier."

"It was no longer broadcasting. Whatever they sent, they were done sending it."

Fred pulled up the comm logs, and confirmed what he'd already suspected: Marama Brown had never gotten to send his manifesto. Fred had been ordered in, and Marama had been busy trying to stay alive. But his last tightbeam to Psych Ops had gotten through just fine. They'd known.

"Sir?" the lieutenant said.

"Doesn't matter. Call up the cyber wonks and have them strip the computer core. I'll go find the liaison officer and start the civilian aid phase."

His lieutenant chuckled.

"Here, kiddies," the lieutenant said. "We blew the shit out of your station, have some free MREs and UN Marine sticker books."

Fred didn't laugh.

"You had to have known that they were desperate out there," Dawes said.

"Of course I did," Fred said. "It was in all the reports. Hell, it was on the news feeds. Increased overhead. People struggling for the basics. You hear it all the time. Turn on a feed now, you'll hear it again."

The blood had stopped flowing from Fred's mouth, but the inside of his lip tasted raw. His shoulder was settling into a low, radiating ache. There was a dark circle of blood on the decking in front of him.

"But this time it was different?" Dawes said. He didn't sound sarcastic or angry. Just curious.

Fred shifted. His legs were dead lumps of meat. He couldn't feel anything. If someone put a knife into his thigh, it would have been like watching it happen to someone else.

"That man had a crippled baby girl," Fred said. "I killed him."

"The UN would just have sent someone else," Dawes said.

"I still killed him."

"You didn't pull the trigger."

"I killed him because he wanted her to have enough air to breathe," Fred said. "I killed her daddy while he was trying to surrender, and they gave me a medal for doing it. So there you go. That's what happened on Anderson Station. What are you going to do about it?"

Dawes shook his head.

"That's too easy. You've killed lots of daddies. What made this one different?"

Fred started to speak, stopped, tried again.

"They used me. They made it about sending messages to everyone that you don't fuck with Earth, because look at the shit we'll do just because you spaced an administrator on a nowhere station. They made me the poster boy for disproportional response. They made me a butcher."

Saying the words was painful, but there was a strange relief too. Dawes was staring at him, his face unreadable. Fred couldn't meet his eyes.

Dawes nodded, seeming to come to a decision, then put a hand in his pocket and took out a utility knife. When he opened it, the blade was old and scored. Fred took a deep breath and let it out slowly. He was ready. Dawes walked behind him. A fast pull across the neck, and Fred could bleed out in four minutes. A stab in the kidney could take hours. Cut the cords that were tying his arms, and it could take years.

Dawes cut the cords.

"This wasn't a trial," Fred said. "You're not here to pass some kind of judgment on me."

"I wasn't expecting to," Dawes said. "I mean, if it really had been just that you'd been boning one of your marines, I'd have dropped you out an airlock, wasteful or no. But I was pretty sure I was right."

"So what happens now?"

Dawes shifted Fred forward. The pins-and-needles feeling was starting in his hands. Dawes cut the binding on his legs.

"If you want the easy way out, you go kill yourself on your own damn time and stop setting the OPA up to take the blame for it. I've got enough bad press without slaughtering the hero of Anderson Station."

"And otherwise?"

Dawes sat back on his haunches and closed the blade with one hand.

"I don't waste resources, Colonel. If you want to die, it will do that girl and her father absolutely no good. If you want to make it up to her and all the people like her, I could use your expertise. You're a rare resource. You've got knowledge and training, and as the man who is famous throughout the whole system for killing Belters, you're in a position to be our strongest advocate. All it means is walking away from everything you know and love. The life you built for yourself. The admiration of everyone who looks up to you. All the things you'd have lost anyway."

"This was a recruitment, then."

Dawes stood up, sliding the knife into his pocket. His smile reached his eyes this time.

"You tell me," Dawes said. Then, to the woman, *"Recanos ai postar. Asi geendig."*

"Aiis," she said, shouldering the rifle like a professional.

The pair walked out together, leaving Fred on the deck, massaging the agony out of his legs as the feeling started to return.

The Butcher of Anderson Station
Author's Note

In the beginning, there weren't going to be any short stories in The Expanse. It wasn't that we were dead set against the idea, it's just that you have to think of these things before you can do them, and it just hadn't occurred to us. In that sense, everything in this book exists because of John Joseph Adams, the editor of *Lightspeed*. He was the first one to ask if we'd thought about writing short fiction in the universe of *Leviathan Wakes*, and as soon as he said it, we had.

"The Butcher of Anderson Station" set the tone of what the short stories would be: a chance to tell some side story or explore some part of the universe that wasn't part of the main storyline but had something interesting about it.

"Butcher" is a little bit of backstory about Fred Johnson, yes. But it's also a chance for us to tell a story about guilt and the lengths to which people will go to get out from under it. Fred is a profoundly moral man, manipulated into being the instrument of something evil. Even though the events at Anderson Station weren't directly his fault, he's haunted by them, and without the intercession of Anderson Dawes, they would have killed him.

There's a line Daniel likes from the gnostic Gospel of Thomas: If you bring forth that which is within you, what you bring forth will save you. If you do not bring forth that which is within you, what you do not bring forth will destroy you. That idea and this story have something to say to each other.

Curiously, John Joseph Adams didn't wind up taking the story. There are a lot of variables that go into editing a magazine, and this particular story didn't fit his needs that month. No blame. We wound up publishing it through Orbit's ebook program, where it's lived happily ever since.

One of the other characters in the story is a frightening woman who holds Fred at gunpoint, ready to shoot him in the head the instant Dawes asks her to. Later, when we were making the show, Cara Gee (who played Camina Drummer) pitched the idea that the unnamed woman with Anderson Dawes might have been Drummer in her early days. Which seemed plausible to us.

Gods of Risk

W hat *kind* of problem?" Hutch asked. Even though he was
from the settlements near Mariner Valley, he didn't have
the relaxed, drawling accent of that part of Mars. Hutch's voice
buzzed like a radio on just the wrong frequency.

"It's not bad," Leelee said, leaping to his defense. "It's not bad,
right, David? Not really a problem. Inconvenience maybe."

"Inconvenience," David echoed.

The silence was uncomfortable. David tugged his fingers, pulling each one straight out from the hand until the knuckle popped,
then moving on to the next. He was half a head taller than Hutch,
but he couldn't seem to bring his gaze up higher than the thin
man's sternum. In two months, David would be sixteen, but he
felt about six. Hutch's meetings were always in small rooms, away
from the main passages and corridors. This one had been a storage hole from the first generation of settlements. The walls were

the polished stone of Mars covered with a clear insulative ceramic that was starting to bubble and gray with age. The light was a construction lantern, the burning white of the LED softened and made ruddy by Leelee's paisley silk scarf draped over it. They sat on metal crates in the cold. Hutch scratched at the scars on his wrist.

"Don't let it choke you, little man," Hutch said. It was an old joke between them—David's family were Polynesian before they were Martian, and between genetics and growing up at barely over a third of Terran g, David was over two meters tall and leaning toward pudgy. "Just say what it is. You got a bad batch, right?"

"No, nothing like that. The batch is fine. It's just my aunt Bobbie's come to live with us for a while. She's always at the place now. Always. Anytime I get home, she's there."

Hutch frowned and tilted his head. Leelee put her arm around his shoulder, draping herself close to the man. Hutch shrugged her back but not off.

"She knows you're cooking?"

"She doesn't know anything," David said. "She just lifts weights and watches video feeds all day."

"Lifts weights?" Hutch asked.

There was an undercurrent of amusement in his voice that made David's guts unknot. He risked a glance at the thin man's tea-brown eyes.

"She used to be a Marine."

"Used to be?"

"Something weird happened. She sort of quit."

"So not a Marine anymore. And now what is she?"

"Just a fucking inconvenience," David said. He took a little joy in the profanity. *Hell* and *damn* were the worst language tolerated in the Draper house. *Fuck* would have gotten him yelled at. Worse than that would be unthinkable. "The batch is fine. But it's going to be harder to get the next one done. I can't do any of the prep work at home now."

Hutch leaned back, his laughter filling the air. Leelee's face relaxed, all the little worry lines vanishing back into the eggshell smoothness of her skin.

"Shit," Hutch said. "You had me thinking there was trouble for a minute there. Thought I was going to have to tell my people that my best cook fell down."

David picked up his satchel, fumbled through it, and came out with a rattling plastic jar. Hutch took it, cracked the seal, and poured four or five of the small pink lozenges into his hand, then passed one to Leelee. She popped it in her mouth like it was hard candy. The 2,5-Dimethoxy-4-n-propylthiophenethylamine was a serotonin receptor agonist that broke down into—among other things—a 2,5 desmethoxy derivative that was a monoamine oxidase A inhibitor. The euphoric effects would start to tighten Leelee's joints and lift her mood in the next half hour. The hallucinations wouldn't kick in for an hour, maybe an hour and a half, and then they'd last her through the night. She rattled the lozenge across the back of her teeth with her tongue, grinning at him. David felt the first stirrings of an erection and looked away from her.

"You do good work, little man," Hutch said, taking out his hand terminal. The small chime meant the transfer was done. David's secret account had a little more money in it, not that he was in this for the money. "Now, this auntie thing. What's it going to do to your schedule?"

"I've still got the lab at school," David said. "I can sign up for more time there. Seniors get preference, so it won't be too hard. It's just—"

"Yeah, no," Hutch said. "Better we play safe. You tell me how much time you need to make the next batch; that's how much time you can take."

"I'm thinking a couple weeks at least," David said.

"Take them, they're yours," Hutch said, waving his scarred hand. "We're in this for the long haul, you and me. No reason to get greedy now."

"Yeah."

The thin man stood up. David was never sure how old Hutch really was. Older than him and Leelee and younger than David's parents. That gulf of years seemed to fill infinite possibilities. Hutch shrugged on his dust-red overcoat and pulled his brown knit tuque out of a pocket, flapped it once like he was whipping the air, and pulled it down over white-blond hair. Leelee stood up with him, but Hutch put a hand on her bare shoulder, turning the girl toward David.

"You see my girl here back to the land of the living, eh, little man? I got a thing to do."

"All right," David said. Leelee pulled her scarf off the lantern, and the dirty little room went brighter. Hutch gave a mocking three-finger salute, then unsealed the door and left. The rule was that Hutch left first, and then ten minutes later David could go. He didn't know exactly where Hutch went, and if Leelee was here with him, he didn't care. She leaned against him, smelling like verbena and girl. She was a year older than him, and he could have rested his chin on the top of her head.

"You're doing all right?" he asked.

"Am," she said, her voice slushy and soft. "It's starting to come on."

"That's good." He gathered her a little closer. She rested her head against his chest, and they waited quietly for the precious minutes to pass.

Seven communities—called the neighborhoods—scattered through the northern reach of the Aurorae Sinus made up Londres Nova. The city, such as it was, had burrowed deep into the flesh of Mars, using the soil as insulation and radiation shielding with only ten domes pressing out to the surface. Forty thousand people lived and worked there, carving new life into the unforgiving stone of humanity's second home. Tube stations made a simple web topology that determined the social forms and structures. Aterpol was the only station with connections to every other neighborhood, and so it became the de facto downtown. Salton was under the biggest agricultural dome and had a surface mono-rail to the observatory at Dhanbad Nova, and so the upper university and technical clinics were concentrated there. The lower university was in Breach Candy, where David and his family lived. Nariman and Martineztown had been manufacturing and energy production sites in the first wave of colonization, and the displacement that came with new technologies meant both neighborhoods were struggling to reinvent and repurpose themselves. Innis Deep and Innis Shallows each had only a single tube route out, making them cul-de-sacs and havens for the sort of Martian who was almost a Belter—antisocial, independent, and intolerant. An address in either Innis was the mark of an outsider—someone dangerous or vulnerable. Leelee lived in the Shallows, and Hutch lived in the Deep.

As much as the neighborhoods differed, the tube stations were the same: high, arched ceilings bright with full-spectrum light and chaotic with echoes; thin-film video monitors pasted to the walls, blaring public information and entertainment feeds; kiosks selling food and clothes, the latest fads and fashions cycled in and out as regularly as tides. Security cameras looked down on everything, identity-matching software tweaking the video feeds to put names with faces in the crowd. The air always seemed to have the faint scents of ozone and cheap food and piss. The plastic-film flyers always looked the same whether they were announcing yoga classes, lost pets, or independent music acts. David had been to the cities in Mariner Valley and the base of Olympus Mons, and the tube stations had been the same there too. The one unifying cultural product of Mars.

David led Leelee through the bustle of the Martineztown station. He shifted his satchel so that she could put her arm around his. The farther they walked the less steady her steps were. Her arm curled around him like ivy clinging to a pillar, and he could feel the stiffness in her muscles and hear it in her voice when she spoke. Her pupils were dilating with pleasure and the chemical cascade in her brain. He wondered what she was seeing.

"You never try the stuff yourself?" she asked again, unaware that it was the third time.

"No," David said again. "I'm finishing up my senior labs. There isn't really time for a night off. Later maybe. When I get my placement."

"You're so smart," she said. "Hutch always says how you're so smart."

Ahead of them, near the platform, a crowd of something close to fifty people were chanting together and holding up signs. A dozen uniformed cops stood a few yards away, not interfering, but watching closely. David ducked his head and turned Leelee away at an angle. Maybe if they headed toward the restrooms there would be a way to the platform that didn't involve walking a tripping girl past the police. Not that the police were paying much attention to the foot traffic. Their attention was all on the protest. The signs were hand lettered or printed on standard-sized paper and glued together. A couple had thin-film monitors playing looped images that fuzzed out to a psychedelic rainbow swirl when the signs flexed.

HIT BACK! and ARE WE WAITING UNTIL THEY KILL US? and EARTH STARTED IT. LET'S FINISH IT. This last slogan was accompanied by a bad homemade animation of a rock slamming into the Earth, a massive molten impact crater looking like a bloody bullet wound in the planet.

The protestors were a mixed group, but most were a little older than David or Leelee. Blood-dark faces and the square-gape mouths sent the sense of rage radiating out from them like heat. David paused, trying to make out what exactly they were chanting through the echoes, but all he could tell was that it had seven syllables, four in a call and three in response. One of the police shifted, looking at David, and he started walking again. It wasn't his fight. He didn't care.

By the time they reached the platform, Leelee had gone quiet. He led her to a formed plastic bench that was intended for three people, but was snug with just the two of them. It ticked and popped under his weight, and Leelee flinched from the sound. There were small, distressed lines between her brows. The arrival board listed six minutes for the tube that would eventually get them to Innis Shallows, the seconds counting down in clean-lined Arabic numerals. When Leelee spoke, her voice was tight. He didn't know if it was from sadness or the expected side effect of the drug.

"Everybody's so angry," she said. "I just wish people weren't so angry."

"They've got reason to be."

Her focus swam for a moment, her gaze fighting to find him.

"Everyone's got reasons to be," she said. "I've got reasons to be. You've got reasons to be. Doesn't mean we are, though. Doesn't mean we want to be. You aren't angry, are you, David?" The question ended almost like a plea, and he wanted to tell her that he wasn't. He wanted to say whatever words would smooth her perfect brow, and then take her back to her room in the housing complex and kiss her and have her strip off his clothes. He wanted to see her naked and hear her laugh and fall asleep, spent, in her arms. He coughed, shifting on the bench. "You aren't angry, are you?" she asked again.

The soft tritone sounded.

"The tube car's here," he said, forcing a smile. "Everything's going to be fine. Just relax, right?"

She nodded and tried to pull away from him.

"It's all red. You're red too. Like a great big cherry. You're so *smart*," she said. "So you never try the stuff yourself?"

On the tube car, things weren't better. This leg of the trip was an express for Aterpol, and the men and women on it were older than he was by a decade. Their demographic weight had the public monitor set to a newsfeed. In some well-appointed newsroom on the planet, a thin, gray-haired man was shouting down a swarthy woman.

"I don't care!" the man said. "The agent they weaponized came from some larger, extra-solar ecosystem, and I don't care. I don't care about Phoebe. I don't care about Venus. What I care about is what they did. The fact is—and no one disputes this—the fact is that Earth bought those weapons and—"

"That's a *gross* oversimplification. Evidence is that there were several bids, including one from—"

"Earth bought those weapons and they fired them at us. At you and me and our children and grandchildren."

The doors slid silently closed and the car began its acceleration. The tubes themselves were in vacuum, the car riding on a bed of magnetic fields like a gauss round. The lurch of acceleration was gentle, though. They'd cover the distance to Aterpol in twenty minutes. Maybe less. Leelee closed her eyes and rested her head against the back of the car. Her lips pressed thin and her grip on his arm tightened. Maybe they should have waited for her to take the pill until she'd gotten to someplace quieter and better controlled.

"And Earth also provided the tracking data that shot them all down," the woman on the screen said, pointing at the gray-haired man with her whole hand. "Yes, a rogue element in the Earth military was involved, but to dismiss the role that the official, *sanctioned* military played—"

"Sanctioned military? You make it sound like there's a civil war on Earth. I don't see that. I don't see that at all. I see Mars under a persistent, existential threat and the government sitting on its hands."

"Tell me a story," Leelee said. "Talk to me. Sing me a song. Something."

"I've got music on the hand terminal if you want."

"No," she said. "You. Your voice."

David tucked his satchel between his feet and turned toward her, dipping his head down close to her ear. He had to hunch a little. He licked his lips, trying to think of something. His mind was blank, and he grabbed at the first thought that came through him. He brought his mouth to the shell of her ear. When he sang, he tried to be quiet enough that no one else would hear him.

"Good King Wenceslas looked out on the feast of Stephen…"

Leelee didn't open her eyes, but she smiled. That was good enough. For ten minutes, David went on, quietly singing Christmas carols to Leelee. Some he got into and didn't remember the right words, so he just made things up. Nonsense that fit the rhythm of the music, or nearly did.

The detonation was the loudest thing David had ever heard, less a sound than a physical blow. The car pitched forward, rattling against the walls of the tube, throwing Leelee into him and then back. The lighting flickered, failed, and then came on in a different color. They were stopped between stations. The monitors clicked to a pinkish-gray as they rebooted, then glowered back to life with the emergency services trefoil.

"Is this happening?" Leelee asked. Her irises were tiny rings of brown around deep black. "David? Is this happening?"

"It is, and it's all right," he said. "I'm here. We're fine."

David checked his hand terminal, thinking that the newsfeeds might tell him what was going on—power failure, rioting, enemy attack—but the network was in lockdown. An almost supernaturally calm male voice came over the public monitors. "The public transport system has encountered a pressure anomaly and has been shut down to assure passenger safety. Stay calm and a maintenance crew will arrive shortly." The message was less important than the tone of voice it was spoken in, and Leelee relaxed a little. She started to giggle.

"Well this is fucked," she said and grinned at him. "Fucked, fucked, fucked, fucked, *fucked*."

"Yeah," David said. His mind was already jumping ahead. He'd be late getting home. His father would want to know why, and when it came out he'd been in Martineztown, there'd be questions. What he'd been doing there, who had he been seeing, why hadn't he told anybody. All around them, the other passengers were grumbling and sighing and arranging themselves into comfortable positions, waiting for the rescuers. David stood up and sat down again. Every passing minute seemed to relax Leelee and shunt that tension into his spine. When he caught a glimpse of his reflection in the glass of the tube doors, the boy looking back seemed furtive and scared.

Half an hour later, the emergency hatch at the end of the car creaked, popped, and opened. A man and a woman in matching blue security uniforms stepped in.

"Hey, folks," the man said. "Everyone all right? Sorry about this, but some jackhole broke the vacuum seals. Whole system's going to be down for about six hours, minimum. Some places longer. We've got service carts out here that can take folks to transport buses. Just line up single file, and we'll get you where you're going."

Leelee was humming to herself as David drew her into line. He couldn't get her to Innis Shallows and get back home. Not with the tubes down. He bit his lips and they moved forward one at a time, the other passengers vanishing through the emergency hatch and into the temporary airlock beyond it. It took forever to reach the front of the line.

"Where are you two headed?" the security man asked, consulting his hand terminal. It was working, even though David's wasn't. The man looked up, concerned. "Hermano. Where are you two headed?"

"Innis Shallows," David said. And then, "She's going to Innis Shallows. I was taking her there, because she's not feeling so good. But I've got to get to Breach Candy. I'm going to miss my labs." Leelee stiffened.

"Innis Shallows and Breach Candy. Step on through."

The temporary airlock was made from smooth black Mylar, and walking through it was like going through the inside of a balloon. The pressure wasn't calibrated very well, and when the outer seal opened, David's ears popped. The hall was wide and low, the dull orange emergency lights filling the passage with shadows and leaching the color out of everything. The air was at least five degrees colder, enough to summon gooseflesh, and Leelee wasn't holding his arm anymore. Her eyebrows were lifted and her mouth was set.

"It'll be okay," he said as they came close to the electric carts. "They'll get you home all right."

"Yeah, fine," she said.

"I'm sorry. I've got to get home. My dad—"

She turned to him. In the dim light, her dilated eyes didn't seem as out of place. Her sobriety made him wonder how much she'd really been feeling it before and how much had been a playful kind of acting.

"Don't worry about it," she said. "Not the first time I've been tripping in public, right? I can behave myself. Just thought you'd come play and I was wrong. Hard cheese for me and moving on now."

"I'm sorry. Next time."

"You call it," she said with a shrug. "Next time."

The driver of the cart for Innis Shallows called out, and Leelee clambered aboard, squeezed between a middle-aged man and a grandmotherly woman, and waved back at David once. The middle-aged man glanced at David, back at Leelee, then down at the girl's body. The cart lurched, whined, and lurched again. David stood, watching it pull away. The mixture of shame, regret, and longing felt like an illness. Someone touched his elbow.

"Breach Candy?"

"Yes."

"Over here, then. Damn. You're a big one, aren't you? All right, though. We'll fit you in."

It was two years almost to the day since David had met Hutch at the lower university. David had been in the commons, the wide, carpeted benches with their soft, organic curves welcoming the students eating lunch. At thirteen, David had already been bio-chemistry track for two years. His last labs had been in tRNA transport systems, and he was reading through the outline for the carbon complex work that would take up his next six months when one of the seniors—an olive-skinned boy named Alwasi— had sat down beside him and said there was someone David should meet.

Hutch had made himself out as more of a scholar back then but still with an edge to him. For months, David had thought the man was an independent tutor; the kind of hired instructor a family might bring on if their children were falling behind. David still had seven rounds of lab to go before his placement, so he hadn't thought too much about Hutch. He'd just become another face in the whirl of the lower university, one more minor character in the cast of thousands. Or hundreds at least.

Looking back, David could sort of see how Hutch had tested him. It had begun with asking innocuous little favors—tell someone who shared David's table that Hutch was looking for her, get Hutch a few grams of some uncontrolled reagent, keep a box for him overnight. They were things that David could do easily, and so he did. Every time, Hutch praised him or paid him back with small favors. David began to notice the people Hutch knew—pretty girls and tough-looking men. Several of the low-tier instructors knew Hutch on sight, and if they weren't overly friendly to him, they were certainly respectful. There hadn't been any one moment when David had crossed a line from being someone Hutch knew to cooking for him. It all happened so smoothly that he'd never felt a bump.

The fact was he would have done the side projects for Hutch without being paid. He couldn't spend the money on anything too extravagant for fear his parents would ask questions, so he used it here and there—a little present for Leelee or lunch on him for the other students at his table or the occasional indulgence that he could explain away. For the most part, it just sat in the account, growing slowly over time. The money wasn't precious because it was money. It was precious because it was secret and it was his.

When he had his placement and moved out to student housing in Salton, he'd have more freedom. Hutch's money would buy him a top-flight gaming deck or a better wardrobe. He could take Leelee out for fancy dinners without having to explain where he'd been or who he'd been with. The workload would be harder, especially if he got placed in medical or development. He'd heard stories about first-year placements on the development teams who pulled fifty-six-hour shifts without sleep. Carving out another six hours after that for Hutch might be hard, but he'd worry about that when he got there. He had more immediate problems.

The transport buses were old, wheezing electrical carts, some of them dating back two generations. The drivetrain clicked under him, and the rubberized foam wheels made a constant sticky ripping noise. David hunched in a seat, trying to pull his elbows close in against his body. Around him, the other travelers looked bored and restless. The system was still locked down, his hand terminal restricted to what it held in local memory. He checked it every few seconds just to feel he had something to do. The wide access corridors passed slowly, the conduits and pipes like the circulatory system of some vast planetary behemoth. It seemed like the corridor would go on forever, even though the distance between Martineztown and Breach Candy wasn't more than forty kilometers.

He was supposed to be in his labs at the lower university. Even if all the public transport was locked down, it wasn't more than a half-hour walk from there to home. David figured he could claim to have been in the middle of something and that it had taken longer than he'd expected to finish up the work. Except that was the excuse he'd been giving to cover the extra time he'd spent cooking for Hutch. His mother had already started wondering in her vague accusation-without-confrontation way whether he was losing focus on his work. If they found out he'd been outside the neighborhood, it would be bad. If they found out why, it would be apocalyptic. David cracked his knuckles and willed the bus to go faster.

It was easy to think of Londres Nova as existing only along its tube lines, but the truth was generations of colonists and proto-terraformers had made a webwork of tunnels under the airless permafrost of Mars. Whole complexes of the original tunnels had gone fallow—sealed off and the atmosphere and heat allowed to flow away into the flesh of the planet. Supply passages linked to electrical maintenance lines. There were shortcuts, and the bus driver knew them. Just when David was about to weep or scream with frustration, he saw the edge of Levantine Park and the north-ernmost edge of Breach Candy. The bus was going faster than he could walk, but just knowing where he was, being able to map his own way home, made the frustration a little less. And the fear maybe a little more.

I didn't do anything wrong, he told himself. *I was in my lab. There was a security alert and the network went down. I had to finish the experiment, and it took a little longer because everyone was trying to find out what had happened. That's all. Nothing else.*

The fifth time the bus stopped, he was as close to his family's hole as he was going to be. He lumbered out into the corridors of his hometown, his head down and his shoulders tucked in toward his chest like he was trying to protect something.

The family lived in a series of eight rooms dug out of the stone and finished with textured organics. Rich brown bamboo floors met soft mushroom-brown walls. The lights were indirect LEDs alleged to match a sunny afternoon on Earth. To David, they were just the color house-lights were. A newsfeed was muttering in the common rooms, so some portion of the system must have been taken off security lockdown. David closed the door behind him and stalked through the kitchen, fists against his thighs, breath shallow and fast.

Aunt Bobbie was alone in the den. In any other family, she'd have been huge. For a Draper, she was only about the middle of the bell curve in height, but athletic and strong. She wore a simple loose-cut outfit that lived somewhere between sweats and paja-mas. It mostly hid the shape of her body. She looked away from the video feed, her dark eyes meeting his, and killed the sound. On the screen, a reporter was speaking earnestly into the camera. Behind him, a lifting mech was hauling a slab of ferrocrete.

"Where's Dad?" he asked.

"Stuck in Salton with your mom," Bobbie said. "The blowout was on that line. Security's saying they'll have everything moving again in about ten hours, but your father said they'd probably be taking a room and coming home in the morning."

David blinked. No one was going to give him any grief. It should have felt like relief. He shrugged, trying to get the tension out of his shoulders, but it wouldn't go. He knew it didn't make sense to be irritated with his parents for not being there to fight with.

"Do we know what happened?" he asked, stepping into the room.

"Sabotage," Aunt Bobbie said. "Someone blew a hole between the tube and the maintenance corridor, sucked in a few thousand kilos of air. They took the vacuum seals off-line too, so the whole tube system popped like a balloon."

"Earth?"

Aunt Bobbie shook her head.

"Earth doesn't think that small," she said. "This is someone local trying to start something."

"Why would someone local blow up our own stuff if they're mad at Earth?"

"Because Earth's too far away."

It didn't sound like an answer to his question, but David let it go with another shrug.

Aunt Bobbie's gaze was on the monitor and not on it. Through it. Seeing something else. He knew she'd been on Ganymede when the fighting started and that something had happened so that she wasn't in the military anymore and she had to live with them. The unfairness of her bringing her problems into his house chafed. She sighed and forced a smile.

"How'd things go at the lab?"

"All right," he said.

"What're you working on?"

"Just labs," he said, not looking at her.

"Your dad said he expected your placement to come through soon. Find out what you'll be doing for the next eight years."

"Guess."

Aunt Bobbie smiled.

"I remember when I first got into training. There was a breakdown in the notification system, and they wound up losing my placement for about six days. I was chewing through rocks until it came through. What about you? Are you more excited, scared, or pissed off?"

"I don't know," he said.

"Your dad's really proud of you," Aunt Bobbie said. "Whatever happens, he's going to be really proud of you."

David felt the flush of warmth rising in his neck and cheeks. For a second he thought he was embarrassed, but then he recognized the rage. He clamped his jaw tight and looked at the monitor so that he wouldn't be looking at Aunt Bobbie. The mech was gesturing to a ragged hole two meters high and half a meter wide, the man controlling it speaking to the reporter as steel claws pointed out the fine cracks fanning unpredictably out from the breach. David's teeth ached and he made himself relax his jaw. Aunt Bobbie turned back to the screen. He couldn't read her expression, but he had the feeling that he'd exposed something about himself he didn't want her to know.

"We have anything for dinner?"

"I didn't make anything," she said. "Could, though."

"It's all right. I'll grab a bowl of rice. I have work I need to do. Lab stuff."

"Okay."

David's room was in the back. It had been cut from the ground with the image of a standard-sized person, and so it felt cramped to him. A standard bed would have left half a meter between the footboard and the wall; David's was almost flush. The gaming deck, the only thing he'd ever spent Hutch's illicit money on, sat at the side of the desk. The wall was set to a still from *Gods of Risk* where Caz Pratihari was about to duel Mikki Suhanam, both men looking strong, dangerous, and a bit melancholy. When the door was locked, he switched the wall to his favorite picture of Una Meing and threw himself to the bed. The newsfeed muttered from the common room, and under it—almost too faint to make out—Aunt Bobbie's slow, rhythmic grunting. Resistance training probably. He wished he could make all the noises go away. That he could have the house to himself for once. He wondered if Leelee was all right. If she'd made it home safe. If she was angry with him. Or disappointed.

His hand terminal chimed. The alert was from the lower university. In response to the terrorist attack on the tube lines, the labs would be closed the following day. Students with ongoing work that couldn't sit for an extra day were to reply to the section proctor who would either give them special authorization to come in or else do part of the work for them. He ran through a mental checklist. He didn't have anything that needed him to be there, and if he got a little behind, everyone else would, too. He didn't have any of Hutch's reagents in his lab, so if there was a security audit, he'd be all right. He had a day off, then.

Leelee's voice spoke in his memory. *You never try the stuff yourself?* Right now, somewhere in Innis Shallows, Leelee's brain chemistry was cascading through a long series of biochemical waterfalls, one imbalance slipping to another, slipping to another. Her visual cortex firing in strange waves, her hippocampus blurring. He rolled to his side, reached between the bed frame and the wall, and plucked out the little felt bag. The pink lozenge looked tiny in his vast palm. It tasted like strawberry flavoring and dextrose.

David laced his fingers behind his head, looked at the woman on his wall looking back at him, and waited, waited, waited for the euphoria to come.

The lower university was one of the oldest complexes in Londres Nova; the first marks had been made by automated construction mechs when there had been only a few thousand people on the planet. The halls were simple, direct, rectilinear, and hard. In the commons area—what everyone referred to as "outside"—there had been some attempt to soften and humanize the space, but within, it was low ceilings and right angles. It didn't help that the original colonial designs hadn't recessed any of the infrastructure. Halls that were narrow already had water pipes and electrical cables crowding in at the corners. The flooring was all metal grate, and David had to duck to get through the doorways. The suction from hundreds of fume hoods venting out to the atmosphere reclamation plants kept a constant breeze blowing against the main doors, pushing the students in and then keeping them from getting out.

David's locker was in the third hall corridor. Senior's row. It was twice as wide as the one he'd had just the year before, and the locking mechanism didn't stick the way the old one had. He'd put a couple decals on the outer face—a picture of Caz Pratihari, a kanji-print cartoon—but nothing like the multicolored glow of the one next to him. It belonged to an industrial engineering girl who he never saw unless they were in the hall at the same time. All the lockers had something, though—a picture, a whiteboard, some in-joke one-liner printed on plastic and fused to the metal. Some little mark to say that this space belongs to someone in particular, someone a little—but only a little—different from the others.

At the end of the cycle, everyone in the senior's row would get their placements, empty the lockers, and go to wherever they were put next. The lockers would be scrubbed clean, decontaminated, sealed, and made anonymous again for whichever student was assigned it next. David had heard about sand castles on beaches being washed away by the tide, but he'd never seen an ocean. The lockers of senior's row were the closest analogue among things he actually knew.

David closed the door and turned down toward his workstation. With the tube stations running, his parents back at the house, and the lower university open, the lab was the place he disliked least. The long muscles in his back and legs still ached a little after his night sampling his own wares, and he was half relieved that he could tell Leelee he'd tried it and half relieved that his schedule wouldn't let him try it again. The whole thing had been like having a very long, pleasant, but kind of boring dream. And it had left his head feeling a little hazy in a way he didn't enjoy.

His lab work was almost at its final phase. The terminal built into his desk was arranged to display the data on all seven studies that were making up the complex tissue of his senior labs. They were all built around the single unified idea of trying to build complex cell structures that would sequester ferrous products. It wasn't a holy grail, but it was a good, solid puzzle with a lot of applications for the terraforming efforts if it worked out. With the day out of lab, he had a double handful of data to look over and incorporate.

And so did everyone else.

"Hey? Big Dave?"

Steppan was one of the other four students under Mr. Oke. He stood in the doorway, leaning on a crutch and smiling uncomfortably. He was pale as bleached flour and allergic to the pharmaceutical cocktail that kept bones dense and muscles functioning in the low Martian gravity. He'd broken his leg twice since the year began.

"Hey," David said.

"Pretty crazy about that tube blowout, eh?"

"Bizarre," David said.

"So look, I was wondering...ah..."

"You need something," David said.

"Yeah."

David tapped his wide fingers across the display screen, letting the data batch process without him. Steppan limped into the room. With both of them there, the lab seemed too small.

"I've got an anomaly on one of my runs. I mean way off. Three standard deviations."

"You're fucked, cousin."

"I know. I think I may have gotten some bad reagent."

"Bad? Or wrong?"

"Wrong would be bad. Anyway, I know you've got some extras, and I was wondering—"

"Extras?"

A little knot squeezed in David's chest. Steppan shrugged and looked away like he'd said something he hadn't wanted to.

"Sure. It's no big deal, right? But my chromium stuff has a lot of the same reagents. If I can scrounge enough together to do another run, I could discard the bad data."

"I don't have that much stuff."

Steppan nodded, his head bowed down, eyes to the floor. He licked his lips, and David could see the desperation in the way he held his shoulders. David had imagined a million times what it would be like if his labs went pear-shaped. Especially right before placements. It was everyone's nightmare.

"Sure you do," Steppan said. "You're always getting equipment and supplies out of that other locker, right? I mean. You know."

"I don't know," David said. His mouth tasted like copper.

"Sure you do," Steppan said, not looking up.

The tension in the room was vicious. Steppan hung his head like a whipped dog, but he wouldn't back away. The walls were too close, the air too stale. Steppan was breathing all the oxygen. The boy's gaze flickered up to meet David's and then away again. How much did Steppan know? How much did he suspect? Who else knew?

"I'll help you," David said, speaking like the words would cut his tongue if he spoke too fast. "You let me know what you need for another run, and I'll help you get it, okay? You can have a fresh run. We'll make the dataset work."

"Sure, thanks," Steppan said. The relief in his shoulders wasn't faked. "Thank you."

"Does Mr. Oke know about the other locker?"

"No," Steppan said with a grin that was almost camaraderie. "And never will, right?"

So instead of working his datasets, David spent the morning going through the labs, looking for anyone he knew well enough to talk to. There were fewer than he'd hoped for, and the tension in the air made people short-tempered. Everyone was behind. Everyone had their own problems. Everyone was worried about their labs and their placements and whatever issues their families put on them. By afternoon, he'd given up. The only option left was to get on the network and order a fresh supply for Steppan from the distributor. It didn't take out too much from his secret account, and he wasn't the only one scrambling at the last minute to supply a lab. It was usually students buying their own things, he thought, but it wouldn't seem that odd to have someone doing a favor for a friend. As long as no one asked where the money came from, he'd be fine. When he got back to his actual labs, he felt like he'd already done a full day's work and he'd hardly started.

The hours passed quickly. By dinnertime, he'd cleared and processed all the data from the day the tubes went down and started on the data for the day after. Just in time for the data that had been accruing while he'd been wandering around the labs to start showing up in the queue. With each batch file that appeared, David felt the night stretching out ahead of him. Maybe he just wouldn't sleep. If he could get through tomorrow, he'd have the whole backlog cleared. Unless someone blew something up, or Steppan decided he wanted something else to keep quiet, or Aunt Bobbie decided to come lift weights at him or something. David tried to stretch the headache out of the base of his skull and got back to work.

At seven minutes past dinnertime, his hand terminal chimed. He accepted the connection with his thumb.

"You aren't coming home for dinner?" his mother asked. Her voice was tinny and small, like air pressed into a straw.

"No," David replied. "I've got to finish my datasets."

"I thought they gave you the daytime to do that," she said. On the hand terminal screen, she looked different than in person. Not older or younger, but both. It was like being shrunk down rubbed out all the wrinkles around her eyes and mouth, but at the same time it made all the gray show in her hair.

"I had some other stuff I needed to take care of."

The small screen version of her face went cool and distant. The tightness in David's shoulders started to feel like a weight.

"Time management is an important skill, David," she said, as if it were just a random thought. Not anything to do with him.

"I know," he said.

"I'll put your meal up for when you get home. Don't be later than midnight."

"I won't."

The connection dropped, and David turned back to his data, growled, and slammed his fist into the display. The monitor didn't break. It didn't even error out. He might as well not have done anything. The next alert came in the middle of the evening when the labs were starting to empty. The voices in the hallways were fainter, almost lost in the drone and drum of music from the construction labs. The maintenance workers were coming through, old men and women with damp mops and desiccant powders. David almost ignored his hand terminal's tritone chime. It only started to bother him a little, wondering who would have sent a message rather than just opening a connection. He looked over. It was from Leelee, and the header read OPEN WHEN YOU'RE ALONE. David's concentration broke. His imagination leapt to the sorts of messages that girls sent to boys to be watched in private. He reached over and closed the door to his lab and hunched over the hand terminal.

She was in a dark place, the light catching her from the side. In the background, a rai song was playing, all trumpets and ululating male voices. She licked her lips, her gaze flicked to the terminal's control display, and then back to him.

"David, I think I'm in trouble," she said. Her voice shook, her breath pressing into the words. "I need help, okay? I'm going to need help, and I know you like me. And I like you too, and I think you'll help me out, right? I need to borrow some money. Maybe… maybe kind of a lot. I'll know soon. Tomorrow maybe. Just send a message back if you can. And don't talk to Hutch."

A woman's voice called from the background, rising over the music, and Leelee surged forward. The display went back to default, and David put in a connection request that timed out with an offer to leave a message instead. Grunting with frustration, he put in another request. Then another. Leelee's system was off-line. He had the powerful urge to get to the tube station and go to Innis Shallows in person, but he didn't know where to find her once he was there. Didn't even know for sure she'd been there when she sent the message. Curiosity and dread spun up a hundred scenarios. Leelee had been caught with some product and had to bribe the police or she'd be jailed. One of Hutch's enemies had found her and was threatening to kill her if she didn't tell how to find him so now she needed to get off planet. Or she was pregnant and she had to get to Dhanbad Nova for the abortion. He wondered how much money she'd need. He imagined the smile on her face when he gave it to her. When he saved her from whatever it was.

But first he had to fix his data and get home. No one could know that something was happening. He set the hand terminal to record and placed himself in the center of the image.

"I'll do whatever I can, Leelee. Just you need to get in touch with me. Tell me what's going on, and I'll do whatever you need. Promise." He felt like there was more. Something else he should add. He didn't know what. "Whatever it is, we'll get through it, right? Just call me."

He set the headers and delivered the message. For the rest of the evening, he waited for the chime of a connection request. It never came.

When he got home, it was near midnight but his father and Aunt Bobbie were still awake. The living room monitor was set to a popular feed with a silver-haired, rugged-faced man talking animatedly. With the sound muted, he seemed to be trying to get their attention. David's father sat on the couch, the mass of his body commanding the space from armrest to armrest like a king on his throne. Aunt Bobbie leaned against the wall, lifting a thirty-kilo weight with one arm as she spoke, then gently letting it descend.

"That's how I see it," she said.

"But it *isn't* like that," his father said. "You are a highly trained professional. How much did Mars invest in you over those years you were in the Corps? The resources that you took up didn't come from nowhere. Mars gave something up to give you those opportunities, those skill sets."

It was a tone of voice David had heard all his life, and it tightened his gut. The man on the monitor lifted his hands in outrage over something, then cracked what was meant to be a charming smile.

"And I appreciate that," Aunt Bobbie said, her voice low and calm in a way that sounded more like shouting than his father's raised voice. "I've served. And those opportunities involved a lot of eighteen-hour days and—"

"No, no, no, no," his father said, massive hands waving in the air like he was trying to blow away smoke. "You don't get to complain about the work. Engineering is just as demanding as—"

"—and watching a lot of my friends die in front of me," Aunt Bobbie finished. The free weight rose and fell in the sudden silence. She shifted it to her other hand. His father's face was dark with blood, his hands grasping his knees. Aunt Bobbie smiled. Her voice was sad. "You're thinking about how you can top me on that, aren't you? Go ahead. Take your time."

David put his hand terminal down on the kitchen table, the click of plastic on plastic enough to announce him. When they turned to look at him, David could see the family resemblance. For a moment, they were an older brother and a younger sister locked in the same conversation they'd been having since they were children. David nodded to them and looked away, unsettled by the thought and vaguely embarrassed.

"Welcome home," his father said, rising up from the couch. "How are things at the lab?"

"Fine," David said. "Mom said she'd put dinner up for me."

"There's some curry in the refrigerator."

David nodded. He didn't like curry, but he didn't dislike it. He put a double serving into a self-heating ceramic bowl and set it to warm. He kept his eyes down, wishing that they'd go on with whatever they'd been talking about so they'd forget about him yet dreading listening to them fight if they did. Aunt Bobbie cleared her throat.

"Did they find anything more about the tube thing?" she asked. David could tell from the shift in her tone of voice that she'd put up the white flag. His father took a deep breath, letting it out slowly through his nose. David's curry tasted more of ginger than usual, and he wondered whether Aunt Bobbie had made it.

"Newsfeed says they have leads," his father said at last. "I imagine they'll get someone in custody by the end of the week."

"Are they saying outside involvement?"

"No. Some idiot protestor trying to make a point about how vulnerable we are," his father said as if he actually knew. "It's happening everywhere. Selfish crap, if you ask me. We were on our way to making the schedule for the month before this happened. Now everyone's lost a day at least. That's not so much when it's just one person, but there were thousands of people thrown off schedule. It's like Dad always says: Three hundred sixty-five people miss one shift, that's a year gone in a day, you know?"

"Yeah, sort of," Aunt Bobbie said. "I remember it being nine thousand people miss an hour."

"Same thought."

David's hand terminal chimed its tritone and his heart raced, but when he pulled it closer, it was only the lower university's automated system posting the lab schedule for the next week. He looked through it without really taking it in. No surprises. He'd get his work done somehow. He killed the sound on his terminal and switched back to Leelee's message just to see her face, the way her shoulders moved. She licked her lips again, looked down, and then up. He heard her voice in his memory. Not the message she'd sent him tonight, but the last thing she said the night the tube broke down. *Just thought you'd come play and I was wrong.*

Oh, God. Had she been thinking about having *sex* with him? Wouldn't Hutch have been angry? Or was that why Hutch had sent them away together? Was that what this was all about? Humiliation and a barely controlled erotic thrill mixed in his blood and left the curry seeming bland. He had to find Leelee. Tomorrow, if he hadn't heard from her, he'd go to Innis Shallows. He could just ask around. Someone would know her. Maybe he could put off his data checking for one day. Or make Steppan do it. Guy owed him one after all…

"Well, kid," his father said, stepping into the room. David flipped his hand terminal facedown. "It's late and I've got work tomorrow."

"Me too," David said.

"Don't stay up too late."

"Fine."

His father's hand gripped his shoulder briefly, the pressure there and gone again. David ate the last few bites of curry and washed it down with a cup of cold water. In the living room, Aunt Bobbie changed feeds on the monitor. A small, old, dark-skinned woman in an orange sari appeared on the screen, leaning forward and listening to an interviewer's question with an expression of polite contempt. Aunt Bobbie coughed out a single sour laugh and turned off the screen.

She walked up to the kitchen, massaging her left bicep with her right hand and grimacing. She wasn't really any bigger than his father, but she was much stronger and it made her carry herself like she was. David tried to remember if she'd killed anyone. He was pretty sure he'd heard a story about her killing someone, but he hadn't been paying attention. She looked down, maybe at his hand terminal turned with its face to the table. Her smile looked almost wistful, which was weird. She leaned against the sink and began pulling her fingers backward, pushing out her palm, stretching out the tendons and muscles of her wrist.

"You ever go free-climbing?" she asked.

David glanced up at her and shrugged.

"When I was about your age, I used to go all the time," she said. "Get a breather and a couple of friends. Head up to the surface. Or down. I went to Big Man's Cave a couple times right before my placement. No safety equipment. Usually just enough bottled air to go, do the thing, and get back to the closest ingress. The whole point was to try and carry as little as we possibly could. The thinnest suits. No ropes or pitons. There was one time, I was on this cliff face about half a kilometer up from the ground with my fist wedged into a crack to keep me in place while a windstorm came through. All I could hear was the grit hitting my helmet and my climbing buddies screaming at me to get out of there."

"Scary," David said flatly. She didn't notice the sarcasm, or she chose not to.

"It was *great*. One of the best climbs ever. Your grandfather didn't like it, though. That was the only time he's ever called me stupid."

David filled another glass of water and drank it. He had a hard time imagining it. Pop-Pop was always praising everyone for everything. To the point sometimes that it seemed like none of it really meant anything. He couldn't imagine his grandfather getting that angry. His father sometimes called Pop-Pop "the Sergeant Major" when he was angry with him. It was almost like he was talking about another person, someone David had never met.

"There was context," Aunt Bobbie said. "A guy I knew died in a fall about a month before. Troy."

"What happened?"

Now it was her turn to shrug. "He was way up on a cliff, and he lost his grip. The fall cracked his air bottle, and by the time anyone could get to him, he'd choked out. I wasn't there. We weren't friends. But to Dad, everyone who free-climbed was the same, and anything that had happened to Troy could happen to me. He was right about that. He just, y'know, thought I didn't know it."

"Only you did."

"Of course I did. That was the point," she said. She pointed to the hand terminal with her chin. "If you flip it like that when he comes over, it makes him curious."

David tasted the copper of fear and pushed back from the table a few centimeters.

"It wasn't anything. It was the lab schedule."

"All right. But when you flip it over, it makes him curious."

"There's nothing to be curious about," David said, his voice getting louder.

"All right," she said, and her voice was gentle and strong and David didn't want to talk about it or look at her. Aunt Bobbie walked back toward the guest room and bed. When he heard her shower go on, he picked up his hand terminal again and checked in case something had come through from Leelee. Nothing had. He put what was left of his dinner into the recycler and headed for his room. As soon as he hit the mattress, his mind started racing. All of the things Leelee might need money for started spinning through his mind—drugs or an attorney or a passage off Mars. As soon as he thought that she might be leaving, he was sure that she was, and it left his chest feeling hollow and hopeless. And she'd told him not to talk to Hutch. Maybe she'd done something to piss him off, and now she had to get away before he caught her.

He drifted to sleep imagining himself standing between Hutch and Leelee, facing him down to protect her. He'd run the scenario from the start. He walked in on the two of them fighting, and he pushed Hutch away. Or was with Leelee and Hutch came after her. He tried out lines—*Hurt her, and I'll make your life hell* or *You think you've got all the power, but I'm David fucking Draper, cousin*—and imagined their effects. Leelee's gratitude shifted into kissing and from there to her taking his hand and slipping it under her shirt. He could almost feel her body pressed against him. Could almost smell her. The dream shifted, and it was all about getting the datasets finished, only Leelee needed the money to change the results of her pregnancy test, and the bank was in a tiny crevasse in the back of his living room, and his hands were too thick to reach it.

When his alarm went off, he thought it had broken. His body still had the too heavy, weak feeling of the middle of the night. But no, it was morning time. He pulled himself to the edge of his bed, let his feet swing down to the floor, and pressed his palms against his eyes. Even through the air filters, he caught the usually welcome scents of breakfast sausage and coffee. Una Meing looked out from his wall, eyes promising him something deep and mysterious. A diffuse resentment flowed through him and he switched the image away from her to a generic preset of sunrise at Olympus Mons. Touristy.

He had to make a plan. Maybe he could talk to Hutch after all. Not say Leelee had talked to him, just that he was worried about her. That he wanted to find her. Because that was true. He had to find Leelee, wherever she was, and make sure she was all right. Then he had to finish his datasets. It was almost two hours to Innis Shallows and back, but if he just planned to work through lunchtime, or else eat in the labs, he'd only be losing one hour for travel. He had to think about how to find her once he was there. He wished there was someone to talk to. Even Hutch. There wasn't, though, and so he was going to have to solve this on his own. Go out, ask, look. She was counting on him. For a moment, he could feel her head resting against him, smell the subtle musk of her hair. So yes. He'd go do this.

No problem.

Only one tube ran to Innis Shallows, back and forth along the same stretch. Since the sabotage of the tube system, there was more security present, men and women with pistols and gas grenades scowling and walking through the cars. The tube station at Innis Shallows didn't even have the usual perfunctory signs announcing that the end destination was Aterpol, like there were only two kinds of places in the universe: Innis Shallows and anywhere else. The official stats said that six thousand people lived and worked in the Shallows, but walking out of the tube station,

David still felt overwhelmed. The main halls were old stone behind clear sealant. White scars marked the places where decades of minor accidents had dug into it. Men and women walked or rode electric carts, moving up ramps from level to level. Most ignored him but a few made a point of staring. He knew he didn't belong there. His clothes and the way he walked marked him. He stood for almost a minute in the center of the corridor, his hand in his pocket, fingers wrapped around his hand terminal. Behind him, the soft chimes of the tube preparing to leave again were like a friend's voice: *Get on. Get out of here. This is dumb.*

He would have, too, turned back around and gotten on the tube and headed back without spending more than five minutes in the neighborhood. Except for Leelee.

David scowled, shook his head, and trudged down the corridor, heading off to his left for no reason. His throat felt tight and uncomfortable and he needed to pee. After about twenty meters of cart rental kiosks and monitors set to entertainment newsfeeds, he found a little restaurant and stepped in. The woman behind the counter could have been a Belter: thin body, too-large head. She lifted her chin at him and nodded back toward half a dozen chipped formed plastic tables.

"Anywhere you want," she said in a thick accent David couldn't place.

David didn't move, looking for the courage to speak for so long the woman raised her eyebrows. He yanked his hand terminal out of his pocket and held it out to her. He'd gotten a still from the message Leelee had left him. It wasn't great, but the shape of her face was clear and she wasn't in the middle of a word or anything.

"I'm looking for her," David said. He sounded terse in his own ears. Almost resentful. "You know her?"

Her eyes flickered down and she shrugged.

"Don't know her. You want to stay, you got to eat. Anywhere you want."

"Her name's Leelee."

She hoisted her eyebrows. David felt a blush rising in his cheeks.

"Do you know where I could look for her?"

"Not here?" the woman suggested. David shoved the terminal back into his pocket and walked out. It was a stupid plan. Walk around the tube station, asking people at random? It was dumb and it was humiliating, but it was Leelee so he did it. The hour was blank stares and shrugs and the growing sense that everyone he talked to was embarrassed for him. When the tube car returned, he'd found nothing. He sat alone on a formed plastic bench. The monitor shifted to a video review by a pretty girl whose voice made it sound like she was shouting every word. "Dika Adalai's best story ever!" David looked up and down the sparsely popu-lated car and came to the conclusion that he was the one who'd triggered the review. It said something about who the ad systems thought he was. What he cared about. Like they knew.

He pulled up his hand terminal. Made another connection request, and Leelee didn't answer. He pulled up her message, playing it low. *I need help, okay?* and *Don't talk to Hutch.* Only there wasn't anyone else to talk to.

He spent the afternoon catching up on his datasets, horrified to realize how far behind he'd let himself fall. He ran through num-ber and correlations, checking the data against expected norms with the practice and contempt of long experience. He needed to put in extra time. Get everything taken care of. If he fell too far behind, Mr. Oke would start noticing, and if there was a full audit, the extra lab work he'd done for Hutch would come out, and then he'd be screwed. He weighed calling in a favor from Steppan, but his mind kept shifting back to Leelee and the closed faces of Innis Shallows. Someone had to know where she was. Who she was.

He had to work.

For the first hour, reviewing and processing the data felt like hard labor, but then slowly, his mind fell into the rhythm. He managed the statistical input and brought out the correlations, fit-ting each one into the larger spreadsheet waiting for meta-analysis, and he could feel himself relax a little. The different catalytic mixes felt more like home than home did, and here like nowhere else in his life, he was in control. Between the comfort and concentration of the work and his exhaustion, he fell into something like a trance. Time passed without any sense of duration. When he came to the end of the run, he could have been going for minutes or hours. Either one seemed plausible. He didn't think to check his hand terminal until he was almost home.

There were four new messages waiting, none of them from Leelee. The first was a correction to the lab schedule, then two posts from a gaming forum he subscribed to even though he barely played any of the games. The last one was from the central educational authority in Salton, the upper university. He flicked it open and his head went as light as a balloon.

He walked into the common room. His mother and father sat before the living room monitor, just far enough away from each other that their legs didn't touch. On the screen, an older man was leaning forward earnestly. "The Martian project is the single most ambitious endeavor in human history. It is all of our duties to see that the threat of Earth…"

"What's the matter?" his father said.

David lifted his hand terminal as if that was explanation enough. And then, when they didn't understand, he spoke. His voice had a distance to it.

"My placement came," he said. "I'm going to development."

His father whooped, stood so violently that the couch almost tipped over. As his dad's arms wrapped around him, lifting him up toward the ceiling, and his mother wept joyful tears into her hands, all David could think was *I'm supposed to be happy about this.*

After that, everything changed and nothing did. He'd been working toward his placement for the last five sections, or looked at another way, his whole life. He'd known it was coming—everyone had—and still it felt like it had snuck up on him. Surprised him. All of the things that had to happen after—the things he hadn't bothered thinking about because they were for later—had to be done now. There was the application for living space in the dormitories of the upper university, the coordination of his long-run experiments with Mr. Oke so that some new second-year could step in and see them to completion, and the preparations and purchases that would, in the coming months, lead to David moving out of his room, out of his home, away from his family for the first time in his life. The times when the idea wouldn't scare him, it couldn't come fast enough.

He could see it in his parents too. The way his mother kept quietly weeping and grinning at the same time, the way his father made a point of sitting with him while he filled out his paperwork and put in for time off so he could go with David to the orientation in Salton next month and brought him sandwiches and coffee for lunch. David had done everything he was supposed to do, had gotten the grades and the attention and the status for the highest placement he'd qualified for, and the reward was even less freedom. It was like his parents had suddenly realized he wouldn't be there forever, and now their love was like a police state; he couldn't escape it. He couldn't go look for Leelee or even send out connection requests. The only one who didn't seem to react one way or the other was Aunt Bobbie who just kept her weird, vaguely intrusive habits of watching the newsfeeds and lifting weights.

Three days after the letter came, David was set to go to the lower university for his first transition meeting with Mr. Oke. His father went with him. Dad held his head high, chin up, beaming like he'd been the one to do something. They walked up the stairs to the lower university commons together, David shrinking into his own chest with the discomfort. This was his world—his friends and enemies, the people who knew him for himself—and Dad didn't belong there. Steppan nodded to him but didn't approach. The girl who'd borrowed his stats array last year frowned at his dad, strutting at David's side. They knew that his being there was wrong, and they drew back, keeping the separation. They all had two lives too, and they weren't supposed to mix like this. Everybody knew that.

"Mr. Oke!" his father said as they rounded one of the seating areas. The research advisor smiled politely, walking toward them.

"Mr. Draper," Mr. Oke said. "It's good of you to come."

"Just want to make sure everything's smooth," Dad said, caressing the air as he said it. "Development's a good placement, but it's a hard one. David doesn't need any distractions."

"Of course not," Mr. Oke agreed.

Over the old man's shoulder, David caught sight of Hutch. He was standing with a couple of the second-years, smiling and listening to a girl whose hands were fluttering and tapping at the air as she explained something. Leelee wasn't with him. David felt his heart rate spike. It was an epinephrine dump. His mind jumped back a section to his physiology labs. Epinephrine was binding to alpha-adrenergic sites, dropping insulin production, upping glycogenolysis and lipolysis. Standard fight-or-flight. Hutch glanced over, nodded politely. David pointed toward the men's room with his chin. Hutch's expression slipped a notch darker and he shook his head, not more than a few millimeters and unmistakable. David scowled and nodded toward the men's room again.

"Are you all right?" his dad asked.

"I have to pee," David said. "I'll be right back."

He left his father and Mr. Oke bantering. The white tile and video mirrors of the men's room were like a retreat to his world. And escape. He stood at the urinal, pretending to piss until the one other student washed his hands and left. Hutch walked in.

"What's the word, friend?" Hutch said, but David could hear annoyance in the syllables. "Saw you got family with you today. Good to see a father so concerned with his son's business."

David zipped his fly and trundled over to Hutch. He kept his voice low.

"He's just being an asshole. It's nothing. We've got to meet," David said. "We have to talk. Not now, but we've got to."

"Slow, slow, slow," Hutch said. "Now's not a good time."

"Tomorrow night," David said. "The usual place."

"Can't do that. Other plans."

"Tonight, then," David hissed.

David's hand terminal chimed, and a moment later, Hutch's did too. The local newsfeed pushing a breaking story. David didn't look away. Hutch's expression shifted from annoyance into anger and then a wary kind of amusement. He shrugged.

"See you tonight then, little man," Hutch said. His lopsided smile looked dangerous. David nodded and trotted back out to the commons. He wouldn't tell Hutch about the message or about Leelee being in trouble. He'd just say he wanted to find her. He'd say it was about his placement because that made it seem like there was something else. Distracting. He got back to Mr. Oke and his father, gathering himself back together, willing himself to act normal, before he noticed that the commons was silent. Everyone was hunched over their hand terminals, their faces gray or flushed. Even his father and Mr. Oke. The newsfeed push had a picture of a public corridor, the air hazed by smoke. A policeman hunched over something, one hand on his hip. The header read EXPLOSION IN SALTON.

"What happened?" he asked.

"Protestors," his father said, and the anger in his voice was startling. "Anti-Earth protestors."

David's hand terminal chimed again. The header shifted. EXPLOSION IN SALTON; THREE CONFIRMED DEAD

Aunt Bobbie was tight-lipped when they got home, sitting in the common room with a massive black weight in her hand that she held without lifting, like a child clutching a favorite toy. The monitor was set to a newsfeed with the sound turned low. Live feeds of the damage in Salton played out in the four corners of the monitor, but she didn't seem to be looking at them. David's mother sat at the table scrolling through her hand terminal. When David and his father walked in, there was a moment of eye contact between his parents that had the weight of significance. He didn't know what it meant. His father tapped David's shoulder in a kind of farewell, then stepped over to the railing.

"Hey, sis."

"Hey," Aunt Bobbie said.

"Did security talk to you?"

"Not yet," Aunt Bobbie said. "They know how to find me if they want to."

David scowled toward his mother. He couldn't think of a reason that security would want to talk with Aunt Bobbie. He tried to make it into a threat against him, that they'd be looking to her for information about the batches he'd cooked for Hutch, but that felt too wrong. It had to be about the bombing, but he couldn't make sense of that either. His mother only lifted her eyebrows and asked how the meeting with Mr. Oke had gone. His father answered for him, and the uncomfortable tension around Aunt Bobbie shifted into the background.

There was going to be a party for the whole family tomorrow night, his mother told him. Pop-Pop and the cousins were coming from Aterpol, and Uncle Istvan and his new wife were making the trip from Dhanbad Nova. They'd rented a room at the best restaurant in Breach Candy. David gave a quiet, generalized thanks to the universe that he'd arranged to see Hutch tonight instead. Slipping away from his own celebration would have been impossible.

After dinner, David said some vague things about friends from school and celebrating, promised not to go to Salton, and ducked out the door before anyone could get too inquisitive. Once he was out walking to the tube station, he felt a moment of relaxation. Almost peace. The whole ride out to Martineztown, David felt almost like he was floating. His datasets were done or else not his anymore, and even with all the rest of it—Leelee and Hutch, the protestors and the bombings, the family party and the prospect of leaving home—just not having the lab work hanging over him was like taking a vise off his ribs. Once he was in Salton, working development would be a thousand times worse than anything in the lower university. But that was later. For now, he could set his hand terminal to play bebapapu tunes and relax. Even if it was only for the length of the tube ride to Martineztown, it was still the most peace he'd had for himself in as long as he could remember.

Hutch was waiting for him when he got there. The construction lamp threw off harsh white light, the battery hissing almost silently. The shadows seemed to have eaten Hutch's eyes.

"Little man," he said as David stepped into the room. "Wasn't thinking to hear from you. Was risky, talking to me with family and authority right there beside us. You were looking jumpy. People notice that kind of thing."

"Sorry," David said. He sat down on a crate, rough plastic clinging to the fabric of his pants and pulling his cuffs up around his ankles. "I just needed to talk to you."

"I'm always here for you, my friend," Hutch said. "You know that. You're my number one guy. Any problem you've got, I've got."

David nodded, picking absently at his fingernail beds. Now that he was here, he found the subject of Leelee was harder to bring up than he'd expected.

"I got into development."

"Knew it. Development's always the place for the smart ones. Play your cards, and you'll be riding this planet like a private cart," Hutch said. "That's not why we're here, though. Is it?"

"No, I was...I wanted to get in touch with Leelee. See if maybe she wanted to come celebrate it with me. Only my hand terminal went corrupt and I didn't have her information on backup and I was thinking that since you..." David swallowed, trying to work the knot out of his throat. "Since you know her better than anyone."

He chanced a look at Hutch's face. The man was expressionless as stone, turned in and silent. It was more threatening than bared teeth.

"She came to you." David had promised himself that he wouldn't tell Hutch about the message, and technically he didn't, but the silence implicated him. Hutch drew a deep breath and ran his hands through his hair. "Don't worry about Leelee. I'm taking care of Leelee."

"She seemed like she was in trouble."

"Okay, little man. You don't follow what's happening here, so I'm going to help. I *own* Leelee. She's mine. Property, see? And she screwed up, started being with the wrong crowd. She got political. People like us don't do that. Earth. Mars. OPA. That shit is for citizens. It just draws attention for people like us."

"She looked scared," David said. He could hear the whine in his voice, and he hated that he couldn't keep it out. He sounded like a kid. "She said she needed money."

Hutch laughed. "Don't ever give that bitch money."

"Property," David said. "She wanted…she wanted to buy herself. Didn't she?"

Hutch's expression softened to something like sympathy. Pity, maybe. He leaned forward and put a hand on David's knee.

"Leelee is a slice of poison with a pretty mouth, little man. That's the truth. She did a bad, stupid thing, and now she's working that mistake off. That's all. I know how much money you have because I'm the guy that gave it to you. You don't have enough to clear her debts."

"Maybe I could—"

"You don't have half. You've got *maybe* a quarter. There's nothing you can do for that girl. She gave you a hard-on, and that was nice for you. Don't make it more than that. You understand what I'm saying to you?"

The deep, sickening tug of humiliation pulled at David's heart. He looked down, willing himself not to cry. He hated the reaction. He was angry with it and with himself and with Hutch and his parents and the world. He burned with embarrassment and rage and impotence. Hutch stood up, his shadow spilling across floor and wall like spent engine oil.

"Best we don't talk for a while," Hutch said. "You got a lot in the air. Don't worry about the cooking. We'll get that all smoothed out when you're in Salton. Then we can go into production for real, eh? See some money worth having."

"Okay," David said.

Hutch sighed and pulled up his hand terminal. As he tapped at its keyboard, he kept talking.

"I'm going to slip a little something in that account of yours, right? Call it a bonus. Take and get yourself something nice, right."

"Right."

And then Hutch was gone, walking out toward Martineztown and the tube station and the world. David sat alone where he'd sat with Leelee not all that long before. The sense of peace and calm was gone. His hands balled in fists, and he had nothing he could hit. He felt cored out. Hollowed. He waited ten minutes the way he was supposed to and then took himself home.

The next night was the party. His party. Pop-Pop was there, smiling a little lopsided since the stroke and thinner than David had ever seen him, but still strong voiced and chipper. Aunt Bobbie sat on one side of him, David's father on the other, like they were propping him up. Muted sounds of silverware against plates and voices raised in conversation competed with a three-piece band set up on a dais by the front doors that filtered into the private back room. Green and gold tablecloths stretched over three tables to make it all seem like it connected. The meal itself had been chicken in black sauce with rice and fresh vegetables, and David had eaten two helpings without really tasting them. His father had taken on the expense of an open bar and Uncle Istvan's new wife was already well on her way to drunk and sort of hitting on one of the older cousins. David's mother paced the back of the room touching shoulders, dropping in and out of conversations like she was running for office. David wanted badly to be anywhere else.

"You know, back in the ancient days," Pop-Pop said, gesturing with a glass of whiskey, "they built cathedrals. Massive churches lifted up to the glory of God. Far, far beyond what you'd expect people to manage with just quarry stone and trees and a few steel knives, you know. Just a few simple tools."

"We've heard about the cathedrals," Aunt Bobbie said. She had a drink too, but David couldn't tell what it was. Legally, David wasn't supposed to drink alcohol for another year, but he had a bulb of beer in his hand. He didn't actually like the taste of it, but he drank it anyway.

"The thing that's important, though, is the time, you see?" Pop-Pop said. "The *time*. Raising up one of those cathedrals would take whole generations. The men who drew the plans, who envisioned the final form of the thing? They would be dead long before it was finished. It might be their grandsons or their great-grandsons or their great-great-grandsons who saw the work complete."

Across the room, one of the younger cousins was crying, and David's mother sloped over and knelt, taking the squalling kid's hand in her own and leading him to his mother. David choked down another mouthful of beer. Next year, he'd be in Salton, so busy that he wouldn't have to come to these things anymore.

"There's a beauty in that," Pop-Pop said earnestly to everyone and no one. "Such a massive plan, such ambition. A man might be setting the final stone and think back to his own father who'd set the stones below him and his grandfather who'd set the stones below that. To have a place in the great scheme, that was the beauty of it. To be part of something you didn't begin and you would not see completed. It was beautiful."

"I love you, Dad," Aunt Bobbie said, "but that's bullshit."

David blinked. He looked from Pop-Pop to his own father and back. The men looked embarrassed. It was like she'd farted. Aunt Bobbie took another sip of her drink.

"Bobbie," David's father said, "maybe you should ease up on that stuff."

"I'm fine. It's just that I've been hearing about the cathedrals since I was a kid, and it's bullshit. Seriously, who were they to decide what everyone was going to be doing for the next four generations? It's not like they asked their however many great-grandkids if they wanted to be stonecutters. Maybe some of them wanted to…be musicians. Hell, be architects and do something of their own. Deciding what everyone's going to do...what we're going to be. It's hubris, isn't it?"

"We're not talking about cathedrals anymore, are we, sis?"

"Yeah, because it was a really obscure metaphor," Aunt Bobbie replied. "I'm just saying that the plan may be great as long as you're inside it. You step outside, though, and then what?"

There was a pain in her voice that David couldn't fathom, but he saw it reflected in his grandfather's eyes. The old man put his hand on Aunt Bobbie's, and she held it like she was a little girl about to be led off to her bath time. David's father, on the other side, looked peevish.

"Don't take her seriously, Pop-Pop. She was talking to security all day, and she's still cranky."

"Is there a reason I shouldn't be? It's like every time anything strange happens, let's go talk to Draper again."

"You had to expect that, Roberta," his father said. He only called her Roberta when he was angry. "It's the consequence of your decision."

"And what decision is that?" she snapped. Her voice was getting louder. Some of the cousins were looking over at them now, their own conversations fading.

David's father laughed. "You aren't working. What are they calling it? Indefinite administrative leave?"

"Psychological furlough," Aunt Bobbie said. "What's your point?"

"My point is that of course they're going to want to talk to you when things get weird. You can't blame them for being suspicious. We were almost killed by Earthers. Everyone in this room and those rooms out there and the corridors. And you were working for them."

"I was not!" It wasn't a shout because it didn't have the gravel and roughness of shouting. It was loud, though, and it carried power along with it like a punch. "I worked *with* the faction that was trying to avert the war. The one that did avert the war. Everyone in these rooms is alive because of the people I helped. But *with* them, not *for* them."

The room was quiet, but David's father was too deep into the fight to notice. He rolled his eyes.

"Really? Who was paying your wages? Earth was. The people that hate us."

"They don't hate us," Bobbie said, her voice tired. "They're afraid of us."

"Then why do they act like they hate us?" David's father said with something like triumph.

"Because that's what fear looks like when it needs someplace to go."

David's mother seemed to appear behind the three of them like some sort of magic trick. She wasn't there, and then she was, her restraining hand on her husband's shoulder. Her smile was humorless and undeniable.

"We're here for David tonight," she said.

"Yes," Pop-Pop said, rubbing his palm against the back of Aunt Bobbie's hand, soothing her. "For David."

His father's face set into an annoyed mask, but Aunt Bobbie nodded.

"You're right," she said. "I'm sorry, David. Dad, I'm sorry. I've just had a really rough day and probably too much to drink."

"It's all right, angel," Pop-Pop said. Tears brightened his eyes.

"I just thought that by now I'd have some idea of…of who I was. Of what I was going to do next, and…"

"I know, angel. We all know what you're going through."

She laughed at that, wiping her eyes with the back of her hand. "All of us but me, then."

The rest of the evening went just the way those things were supposed to go. People laughed and argued and drank. His father tried to call for silence and make a little speech about how proud he was, but one of the kid cousins was whispering and tapping on his hand terminal all the way through it. A few people gave David small, discreet presents of money to help him set up his dorm in Salton. Uncle Istvan's new wife gave him an unpleasant, boozy kiss before gathering herself up and walking out with Istvan on her arm. They took a rental cart back home, his parents and Aunt Bobbie and him. He couldn't shake the image of her weeping at the table. *You step outside, though, and then what?*

The cart's wheels sounded sticky against the corridor floors. The lights had dimmed all through Breach Candy, simulating a twilight he'd never actually seen. Somewhere, the sun would slip below a horizon, a blue sky darken. He'd seen it in pictures, on video. In his life, though, it was just that the LEDs changed color and intensity. David leaned his head against one of the cart's support poles, letting the vibration of the engines and the wheels translate directly into his skull. It felt comfortable. His mother, sitting beside him, pressed her hand against his shoulder, and he had the powerful physical memory of coming back from a party when he'd been very young. Six, maybe seven years old. He remembered putting his head in her lap, fading into sleep with the texture of her slacks against his cheek. That was never going to happen again. The woman beside him hardly even seemed to be the same person, and in a few months, he wouldn't see her anymore. Not like he did now. And what would she have done if she knew about Hutch? About Leelee? His mother smiled at him, and it looked like love, but it was love for some other boy. The one she thought he was. He smiled back because he was supposed to.

When they got home, he went straight back to his room. He'd been around people enough. The cheesy generic wall was still up, and he shifted it back to Una Meing. Massive dark eyes with mascara on the lashes looked out at him. He dropped to the bed. Outside, Aunt Bobbie and his father were talking. He listened for a buzz of anger in their voices, but it wasn't there. They were just talking. The water pipes started to whine. His mother taking her evening bath. Everything small and domestic and safe, and out there somewhere, Leelee was working off her debt. She'd asked for his help, and he'd failed. And Hutch. Maybe he'd always been scared of Hutch. Maybe that was what had made cooking for him seem like the right thing. The wise thing, even. Hutch was the kind of dangerous that could make people into property. Could take them and make them disappear. Being part of that world was fun. Exciting. It was a way to step outside all the good student, good son, good prospects crap that was his life. So what that it scared him now? So what that Leelee was probably being rented out to whoever had the money and David wouldn't see her again? He'd made his choice, and this was the consequence.

Una Meing stared out at him, soulful and erotic. David turned out the lights, grabbed a pillow, and pulled it over his head. As his mind began to fragment down into sleep, Leelee kept coming back to him. Her face. Her voice. The soft, almost gentle way Hutch had said, *I* own *Leelee* and *You don't have enough to clear her debts.* He wished that he did. He walked into a bleak, prison-like room that was half dream and half imagination. Leelee shied back from the sudden light and then saw who it was, and her face lit up. *David,* she said, *how did you do it? How did you save me?*

And with an almost electrical shock, he knew the answer.

He sat up, turned on the light. Una Meing's sly-sad smile seemed more knowing than it had before. *Took you long enough.* He checked the time: well past midnight. It didn't matter. It wouldn't wait. He listened at his door for a few seconds. No voices except the professional enunciation of the newsfeed announcer. David took his hand terminal out of his satchel, sat on the edge of his bed, and put in the connection request. He didn't expect an answer, but Steppan's face appeared on the screen almost instantly.

"Big Dave! Hey," Steppan said. "Heard about your placement. Good going, cousin."

"Thanks," David said, keeping his voice low. "But look, I need a favor."

"Sure," Steppan said.

"You have lab time?"

"More time than sleep," Steppan said ruefully. "But you've got placement. You don't need to scrounge for lab hours anymore."

"Kind of do. And I could use an extra hand."

"How long are we talking about?"

"Ten hours," David said. "Maybe a little more. But some of that's waiting, so you can do your own stuff too. And I'll help with your work if you help with mine."

Steppan shrugged.

"All right. I've got hours tomorrow starting at eight. You know where my space is?"

"Do," David said.

"See you there," Steppan said and dropped the connection. So that was the first part. David's mind was already leaping ahead to the rest. He had enough tryptamine to build from, and the catalysts were always easy. What he didn't have was sodium borohydride or amoproxan in anything like the volume he'd need. Closing his eyes, he went through the inventory of his secret locker, thinking about each reagent and what he could gracefully change it into. Carbon double bonds cleaved, ketones formed, inactive isomers were forced into different configurations. Slowly, certainly, a clear biochemical path formed. He opened his eyes, jotted down a quick flowchart of the reactions, and built a wish list. When he was done, he switched his hand terminal over to the main distributor's site and ordered the reagents he'd need with immediate delivery to Steppan's lab. The total bill was enough to clean out his secret account, but that was fine with him. He'd never cared about the money.

When his hand terminal chirped the morning's alarm, he'd managed a two-hour nap. He changed into clean clothes, ducked into the bathroom to wet down his hair and shave. His mind was already three steps ahead. His hand terminal chimed with breaking news, and he almost dreaded to look, but for once it was something good. Eight people had been arrested in connection with the pressure loss on the tube system and were being actively questioned about the bomb in Salton. While David brushed his teeth, he watched the newsfeed play. When the scroll of mug shots came, he had a moment's anxiety—*What if Leelee was one of them? What if that was what Hutch meant by her getting political?*—but none of the faces was familiar. They were young people, none of them over eighteen, but well-worn. Two had black eyes and one of the women had been crying. Or else she'd been teargassed. David dismissed them.

"Where are you going?" his mother asked as he walked, head bowed and shoulders hunched, for the door.

"Friend needs help," he said. He'd meant the lie that Steppan needed an extra hand at the labs, but halfway to the lower university, he noticed that by not elaborating, he'd sort of told the truth. The fact was weirdly disturbing.

The day was a massive cook. With the two of them in the space, it was crowded, and Steppan, sleepless, hadn't showered recently. Between the chemical vapors that the fume hood didn't whisk away and the stink of adolescent boy, the heat of the burners, and Steppan's constant, nearly intimate presence, the day passed slowly. But it passed well. Steppan didn't ask what David's experiment was, and during the quiet times, David ran Steppan's datasets and even pointed out a flaw in the statistical assumptions he was making that made the final data prettier when he corrected it. When the early afternoon came and they were flagging, David measured out a small dose of amphetamine and split it between them. When his mother requested a connection, he didn't answer, just sent back the message that he'd be home late, to eat dinner without him. Instead of the usual indirect disapproval, she sent back a note that she supposed she'd have to get used to that. It left him sad until the timer went off and he had to cool the batch and add catalyst and the work took his attention. There was a real pleasure to the work, something he hadn't felt in years. He knew each reaction, each bond he was breaking, each molecular reconfiguration. He could look at the milky suspension, see a subtle change in the texture, and know what had happened. This, he thought, was what mastery felt like.

The last of his run was finished, the powder measured out into pale pink gelcaps and melted into sugared lozenges. His satchel was thick with them and heavy as a bowling ball. At a guess, he had the equivalent of his father's retirement account on his hip.

The public LEDs were dim as he walked home. His eyes felt bloodshot and gritty, but his step was light.

Aunt Bobbie was in the common room, the way she always was, doing deep lunges and watching the monitor. A young woman with skin the color of coffee and cream and pale lips was speaking seriously into the camera. A red band around her had SECURITY ALERT HIGH scrolling in four languages. David paused. When Aunt Bobbie looked back at him, not pausing in her exercises, he nodded toward the screen.

"They found plans for another bomb," Aunt Bobbie said.

"Oh," David said, then shrugged. It was probably better that way. Let security focus on the political intrigue. It just meant there'd be fewer eyes looking at him.

"Your mother's asleep."

"Where's Dad?"

"Nariman. Work emergency."

"All right," David said and headed back to his room. Aunt Bobbie hadn't noticed the bulk of his satchel, or if she had, she hadn't mentioned it. With his door safely closed, he checked the time. Late but not too late, and between the late afternoon amphetamines and the excitement and anxiety, trying to rest wasn't an option. Now that he had the product, all he wanted to do was get rid of it. Get it all away from him so that no one would stumble across it, get this all over with. He pulled out his hand terminal and put through a connection request to the contact Hutch had given him for emergencies only. He waited. Seconds stretched. A minute passed, and the tight feeling of panic grew in David's gut.

The screen jumped, and Hutch was there, scowling into the camera. He was naked from the waist up, his pale hair messy. The hardness in his expression was clear, even through the connection.

"Yeah?" Hutch said. It was a noncommittal greeting. If security had been watching over David's shoulder, they wouldn't even be sure that he and Hutch knew each other.

"We need to meet," David said. "Tonight. It's important."

Hutch was silent. A dry tongue ran across the man's lower lip and he shook his ragged head. David's heart was thudding like little hammer blows against his rib cage.

"Don't know what you mean, cousin," Hutch said.

"No one's listening in. I'm not busted. But we have to talk. Tonight," David said. "And you have to bring Leelee."

"You want to say that again?"

"One hour. The usual place. You have to bring Leelee."

"Yeah, I thought maybe you were giving me some kind of order there, little man," Hutch said, his voice buzzing with anger. "I'm going to tell myself that you burned this number because you got a little drunk or some shit. Out of my deep fucking kindness, I'm going to pretend you didn't forget yourself, yeah? So you get yourself back to bed and sleep until you're sober."

"I am sober," David said. "But it has to be tonight. It has to be now."

"Not going to happen," Hutch said and leaned forward to shut off the connection.

"I'll call security," David said. "If you don't, I'll call security. I'll tell them everything."

Hutch froze. Sat back. He pressed his hands together palm to palm, index fingers touching his lips like he was praying. David squeezed his hands into fists, then released them, squeezed and released. An uncomfortable creeping moved up the back of his neck and onto his scalp. Hutch drew in a long breath and let it out slow.

"All right," he said. "You come to me. One hour."

"And Leelee."

"Heard you the first time," Hutch said, his voice cool and gray as slate. "But anything smells like a setup, and your little girl-friend dies first. You savvy?"

"You don't need to hurt her. This isn't a setup. It's business."

"So you say," Hutch said and cut the feed. David's hands were trembling. He shouldn't have said that about going to security, but it was the only leverage he had. The only thing that would make Hutch listen. When he got there, he could explain it all. It would be all right. He stuffed the hand terminal in his pocket, stood silently for a moment, then shifted the wall to the still from *Gods of Risk*. Two men facing each other with the fate of everything in the balance. David lifted his chin and picked up the satchel.

When he came into the common room, Aunt Bobbie frowned.

"Going somewhere?" she asked.

"Friend," he said, shrugging and pulling the satchel closer to his hip. "Just a thing."

"But it's here, right? In Breach Candy?"

A new tickle of anxiety lifted the hair at the back of his neck. Her tone wasn't accusing or suspicious. That made it worse.

"Why?"

Aunt Bobbie nodded toward the monitor with its red border and earnest announcer.

"Curfew," she said.

David could feel the word trying to get into his mind, trying to mean something that he didn't let it mean.

"What curfew?"

"They put the whole city on first-stage lockdown. No unaccompanied minors on the tube system or service tunnels, no gatherings in the common areas after seven. Doubled patrols too. If you're heading out of the neighborhood, you may have to send your regrets," she said. Then, "David? Are you okay?"

He didn't remember sitting down. He was just on the kitchen floor, his legs folded under him like some kind of Zen monk. His skin was slick with sweat even though he didn't feel hot. Hutch was going to meet him and he wouldn't be there. He'd think it was a setup. And he'd have Leelee with him because David had told him to. Had insisted. Threatened even. Without thinking, he pulled out his hand terminal and requested a connection to Hutch. The address came back invalid. It had already been deleted.

"David, what's the matter?"

She was leaning over him now, her face a mask of concern. David waved his hand, feeling like he was underwater. No unaccompanied minors. He had to get to Martineztown. He had to go now.

"I need a favor," he said, and his voice sounded thin and strangled.

"All right."

"Come with me. Just so I can use the tube."

"Um. Okay," she said. "Let me grab a clean shirt."

They walked the half kilometer to the tube station in silence. David kept his hands in his pockets and his satchel on the other side of his body so that Aunt Bobbie might not see how full it was. He hated this. His chest felt tight and he needed to pee even though he didn't really. At the tube station, a red-haired security man in body armor and carrying an automatic rifle stopped them. David felt the mass of the drugs pulling at his shoulder like a lead weight. If they asked to see what was in the satchel, he'd go to prison forever. Leelee would be killed. He'd lose his place in Salton.

"Name and destination, please?"

"Gunnery Sergeant Roberta Draper, MMC," Aunt Bobbie said. "This is my nephew, David. He just got his placement, and I'm taking him to a party."

"Sergeant?" the security man said. "Marines, huh?"

A shadow passed over her face, but her smile dispelled it.

"Yes, sir."

The security man turned to David. His expression seemed friendly. David tasted vomit and fear at the back of his throat.

"Party?"

"Yes. Sir," he said, "yes, sir."

"Well, don't do any permanent damage, son," the security man said, chuckling. "Carry on, Sergeant."

And then they were past him and into the tube station proper. The white LEDs seemed brighter than usual, and his knees struggled to support him as he walked up to the kiosk. When he got the tickets for Martineztown, Aunt Bobbie looked at him quizzically but didn't say anything. Fifteen minutes to Aterpol, then a change of cars, and twenty to Martineztown. The other people in the car were grubby, their clothes rough at the edges. An old man with an exhausted expression and yellowed eyes sat across from them with a crying infant ignored in his arms. An immensely fat woman in the back of the car shouted obscenities into her hand terminal, someone on the other side of the connection shouting back. The air smelled of bodies and old air filters. With every passing kilometer, Aunt Bobbie's expression grew cooler and less trusting. He wanted to be angry with her for thinking that he wouldn't have friends in Martineztown, for being prejudiced against the neighborhood just because it was older and working class. It would have been easier if she hadn't been right.

At the Martineztown station, David turned to her and put his hand to her, palm out.

"Okay, thank you," he said. "Now just stay here, and I'll be right back."

"What's going on here, kid?" Aunt Bobbie asked.

"Nothing. Don't worry about it. Just wait for me here, and I'll be right back."

Aunt Bobbie crossed her arms. All warmth was gone from her face. A bright flare of resentment lit David's mind. He didn't have time to reassure her.

"Just wait," he said sharply, then spun on his heel and hurried off. A few seconds later, he risked a glance back over his shoulder. Aunt Bobbie hadn't moved. Her crossed arms and disapproving scowl could have been carved into stone. The LEDs of the tube station turned her into a black silhouette. David turned the corner, and she was gone. His satchel bounced against his hip, and he ran. It wasn't more than fifty meters before he was winded, but he pushed on the best he could. He didn't have time. Hutch might be there already.

And in point of fact, he was.

The crates had been rearranged. All of them were stacked against the walls, packed tight so that no one and nothing could hide behind them. The only exception was a doubled stack standing to Hutch's left and right like bodyguards. Like the massive sides of a great throne. Hutch stood in the shadows between them, a thin black cigarette clinging to his lip. His yellow shirt hung loose against his frame, and the muscles of his arms each seemed to cast their own shadows. The brushed black pistol in his hand made his scars seem like an omen.

Leelee knelt in front of him, in the center of the room, hugging herself. Her hair was lank and greasy looking. Her skin was pale except right around her eyes where the rash-red of crying stained her. She was wearing a man's shirt that was too big for her and a pair of work pants stained by something dark and washed pale again. When David cleared his throat and stepped into the room, her expression went from surprise to despair. David wished like hell he'd thought to stop at a bathroom.

"Hey there, little man," Hutch said. The insincerity of his casualness was a threat. "Now then, there was something you wanted to see me about, yeah?"

David nodded. The thickness in his throat almost kept him from speaking.

"I want to buy her," David said. "Buy her debt."

Hutch laughed softly, then took a drag on his cigarette. The ember flared bright and then dimmed.

"Pretty sure we covered that already," Hutch said, and the words were smoke. "You don't have that kind of cash."

"A quarter. You said I had a quarter."

Hutch's eyes narrowed and he tilted his head to the side. David dropped his satchel to the floor and slid it toward Leelee with his toe. She reached out a thin hand toward it.

"If you touch that bag, I will end you," Hutch said to Leelee, and she flinched back. "How about you tell me what that's supposed to be?"

"I cooked a batch. A big one. The biggest I've ever done," David said. "Mostly, it's 3,4-methylenedioxy-N-methylamphetamine. I did a run of 5-hydroxytryptophan too since I didn't need to order anything extra to do it. And 2,5-Dimethoxy-4-bromophenethylamine.

Some of that too. I got all the reagents myself. I did all the work. It's got to be worth more than four times what I put into it, and you get all of it free. That's the deal."

"You...," Hutch said, then paused, bit his lip. When he spoke again, he had a buzz of outrage in his voice. "You cooked a batch."

"It's got plenty. Lots."

"You. Stupid. Fuck," Hutch said. "Do you have any idea how much trouble you just handed me? How am I going to move that much shit? Who's going to buy it?"

"But you get it free."

Hutch pointed the gun at the satchel.

"I flood the market, and the prices go down. Not just for me. For everybody. You understand that? Everyone. People start coming up from Dhanbad Nova because they hear we've got cheap shit. All the sellers up there start wondering what I mean by it, and I've got drama."

"You could wait. Just hold on to it."

"I'm going to have to, right? Only it gets out that I'm sitting on an egg like that, someone gets greedy. Decides maybe it's time to take me on. And boom, I got drama again. Cut it how you want, kid. You just fucked me."

"He didn't know, Hutch," Leelee said. She sounded so tired.

Hutch's pistol barked once, shockingly loud in the small space. A gouge appeared in the floor next to Leelee's knee like a magic trick. She started crying.

"Yeah," Hutch said. "I didn't think you wanted to interrupt me again. David, you're a sweet kid, but you're dumb as a fucking bag of sand. What you just handed me here? It's a problem."

"I'm...I'm sorry. I just..."

"And it's going to require a little"—Hutch took a drag on his cigarette and raised the pistol until David could see him staring down the black barrel—"risk management."

The air in the room changed as the door behind him opened. He turned to look, but someone big moved past him too fast to follow. Something quick and violent happened, the sounds of a fight. David was hit in the back, hard. He pitched forward, unable to get his hands out fast enough to stop his fall. His head bounced off the sealed stone floor, and for a breathless second, he was sure he'd been shot. Been killed. Then the fight ended with Hutch screaming, crates crashing. The crackle of plastic splintering. David rose to his elbows. His nose was bleeding.

Aunt Bobbie stood where Hutch's crate shelter had been. She had the pistol in her hand and was considering it with a professional calm. Leelee had scooted across the floor toward David, as if to seek shelter behind him. Hutch, his cigarette gone, was cradling his right hand in his left. The index finger of his right hand—his trigger finger—stood off at an improbable angle.

"Who the fuck are you!" Hutch growled. His voice was low. Feral.

"I'm Gunny Draper," Aunt Bobbie said, ejecting the clip. She cleared the chamber and grabbed the thin brass glimmer out of the air. "So we should talk about this."

Leelee pressed her hand against David's arm. He shifted, gathered her close against him. She smelled rank—body odor and smoke and something else he couldn't identify—but he didn't care. Aunt Bobbie pressed something, and the top of the gun slipped off the grip.

"What've you got to say to me, dead girl?" Hutch asked. His voice didn't sound as tough as he probably hoped. Aunt Bobbie pulled the barrel out of the gun and tossed it into a corner of the room, in the narrow space between some crates and the wall. She didn't look up from the gun, but she smiled.

"The boy made a mistake," she said, "but he treated you with respect. He didn't steal from you. He didn't try to track the girl down on his own. He didn't go to security. He didn't even try to sell the product and get the money."

Leelee shivered. Or maybe David did and it only seemed like it was her. Hutch scowled, but a thoughtful look stole into his eyes.

Aunt Bobbie plucked a long, thin bit of metal out of the gun and then a small black spring and tossed both behind a different crate. "You're a tough guy in a tough business, and I respect that. Maybe you've killed some people. But you're also a businessman. Rational. Able to see the big picture." She looked up at Hutch, smiled, and tossed him the grip of his gun. "So here's what I'm thinking. Take the bag. Sell it, bury it. Drop it in the recycler. It's yours. Do what you want with it."

"Would anyway," Hutch said, but she ignored him.

"The girl's debt's paid, and David walks away. He's out. You don't come for him, he doesn't come for you. I don't come for you, either." She tossed him the empty top half of his gun, and he caught it with his uninjured hand. From where David was, hunched on the floor, both of them looked larger than life.

"Girl's nothing," Hutch said. "All drama and easy to replace. Boy's something special, though. Good cooks can't be swapped out just like that."

Aunt Bobbie started working the bullets out of the magazine with one thumb, dropping each one into her wide, powerful palm. "Everyone's replaceable in work like yours. You've got four or five like him already I bet." She took out the last of the bullets and put them in her pocket, then passed him the empty magazine. "David's the one that got away. No disrespect. Not a risk to the operation. Just worked out until it didn't. That's the deal."

"And if I say no?"

"I'll kill you," Aunt Bobbie said in the same matter-of-fact tone. "I'd prefer not to, but that's what happens if you say no."

"That easy?" Hutch said with a scowl. "Maybe not that easy."

"You're a tough guy, but I'm a nightmare wrapped in the apocalypse. And David is my beloved nephew. If you fuck with him after this, I will end every piece of you," Bobbie said, her own smile sad. "No disrespect."

Hutch's scowl twitched into a flicker of a smile.

"They grow 'em big where you come from," he said and held up the disassembled pistol. "You broke my gun."

"I noticed the spare magazine in your left pocket," she said. "David, stand up. We're leaving now."

He walked ahead, Leelee holding him and weeping quietly. Aunt Bobbie took the rear, keeping them going quickly without quite making them run and looking back behind her often. When they got near the tube station, Aunt Bobbie put a hand on David's shoulder.

"I can get you through the checkpoint, but I can't get her."

Leelee's eyes were soft and wet, her expression calm and serene. Filthy and stinking, she was still beautiful. She was redeemed.

"Do you have somewhere you can go?" David asked. "Someplace here in Martineztown where he can't find you?"

"I've got friends," she said. "They'll help."

"Go to them," Aunt Bobbie said. "Stay out of sight."

David didn't want to let her go, didn't want to lose the contact of her arm against his. He saw her understand. She didn't step into his arms as much as flow there, soft and supple and changing as water. For a moment, her body was pressed against his perfectly, without a millimeter of space in between. Her lips were against his cheek, her breath in his ear. She was Una Meing for a moment, and he was Caz Pratihari, and the world was a heady, powerful, romantic place. She shifted against him and her lips against his were soft and warm and they tasted like a promise.

"I'll find you," she whispered, and then the moment was over, and she was walking a little unsteadily down the corridor, her head high. He wanted to run after her, to kiss her again, to take her home with him and fold her into his bed. He could feel his heartbeat in his neck. He had an erection.

"Come on," Aunt Bobbie said. "Let's go home."

From Martineztown to Aterpol, she said nothing, just sat with her elbows resting on her knees, squeezing one of the bullets she'd taken between two fingers, then running it across her knuckles like a magic trick. Even through the chemical rush of relief, he dreaded what would come next. The disapproval, the lecture, the threats. When she spoke, with five minutes still before they reached Breach Candy, it wasn't what he'd expected to hear.

"That girl. You saved her. You know that? You saved her."

"Yeah."

"You feel good about that. You did a right thing, and that feels good."

"Yeah," he said.

"That good feeling is the most that girl will ever be able to give you."

The tube car's vibration was almost imperceptible. The monitors had tuned themselves to a newsfeed, unable to find any common ground between him and his aunt. David looked at his hands.

"She doesn't like me," he said. "She just acted like she did because he told her to. And then she knew I had money."

"She knew you had money and she knew you were a good guy," Aunt Bobbie said. "That's different."

David smiled and was surprised to kind of mean it. Aunt Bobbie leaned back, stretched. When she shifted her head, the joints in her neck popped like firecrackers.

"I need to move out," she said.

"Okay," David said, suddenly finding himself wishing she wouldn't. Too many losses today already, and this was one he hadn't even known would hurt. "Where will you go?"

"Back to work." Bobbie flipped the bullet up and caught it, then juggled it across her fingers again. "I need to find something to do." She pointed at the news on the monitors with her chin. It was all about Earth and Mars and angry people with bombs. "Maybe I can help."

"Okay," David said again. Then a moment later, "I'm glad you stayed with us."

"I should take you free-climbing," she said. "You'd love it."

David only saw Leelee one more time. It was his second year in development, about three weeks after he'd turned eighteen. He was in a noodle bar with the three other members of his team and their advisor, Dr. Fousek. The wall was playing a live feed of the football match from the Mariner Valley with the sound turned low enough to talk over. The table screen, on the other hand—they'd tunneled into the arrays at the upper university, and between bottles of beer and tea and black ceramic bowls of noodles and sauce, their latest simulation models were running.

Jeremy Ng, his dorm mate and the only other biochemist on the team, was shaking his head and pointing at the imagined surface of Mars that the computers back at their official labs were generating.

"But the salt—"

"Salinity's not an issue," David said, his frustration clear in his voice. "That's why we put the sodium pumps in, remember? It won't build up across the membrane."

"Gentlemen," Dr. Fousek said, her tone both authoritative and amused. "You have spent fifty hours a week arguing this for the last seven months. No point rethinking it now. We'll have solid projections soon enough."

Jeremy started to object, then stopped, started again, and ground to a halt. Beside him Cassie Estinrad, their hydro systems expert, grinned. "If this really works, you guys will put the terraforming project a couple decades ahead of schedule. You know that."

Dr. Fousek raised her hand, commanding silence. The simulation was almost done. Everyone at the table held their breath.

David couldn't say what made him look up. A sense of being watched maybe. A feeling of unease crawling up the back of his neck. Leelee was there at the back by the bar, looking toward him without seeing him. The years hadn't been kind. Her skin belonged on a woman twice her age and the elfin chin now just looked small. She had a child on her hip that looked about six months old and still too unformed to have a gender. She could have been anyone, except he had no question. A thin, electric jolt passed through him. For a split second he was fifteen again, on the edge of sixteen, and reckless as a fire. He remembered the way her kiss had felt, and almost without meaning to, he lifted his hand in a little wave.

He saw it when she recognized him; a widening of the eyes, a shift in the angle of her shoulders. Her expression tightened with something like anger. Fear looking for somewhere to go. The man sitting beside her touched her shoulder and said something. She shook her head, faced away. The man turned, scowling at the crowd. He met David's eyes for a moment, but there was nothing like understanding in them. David looked away from her for the last time.

"Here we go," Cassie said as the first results began to come. David put his elbows against the table as one by one values within his error bars clicked into place. He watched Dr. Fousek's eyebrows lift, watched Jeremy start to grin.

The euphoria came.

Gods of Risk
Author's Note

When the time came for the second contract—the one that covered *Cibola Burn*, *Nemesis Games*, and *Babylon's Ashes*, the fine folks at Orbit had started taking notice of the short fiction. We talked about it and came up with a plan. The contract also called for five novellas that would come out more or less between the novels. "Gods of Risk" was the first one.

Only it wasn't originally "Gods of Risk."

One of the weird things is how many of the stories were written under different titles than what they finally came out with. *Abaddon's Gate* was originally *Dandelion Sky*. "The Churn" was "Belovèd of Broken Things." "The Vital Abyss" was "The Necessary Abyss" (which we'll get into later). And "Gods of Risk"? Its working title was "Chemistry."

Mars was one of the big three factions in the storytelling

universe from the start, but while we'd spent a fair amount of time on Martian ships in the novels, we didn't spend much time on the planet. This way we got to.

The story itself was a little crime story confection, but more than that, it was a moment with two characters who were in moments of transition: David, who is in the unfortunate dumb-fuck phase of adolescence that everyone has to suffer through, and Bobbie, who had a career path mapped out that didn't come to pass and is trying to figure out who she is now that her old life has fallen apart. And through them, the country and government and planet that we, as the authors, knew was about to be in a phase change of its own.

A lot of these stories are about loss and rebirth and redemption. This one too.

We still think "Chemistry" would have been a great title for it. Tricky to find in a search engine, though.

The Churn

Burton was a small, thin, dark-skinned man. He wore immaculately tailored suits, and kept the thick black curls of his hair and the small beard on his chin neatly groomed. That he worked in criminal enterprises said more about the world than about his character. With more opportunities, a more prestigious education, and a few influential dorm mates at upper university, he could have joined the ranks of transplanetary corporate executives with offices at Luna and Mars, Ceres Station and Ganymede. Instead, a few neighborhoods at the drowned edges of Baltimore answered to him. An organization of a dozen lieutenants, a couple hundred street-level thugs and knee-breakers, a scattering of drug cooks, identity hackers, dirty cops, and arms dealers followed his dictates. And a class of perhaps a thousand professional victims— junkies, whores, vandals, unregistered children, and others in possession of disposable lives—looked up to him as he might look up at Luna: an icon of power and wealth glowing across an impassable void. A fact of nature.

Burton's misfortune was to be born where and when he was, in a city of scars and vice, in an age when the division in the popular mind was between living on government-funded basic support or having an actual profession and money of your own. To go from an unregistered birth such as his to having any power and status at all was an achievement as profound as it was invisible. To the men and women he owned, the fact that he had risen up from among the lowest of the low was not an invitation but a statement of his strength and improbability, mythical as the seagull that flew to the moon. Burton himself never thought about it, but that he had managed what he did meant only that it was possible. Anyone who had not had his determination, ruthlessness, and luck deserved pretty much whatever shit he handed to them. It didn't make him sympathetic when someone stepped out of line.

"He...what?" Burton said

"Shot him," Oestra said, looking at the table. Around them, the sounds of the diner made a white noise that was like privacy.

"Shot. Him."

"Yeah. Austin was talking about how he was good for the money, and how he just needed a few more days. Before he could finish, Timmy took that shitty homemade shotgun of his and—" Oestra made a shooting motion with two fingers and a thumb, the movement turning seamlessly into a shrug: a single gesture of violence and apology. Burton leaned back in his chair and looked over at Erich as if to say, *I think your puppy peed on my rug.*

Erich had recommended Timmy, had vouched for him, and so was responsible if things went wrong. It felt like they were going very wrong. Erich leaned forward, resting on his good elbow, hiding his fear with forced casualness. His bad arm, the left, was no longer than a six-year-old's and scarred badly at the joints. His disfigurement was the result of a beating he'd suffered as a child or something. It wasn't a fact that he'd shared with Burton, nor would he mention it now, though it did figure into the calculations that were his life. As did Timmy.

"He had a reason," Erich said.

"He did?" Burton said, raising his eyebrows with feigned patience. "And what was it?"

Erich's stomach knotted. His bad hand closed in a tiny fist. He saw the hardness in Burton's eyes, and it reminded him that even with his knowledge, even with his skills, there were others who could fake identity records. Others who could fake DNA profiles. Others who could do for Burton what he did. He was expendable. It was the message Burton meant him to take.

"I don't know," he said. "But I've known Timmy since forever, yeah? He doesn't do anything unless there's a reason."

"Well," Burton replied, pulling the word out to two syllables. "If it's since *forever*, I guess that makes it all right."

"Just, you know, if he did that, he did it for something."

Oestra scratched his arm, scowling to hide the relief he felt at Burton's focus turning to Erich. "I got him in the storage room."

Burton stood up, pushing back his chair with the backs of his knees. The waitress made a point not to look at the three as they moved across the room and out through the doors marked EMPLOYEES ONLY, Burton and then Oestra and Erich limping at the back. She didn't even start cleaning the table until she was sure they were gone.

The storage room was claustrophobic to begin with and lined with boxes, making it even smaller. Cream-colored degradable storage boxes with flat green adhesive readouts on the side that listed what they contained and whether the cheap, disposable sensors in the foam had detected rot and corruption. The table in the cramped open space at the center was pressed particleboard, as much glue as wood. Timmy sat at it, the LED fixture overhead throwing the shadow of his brow down into his eyes. He was barely halfway into his second decade of life, but the red-brown hair was already receding from his forehead. He was strong, tall, and had an unnerving capacity for stillness. He looked up when the three men came in, dividing his smile equally among his childhood friend, the professional thug he'd just disappointed, and the thin, well-dressed man who controlled everything important in his life.

"Hey," Timmy said to any of them.

Erich moved to sit at the table, saw that Oestra and Burton were standing motionless, and pulled back. If Timmy noticed, he didn't say anything.

"I hear that you killed Austin," Burton said.

"Yeah," Timmy said. The empty smile changed not at all.

Burton pulled out the chair opposite Timmy and sat. Oestra and Erich carefully didn't look at each other or at Burton. The object of all their attention, Timmy waited amiably for whatever came next.

"You care to tell me why you did that?" Burton asked.

"It's what you said to do," Timmy said.

"That man owed me money. I told you to get whatever you could from him. This was your tryout, little man. This was your game. Now, how do you go from what I actually *said* to what you *did*?"

"I got whatever I could get," Timmy replied. There was no fear in his voice or his expression, and it left Burton with the sense he was talking to an idiot. "I couldn't get money out of that guy. He didn't have any. If he had, he'd have given it to you. Only thing you were getting from him was a way to make sure everyone else pays you on time. So I took that instead."

"Really?"

"Yup."

"You're positive—you're *convinced*—that Austin wouldn't have gotten my money?"

"I don't mean to second-guess why anybody gave it to him in the first place," Timmy said, "but that guy never met a dollar he didn't snort, shoot, or drink away."

"So you thought it through, and you came to the conclusion

that the wise and right thing to do was escalate this little visit from a collection run to a murder?"

Timmy's head tilted a degree. "Didn't spend a lot of time thinking about it. Water's wet. Sky's up. Austin gets you more dead than alive. Kind of obvious."

Burton went silent. Oestra and Erich didn't look at him. Burton rubbed his hands together, the hiss of palm against palm the loudest noise in the room. Timmy scratched his leg and waited, neither patient nor impatient. Erich felt a growing nausea and the certainty that he was about to watch an old friend and protector die in front of him. His stunted hand opened and closed and he tried not to swallow. When Burton smiled his small, amused smile, the only one who saw it was Timmy, and if he understood it, he didn't react.

"Why don't you wait here, little man," Burton said.

"Arright," Timmy said, and Burton was already walking out the door.

Out in the café, the lunch rush had started. The booths and tables were filled, and a crowd loitered in the doorway, scowling at the waitresses, the diners who had gotten tables before them, and the empty place reserved for Burton and whoever he chose to have near him. As soon as he took his chair, the waitress came over, her eyebrows raised, as if he were a new customer. He waved her away. There was something about sitting at an empty table in full view of hungry men and women that Burton enjoyed. *What you want, I can take or I can leave*, it said. *All I want is to keep your options for myself.* Erich and Oestra sat.

"That boy," Burton said, letting the words take on an affected drawl, "is some piece of work."

"Yeah," Oestra said.

"He's good at what he does," Erich said. "He'll get better."

Burton was quiet for a long moment. A man at the front door pointed an angry finger toward Burton's table, demanding something of the waitress. She took the stranger's hand and pushed it down. The angry man left. Burton watched him go. If he didn't know any better, this wasn't the place for him.

"Erich, I don't think I can take your friend off his probation period. Not with this. Not yet."

Erich nodded, the urge to speak for Timmy and the fear of losing Burton's fickle forgiveness warring in his throat. Oestra was the one to break the silence.

"You want to give him another job?" The words carried a weight of incredulity measured to the gram.

"The right job," Burton said. "Right one for now, anyway. You say he watched out for you, growing up?"

"He did," Erich said.

"Let him do that, then. Timmy's going to be your personal bodyguard on your next job. Keep you out of trouble. See if you can keep him out of trouble too. At least do better than Oey did with him, right?" Burton said and laughed. A moment later Oestra laughed too, only a little sourly. Erich couldn't manage much more than a sick, relieved grin.

"I'll tell him," he said. "I'll take care of it."

"Do," Burton said, smiling. An awkward moment later, Erich got up, head bobbing like a bird's with gratitude and discomfort. Burton and Oestra watched him limp back toward the storage room. Oestra sighed.

"I don't know why you're cultivating that freak," Burton's lieutenant said.

"He's off the grid and he cooks good identity docs," Burton said. "I like having someone who can't be traced keeping my name clean."

"I don't mean the cripple. I mean the other one. Seriously, there's something wrong with that kid."

"I think he's got potential."

"Potential for what?"

"Exactly," Burton said. "Okay, so tell me the rest. What's going on out there?"

Oestra hoisted his eyebrows and hunched forward, elbows on the table. The kids running unlicensed games by the waterfront weren't coming up with the usual take. One of the brothels had been hit by an outbreak of antibiotic-resistant syphilis; one of the youngest boys, a five-year-old, had it in his eyes. Burton's neighbors to the north—an Earthbound branch of the Loca Griega—were seeing raids on their drug manufacturing houses. Burton listened with his eyelids at half-mast. Individually, no one event mattered much, but put together, they were the first few fat raindrops in a coming storm. Oestra knew it too.

By the time the lunch rush ended, the booths and tables filling and emptying in the systole and diastole of the day's vast urban heart, Burton's mind was on a dozen other things. Erich and Timmy and the death of a small-time deadbeat weren't forgotten, but no particular importance was put on them either. That was what it meant to be Burton: those things that could rise up to fill a small person's whole horizon were only small parts of his view. He was the boss, the big-picture man. Like Baltimore itself, he *weathered* storms.

Time had not been kind to the city. Its coastline was a ruin of drowned buildings kept from salvage by a complexity of rights, jurisdictions, regulations, and apathy until the rising sea had all but reclaimed them for its own. The Urban Arcology movement had peaked there a decade or two before the technology existed to make its dreams of vast, sustainable structures a reality. It had left a wall seven miles long and twenty stories high of decaying hope and structural resin that reached from the beltway to Lake Montebello. At the street level, electric networks laced the roadways, powering and guiding the vehicles that could use them. Sparrows Island stood out in the waves like a widow watching the sea for a ship that would never come home, and Federal Hill scowled back at the city across shallow, filthy water, emperor of its own abandoned land.

Everywhere, all through the city, space was at a premium. Extended families lived in decaying apartments designed for half as many. Men and women who couldn't escape the cramped space spent their days at the screens of their terminals, watching newsfeeds and dramas and pornography and living on the textured protein and enriched rice of basic. For most, their forays into crime were halfhearted, milquetoast affairs—a backroom brewer making weak, unregulated beer; a few kids stealing a neighbor's clothes or breaking their furniture; a band of scavengers with scrounged tools harvesting metal from the buried infrastructure of the city that had been. Baltimore was Earth writ small, crowded and bored. Its citizens were caught between the dismal life of basic and the barriers of class, race, and opportunity, vicious competition and limited resources, that kept all but the most driven from a profession and actual currency. The dictates of the regional administration in Chicago filtered down to the streets slowly, and the local powers might be weaker than the government, but they were also closer, the gravities of law and lawlessness finding their balance point somewhere just north of Lansdowne.

Time had not been kind to Lydia either. She wasn't one of the unregistered, but very little of what was important in her life appeared in the government records. There, she was a name—not Lydia—and an address where she had never lived. Her real home was four rooms on the fifth floor of a minor arcology looking out over the harbor. Her real work was keeping track of inventory for Liev, one of Burton's lieutenants. Before that, she had been his lover. Before that, she had been a whore in his stable. Before that, she had been someone else who she could hardly remember anymore. When she was alone, and she was often alone, the narrative she told herself was of how lucky she was. She'd escaped basic, she'd had dear friends and mentors when she was working, she'd been able to retire up in the ad hoc structure of the city's underworld. Many, many people hadn't been anywhere near as fortunate as she had been. She was growing old, yes. There was gray in her hair now. Lines at the corners of her eyes, the first faint liver spots on the backs of her hands. She told herself they were the evidence of her success. Too many of her friends had never had them.

Never would. Her life had been a patchwork of love and violence, and the overlap was vast.

Still, she hung warm-colored silk across her windows and wore the silver bells at her ankles and wrists that were the fashion among much younger women. Life, such as it was, was good.

The evening sun hung over the rooftops to the west, the late summer heat thickening the air. Lydia was in the little half-kitchen warming up a bowl of frozen hummus when the door chimed and the bolts clacked open. Timmy came in, lifting his chin in greeting. She smiled back, raising an eyebrow. There was no one with him, and there never would be. They had never allowed someone else to be with them when they were together. Not since the night his mother died.

"So, how did it go?"

"Kind of fucked it up, me," Timmy said.

Lydia's heart went tight and she tried to keep her voice calm and light. "How so?"

"Burton told me to get what I could out of this guy. Looking back, I think he just meant money. So." Timmy leaned against the couch, hands deep in his pockets, and shrugged. "Oops."

"Was Burton angry?"

Timmy looked away and shrugged again. With that motion, she could see him again as he'd been as a young boy, as a child, as a baby. She had known his mother when they'd worked together, each watching out for the other when they turned tricks. Lydia had been there the night Timmy was born among the worn tiles and cold lights of the black-market clinic. She'd made him soup the night Liev had turned him out the first time and while he ate told him lies about her first time with a john to make him laugh. She'd picked music with him for his mother's memorial and told him that she'd died the way she'd lived, and not to blame himself. She had never been able to protect him from anything, so she'd helped him live in the jagged world, and he gave her something she couldn't describe or define but that she needed like a junkie craved the needle.

"How angry is he?" she asked carefully.

"Not that bad. I'm gonna be watching Erich's back for a while. He's got some things need doing, and the boss doesn't want anything going pear-shaped. So that's all right."

"And you? How are you?"

"Eh. I'm good," Timmy said. "I think I'm coming down with something. Flu, maybe."

She walked out from the kitchen, her food abandoned, and put the back of her hand to his forehead. His skin felt cool.

"No fever," she said.

"Probably nothing," he said, pulling his shirt up over his head. "I got the shakes a little, and I got dizzy a couple times on the way back. It ain't serious."

"What happened to the man Burton sent you to?"

"I shot him."

"Did you kill him?" Lydia asked as she walked back to her bedroom. The ruddy light of sunset filtered through yellow silk. An old armoire stood against one wall, its silver finish stained and corroded by years. The bed was the same cheap foam queen-sized she'd had when she was working, the sheets old and thin, softer than skin with wear.

"Used a shotgun about a meter from his chest," Timmy said, following her. "Could have stuck your fist through the hole. So, yeah, pretty much."

"Have you ever killed a man before?" she asked, lifting her dress up over her thighs, her hips, her head.

Timmy undid his belt, frowning. "Don't know. Beat some guys pretty bad. Maybe some of 'em didn't get back up, but no one I know about. You know, not for sure."

Lydia unhooked her bra, letting it slide to the cheap carpet. Timmy took his pants down, kicking them off with his shoes. He didn't wear underwear, and his erect penis bobbed in the air like it belonged to someone else. There was no desire in his expression, and only a mild distress.

"Timmy," she said, lying back on the bed and lifting her hips. "You aren't getting ill. You're traumatized."

"Y'think?" He seemed genuinely surprised by the thought. And then amused by it. "Yeah, maybe. Huh."

He pulled her underwear down to her knees, her ankles. "My poor Timmy," she murmured.

"Ah shit," he said, lowering his body onto hers. "I'm all right. At least I'm not getting sick."

Sex held few mysteries for Lydia. She had fucked and been fucked by more men than she could count, and she'd learned things from each of them. Ugly things sometimes. Sometimes beautiful. She understood on a deep, animal level that sex was like music or language. It could express anything. Love, yes. Or anger, or bitterness, or despair. It could be a way to grieve or a way to take revenge. It could be a weapon or a nightmare or a solace. Sex was meaningless, and so it could mean anything.

What she and Timmy did to and for and with each other's bodies wasn't a thing they discussed. She felt no shame about it. That other people would see only the perversion of a woman and the boy she'd helped raise pleasuring one another meant that other people would never understand what it meant to *be* them, to survive the world they survived. They were not lovers, and never would be. They were not surrogate mother and incestuous son. She was Lydia, and he was Timmy. In the bent and broken world, what they did fit. It was more than most people had.

After, Timmy lay beside her, his breath still coming in small, reflexive gulps. Her body felt pleasantly tender and bruised. The yellow over the window was fading into twilight, and the rumble of air traffic was like constant thunder in the distance, or a city being shelled two valleys over. A transport ship for one of the orbital stations, maybe. Or a wing of atmospheric fighter planes on exercises. So long as she didn't look, she could pretend it was anything. Her mind wandered, delivering up what had been nagging at her since Timmy had told her all that had happened.

Burton had sent Timmy to collect a debt, Timmy had killed the man instead, and Burton hadn't cut him loose. Two points defined a line, but three defined the playing field. Burton didn't always have need of boys like Timmy, but sometimes he did. Right now, he did.

Lydia sighed.

The churn was coming. It was the name Liev had given it, back before. All of nature had its rhythms, its booms and busts. She and Timmy and Liev and Burton were mammals, they were part of nature, and subject to its rules and whims. She had lived through perhaps three, perhaps four such catastrophes before. Enough that she knew the signs. Like a squirrel gathering food before a hard winter, Burton collected violent men before the churn. When it came, there would be blood and death and prison sentences and maybe even a curfew for a time. Men like Timmy would die by the dozen, sacrificed for things they didn't know or understand. Maybe even some of Burton's lieutenants would fall the way Tanner Ford had back when she'd been Liev's lover. Or Stacey Li before him. Or Cutbreath. The history of her corrupted world echoed with the names of the dead; the expendable and the expended. If Burton had kept Timmy on, it was because he thought it was coming. And if Burton thought it was coming, it probably was.

Timmy's breath was low and deep and regular. He sounded like a man asleep, except his eyes were open and fixed on the ceiling. Her own skin was cool now, the sweat dried or nearly so. A fly swooped through the air above them, a gray dot tracing a jagged path, turning and dodging to avoid dangers that weren't there. She lifted her first two fingers, cocked back her thumb, and made a thin cartoon shooting sound with her teeth and tongue. The insect flew on, undisturbed by her small and violent fantasy. She turned her head to look at Timmy. His expression was blank and empty. He was still, and even in the warmth that followed orgasm, there was a tension in his body. He wasn't a beautiful boy. He'd never be a beautiful man.

Someday, she thought, *I will lose him. He will go off on some errand and he will never come back. I won't even know what happened to him.* She probed at the thought like a tongue-tip against the sore gum where a tooth has been knocked out. It hurt and hurt badly, but it hadn't happened yet, and so she could bear it. Best to prepare herself now. Meditate upon the coming loss so that when it came, she was ready.

Timmy's eyes clicked over toward her without his head shifting at all, without any expression coming to his face. Lydia smiled a slow, languorous smile.

"What are you thinking?" she asked.

He didn't answer.

The catastrophe began four days later. Quietly, and with near-military precision, the city opened a contract with Star Helix security. Soldiers from across the globe arrived in small groups and sat through debriefings. The plan to end the criminal networks operating in Baltimore would be announced after the fact, or at least after the first wave. The thought, widely lauded by the self-congratulatory minds in administration, was to take the criminal element by surprise. In catching them flat-footed, the security teams could cripple their networks, break their power, and restore peace and the rule of law. The several unexamined assumptions in the argument remained unexamined, and the body armor and riot control weapons were distributed in perfect confidence that the enforcers would arrive unanticipated.

In fact, what Burton and Lydia knew from experience, many, many others felt by instinct. There was a discomfort in the streets and alleys, on the rooftops, and behind the locked doors. The city knew that something was near. The only surprise would be in the details.

Erich felt it like an itch he couldn't scratch. He sat on the rotting concrete curb, drumming the fingers of his good hand against his kneecap. The street around him was the usual mix of foot traffic, bicycles, and wide blue buses. The air stank. The sewage lines this near the water were prone to failures. A few doors to the east, a group of children were playing some kind of complex game with linked headsets, their arms and legs falling into and out of phase with each other. Timmy stood on the sidewalk, squinting up into the sky. Behind them was a squatters' camp in an old ferrocrete apartment block. In a locked room at its center, Erich's custom deck was set up and primed, connected to the network and prepared to create a new identity from birth records to DNA matching to backdated newsfeed activity for the client, as soon as she arrived. Assuming she arrived. She was fifteen minutes late and, though they had no way to know it, already in custody.

Timmy grunted and pointed up. Erich followed the gesture. Far above, a star burned in the vast oceanic blue, a plume of fire pushing a ship out of the atmosphere. Near the horizon, the half moon glowed pale, a network of city lights crossing the shadowy meridian.

"Transport," Erich said. "They use mass drivers for the stuff that can take the gees."

"I know," Timmy said.

"Ever want to go up there?"

"What for?"

"I don't know," Erich said, staring down the street for the client. He'd seen her picture: a tall Korean woman with blue hair. He didn't know who she'd been before, and he didn't much care. Burton wanted her made into someone new. "Piss out the window and make everyone down here think it was raining, maybe."

Timmy's chuckle sounded polite.

"It's what I'd do, if I could," Erich said, making a swooping gesture with his good hand. Zoom. "Get up the well and out of here. Go where no one cares about who you are so long as you're good at what you do. Seriously, it's the wild fucking west up there. You want nineteenth-century Tombstone, Arizona, it's alive and well on Ceres Station. From what I heard, anyway."

"Why don't you go, then?" Timmy said. With a different intonation, it could have been dismissive. Instead it was only a mild kind of curiosity. It was part of what Erich liked about Timmy. There was almost nothing he seemed to feel deeply.

"Starting from here? I'd never make it. I'm not even a registered birth."

"You could tell them," Timmy said. "People get registered all the time."

"And then they get tracked and monitored and wind up dying on basic," Erich said. "Anyway, no one's taking me for a vocational. Waiting lists for that are eight, ten years long. By the time I came up, I'd have aged out."

"Could build one, couldn't you?" Timmy asked. "Make a new identity and put it at the front of the list?"

"Maybe," Erich said. "If you gave me a couple years to layer it all in like I did for Burton. He can go *anywhere* with docs I built for him."

"So why don't you go, then?" Timmy asked again, his inflection as much an echo as his words.

"Guess I don't want it bad enough. Anyway, I've got real stuff to do, don't I? I wish she'd fucking get here, right?" Erich said, unaware that he made everything a question when he wanted to change the subject. Unconsciously, he made a fist with the hand of his bad arm. Timmy nodded, squinting down the street for the client that wasn't coming.

Most of their lives had been spent on streets like this. The trade that exploited prostitutes and their illegal children was the second largest source of unregistered births in the city. Only religious radicals accounted for more. It was impossible to know how many unregistered men and women were eking out lives on the margin of society in Baltimore or how many had lived and died unknown to the vast UN databases. Erich knew of perhaps a hundred scattered among the legitimate citizens like members of a secret society. They congregated in condemned buildings and squats, traded in the gray-market economy of unlicensed services, and used their peculiar anonymity where it was most helpful. Looking down the pocked asphalt street, Erich could count three or four people that he personally knew were ghosts in the great world machine. Counting him and Timmy, that was half a dozen all breathing the same air while the plume of the orbital transport marked the sky gold and black above them. There was old water in the gutters, black circles of gum and tar on the sidewalk, the combined smell of urine and decay, and ocean all around them. Erich looked up at the sky with a longing he resented.

He knew himself well enough to recognize that he was a man of desires and grudges, so well in fact that he'd come to peace with it. The blackness of space where merit counted more than the placement on a bureaucrat's list, where the brothels were licensed and the prostitutes had a union, where freedom was a ship and a crew and enough work to pay for food and air. It called to him with a romance that made his heart ache. On Ceres or Tycho or Mars, the medical technology was available to regrow his crippled arm, to remake his shortened leg. The same technology could be found fewer than eight miles from the filthy curb where he sat, but with the triple barriers of being unregistered, basic medical care waiting lists, and his own ability to function despite his disabilities, space was closer. Out there, he could be the man he should have been. The thought was like the promise of sex to a teenager, rich and powerful and frightening. Erich had resolved a thousand times to make the effort, to build himself an escape identity and shrug off the chains of Earth, of Baltimore, of the life he'd lived. And a thousand and one times, he had postponed it.

"Get up," Timmy said.

"You see her?" Erich said.

"Nope. Get up."

Erich shifted, frowning. Timmy was looking east with an expression of mild curiosity, a casual witness at someone else's wreck. Erich stood. At the intersection a block down, two armored vans had pulled to a stop. The logo on their sides was a four-pointed star. Erich couldn't tell if the people getting out were men or women, only that they were wearing riot gear. Metallic fear flooded his mouth. Timmy put a strong hand on his shoulder and pushed him gently but implacably across the street. Two more vans came to a halt at the intersection to the north.

"What the fuck?" Erich said, his voice distant and shrill in his own ears.

Timmy got him across the street and almost up to the doors of a five-story squat before Erich pulled back. "My deck. My setup. We've got to go back for it."

A deep, inhuman voice broke the air, the syllables designed in a sound lab to be sharp, clear, and intimidating. *This is a security alert. Remain where you are with your hands visible until security personnel clear you to leave. This is a security alert.* At the intersection, teams of armored figures were already questioning three men. One of the civilians—a thin, angry man with close-cropped black hair and dark olive skin—shouted something, and the security team pushed him to his knees. The biometric scan—fingerprints, retina scan, fast-match DNA—took seconds while the man's arms were held out at his sides, his elbows bent back in restraint holds.

"I think maybe you used to have a deck," Timmy said. "I don't think you got one right now."

Erich stood unmoving, caught between the animal urge to flee and to protect himself by hiding the evidence. Timmy's thick fingers closed around his good shoulder. The big kid's expression was mildly concerned. "We don't go right now, they're gonna have you and it both. I sorta screwed up the last thing Burton told me to do. Let's not burn my second chance getting you caught."

This is a security alert. Remain where you are with your hands visible until security personnel clear you to leave.

Erich swallowed and nodded. It was the nearest he could come to speech. Timmy turned him toward the squat and pushed him forward.

In the streets, the security teams converged slowly, moving from person to person, door to door, floor to floor. Before the operation was through, they would identify three hundred forty-three people and detain four who appeared in the operational database as persons of interest. Three unregistered individuals would be identified, entered into the system, and held pending investigation. The two of the unregistered who refused to provide a name would have names assigned to them. The operation, covering three city blocks, would locate an unlicensed medical clinic, three children in distressed circumstances, seven pounds of S-class psychoactives, eighty-two instances of illegal occupation, and the network interface deck and data collection setup offered up by a blue-haired detainee in exchange for a reduced penalty. The process would take ten hours, and so it was still hardly under way when Timmy and Erich emerged from the undocumented access tunnel that connected the squat with an abandoned seawater pumping station. They walked together, Erich with his good hand stuffed deep in his pocket, Timmy with the same amiable air that was his default. Erich was weeping silently. Above them, the transport ship was gone, the golden exhaust plume now only a streak of smoke against the sky.

"I'm dead," Erich said. "Burton's going to fucking kill me. They got my deck. They got everything."

"Wait a minute," Timmy said. "*Everything* everything? Burton's stuff was on the—"

"No. I'm not stupid. I don't store records of how I keep Burton clean. But I didn't wash it down after the setup. I was going to do it after we were done. It's going to have DNA on it. Shit, it may even have fingerprints. I don't know."

"So what if it does?" Timmy asked with a shrug. "You're not in the system."

"Not now," Erich said. "But if they pick me up ever, for *anything*, it's going to be with a little highlight alert linking back to that fucking deck. They'll know what I do. And then they'll know to ask."

"You don't gotta say anything," Timmy said, his tone almost apologetic.

"I won't get a chance. Burton finds out they've got my DNA, all he's gonna see is a path back to him. I'm a loose end, man. I'm dead."

All around the city, traps shut.

In the north, five dozen armored security personnel blocked intersections and shut down metro stations. The door-to-door search and control operation converged on a seven-story office building controlled by the Loca Griega. The local men and women took shelter where they could, hiding in bathtubs and basements and soot-caked hard-brick fireplaces. Things dense enough to hopefully block the infrared and backscatter and heartbeat sensors Star Helix carried. Network signals went dark. The Star Helix employees moved forward in tight formation, forced to use their eyes instead of their tech, the plates of armor on their chests and backs and bellies making them seem like vast beetles in the autumn sunlight. When the perimeter around the building was established, monitoring stations were constructed, watching the windows for the vibrations made by voices. A wave of dragonfly-small surveillance drones swept in, and for a moment it seemed like perhaps the violence wouldn't come. And then, as one, the hundreds of small, cheap Star Helix robots fell to the ground, victims of Loca Griega countermeasures, and the building bloomed with gunfire. Seventeen Loca Griega died before the sun went down, including Eduard Hopkins and Jehona Dzurban, reputed to be the Earth-surface coordinators of the Belt-based syndicate. The plume of smoke that rose from the building darkened the air for hours and left the city air gray and hazy the next morning.

At the same time in the west, where the municipal limits gave way invisibly to the regional jurisdiction, a warehouse owned and operated through a complex web of shell companies was locked down. The security teams emptied a three-block radius using a small fleet of armored buses and an operational procedure designed for response to sarin gas attacks. When the warehouse's perimeter was breached shortly before midnight, it contained ten thousand unrecorded assault rifles, half a million rounds of tracer-free ammunition, seventy cases of grenades, and a computer room ankle deep in melted slag. There was no evidence of anyone having been present in the warehouse, and no trail of ownership for any of it.

Checkpoints at the evacuated rail terminal, the spaceport, and the docks identified seventy people traveling on falsified accounts.

All of them were independents or small fry in a larger organization. The security forces hadn't expected to catch anyone high on their priorities list in the first pass. The more powerful, better-connected targets were either smart enough not to travel during a crackdown or else had cleaned accounts to move under. Instead, the thought was that among the small-time thugs and operatives, there might be one or two desperate and foolish enough to provide them a lead to someone bigger. Someone worth having. And so without knowing who Burton was, what he looked like, his name or description or precise role in the criminal ecology of Baltimore, they were hunting him. And they were also hunting others, many of them much higher-priority than himself. Organizace Bayyo had a presence in the city, as did the Golden Bough. Tamara Sluydan controlled several blocks north of the arcology, and Baasen Tagniczen an area twice Burton's—though not so profitably run—in the Patapsco Valley Housing Complex. There was a great deal of crime, organized and otherwise, for the forces of law to concern themselves with, and no net was so strong or fine that nothing slipped through.

In times like these, when he couldn't know whether he had been compromised, Burton played it safe. He had half a dozen apartments and warehouses outfitted to act as temporary command centers, and he moved between them almost at random. Some of his people, he knew, would be caught up. Some of those who were would buy short-term leniency with the coin of information. He knew that would happen, and he had plans in place that would protect him from discovery, obscure his involvement in anything actionable, and punish brutally and irrevocably whoever had chosen to make that trade. It was understood that anyone captured would be wiser to trade their own underlings to the security forces than to sell out Burton. The risk devolved on the little guy. Shit rolling downhill, as it had since the beginning of time. Which was, in part, why what happened to Liev was so unfortunate for everybody.

Liev Andropoulous had worked for Burton since coming to

Baltimore from Paris more than twenty years before. He was a thickly built man, as round in the chest as the belly, and strong enough that he rarely had to prove it. His appetite for women occasioned jokes, though rarely the sort made in front of him, as did his habit of placing his long-term lovers in positions of comfort within his organization when he ended their relationships. As one of Burton's lieutenants, he oversaw three full-time whorehouses, a small network of drug dealers specializing in low-end narcotics and psychoactives, and an unlicensed medical facility that catered to the unregistered population. By custom, he worked from a small concrete building at the edge of the water, but when the churn began, he was leaving his lover's apartment on Pratt. The woman's name was Katie, and she had the olive skin and brown lips that Lydia had had twenty years before. Liev was a man of deep habits and consistent tastes. He kissed her goodbye for the last time on the street outside the apartment building, then walked away to the north while she went south. It was a perfunctory gesture, meaningful only in retrospect, as so many last kisses are.

The streets were crowded, the air muggy and close. The saltwater and rotting fish smells of the encroaching Atlantic were omnipresent, as they always were on hot days. Private transport wasn't allowed, and the lumbering buses moved like slow elephants in the press of midday bodies. A beggar plucked at Liev's sleeve and then backed away in fear when Liev turned to scowl at him. In the cacophony of the city, the whine of the flying drones should have been inaudible, but something caught Liev's attention, tightening the skin across the back of his wide neck. His footsteps faltered.

From above, the ripples in the crowd would have looked like the surface of still water disturbed by the convergence of half a dozen fish intent on the same fly. For Liev, it was only a sense of dread, a burst of useless adrenaline, and the offended shouts of the civilians pushed aside by the armored security men. As if by magic, a bubble of open space appeared around him. Liev could see clearly the scuffed and stained concrete on which he walked.

The man in the Star Helix uniform before him held a pistol in both hands, the barrel fixed on Liev's chest. Center of mass. By the books. Behind the helmet's clear face shield, the man looked to be somewhere in his middle twenties, focused and frightened. Liev felt a pang of amusement and regret. He held his arms out at his sides, cruciform, as five more security men boiled out of the gawking crowd.

"Liev Andropoulous!" the boy shouted. "You are under arrest for racketeering, slavery, and murder! You are not required to participate in questioning without the presence of an attorney or union representative!" Tiny flecks of spittle dotted the inside of the face shield. The boy's wide eyes were almost jittering with fear. Liev sighed.

"Ask me," he said slowly, enunciating very clearly, "if I understand."

"What?" the boy shouted.

"You've told me the charges and made the questioning statement. Now you have to ask me if I understand."

"Do you understand?" the boy barked, and Liev nodded.

"Good. Better," Liev said. "Now go fuck yourself."

The prisoner transport blatted its siren, shouldering its way through the crowd, but before it had crossed the distance to Liev, before he had been slotted into the steel cell and made secure, news of his capture was radiating out through the neighborhood. By the time the transport began moving again, making its way north toward the nearest tactical center, Burton had already seen a recording of the arrest. Katie, sitting at a noodle café with her little brother, got the news on her hand terminal and broke down weeping. Dread passed through the network of Liev's employees and underlings. Everyone knew what would happen next, and what would not. Liev would be taken to a holding cell, processed, and interrogated. If he kept quiet, he would be remanded to state custody, tried, and sent to a detention center, likely in North Africa or the west coast of Australia. More likely, he would cut a deal, parting out the network of crime he'd controlled bit by bit in exchange for clemency—the names and ID numbers of his pimps in order to serve his time in North America or Asia, the details of how he laundered the money for a private cell, which physicians had moonlighted in his clinic for library access.

They would ask him who he worked for, and he wouldn't say.

For Burton's other lieutenants, it complicated the future and simplified the present. One of their own was gone and unlikely to return. When the worst had passed and something like normalcy returned to Burton's little kingdom, business that had been Liev's would be shared among them, granted to some newly promoted member of the criminal nobility, or a combination of the two. How exactly that played out would be the subject of weeks of negotiations and struggle, but later. Later. In the short term, all such agendas gave way to the more immediate problems of avoiding the security forces, protecting the assets they had, and making it very clear to everyone under them that selling out information for the favor of the court's mercy was a very, very bad idea.

In a basement lab at the corner of Lexington and Greene, eighty gallons of reagents used in alkaloid synthesis were poured into the water recycling stream. At the locally renowned Boyer Street house, two overly talkative prostitutes went quietly missing and the doors were locked. The body of Mikel "Batman" Chanduri was discovered in his two-room apartment at sundown, and though it was clear his death had been both violent and protracted, none of his neighbors had anything to report to the security men who'd come to interview him. Before the sun had set, Burton's lieutenants—Cyrano, Oestra, Simonson, Little Cole, and the Ragman—went to ground like foxes, ready to wait out the worst of the crackdown, each hoping that they would not be another gap in the organization like Liev, and each hoping that the others—not all, of course, but a few—would. One or two, perhaps even three, harbored some plots of their own, ways to see that their rivals within Burton's organization fell prey to the dangers of the churn. But they didn't speak of them to anyone they didn't trust with their lives.

And in an unlicensed rooftop coffee bar that looked down over the human-packed streets, Erich hunched over a gray-market network deck the owner had bolted to the table. He was trying to keep his panic from showing, wondering if Burton had heard about the capture of his deck, and hoping that wherever Timmy had rushed off to when they'd heard of Liev's arrest, he'd get back soon. The coffee was black and bitter, and Erich couldn't tell if the coppery flavor was a problem with the beans or the lingering taste of fear. He sat on his newsfeed, set to passive for fear that his search requests would be traced, and watched as all around him more traps snapped shut, his gut knotting tighter with every one.

When Lydia heard what had happened to Liev, her first action was to put on her makeup and style her long, gray-streaked hair. She sat at the mirror in her bedroom and rubbed on the flesh-toned base until the lines in her skin were gone. She painted her lips fuller and darker and redder than they had ever been in nature. The black eyeliner, reddish eyeshadow, rust-colored blush. Despite the danger she was in, she didn't hurry. A lifetime of experience had drawn connections in her mind that linked sexual desirability, fear, and fatalism in ways she would have recognized as unhealthy if she'd seen them in someone else. She pulled her hair around, piling it high and pinning it in place until it cascaded, three-quarters contained, to her shoulders in the style Liev had enjoyed back when he had lifted her up from the working population of the house and made her his own. She thought of it as a last act of fidelity, like dressing a corpse.

She shrugged out of her robe and pulled on simple, functional clothes. Running shoes. Her go-bag was a nondescript blue backpack with a three-month supply of her medications, two changes of clothes, four protein bars, a pistol, two boxes of ammunition, a bottle of water, and three thousand dollars spread across half a dozen credit chips. She pulled it down from the top of her closet, and without opening it to check its contents, went to the chair by her front window. The curtains were pale gauze that scattered and softened the afternoon light, graying everything. She pulled a sheer yellow scarf over her hair, swathed her neck, and tied it at her sternum, the ironic echo of her old hijab. Then sat very still, feet side by side, ankles and knees touching. Primly, she thought. She waited in silence to see who would open her door, a security team or Timmy. The darkness, or else the light.

The better part of an hour passed. Her spine hurt, and she savored the pain, keeping her face placid. Smiles or grimaces, either one would disturb her makeup. Then footsteps in the hall, like someone clearing their throat. The door opened, and Timmy stepped in. His gaze flicked down to her back, up to her face. He shrugged and nodded to the hall in a gesture that said, *Can we go?* as clearly as words. Lydia stood, pulled on her pack as she walked to the door, and left her room for the last time. She had lived there for the better part of a decade. The necklace that Liev had given her the night he'd told her he was moving on, but that she would be cared for, hung from a peg in the bathroom. The cheap earthenware cup that Timmy had painted with glaze when he was eight years old and given her for what he'd mistakenly thought was her birthday remained in the cupboard. The half-finished knitting that an old roommate had left when she disappeared twenty years before sat hunched in a plastic bag under the bed, stinking of dust.

Lydia didn't look back.

"My spirit animal is the snake," she said as they walked south together. They went side by side, but not touching. "I shed my skin. I just let it slough away."

"Okay," Timmy said. "Come on this way. I got a thing waiting."

The waterline was cleanest near the new port. There, the ships and houseboats rested in clean slips made of flexible ceramic and the bones of the drowned buildings had been cut free and hauled away. With every mile farther from the port, the debris grew less picturesque, the charm of the reclaimed city giving way to the debris of its authentic past. Little beaches formed over asphalt, gray sand swirling around old blocky concrete pillars standing in the waves green with algae and white with bird shit. The stink of rot came from the soupy water and the corpses of jellyfish melting where the tide had left them.

Timmy's boat was small. White paint flaked off the metal where it hadn't been scraped well enough before being repainted. Lydia sat in the bow, her legs folded under her, her chin high and proud. The motor was an under-the-waterline pulse drive, quiet as a hum. The water in their wake was louder. The sun was near to setting, the city casting its shadow on the waves. A handful of other boats were on the water, manned by children for the most part. The citizens of basic with nothing better to do with their time than spend the twilight on the water, then go home.

Timmy ran them along the coast for a time, and then turned east, out toward the vast ocean. The moon had set, but the lights of the city were bright enough to travel by. The islands had once been part of the city itself, and now were ruins. Timmy aimed for one of the smaller, a stretch not more than two city blocks long by three wide humped up out of the water. A few ancient walls still stood. The boat ran up onto the hard shore, and Timmy jumped out, soaking his pants to the thighs, to pull it the rest of the way up. The metal screeched against the rotting concrete sidewalk.

The ruin he led her to was little more than a camp site. A bright yellow emergency-preparedness sleeping bag lay unrolled on a foam mattress. An LED lamp squatted beside it with a cord snaking up the grimy wall to a solar collector in the window. A small chemical camping stove stood on a driftwood board placed over two cinderblocks, a little unpowered refrigerator beside it to store food. Two more rooms stood empty through the doorway. If the house had ever had a kitchen or a bathroom, it was lost in the tumble of rubble beyond that. Outside, the city glowed, the violence and bustle made calm and beautiful by even such a small distance. The wail of the sirens and angry blat of the security alerts became a kind of music there, transformed by the mystical act of passing above waves.

Timmy pulled off his water-soaked pants and dug a fresh pair out from under the sleeping bag.

"This is where you go?" Lydia said, putting her hand on the time-pocked window glass. "When you aren't with me, you come to this?"

"Nobody bugs you here," Timmy said. "Or, you know. Not twice."

She nodded, as much to herself as for his benefit. Timmy looked around the room and rubbed his hand across his high forehead.

"It's not as nice as your place," he said. "But it's safe. Temporary."

"Yes," she said. "Temporary."

"Even if Liev does tell 'em about you, it's not like it's over. You can get a new name. New paper."

Lydia turned her gaze back from the city, her right hand going to her left arm as if she were protecting herself. Her gaze darted to the empty doorway, and then back. "Where's Erich?"

"Yeah, the meet didn't happen," Timmy said, leaning against the wall. She never ceased to be amazed by his physicality. The innocence and vulnerability that his body managed to project while still being an instrument of violence.

"Tell me," she said, and he did. All of it, slowly and carefully, as if worried he might leave something out that she wanted to know. That she found interesting. The low rumble of a launch shuddered like an endless peal of thunder, and the exhaust plume rose into the night sky as he spoke. It had not yet broken into orbit when he stopped.

"And where is he now?" she asked.

"There's a coffee bar. The one at Franklin and St. Paul? On top of the old high-rises there. I got him there when it was done. They've got a deck there you can rent by the minute, and since his got taken, I figured he'd like that. Gotta say, he was pretty freaked out. That DNA thing? I don't see how that's gonna end well. If he's right about how Burton's gonna react..."

Lydia shook her head once, a tiny gesture, almost invisible by the light of the single LED lamp. "I thought you were his body-guard. You were assigned to protect him."

"I did," Timmy said. "But then the job was done. Burton didn't tell me I was supposed to go to the bathroom with him for the rest of his life, right? Job was done, so the job was done."

"I thought you were his friend."

"I am," Timmy said. "But, y'know. *You.*"

"Don't worry about me. Whatever comes to me, I have earned it a thousand times over. Don't disagree with me! Don't interrupt. Burton asked you to protect Erich because Erich is precious to him. The particular job he assigned you may be over, but worse has come to the city, and Erich is still precious."

"And I get that," Timmy said. "Only when they got Liev—"

"I have lived through the churn before, darling boy. I know how this goes." She turned to the window, gesturing at the golden lights of the city. "Liev was only one. There will be others. Perhaps many, perhaps few, but Burton will lose some part of his structure to the security forces or to death. And the ones who remain afterward will become more important to him. He is a man who values survivors. Who values loyalty. What will he think, dear, when he hears that you left Erich to come spirit me away?"

"Job was done," Timmy said, a little petulantly she thought.

"Not good enough," she said. "Not anymore. You aren't the boy Erich drinks with anymore. You aren't even your mother's son now. Those versions of you are gone, and they will never come back. You are the man who took a job from Burton."

Timmy was silent. Far above them, the transport's exhaust plume went dark. Lydia stepped close to him and put her hands on his shoulders. He wouldn't meet her eyes. She thought that was a good sign. That it meant she was getting through to him.

"The world changes you and you can't stop it from doing so. You have to let go of being someone who doesn't matter now. Because if you live through this time—just live through it and nothing more—you will be more important to Burton. You can't avoid it. You can only choose what your importance is. Will you be someone he can rely upon, or someone he can't?"

Timmy took a deep breath in through his nose and sighed it out. His eyes were flat and hard. "I think I maybe fucked up again."

"Only maybe," Lydia said. "There still may be time to repair the error, yes? Go find your friend. You can bring him here."

Timmy's head jerked up. Lydia rubbed his shoulders gently, beginning at the base of his neck and stroking out to the bulges of muscle where his arms began, then back again. It was a gesture she had made with him since he was a child, a physical idiom in their own private language. Her heart ached at the sacrifice she was making. *The world changes you*, she thought. Hadn't she just said that?

"Bring him here? Y'sure about that?"

"It's all right," she said. "It's temporary."

"Okay then," he said. She felt a tug of regret that he had given in so quickly, but it passed quickly. "I'll leave you the good boat."

"The good boat?" she said to his retreating back.

"The one we came in."

The door closed. The gray that passed for darkness swallowed him up, and five minutes later she heard what might have been a skiff splashing in among the waves. Or it might only have been her imagination. She pulled herself into the warm, stinking, plastic embrace of the sleeping bag and stared at the ceiling and waited to see whether he returned.

All through Baltimore, the struggle between law and opportunity continued, but most of the citizens allied themselves with neither side. The unlicensed coffee shop filled with customers looking for a cheap way to make their dinners on basic seem more palatable, and then with younger people who either didn't have the currency or else the inclination to take amphetamines before descending to the one-night rai clubs on barricaded streets. A few parents came home from actual jobs, proud to spend real money for a stale muffin and give their credits to the gray-market daycares run out of neighborhood living rooms. Very few people stood wholly for the law or wholly against it, and so for them the catastrophe of the churn was an annoyance to be avoided or endured or else a titillation on the newsfeeds. That it was a question of life and death for other people spoke in its favor as entertainment.

Erich, sitting at the rented deck with a newsfeed spooling past, felt the distance between himself and the others who shared his space more keenly than they did. His sense of dread, of a chapter of his own life ending, was unnoticed by the heavyset woman who brewed the coffee and the thin man at the edge of the rooftop who spent his hours sending messages about tangled romantic involvements. To the other habitués of the coffee shop, Erich was just the crippled man who was hogging the deck. An annoyance and an amusement, and no one would particularly notice or care if he vanished from the world.

Timmy arrived just after midnight, his broad, amiable smile softening the distance in his eyes. To anyone who didn't look at him closely, he seemed unthreatening, and no one looked at him closely. He pulled a welded steel chair up to the bolted-down deck and sat at Erich's side. The newsfeed was set to local. A pale-skinned woman with the Outer Planets Association split circle tattooed on her sternum and Loca Griega teardrops on her cheeks had blood pouring from her nose and left eye while she struggled against two Star Helix enforcers in gear so thick they barely seemed human. Erich smiled, trying to hide the relief he felt at Timmy's return.

"Loca," Erich said, nodding at the feed. "They're having a bad night too."

"Lot of that going around," Timmy said.

"Yeah, right? You...heard from Burton?"

"No. Didn't try to find him yet either," Timmy said with a shrug. "You want to hang out here some more, or you about ready to go?"

"I don't know where to go," Erich said, a high violin whine coming in at the back of his voice.

"I got that covered," Timmy said.

"You got a bolt-hole? Jesus, that's where you've been all this time, isn't it? Getting someplace safe to hide?"

"Kind of. But, you know, you ready?"

"I need to stop someplace. Get a deck."

Timmy frowned and nodded at the table before them. *There's one right there* was in his eyes. Erich pointed at the bolts anchoring the machine to the wooden tabletop. Timmy's expression went empty and he stood up.

"Hey," Erich said. "What're you...Timmy? What are you—"

The thick woman who brewed the coffee looked up at the broad-shouldered young man. The coffee bar had been hers for three years, and she'd seen enough of the regulars to recognize trouble.

"Hey," the large man—boy, really—said, his voice making the word half apology. "So look. I don't mean to be a dick or anything, but I kind of need that deck."

"You can use it here, you buy some coffee. Or rates are printed on the side," the woman said, crossing her arms.

The big kid nodded, his brow knotting. He took a scuffed and stained black-market credit chip and pressed it into her palm.

"Shit, Jones," she said, blinking at the credit balance on the tiny LED display. "How much coffee you want?"

The kid had already turned back to the table where the cripple with the baby arm had been sitting all day. He hit the table with his fist hard enough that everyone on the rooftop turned to look at him. After the third hit, the wood of the tabletop started to splinter. There was blood on the big boy's knuckles, and the cripple was shifting back and forth anxiously as the table fell to sticks and splinters. The boy pulled her little deck free with a creaking sound. The bolts still hung from it, the wood torn out from around them. Blood dripped from his hands as he tucked the machine under his arm and nodded to the cripple.

"Anything else you need?" Timmy asked.

Erich had to fight not to smile. "No, I think I'm good now."

"All right then. We should go." Timmy turned to the woman and lifted his swelling hand to her in a wave. "Thanks."

She didn't say anything, but pushed the credit stick into her apron and waddled back to get a broom. They were gone before she returned, walking down the stairway to the street.

"That was incredible," Erich said. "The way you did that? I mean, damn it. Everyone in there was cold as stone, and you were just madness and power, man. Did you see that? Did you see how gassed they were at you?"

"You said you needed the deck," Timmy said.

"Come on! That was critical. You can brag about it some."

"Tables don't fight back," Timmy said. "Come on. I got a boat."

Erich's relief left him chatty, but he didn't talk about the fear he'd felt when Timmy had left him. Instead, he filled the trip with everything he'd seen on the feeds, and he told it all like he was telling ghost stories. The security forces were watching the ports, the trains, the transports up to the orbitals and Luna. Eighteen dead today, maybe three times that many in custody. It was news all over the world, and farther. There had even been a lady from Mars who'd come on for a while talking about the history of Earth-based police states. Wasn't that cool? All the way to Mars, they were talking about what was going on right then in Baltimore. They were everywhere.

Timmy listened, adding in a few words here and there, but mostly he walked until they reached the water, and then he rowed. The ceramic oars dipped into the dark water and lifted out again. Erich drummed his fingertips against the stolen deck, anxious to reconnect it to the network, to see what was happening and what had changed in the time since they'd left the coffee bar. That being connected would somehow protect him was an illusion, and Erich half knew that. But only half.

At the little island, Timmy pulled the boat onto shore and marched into the ruins where a light was burning. An old woman was sitting beside a chemical stove, stirring a small tin pot. The smell of brewing tea competed with the brine and the reek of decaying jellyfish. She looked up. Her face was like a mask, the makeup applied so perfectly it shoved her back into the uncanny valley.

"I found your tea," she said. "I hope you don't mind."

"Nope," Timmy said, not breaking stride. "Come on, Erich. I'll get you set up."

They walked through a doorway without a door and into a small room. It was even less comfortable than the one with the old lady. There was nothing on the floor but the glue marks where there had once been carpeting. Mold grew up along one wall, black and branching like tree limbs. Timmy put the deck on the ground. His knuckles were black with blood and forming scab.

"You be able to get a signal here?" Timmy asked.

"Should be. May need to find a way to power up in the morning."

"Yeah, well. We'll come up with something. So this is your room, okay? Yours. That one's hers," Timmy said, pointing a thumb at the lighted doorway. "Hers. She asks you in, you can go in, but she asks you to leave, you do it, right?"

"Of course. Sure. Christ, Timmy. Your place, your rules, right?" Erich smiled, hoping to coax one in response. "We've always respected each other, right? Only, seriously, who is she? Is that your mom?"

It was like Timmy hadn't heard him. "I'm gonna get some sleep, but come morning, I can go back in, get some food. And I'll check in with the man."

Erich felt his belly go cold. "You're going to talk to Burton?"

"Sure, if I can find him," Timmy said. "He's got the plan, right?"

"Right," Erich said. "Of course."

He opened the deck, ran it through its startup options, and connected to the network. The signal strength wasn't great, but it wasn't awful. He'd been in half a dozen basement hack shacks with worse. He opened the newsfeed, still set to passive. The glow from the screen was the only light. Erich was cold, but he didn't complain. Timmy stood, stretched, considered the skinned knuckles of his hand with what could have been a distant sort of ruefulness, and turned to go back to the old woman and the light.

"Hey, we're friends, right?" Erich said.

Timmy turned back. "Sure."

"We've always watched out for each other, you and me."

Timmy shrugged. "Not *always*, but when we could, sure."

"Don't tell him where I am, okay?"

Security crackdowns, like plagues, had a natural progression. A peak, and then decline. As terrible as they might be at their height, they did not last forever. Burton knew this, as did all of his lieutenants, and he made his plans accordingly. Burton moved through his safe houses, playing shell games with the security forces. The first night, while Erich and Lydia slept in their respective rooms in the little island ruin and Timmy tried to find someone in the organization to report to, Burton slept in a loft above a warehouse with a woman named Edie. In the morning, he moved to the storage in the back of a medical clinic, locking the door and hijacking an untraceable connection so that he could speak to his people with relative safety. Little Cole had closed down her houses, locked away her reports, buried a month's supply of drugs, and taken a bus to Vermont to stay with her mother until things died down. Oestra was still in the city, moving from place to place in much the same fashion that Burton was. Ragman and Cyrano were missing, but it was early enough that Burton wasn't concerned yet. At least they weren't in the newsfeeds. Liev and Simonson were.

And there was other evidence, indirect but convincing, of where the little war stood. Even in the first morning after the catastrophe began, security teams were calling on Liev's underlings, sweeping them up for questioning. Some, they held. Others, they released. Burton had no way of knowing which of those who had been set free had cut deals with security and which had been lucky enough to slip through the net. It hardly mattered. That branch of the business had been compromised, and so it would die. The demand for illicit drugs, cheap goods, off-schedule medical procedures, and anonymous sex could be neither arrested nor sated, and so the thing that mattered most for Burton's little empire was safe. Would always be safe. The question of how to feed the city's subterranean hungers was only a tactical one, and Burton could be flexible.

The temptation, of course, was to fight back, and in the following days, some did. Five soldiers from the Loca Griega left a bomb outside a Star Helix substation. It exploded, injuring two of the security contractors and damaging the building, and all five bombers were identified and taken into custody. Tamara Sluydan, who really should have known better, organized street-level resistance, starting a two-day riot that ended with half of her people hospitalized or in custody, eighteen local businesses looted or set afire, and the goodwill of her client base permanently damaged. Burton understood. He wasn't a man without passions. If someone hurt him, of course he wanted to hurt them back. Phrases like "even the score" or "blood for blood" came to mind, and each time they did, he made the practice of tearing them apart to himself. "Even the score" was the metaphor of a game, and this wasn't a game. "Blood for blood" made it sound as if through more violence, past wrongs could be balanced, and they couldn't. The hardest lesson Burton had ever learned was to endure the blows, accept the damage, and let someone else strike back. Soon, very soon, the crackdown would shift from its great, overwhelming force to individual struggles. It was in his interests to see that those struggles were with the Loca Griega and Tamara Sluydan, not with him. As soon as the enemy was clearly defined in the collective mind of Star Helix and Burton's name and organization were not central to their plans, the storm would move on and he could begin to reopen the folded fronds of his business.

In the meantime, he moved from one place to the next. He told people he would go one place, and then arrived at another. He considered all his habits with the uncompromising eye of a predator, and killed the ones with flaws. Anything that connected him with the patterns of the past was a vulnerability, and wherever possible, he chose to be invulnerable. It wasn't the first time he'd been through this. He was good at it.

And so when it took Timmy the better part of a week to find him, Burton's annoyance was balanced against a certain self-centered pride.

The office was raw brick and mortar, newsfeeds playing on five different screens. A sliding wooden door stood half open, the futon where Burton had slept the night before half visible through it. Oestra, whose safe house it was, sat by the window looking down at the street. The automatic shotgun across his legs seemed unremarkable. Timmy had been searched by three guards on the street, and he'd been clean. Even if he'd swallowed a tracking device they would have found it, and the big slab of human meat would have been bleeding out in a gutter instead of smiling amiably and gawking at the exposed ductwork.

"Timmy, right?" Burton said, pretending uncertainty. Let the boy feel lucky he'd remembered that much.

"Yeah, chief. That's me." The openness and amiability was annoying. Burton glanced toward Oestra, but the lieutenant was squinting at the brightness of the day. Burton scratched his leg idly, his fingernails hissing against the fabric of his pants.

"You got something for me?"

Timmy's face fell a little. "Just news. I mean, I didn't have any stuff. Nothing to deliver or anything."

"All right, then," Burton said. "What's the news, Tiny?"

Timmy grinned at the irony of the nickname, then sobered and began his report. Burton leaned forward, drinking in all the words as fast as they spilled from Timmy's lips. When Oestra risked a glance back, it was like watching a bird singing away while a cat stood in the too-still pose of a carnivore waiting to pounce. The details came out in no particular order: Erich was in a safe place, Timmy had been taking food to him, the fake profile deal had been interrupted by the security crackdown, Erich's original deck was gone but he had a replacement, the police probably had his DNA profile now. Oestra sighed to himself and looked back out the window. On the street, a half dozen young men who hadn't just condemned their friends to death slouched down the street together.

"He's sure about that?" Burton asked.

"Nah," Timmy said. "We didn't hang around and watch them find the deck or anything. I figured it'd be better, you know. To get out."

"I see."

"Erich wanted to go get it. Grab the hardware, I mean."

"That would have been a mistake," Burton said. "If security had the deck and the man, that...well, that'd be bad."

"Was what I thought too," Timmy said.

Burton sat back, the leather of the chair creaking. Back past the bedroom, Sylvia started running the shower. Sylvia or Sarah. Something like that. One of Oestra's, provided with the bed. "Where's the safe house?"

"I'm not supposed to say," Timmy said.

"Not even to me?"

The boy had the good sense to look uncomfortable. "Yeah, not to anyone. You know how it is."

"Is there anyone there with him?"

"Yeah, I got a friend there."

"A guard?"

"Not really, no. Just a friend."

Burton nodded, thinking hard. "But he's secure?"

"He's on the water. Anyone starts coming in, he's got a boat and about a dozen decent places to hide. I mean, nowhere's a hundred percent."

"And you're protecting him."

"That's the job," Timmy said, with a shrug and a smile. Burton couldn't quite put his finger on what it was about the boy that was so interesting. Over the years, he'd had hundreds just like him who came through, worked, disappeared, died, were fed to security or found God and a ticket out of town. Burton had a nose for talent, though, and there was something about this one that kept bringing him back to the sense of the boy's potential. Perhaps it was the casual logic he'd used when he'd killed Austin. Maybe it was the deadness in his eyes.

Burton got up, raising a finger. Timmy sat deep in his chair like a trained dog receiving a command. Sylvia—whoever—was singing in the bathroom. The splash of water against porcelain covered the sound of Burton opening the gun safe, pulling out the pistol and its magazine. When he stepped back into the main room, Timmy hadn't so much as crossed his legs. Burton held the gun out.

"You know what this is?" he asked.

"It's a ten-millimeter semi-auto," Timmy said. He put his hand out halfway to it, and then looked up at Burton, his eyes asking permission. Burton nodded and smiled. Timmy took the gun.

"You know guns?"

Timmy shrugged. "They're around. It feels...sticky."

"It's got a resin of digestive enzymes," Burton said. "Won't hurt your skin much, but it won't hold prints and it breaks down any trace evidence. No DNA."

"That's cool," Timmy said, and started to hand it back. Burton tossed the magazine onto the boy's lap.

"Those are plastic-tipped. Organ shredders, but they don't work on armor," Burton said. "Still, step up from that homemade shotgun you've used, right?"

"Right."

"You know how those things all go together?"

Timmy weighed the pistol in one hand, the magazine in the other. He slid them together, checked the chamber, flicked the safety on and off. It wasn't the practiced action of a professional, but talented amateur was good enough for his purposes. Timmy looked up, his smile blank and empty. "New job?" he asked.

"New job," Burton said. "I know you and Erich grew up together. Is this going to be a problem for you?"

"Nope," Timmy said, slipping the gun into his pocket. There hadn't even been a pause.

"You're sure?"

"Sure, I'm sure. I get it. They've got him in the system now. If they get him too, there's all kinds of things he compromises. If they can't get him, nothing gets compromised, and I'm the only guy who can get close to him without him seeing it coming."

"Yes."

"So I kill him for you," Timmy said. He could have been saying, *So I'll pick up dinner on my way.* There was no bravado in it. Burton sat, tilted his head. The friendly smile and the empty eyes met him.

"All right, I'm curious," Burton said. "Did you game this? This was your plan?"

"Shit no, chief," Timmy said. "This here's just happy coincidence."

Either it was truth or the best deadpan Burton had seen in a long time. The shower water turned off. On the newsfeeds, a woman in a Star Helix uniform was saying something, a dour expression on her face. Burton wanted to turn up the volume, see if the press statement was something useful to him like reading fortunes in coffee grounds. He restrained himself.

"I will need proof," Burton said. "Evidence, yeah?"

"So what, you want his heart?"

"Heart. Brain. Windpipe. Anything he can't live without."

"Not a problem," Timmy said. Then a moment later, "Is there anything else, or should I go?"

"You watched out for this kid your whole life," Burton said. "He vouched for you. Got you in with me. And you're really going to put a slug in his brain just like that?"

"Sure. You're the man with the plan."

When the boy left, Burton came to stand beside Oestra, watching him walk away down the sunlit street. The thinning reddish-brown hair and wide shoulders made him look like some kind of manual laborer twice his age. His hands were shoved deep in his pockets. He could have been anybody.

"Think he'll do it?" Burton asked.

Oestra didn't answer for a long moment. "Might."

"He does this for me, he'll do anything," Burton said, clapping Oestra's shoulder. "Potential for a man like that."

"If he doesn't?"

"There are a lot of ways to dispose of someone disposable," Burton said.

Burton walked back to the chair, shifted the newsfeed buffer back to the start of the Star Helix woman's press announcement. The woman started talking, and Burton listened.

Timmy's ruin had long since become a misery for Lydia, and misery had become a kind of pleasure. Their days had taken a kind of rhythm. Erich woke first in the morning, his uneven footsteps playing a tentative counterpoint to the rough sound of the waves. Lydia lay in the warmth of her cocoon, the slick fabric wrapped around her until only her mouth and nose were in the free air. When she could no longer pretend sleep, she emerged and made tea on the little stove, and when she was done, Erich transferred the solar charger to his deck and squatted over it, scanning the newsfeeds with a ferocity and single-mindedness that made her think of a poet chasing the perfect rhyme. If Timmy was there, she would walk with him to the boats or survey the newest supplies he had smuggled to their private island: fresh clothes, carryout tandoori, charged batteries for the deck and the lamp. More often, he was not there, and she haunted the shore like a sea widow. The city glowered out at her from across the water, like a great angry gray face, condemning her for her sins.

Is this the time? she would wonder. *Has he left now, never to return? Or will there be one more? Another time to see his face, to hear his voice, to have the conversations that we can only ever have with each other?*

She knew that the churn was playing itself out there, across the narrow waves. Security had likely come to her rooms on Liev's word and found them already abandoned. The men and women she'd worked with these last years were part of the past now. Part of a life she'd left behind, though nothing else had begun. Only this island exile and its waiting.

At night, Erich would eat with her. Their conversations were awkward. She knew that she was uncanny to him, that he thought of Timmy as his own friend, a character from his own past. Her appearance and the reticence she and Timmy had to making her explicable were as odd to Erich as if lobsters had crawled up out of the sea and started speaking Spanish. And yet if they did, what could anyone do but answer them, and so Erich and Lydia reached the odd peace of roommates, intimate in all things and nothing.

That night, Timmy crossed the waves unnoticed by her or Erich. Lydia was looking east over the ruined island to the greater sea beyond. Erich curled in the room that common habit designated as his, snoring slightly as the deck ran down its charge to nothing beside him. Timmy arrived quietly and alone, announced only by his footsteps and the smell of fresh ginger.

When he emerged from the darkness, two thin plastic sacks hung from his left fist. Lydia shifted, not rising, but coming up to rest on her knees and ankles in a posture she imagined to be like a geisha, though she'd never met a real geisha. Timmy put the sacks down beside her, his eyes on the shadows past the doorway. Far away across the water, gulls complained.

"Two?" she said.

"Hmm?" Timmy followed her gaze to the sacks. A glimmer of something that might have been chagrin passed through his eyes fast as a blink. "Oh. The dinners. Hey, is Erich back there?"

"He is," Lydia said. "I think he's asleep."

"Yeah," Timmy said, straightening. He put a hand into his pocket. "Hang on a minute." He walked back toward the black doorway as if he were going to check on the other boy, perhaps wake him for his supper.

"Wait," Lydia said as Timmy reached the doorway.

He looked back at her, twisting at the shoulders, his body and feet still committed.

"Come sit with me."

"Yeah, I just gotta—"

"First," she said. "Come sit with me first."

Timmy hesitated, fluttering like a feather caught between contradictory breezes. Then his shoulders sank a centimeter and his hips turned toward her. He pulled his hand from his pocket. Lydia opened the sacks, unpacked the food, laid the disposable forks beside the plates. Every movement had the precision and beauty of ritual. Timmy sat facing her, his legs crossed. The bulge of the gun stood out from his thigh like a fist. Lydia bowed her head, as if in prayer. Timmy took up his fork and stabbed at the ginger beef. Lydia did the same.

"So you're going to kill him?" Lydia asked, her voice light.

"Yeah," Timmy said. "I mean, I ain't happy about it, but it's what needs to get done."

"Needs," Lydia said, her intonation in the perfect balance point between statement and question.

Timmy ate another bite. "I'm the guy that took a job from Burton. Used to be the job was one thing. Now it's something else. It's not like I get to tell him what to do, right?"

"Because he's Burton."

"And I'm not. You were the one who said I'd be important to him if I made it through this shitstorm. This is part of that."

"I said Burton would *see* you as important," Lydia said. "There is more to you than what he sees. There's more to you than what anybody sees."

"Well," Timmy said. "You."

Even I do not know your depths floated at the back of her throat like a cough. She didn't have it in her to say the words. If it was true, so what? When had truth ever been her friend? Instead she took another bite of the beef. He did the same. She imagined that he was giving her the time to gather herself. It might even have been true. The perfectly straight lightning bolt of a railgun transport lit the black sky, its thunder rolling after it like a wave. The ginger and pepper burned her lips, her throat, her tongue, and she took another bite, welcoming the pain. It was always pleasant when pain was on the outside.

"And who will you be to yourself?" she said at last. "Doesn't what you think matter more than what he does?"

Timmy's brow furrowed. "Yeah, I don't know what you just said."

"Who are you going to be to yourself, if you do this?" She put down her fork, leaned across the space between them. She lifted his shirt as she had countless times before, and the erotic charge of it was still there. Never absent. She pressed her palm against his breast, her skin against his skin in the place above his heart. "Who will you be in there?"

Timmy's face went perfectly still in the unnerving way it sometimes did. His eyes were flat as a shark's, his mouth like a plaster cast mold of himself. Only his voice was the same, bright and amiable.

"You know there ain't no one in there," he said.

She let her fingertips stray to the side, brushing through the coarse hair she knew so well. She felt the hardness of his nipple against her thumb. "Then who will you put there? Burton?"

"He's the guy with the power," Timmy said.

"Not the power to kill Erich," she said. "Not the power to make *you* kill him. That is you and only you. People like us? We aren't righteous. But we can pretend to be, if we want, and that's almost the same as if it were true."

"I get the feeling you're asking me for something. I don't know what it is."

"I am not a good person," she said.

"Hey. Don't—"

"If I were, though? If I *were* that woman? What would I want you to do?"

Timmy took another mouthful of beef, his jaw working slowly. In his concentration, she saw the echoes of all the versions of himself that she had known from baby to toddler to young man to this, now before her. She folded her hands on her lap.

"That's a long way to say I shouldn't do it," he said.

"Is that what I said?" she asked.

Erich's yawn came from the doorway. Lydia felt the blood rush from her face, tasted the penny-bright flush of fear as if she had been caught doing something illicit. Erich came into the light, scratching his sleep-tousled hair with his good hand. "Hey," he said. "Did I hear you get back, big guy? What's the word?"

Timmy was quiet, his gaze fixed on Lydia, his expression empty as a mask.

"Guys?" Erich said, limping forward. "What's the matter? Is something wrong?"

Timmy's sigh was so low that Lydia barely heard it. The boy she had loved for so long, and in so many ways, put on his cheerful smile and looked away from her. She felt tears pricking her eyes.

"Yeah, bad news," Timmy said. "Burton's not taking the whole thing very well. He's put out paper on you."

Erich sat down, the blood draining from his face. He grabbed his bad arm reflexively, unaware that he was doing it, and looked from Timmy to the woman and back. His heart thudded like a drum in his ears. Timmy licked his fork clean and put it down. The woman was still as stone. Erich felt his world fall out from underneath him, and that he had known it would was less of a comfort than he'd expected. Anyone looking in at the little circle of light from the shadows would have seen only three faces in the black, like a family portrait of refugees. Erich broke the silence.

"Are you *sure*?"

"Yeah, pretty sure," Timmy said. "Seeing as how I got the contract."

Erich stopped breathing. Timmy stared at him, expressionless for several infinitely long seconds.

"We've gotta find a way to get you out," his big friend finally said, and Erich started breathing again.

"There's no way out," he said. "Burton'll track me down anywhere."

"What about that deck?" Timmy asked. "It ain't your old one, but can you still sample with it?"

"What do you mean?" Erich said.

"You've got the escape plan for Burton. The clean one. Why don't you put your sequence on it? Use it to get out of here?"

"I can, sure, but they've already got my *other* deck, remember? I put my DNA on a record, the flag goes up, and I'm in for questioning."

"Yeah," Timmy said. "Well maybe you could…Shit. I don't know. Maybe you could think of something."

"I knew," Erich said. "The second I saw those bastards coming down the street, I knew it was over for me. I'm dead. It's just a matter of time is all."

"That's always true," Lydia said, her mind taken with other matters. "For everyone."

"Might as well be you," Erich said to Timmy, giving his friend permission. Terror and love warring in his chest.

"Nope," Timmy said, cocking his head to one side as if he'd only just made the decision in that moment.

"Erich," Lydia started.

"As long as I'm alive," Erich said, ignoring her, "Burton's not safe. He's not going to let me slide."

Timmy frowned, then grunted in surprise. Maybe pleasure.

"What?" Erich said.

"Just that it works the other way too," Timmy said, levering himself up to his feet. "Anyway, I gotta go back in."

"Back in?" Erich said.

Timmy brushed his hands across his wide thighs. "The city. I gotta go back to the city. Burton's expecting me."

"You're not going to tell him where I am, are you?" Erich asked. Timmy started laughing and Lydia took it up. Erich looked from one to the other, confused.

"Nah, I'm not going to tell him where you are. I got something of his I need to give back is all. Nothing you have to worry about."

"Easy for you to say," Erich said, ashamed of the whine in his voice.

"I'll leave you the good boat," Timmy said, turning toward the darkness.

"Will you be back?" Lydia said. She hadn't meant to, because she knew in her heart, in her bones, and deeper than that what the answer was. Timmy smiled at her for the last time. *I take it back*, she thought. *Kill him. Kill the boy. Kill everyone else in the world. Shoot babies in the head and dance on their bodies. Any atrocity, any evil, is justified if it keeps you from leaving me.*

"Eh," Timmy said. "You never know."

The darkness folded around him as he walked away. Her hands were made of lead and tungsten. Her belly felt hurt and empty as a miscarriage. And underneath the hurt and the horror, the betrayal and the pleasure she took in her distress, something else stirred and lifted its head. It took her time to recognize it as pride, and even then she couldn't have said who or what she was proud of. Only that she was.

The boat splashed once in the water, her almost-son and sometime-lover leaving the shore for the last time. Her lifetime was a fabric woven of losses, and she saw now that all of them had been practice, training her to teach her how to bear this pain like a boxer bloodying knuckles to make them strong and numb. All her life had been preparation for bearing this single, unbearable moment.

"Shit," Erich said. "Were there only two dinners? What am I going to eat?"

Lydia plucked up the fork that had been Timmy's, gripping the stem in her fist like holding his hand again, one last time. Touching what he had touched, because she would never touch him again. Here this object had opened his lips, felt the softness of his tongue, and been left behind. It held traces of him.

"What's the matter?" Erich said. "Are you all right?"

I stopped being all right before you were born, she thought. What she said was, "There's something I'd like you to do for me."

The streets of Baltimore didn't notice him pass through them this one last time. More than three million people lived and breathed, loved and lost, hoped and failed to hope that night, just as any other. A young woman hurrying home later than her father's curfew dodged around a tall man with thinning hair and pants wet to the knee at the corner of South and Lombard, muttering obscenities and curses at him that spoke more of her own dread and fear than anything the man had done. Four Star Helix security employees, out of uniform and off-shift, paused at the entrance to an Italian restaurant to watch a civilian pass. None of them could have said what it was about him that caught their attention, and it might only have been that they'd operated on high alert for so many days at once. The civilian went on, minding his own business, keeping himself to himself, and they went into the building's garlic and onion smells and forgot him. A bus driver stopped, let two old women, a thin-faced man, and a broad-shouldered amiable fellow come on board. Bus service was part of basic, and the machine followed its route automatically. No one paid, no one spoke, and the driver went back to watching the entertainment feeds as soon as the bus pulled back into traffic.

Nearer Oestra's safe house, things changed. There were more eyes, more of them alert. The catastrophe of the churn hung thick in the air, the sense that doom might come at any moment in the shape of security vans and riot gear and voices shouting to keep hands visible. Nothing like it had happened that day or the one before, but no one was taking comfort in that yet. The guards who stopped Timmy were different than the ones he'd seen earlier, but their placement on the street was the same. They stopped him, took the pistol that Burton had given him, scanned him for tracking devices, firearms, explosives, chemical agents, and when they found he was clean, they called in. Oestra's voice through their earpieces was less than a mosquito but still perfectly recognizable, a familiar buzz and whine. They waved Timmy on.

Oestra opened the door to him, automatic shotgun still in the lieutenant's hand, as if he hadn't put it down all day. Probably, he hadn't.

Timmy stepped into the main room, looking around pleasantly. The newsfeeds flickered silently on their screens: a street view from sometime earlier in the day with five security vans lined up outside a burning apartment building, a serious-faced Indian woman speaking into the camera with a dour expression, an ad with seven bouncing monkeys reaching for a box of banana-flavored cakes. The world cast its shadows on the bare brick wall and threw stories into the gray mortar. The churn, running itself to exhaustion. New stories from around the world and above it filling in the void.

"You're back," Oestra said.

"Yup."

"You do the thing?"

"It got a little complicated," Timmy said. "The man still here?"

"Wait. I'll get him."

Oestra walked to the back, one set of footsteps fading into the safe house, then a long pause made rich by the murmur of voices, then two sets of footsteps coming back. The timestamp beside the dour Indian woman read 21:42. Timmy considered the curtains. Blue-dyed cotton with cords of woven nylon. The chair Oestra had been sitting on before, leather stretched over a light metal frame. A kitchen through a wide brickwork archway. The bedroom in the back with its futon, and a bathroom somewhere behind that.

"Tiny," Burton said. "What's the news, little man?"

Burton's white shirt caught the light from the screens, dancing in a hundred colors. His slacks were dark and beautifully cut. Timmy turned to him like he was an old friend. Oestra walked past them both, taking his place by the window. Timmy glanced back at him only a few feet away, a shotgun across his thighs.

"Well," Timmy said. "Truth is, I ran into a little hiccup."

Burton crossed his arms, squared his shoulders and hips.

"Something you couldn't handle?" he asked, his voice hard with disapproval.

"I'm waiting to see," Timmy said.

"Waiting to see if you can handle it?"

"Well, yeah," Timmy said with a wide, open smile. "Actually, it's kind of funny you put it that way."

When the big man stepped back toward the window, the movement was so casual, so relaxed, that neither Oestra nor Burton recognized what was happening. Timmy's thick fingers grabbed the back of the leather chair, pulling back and down fast and hard. Oestra twisted trying to keep from falling and also bring the shotgun to bear at the same time, managing neither. He spilled to the floor, Timmy's knee coming down hard on his neck. Oestra's muffled roar was equal parts outrage and pain. Timmy reached down and ripped the man's right ear off, then punched down twice, three times, four. Burton ran for the back bedroom. There wasn't much time.

Unable to use it with Timmy on his neck, Oestra dropped the shotgun and twisted, trying to get his arms and legs under himself, trying to get the leverage to push Timmy back. Timmy reached down and hooked his finger into the gunman's left eye, bracing the head with his knee and turning his wrist until he felt the eyeball pop. Oestra's screams were wilder now, panic and pain taking over. Timmy let the pressure up, scooted to the left, and picked up the abandoned shotgun. He fired once into Oestra's head and the man stopped screaming.

Timmy trotted across the room, shotgun in one hand. Burton boiled out of the bedroom, pistols in either fist and teeth bared like a dog's. The front window shattered. Timmy ducked through the brick archway into the kitchen, shifted his grip on the shotgun, and swung it hard and low, leading with the elbow like a cricket player at the bat as Burton roared in after him. The sound of the connection was like a piece of raw steak being dropped on concrete. Burton's feet flew out from under him, but the momentum of his rush carried him stumbling into the space beyond. Timmy lowered the shotgun toward the man's head, but Burton whirled, dropping his own guns and grabbing the shotgun's barrel. The smell of burning skin was instantaneous. Timmy tried to pull back, but Burton kicked out. His right foot hit Timmy's knee like he'd kicked a fire hydrant, but Timmy still stumbled. The shotgun roared again, and the refrigerator sprouted pocks of twisted metal and plastic. Burton twisted, pulling himself in close. Too close for the shotgun's long barrel. He hammered his elbow into Timmy's ribs twice and felt something give the third time. Timmy dropped the shotgun, and then they were both down on the floor.

They grappled, caught in each other's arms, each man shifting for the position that would destroy the other in a parody of intimate love. The fingers of Burton's left hand worked their way under Timmy's chin, digging at his neck, pushing into the hard cartilage of his throat. Timmy choked, gagged, pulled back the centimeter that was all Burton needed. He pulled his right arm up into the gap, braced himself, twisted, and now Timmy's arm and head were locked. Burton gasped out a chuckle.

"You just fucked the wrong asshole," he hissed as Timmy bucked and struggled. "Your little cripple boyfriend? I'm gonna burn him down for days. I'm gonna find everyone you ever loved and kill them all slow."

Timmy grunted and pushed back, but the effort only made Burton's lock on him tighter.

"You thought you could take me, you dumbfuck piece of shit?" Burton spat into Timmy's ear. "You thought you were tougher than *me*? I owned your momma, boy. You're just second-generation *property*."

All along their paired bodies, Burton felt Timmy tense and then, with a vast exhalation, relax, melting into the hold. Burton pulled tighter, squeezing. There was a report like a pistol shot when Timmy's shoulder dislocated and the resistance stuttered. Burton's grip broke. Timmy rolled, cocked back his fist and brought it down on the bridge of Burton's nose. The pain was bright. The volume of the world faded. The fist came down again, jostling the kitchen. The light seemed strange, reducing the red of the bricks and the yellow of the stove to shades of gray. Burton tried to bring his arms up to cover his face, to shield him from the violence, but they were a very long way away, and he kept losing track of them. He had them up, but they were numb and boneless. The attacks easily brushed them aside. The fist hit his nose again, and he didn't know if it was for the third time or the fourth.

Shit, he thought. *This is just going to keep going on until that fucker decides to stop.*

The impact came again, and Burton tried to say something, to scream. The impact came again, and afterward followed a few seconds of darkness and silence and calm. Burton felt very sleepy. The impact came again. Calm. The impact came again and again and again. Each time, the violence felt more distant and the emptiness between more profound until a kind of forgetfulness came over him.

Once Timmy was sure that he was alone in the apartment, he rolled onto his back. His left arm hung from the socket, limp, useless, and disconnected. He levered himself up to his knees, breathing hard between clenched teeth. Then stood. He took the automatic shotgun in his one good hand and stepped out to the main room. On the screen, the Indian woman was still speaking, wagging a finger at the camera to make a point. The timestamp beside her read 21:44. Two minutes. Maybe a little less. Timmy walked to the front window. The guards from the street weren't at their posts. He nodded to himself and went to stand by the front door. When the knob turned, he waited. The door flew open, and he fired three times, once straight ahead, and then angling to the left and right. Someone started screaming and the door banged closed again.

Timmy went back to the kitchen. He flipped on the burners, pulled down the roll of cheap paper towels from the wall. He found a bottle of peanut oil in the cabinet and doused the towels with half of it before he put them directly on the heating element. A flurry of footsteps came from the front and he fired the shotgun again, not aiming at anything. They retreated. The oil-soaked paper caught fire, and Timmy picked up the burning roll, trotted to the bedroom, and threw the flaming mass into the bunched covers. By the time he was back in the kitchen, the flame shadows were already dancing in the archway behind him. Timmy put the half-full bottle of oil directly onto the heating element and walked to the back of the safe house. The stairway leading to the alley was narrow and white. He didn't see anyone, but he fired the shotgun twice anyway then tossed the gun back into the fire. If there had been a guard there, they'd fled. Timmy walked out into the night.

He moved slowly, but with purpose. When his path crossed with other people's he smiled and nodded. Once, when he had almost reached his destination, an old man in a black coat had stopped and stared at his bruised and bloody hand. Timmy smiled ruefully, shrugged, and didn't break stride. The old man didn't raise an alarm. Around here, a muscle-bound thug with blood on his cuffs and skinned knuckles didn't warrant anything more than a disapproving look.

The security forces had put a fresh lock on Lydia's door, but Timmy knew the back way in. He slid through the window into the bathroom he'd known so well over the last few years. It still smelled like her. They'd gone through everything. Her towels and the shower curtain were on the floor. Bottles of medications littered the sink. He dug through until he found some painkillers and dry swallowed three. In the kitchen, he wrapped his shoulder in ice, then waited motionless until the swelling was down as far as it was going to go. Putting his shoulder back in its socket was a question of lying on the bed, his grip on the mattress bottom hard and unforgiving, and then pulling back slowly, relaxing into the pain, until it slid back into place with a wet, angry pop. He stripped, washed himself with wet hand towels, and changed into a fresh set of his clothes. Ones that didn't have anybody's blood on them.

The churn, the crackdown, the catastrophe. The cycle of boom and bust. The turn of the seasons. Whatever name was applied to it, the inevitable cascade of events in the city rolled on just the same. When the fire trucks came and put out the blaze, they identified the two bodies as Feivel Oestra and an unregistered man. The unregistered was a small, compact, dark-skinned man in an expensive shirt and tailored slacks. He had no tattoos, and a wide birthmark on his right shoulder blade in the shape of a rough triangle. Both men had died by violence. If the fire had been meant to conceal that, it failed. If it was only meant to foul any trace DNA or fingerprint evidence, it did well enough. Add to that the fact that Oestra was on the Star Helix lists as someone to bring in for questioning, and the broad strokes of the story came clear.

The same night, fifteen men loyal to the Loca Griega were surrounded in a nightclub. The hostage situation that rose out of it left two people dead and ten in custody, and the attendant lawsuits against Star Helix and the owners of the nightclub were the top of the local and regional newsfeeds. Oestra's death was little more than a footnote, something mentioned and then moved on from. Other things—smaller things—fell even below that level of obscurity. A woman selling illicit painkillers out of her apartment beside the arcology had a screaming fight with one of her clients, called security, and was taken away for questioning. A sweep of the ruins on the bay islands found a small squatters' camp with an LED lamp, an emergency prep sleeping bag, and an exhausted chemical stove, but anyone who had been living there was gone. An art dealer contacted with a request for assistance with an investigation killed himself rather than come in. None of those events raised any notice at all.

Soon, the paroxysm of violence, legal and otherwise, would thin back down to the normal background radiation of human vice. Very serious people would argue about whether the program had worked. Some would argue that crime had gone down, others that it had actually risen. Star Helix would take its payment from the government and settle out of court most of the complaints made against it. One of the remaining lieutenants would rise to the top, or the whole criminal apparatus would turn over to a new organization, a new generation. Within a year, there would be a new working normal that would run more or less gracefully until the next time. People of little importance would survive and make names for themselves. The mighty would fall, the meek would rise up in their places and become mighty. But all that would come later.

In the pearly light that came before the dawn, one other thing happened that went unnoticed, meaningless to anyone but those involved.

It was on a street down near the water's edge. The eastern sky was brightening with the coming dawn, the western sky still boasted a scattering of stars. Traffic on the street was thick, but not yet the immobile crush that would come with the light. Sea and rot perfumed the air, but the cool made the scent seem almost pleasant. A tea-and-coffee stand was opening, sporting the blue-and-pink logo of a popular chain and a tray of baked goods just the same as a million other trays on five continents and two worlds. Old men and women on basic huffed down the side-walk, getting in the day's exercise before the sun came up. Young men and women staggered home from long nights at the street clubs and rairai joints, exhausted from hours of dancing, drinking, sex, and frustrated hope. Soon, the streets and tube stations would thicken with the traffic of those who had jobs to go to, and then be released to the masses for whom basic was a way of life.

A boy on the verge of manhood stood on a corner near the tea-and-coffee stand. He was taller than average, and muscular. His close-cropped reddish-brown hair was receding, though he was young. His expression was blank, and he held himself in a tight, guarded way that could have been grief or the protecting of some physical injury. His right hand was swollen, the knuckles skinned. If it hadn't been for that last detail, the security team might have passed him by. Three women and two men, all in the ballistic armor and helmets of Star Helix.

"Morning," the team lead said, and half a beat later the tall man smiled and nodded. He turned to walk away, but the other personnel shifted to block his path.

The man tensed, then made the visible decision to relax. His smile was rueful. "Sorry. I was just heading out."

"I respect that, sir. We appreciate you taking a moment," the team lead said, placing a hand on the butt of his pistol. "Really did a number on your hand."

"Yeah. I box."

"Can be a good workout. I'm going to need to see your ID."

"Don't got it on me. Sorry."

"We'll need to check you against the database, then. That isn't a problem, is it?"

"Think I got the right to refuse that, don't I?"

"You do," the team lead said, letting a hint of hardness slip into his voice beneath the casual words. "But then we'd need to take you to the substation and do the full biometric scan to exclude you from the persons of interest list, and there are a whole lot of very unpleasant people who are in that queue. You don't want to hang out with them. Not if you have someplace you need to be."

The big man seemed to consider this. He glanced back over his shoulder.

"Looking for someone?" the team lead asked.

"Was more thinking there might be some folks looking for me."

"So. How do you want to play this?"

The man shrugged and held out his hand. The team's data analyst stepped forward and tapped the collector against the thick wrist. The readout stuttered red, then went to solid green. The seconds ticked away.

"If there's something you want to tell me," the team lead said, "this would be the time."

"Nah," the big man said. "I think I'm good."

"Yeah?"

"You know," he said, "good enough."

The team lead's hand terminal chimed. He pulled it out with his left hand, his right still on the butt of his gun. The readout had the red border of a flagged profile. The big man's body went very still while they read. It was a long moment before the team lead spoke.

"Amos Burton."

"Yeah?" the big man said. It could have meant, *Yes, I killed him*, or *What about him?* All the team lead heard was the affirmation.

"I've got a travel flag on you here. You're cutting it pretty close."

Amos Burton's eyebrows rose and the corners of his mouth turned down. "I am?"

"You're shipping out to Luna on the noon launch from Bogotá station, Mr. Burton. These apprenticeship programs are tough to get into, and last I heard, they take it mighty poorly if you miss your berth. Might wind up waiting another decade to get back on the list."

"Huh," the big man said.

"Look, there's a high-speed line about nine blocks north of here. We can take you there if you want."

"Erich, you sonofabitch," the big man said. Instead of looking north, he turned to the east, toward the sea and rising sun. "I'm not Mr. Burton."

"Sorry?"

"I'm not Mr. Burton," the man said again. "You can call me Amos."

"Whatever you want. But I think you'd better haul ass out of town if you don't want to get in some serious shit, Amos."

"You ain't the only one that thinks that. But I'm good. I know where the high-speed lines are. I won't miss my ride."

"All right then," the team lead said with a crisp nod. "Have a better one."

The security team moved on, flowing around the big man like river water around a stone. Amos watched them go, then went to the tea-and-coffee stand, bought a cup of black coffee and a corn muffin. He stood on the corner for a long minute, eating and drinking and breathing the air of the only city he'd ever known. When he was done, he dropped the cup and the muffin wrapper into the recycling bin and turned north toward the high-speed line and Bogotá station and Luna. And, who knew, maybe the vastness beyond the moon. The sweep of planets and moons and asteroids that humanity had spread to, and where the chances of running into anybody from Baltimore were vanishingly small. A needle in a haystack all of humanity wide.

Amos Burton was a tall, stocky, pale-skinned man with an amiable smile, an unpleasant past, and a talent for cheerful violence. He left Baltimore to its dynamic balance of crime and law, exotics and mundanity, love and emptiness. The number of people who knew him and loved him could be counted on one hand and leave most of the fingers spare, and when he was gone, the city went on without him as if he had never been.

The Churn
Author's Note

From a technical standpoint, this was probably the hardest thing we ever wrote. The critical bit—that Timmy was going to grow up to be the Amos we know and love—was the big reveal, but we couldn't be sure when the penny was going to drop for any individual reader, so the story had to work with and without the surprise coming at the end.

Partly because of that, "The Churn" is the only part of The Expanse written in an omniscient voice. Almost everything else we do is close third. In the novels, we use a wide variety of close thirds, usually (but not always) mapping to the chapters. "The Churn" dips into a lot of different people's minds—though never Timmy's—and even shows things that no one could have seen. The "crane shot" image when the police are converging on Liev through the crowd, for instance, isn't one anybody in the story could have seen, but the narrator can, and so the reader can. It changes the voice of the story in ways that were tricky and interesting.

The stories don't just let us explore parts of the universe that the novels didn't, they also let us play with the writing process a little.

It's also probably the darkest story we wrote. The sexual relationship between Lydia and Timmy is deeply messed up—for both of them—and the story doesn't condemn or celebrate it. When the show was cast, Wes Chatham (who plays Amos Burton/Timmy) took this story to a psychotherapist and talked about what kinds of things an upbringing like this would do to someone.

A lot of Amos' character requires forgoing the customary moral judgments. For better or worse.

The Vital Abyss

They kept us in an enormous room. Ninety meters by sixty with a ceiling eight meters above us, a bit less than a football pitch, with observation windows along the top two meters all the way around from which our guards could look down on us if they chose to. Old crash couches salvaged from God knew where lay scattered around the floor. Eventually I came to recognize a certain subtle smell like alcohol and plastic when the air scrubbers were replaced, and the humidity and temperature would sometimes vary, leaving runnels of condensate coming down the walls. Those were the nearest things we had to weather. The gravity, somewhere in the neighborhood of one-quarter g, suggested we were on a spin station. Our guards never said as much, but I could think of no planetary bodies that matched that.

For most of us there was a sense that this shabby, empty room was the final destination for us, the former science team from

Thoth Station. Some wept at the thought. The research group did not.

We had toilets and showers, but no privacy. When we washed ourselves, it was in front of anyone who cared to observe. We learned to shit with the casualness of animals. When, as was inevitable, we began to turn to each other to fulfill our sexual needs, it was without the veneer of privacy we had once enjoyed, though eventually several of the crash couches were sacrificed to create a small area visually cut off from the rest of the room and that we began calling "the hotel." There was never anything sufficient to absorb sound. Our enforced physical intimacy with one another was a source of shame for many of the prisoners who didn't come from the research groups. Those of us who had—myself included—held a different perspective. I think our shamelessness was part of what made it hard for the others, the ones who had worked security or maintenance or administration, to accept us. There were other reasons too, but I think the shamelessness was the most visible. I might be wrong about that. I have learned to question my assumptions about what other people feel.

The lights in the room went on at what became morning, turned off again at what we agreed to call night. Water, we took from a pair of spigots beside the showers, drinking directly from them using our own cupped hands. For want of razors or depilatories, the men among us grew beards. Guards and jailers would come through whenever they saw fit, armor-clad and carrying guns sufficient to slaughter us all. They brought Belter food, vat-grown and yeasty. Sometimes they joked with us, sometimes they pushed us away or beat us, but they always brought us sustenance and the thin paper jumpsuits that were our only clothes. All of our guards were Belters, with the elongated bodies and slightly enlarged heads that spoke of childhoods in low gravity and long exposure to the pharmaceutical cocktails that made such lives possible. They spoke in the polyglot cant of the Belt: a hundred different vocabularies all crushed together until understanding it was as much music appreciation as grammar.

During the first year, they occasionally took us out of the room for periods of interrogation. The times that I was taken, the sessions were held in small, dirty rooms, often without chairs. The techniques varied from threats and violence, to offers of privileges, to a thin-faced woman who just sat in silence and stared at me as if she could force me to speak through raw, unspoken will. As time went on, these occasions grew fewer and farther between. Sometime in the third year, they stopped entirely, and the room became the totality of our collective world. We were a community of thirty-seven people living under the eyes of cold and unsympathetic jailers.

Though we came to know each other quite well, the taxonomy of our previous employment remade itself into a kind of tribalism. Van Ark and Drexler might disagree about everything from the best use of our "daylight" time to who had starred in the entertainment videos of our youth, but they had both been maintenance, and so when any conflict arose, they took each other's side against the rest of us. Fong had enjoyed the highest rank among the security team in our random organizational slice, and so she was not only the unspoken head of that group but through them the ersatz leader of our community. Research was kept separate, and even then divisions by work group made a web of subdivisions. Of the several dozen large signaling and communications work group, only Ernz and Ma had come to the room. Imaging was the largest with five: Kanter, Jones, Mellin, Hardberger, and Coombs. Nanoinformatics had three: Quintana, Brown, and myself.

Of the system outside the room—Earth and Mars and the Belt—we knew essentially nothing. For us, history had ended on Thoth Station with our experiment on Eros only half-done. Even years after the fact, I would find myself ruminating on some peculiarity of the dataset. I no longer trusted my memory enough to say whether the issues that absorbed my hours were accurate or figments of my somewhat fragile and altered mind.

During my bitterest times, I would lie in a crash couch for days at a time, thinking of Isaac Newton and the way that, by having his mind and his peculiar history, he had refashioned all of human understanding. I had stood on a precipice as great as his and been pulled back against my will. But more often, I was able to ignore such thoughts for weeks, sometimes months, at a time. I took a lover. Alberto Correa. He worked in administration and spent his childhood taking odd jobs at the spaceport complex at Bogotá. He had an advanced degree in political literature, and he said both my names—Paolo and Cortázar—reminded him of authors he had studied. He would talk for hours sometimes about the effects of class systems on poetic forms or Butler-Marxist readings of the action videos of Pilár Eight and Mikki Suhanam. I listened, and I like to think I absorbed some of it. The sound of his voice and the presence of his body were comforting, and the moments we spent together in the hotel were pleasant and calming. He said that if he'd known he would end here, he'd have stayed on Earth and lived on basic. When I pointed out that then he and I wouldn't have met, he would either agree that I made it worthwhile or else tell me about the beautiful men he had loved in Colombia.

Time, of course, became difficult to track, but I was fairly certain we were into the fourth year in the room when Kanter died. He'd been complaining of feeling ill, then grew agitated and delusional. The guards, seeing all as they did, brought medicine that I suspect was merely a sedative. He died a week later.

It was the first death, and reinforced to us the idea that we would likely never again be free. I watched as the others went through a period of mourning that was less for Kanter than for the lives we'd had and left behind. Not the research group, but the others. Alberto became a much more ardent lover for a time, and then lapsed into a funk in which he barely spoke to me and shied away from my touch. I was patient with him because I found patience easier when there was no alternative.

Day by day, we were ground down. Our experiential worlds narrowed to who was having sex with whom, whether someone's comment about a fellow inmate was innocuous or provocative, and fighting—sometimes violently—over who among us slept in which of the crash couches. We were petty and cruel, despairing and restless, occasionally humane and even capable of moments of actual if ephemeral beauty. Perhaps all periods of prosperity and calm go unnoticed when they occur. Certainly I didn't look on those days with any fondness until after the Martian came.

I didn't see him arrive myself. I was talking with Ernz when it happened, so my introduction to the man was Quintana barking my name. When I turned, the Martian was simply there. He was pale-skinned with nut-brown hair and a bad complexion, and he wore the familiar uniform of the Martian Congressional Republic Navy. Our customary Belter guards flanked him, chins lifted a bit higher than usual. Quintana and Brown stood before them, waving me impatiently to them. I didn't hesitate. The pull of something new after so much sameness called forth an excitement that left my hands trembling. I plucked at my beard as I strode over, hoping against all reason that it would make me look more respectable. When we stood before the new man, the three of us together, Brown took a little half-step ahead. I stifled the urge to move forward as well, certain that it would end in all of us crowding in on our visitor. I would swallow Brown's little physical dominance play in order to keep the Martian from leaving.

"This is all of them?" he said. He had a pleasant voice, barely accented with the drawl of the Mariner Valley.

"Bist," the Belter guard said with a nod. "Nanoinformatic, you wanted. This them."

The Martian looked at us each in turn, studying us like we were fresh recruits. It felt as if the floor was shuddering, but it was only my body. There was always an electricity in the unknown, a sense of impending revelation like the last moments before orgasm. Seeing this man and being seen by him, I felt more naked than I had since my first sexual experiences; though the longing and desire sprang from my heart and throat now, they were as commanding. All the things that the room had taken from me—my curiosity, my hope, my sense that a life outside of my nameless prison was possible—were distilled into his cool brown eyes. One of the occupational hazards of my career path is a kind of solipsism, but I truly felt at that moment that God had sent an angel to deliver me and whisper the secrets that had been hidden from me so long into my ear, which made the actions that followed so devastating.

"All right," the Martian said.

The filthy little half-step Brown had taken reaped its reward. The Martian took a dedicated hand terminal from his pocket and held it out. "Take a look at this. See what you make of it."

Brown snapped it up. "I will have a reaction prepared, sir," he said, as if he were team lead again and not a filthy, long-bearded captive in a paper suit.

"Can we have copies?" Quintana asked.

I was going to add my voice to his, but the guard cut me short. "One trade, one terminal. Sus no neccesar."

The Martian turned to leave, but Quintana surged forward. "If you need someone to interpret data for you, Brown's not the right person. He was only team lead so he could spend more time talking to administration. If he'd been a better mind, they'd have kept him in the *labs*." The same sentiment was forming in my own throat, but my hesitation in finding the words saved me. The nearest of the Belter guards shifted his weight, turned, and sank the butt of his rifle into Quintana's gut, folding him double. The Martian scowled, disapproving of the violence, but he did not speak as the guards led him to the doorway and out of the room. Brown, his beard jutting and his face flushed, half-ran and half-strutted to the hotel, the hand terminal clutched to his chest. Triumph and fear widened his eyes. Quintana retched, and I stood over him, considering. The others watched from all around the room, and when I looked up, there were more figures behind the glass staring down at us. At me.

Quintana had made a mistake, and one I would have made as well. He'd called the Martian's judgment—capricious as it was—into question. He'd tried to take a position of authority when we were all here specifically because we had no authority. Seeing that was like remembering something I'd forgotten.

One trade, one terminal. The words meant two things to me: first, that after all this time someone was trading for either our freedom or possession of us, and second, that only one of us would be required. Needless to say, I determined in that moment that the traded prisoner would be me.

"Come on," I said, helping him to his feet. "It's all right. Come on, and I'll help you get washed up." I let them see me assist him. With any luck it would get back to the Martian that one of the three was a team player, the kind of man who helped someone when they were down. Quintana, I felt sure, had lost his chance. Brown, by having the hand terminal and whatever was on it, was ahead. I didn't see yet how to arrange things so that I could gain the advantage, but simply having a real problem to solve again felt like waking up after a long and torpid sleep.

Brown didn't leave the hotel for the rest of the day, and while he did venture out when the guards brought our evening rations, he sat apart, the hand terminal stuck down the neck of his jumpsuit. Quintana glowered at him from under storm cloud brows and I kept my own counsel, but the effect of the day's actions went well beyond the three of us. Everyone in the room buzzed. There was no other subject of conversation. Mars knew we were here, and what was more, they wanted something of us. Or at least of one of us. It changed everything from the taste of the food to the sound of our voices.

Keep a man in a coffin for years with just enough food and water to live, and then—just for a moment—crack the lid open and let him see daylight. We were all that man, stunned and confused and elated and afraid. The numbness of captivity fell away for a few hours, and we lived that time deeply and desperately.

After the meal, Brown retreated to a crash couch near the wall, curling into it so that no one could sneak up behind him. I, pretending nothing had changed, went through my customary nighttime rituals—voiding my bowels, showering, drinking enough water that I would not wake thirsty before the lights came back. By the time our sudden toggle-switch nighttime came, I was curled in my couch with Alberto. His body was warm against my own. Brown, whose movements I had become profoundly aware of, remained in his crash couch by the wall. The glow of the terminal was dim as an insult. I pretended to sleep and thought I had fooled Alberto until he spoke.

"And so they've thrown us the apple, eh?"

"The fruit of knowledge," I said, but I had misunderstood which apple he meant.

"Worse than that, the golden one," he said. "Private property. Status. Now it's all going to be about fighting over who's the prettiest one, and war will come out of it."

"Don't be grandiose."

"It isn't me, it's history. Differences in status and wealth are always what drives war."

"Have we been a Marxist paradise this whole time and I didn't notice?" I said, more acidly than I'd meant to.

Alberto kissed my temple and brushed his lips along my hairline to the cup of my ear. "Don't kill him. They'll catch you."

I shifted. In the darkness, I couldn't see more than a limn of his face, floating over me. My heart beat faster and the coppery taste of fear flooded my mouth. "How did you know what I was thinking?"

When he answered, his tone was soft and melancholy. "You're from *research*."

I wasn't always the thing I became. Before I was *research*, I was a scientist who had educated himself into too fine a specialty. Before that, a student at Tel Aviv Autonomous University, caught between investing in a future I couldn't imagine and losing myself in a grief I couldn't fully encompass. Before that, I was a boy watching his mother die. I was all of those men before I was a researcher for Protogen Corporation based on Thoth Station. But it is also true that I remember many of those former selves with a distance that is more than time. I tell myself that remove allows me to trace the path from one to another, but I'm not sure that this is true.

My mother—a heart-shaped face above a pear-shaped body who rained love on me as if I were the only one in the world who mattered—lived on basic most of her life, sharing a room in a UN housing complex at Londrina. She wasn't educated, though I understand she was a good enough musician when she was younger to play in some local underground bands. If there were recordings of her on the network, I never found them. She was a woman of few ambitions and tepid passions until she reached thirty-two. Then, to hear her tell it, God had come to her in her sleep and told her to have a baby.

She woke up, marched to the training center, and applied for any program that would earn her enough money to legally go off contraception. It took her three years of fourteen-hour days, but she managed it. Enough money for both a licensed child and the donation of germ plasm that would help begin my life. She said that it was her choice to purchase sperm from a trading house that gave me my intelligence and drive, that the only fertile men in the housing complex were criminals and thugs too far outside of civilization to be on the basic rolls, and that I couldn't have gotten it from her because she was lazy and stupid.

As a child, growing up, I used to fight back on the last point: She was smart and she was beautiful and anything good about me surely had its roots in her. I believe now she used to denigrate herself in front of me in order to hear praise from someone, even if it was only a beloved child. I don't resent the manipulation. If intellect and focus were indeed the legacies of my invisible father, emotional manipulation was my mother's true gift, and it was as valuable. As important.

Because I was an adolescent when it began, I did not notice her symptoms until they were fairly advanced. My time was largely spent out of the house by then, playing football at a dirt-and-weed pitch south of the housing complex, running badly designed experiments with some garage-level makers and artists, exploring my own sexuality and the limits of the young men of my cohort. My days were filled with the smell of the city, the heat of the sun, and the promise that something joyous—a football win, a good project, a transporting affair—might come at any moment. I was a street rat living on basic, but the discovery of life was so rich and dramatic and profound that I wasn't concerned with my status in the larger culture. My social microenvironment seemed to stretch to the horizon, and the conflicts within it—whether Tomás or Carla would be goalie, whether Sabina could tweak off-the-shelf bacterial cultures to produce her own party drugs, whether Didi was homosexual and how to find out without courting humili-ation and rejection—were profound dramas that would resonate through the ages. When, later, my project lead said *There is a period of developmental sociopathy in every life*, this is the time I thought of.

And then my mother dropped a glass. It was a good one, with thick, beveled sides and a lip like a jelly jar, and when it shattered, it sounded like a gunshot. Or that's how I remember it. Moments of significance can make maintaining objectivity difficult, but that is my memory of it: a thick, sturdy drinking glass catching the light as it fell from her hands, twirling in the air, and detonat-ing on our kitchen floor. She cursed mildly and went to fetch the broom to sweep up the shards. She walked awkwardly and fum-bled with the dustpan. I sat at the table, an espresso growing cold in my hands while I watched her try to clean up after herself for five minutes. I felt horror at the time, an overwhelming sense of something wrong. The metaphor that came to me in the moment was my mother was being run remotely by someone who didn't understand the controls very well. The worst of it was her confu-sion when I asked her what was wrong. She had no idea what I was talking about.

After that, I began paying attention, checking in on her through the day. How long it had been going on, I couldn't say. The trouble she had finding words, especially early in the morning or late at night. The loss of coordination. The moments of confusion. They were little things, I told myself. The products of too little sleep or too much. She spent whole days watching the entertainment feeds out of Beijing, and then stayed up all night rearranging the pantry or washing her clothes in the sink for hours on end, her hands growing red and chapped from the soap as her mind was trapped, it seemed, by minor details. Her skin took on an ashen tone and a slackness came to her cheeks. The slow way her eyes moved reminded me of fish, and I began having the recurring nightmare that the sea had come to take her, and she was drowning there at the breakfast table with me sitting beside her powerless to help.

But whenever I talked about it, I only confused her. Nothing was wrong with her. She was just the same as she had ever been. She didn't have any trouble doing her chores. She wasn't uncoordinated. She didn't know what I was talking about. Even as her words choked her on their way out, she didn't know what I meant. Even as she listed like a drunk from her bed to the toilet, she experienced nothing out of the ordinary. And worse, she believed it. She genuinely thought I was saying these things to hurt her, and she didn't understand why I would. The sense that I was betraying her through my fear, that I was the cause of her distress rather than only a witness to something deeply wrong, left me weeping on the couch. She wasn't interested in going to the clinic; the lines there were always so long and there was no reason.

I got her to go the day before Ash Wednesday. We arrived early, and I had packed a lunch of roast chicken and barley bread. We made it to the intake nurse even before we ate, and then sat in the waiting area with its fake bamboo chairs and worn green carpet. A man just older than my mother sat across from us, his hands in fists on his knees as he struggled not to cough. The woman beside me, my age or younger, stared straight ahead, her hand on her belly like she was trying to hold in her guts. A child wailed behind us. I remember wondering why anyone who could afford to have a child would bring it to a basic clinic. My mother held my hand, then. For hours we sat together, her fingers woven with mine. For a time I told her everything would be all right.

The doctor was a thin-faced woman with earrings made of shell. I remember that her first name was the same as my mother's, that she smelled of rose water, and that her eyes had the shallow deadness of someone in shock. She didn't wait for me to finish telling her why we'd come in. The expert system had already pulled the records, told her what to expect. Type C Huntington's. The same, she told me (though my mother never had), that had killed my grandfather. Basic would cover palliative care, including psychoactives. She'd make the notation in the profile. The prescriptions would be delivered starting next week and would continue as long as they were needed. The doctor took my mother's hands, urged her in a rote and practiced tone to be brave, and left. Off to the next exam room, hopefully to someone whose life she might be able to save. My mother wobbled at me, her eyes finding me only slowly.

"What happened?" she asked, and I didn't know what to tell her.

It took my mother three more years to die. I have heard it said that how you spend your day is how you spend your life, and my days changed then. The football games, the late night parties, the flirtation with the other young men in my circle: all of it ended. I divided myself into three different young men: one a nurse to his failing mother, one a fierce student on a quest to understand the disease that was defining his life, and the last a victim of depression so profound it made bathing or eating food a challenge. My own room was a cell just wide enough for my cot, with a frosted glass window that opened on an airshaft. My mother slept in a chair in front of the entertainment screen. Above us, a family of immigrants from the Balkan Shared Interest Zone clomped and shouted and fought, each footfall a reminder of the overwhelming density of humanity around us. I gave her ramen soup and a collection of government pills that were the most brightly colored things in the apartment. She grew impulsive, irritable, and slowly lost her ability to use language, though I think she understood me almost to the end.

I didn't see it at the time, but my options were to weave myself a lifeline from what I had at hand, abandon my mother in her final decline, or else die. I would not leave her, and I did not die. Instead I took her illness and made it my salvation. I read everything there was on type C Huntington's, the mechanism as it was understood, the research that was being done with it, the treatments that might someday manage it. When I didn't understand something, I found tutorials. I sent letters to the outreach programs of medical care centers and hospitals as far as Mars and Ganymede. I tracked down the biomakers I had known and drilled them with questions—What was cytoplasmic regulation delay? How did mRNA inhibitor proteins address phenotypic expressions of primary DNA sequences? What did the Lynch-Noyon synthesis mean in respect to regrown neural tissues?—until it was clear they didn't understand what I was saying. I dove into a world of complexity so deep even the research watsons couldn't encompass it all.

What astounded me was that the cutting edge of human knowledge was so close. Before I educated myself, I assumed that there was a great depth of science, that every question of importance had been cataloged, studied, that all the answers were there, if only someone could query the datasets the right way. And for some things, that was true.

But for others—for things that I would have thought so important and simple that everyone would have known—the data simply wasn't there. How does the body flush plaque precursors out of cerebrospinal fluid? There were two papers: one seventy years out of date that relied on assumptions about spinal circulation that had since been disproved, and one that drew all its data from seven Polynesian infants who had suffered brain injuries from anoxia or drug exposure or trauma.

There were explanations, of course, for this dearth of information: Human studies required human subjects, and ethical guidelines made rigorous studies next to impossible. One didn't give healthy babies a series of monthly spinal taps just because it would have been a good experimental design. I understood that, but to come to science expecting the great source of intellectual light and step so quickly into darkness was sobering. I began to keep a book of ignorance: questions that existing information could not answer and my amateurish, half-educated thoughts about how answers might be found.

Officially, my mother died of pneumonia. I had learned enough to understand what each of her drugs did, to read her fate from the pills that arrived. I knew by their shapes and colors and the cryptic letters pressed into their sides when the vast bureaucracy that administered basic health care had moved her from palliative care to full hospice. In the end, she was on little more than sedatives and antivirulence drugs. I gave them to her because it was what I had to give her. The night she died, I sat at her feet, my head resting on the red wool blanket that covered her wasted lap. Heartbreak and relief were my soul's twin bodyguards. She moved beyond pain or distress, and I told myself the worst was over.

The notification from basic came the next day. With my change in status, the rooms we had been in were no longer appropriate. I would be reassigned to a shared dormitory, but should be prepared to relocate to São Paulo or Bogotá, depending on availability. I thought—mistakenly, as it turned out—that I wasn't ready to leave Londrina. I moved in with a friend and former lover. He treated me gently, making coffee in the mornings and playing cards through the empty afternoons. He suggested that it might be less that I needed to stay in the city of my birth, the city of my mother, and more that I needed some control over the terms of my departure.

I applied to apprentice programs at London, Gdansk, and Luna and was rejected by all of them. I was competing against people who had years of formal schooling, political connections, and wealth. I lowered my expectations, searching for uplift programs that aimed specifically for autodidacts who had been living on basic, and six months later, I arrived in Tel Aviv and met Aaron, a former Talmudic scholar who had researched his way to atheism and was now my dorm mate.

The third night, we sat together on our little balcony looking out over the city. It was sunset, and we were both a little high on marijuana and wine. He asked me what my ambitions were.

"I want to understand," I told him.

He shrugged only his left shoulder. "Understand what, Paolo? The mind of God? The reason for suffering?"

"Just how things work," I said.

It became clear immediately that Brown had become the most important person not only among the nanoinformatics group or even research in general, but in the entire room. Over the following days, Fong, who had never treated anyone in research as better than suspicious, deferred to him when the guards brought food. Drexler sat near him before lights-out, laughing at anything he said that might pass for a joke. When Sujai and Ma fell into one of their singing mock competitions, they invited Brown in, though he demurred.

Speculation ran in all directions: We would be extradited and tried for the dead Martians on Phoebe; the company had found diplomatic channels to negotiate for our release; the Outer Planets Alliance and the Martian Republic were at war and our fates were going to be part of the settlement. My own theory—the only one that really made sense to me—was that the experiment had been running all this time and something new had happened. Grave or miraculous, it carried a weight of importance and inscrutability that brought us back from our forgotten place in a Belter prison and into the light. The Martian had come because he needed the things that only we knew, and possibly needed it badly enough to overlook our previous sins. In the observation windows above us, guards appeared more often now, usually with their attention fixed on Brown. It was not only the prisoners who found his new status of interest.

Brown himself changed, but not in the way others might have. While I believe he made use of the opportunities his new status afforded him, he did so rationally. He didn't hold himself more grandly, did not deepen the timbre of his voice. He did not hold court or bask in the new attention given to him. Humanity is social, and the self-image of humans is built from the versions of ourselves we see and hear reflected in others; that this is not true of the research group—of Coombs or Brown or Quintana or me—was, after all, precisely the point. Instead, Brown balanced his new power with the new risks it carried. He made an unofficial alliance with Fong, staying near her and her people so that, should Quintana or I try to take the hand terminal by force, there were others who could interfere in an attempt to curry favor with him.

Van Ark responded by eating and sleeping closer to Quintana and Alberto and myself. He'd had no love of Brown, and treated his elevation as an insult. The room was pulling itself apart like a cell preparing to divide. Brown and the Martian's hand terminal formed one locus. Quintana and I, the other.

We planned our theft quietly. When Brown sat bent over the terminal, he could not watch us talk, but Quintana and I were discreet all the same. I squatted at the side of a crash couch while he lay in it, facing away from me. The metal and ceramic made too hard a backrest, my spine aching where it pressed. I tried not to move my lips while we spoke. Fong, I felt sure, noticed us, but did nothing. Or perhaps she didn't see us. Fear kept me from looking around to find out.

"He has to sleep," Quintana said.

"He also has to wake up," I said, recalling Alberto's advice.

Quintana shifted on the couch, the gimbals hissing as the cup of the couch readjusted. Across the room, Brown sat near the hotel. The hand terminal flickered, throwing subtle shadows onto his cheeks and the hollows around his eyes. With the right equipment, I could have modeled his face, its reflectivity, and rebuilt the image he was looking at. I realized that Quintana had been speaking, and I didn't know what he'd said. When I asked him to repeat himself, he sighed with a sound very much like the gimbals.

"Once I get it, you hide it," he said. "They'll question me. Search where I went. Then they'll have to give him another copy. Once that happens, we'll be safe. They won't care anymore. You can get it back out and give it to me. You won't even have to get in trouble."

"Won't they punish us?"

"He'll have the copy. Why would anyone care about the original?"

I suspected that analysis had some holes in it, but I didn't object, out of concern that Quintana would grow impatient and scrap the plan. I resolved instead to ask Alberto if he thought the stolen hand terminal would be trivial once a copy was delivered, but as things fell out, I didn't have the chance. Navarro, one of Fong's leadership from security, walked toward us. I coughed, alerting Quintana, and he changed to talking about the nutritional value of Belter food compared to the fare we'd had before the room, and the probable health effects that we could expect from our systematic malnutrition. Navarro sat at the next couch over, watching the guards at the window watch us. She didn't say anything. She didn't need to. The message—you're being watched—was clear.

That afternoon, the guards came early and took Brown away. They offered no explanation, simply found him there among us, nodded to the doors they'd entered through, and escorted him away. I watched him leave. My heart was in my throat, and I was certain it was already too late. If they were taking him to the Martian, he might never come back. When Brown returned to the room just before nightfall, confusion and worry pressed on his brow, but he carried the hand terminal with him.

That night as we curled up to sleep, I told Alberto of my fear that Brown and the hand terminal might vanish before I could see what was on it.

"Better if it did," Alberto said, holding my hand. I didn't know if he meant that with the irritant of hope gone, the room could return to something like its resting state, or something more personal between the two of us. I intended then to sound him out about Quintana's plan, but he had other intentions that were more urgent and immediate, and when we were spent, I curled in his arms, warm and content in the way that being a masculine animal allows.

Either Brown's temporary absence spurred Quintana to action sooner than planned, or he had told me his timetable when my attention was elsewhere. The first I knew that action had been taken was the screaming, then pelting footfalls going one way and the next. I tried to stand, but Alberto impeded me, and then, from the darkness, a dim glow. The plate of a hand terminal, moving toward me. Quintana loomed up out of the darkness, pressing hard ceramic into my hand. He didn't speak, but ran on past me. I curled back with Alberto and waited. Brown was shrieking now, his voice bansheeing up until it threatened to rise above the wavelengths of human perception. And then Fong. And then Quintana proudly announcing that Brown didn't deserve the data, couldn't understand the data, and was going to doom us all to living and dying in the room out of his own misplaced pride.

I lay with my head against my lover's shoulder, the hand terminal tucked beneath our bodies, while the other prisoners screamed and fought in the darkness, the first open combat in the war Alberto had foreseen. The Belter guards did not come. I felt sure their absence meant something, but I couldn't say what.

I didn't want to leave the relative safety and warmth of the crash couch, but I knew that the battle raging in the darkness was also my best cover. Quintana's belief that I wouldn't be questioned because he had taken the credit for stealing the terminal seemed optimistic to me. Worse, it seemed like the kind of asserted reality—the willful decision to believe that people would act the way you preferred that they would—that posed a constant threat to those of us in research. I slid the terminal down the front of my already open jumpsuit and moved to rise from the couch, hoping the sound of the gimbals would be lost under the shouting.

Alberto took my hand for the space of a breath, and then released it. "Be careful," he whispered.

As I moved through that darkness, the room felt even bigger than it was. I had the most precious thing in my life pressed against the skin of my belly while men and women whose voices I knew intimately, the compatriots of my years-long captivity, threatened and defied and wheedled and cried out in sudden pain. Like a stage magician's arcing gesture, they commanded the attention and gave me the cover to do what needed to be done. I slid the hand terminal under one of the crash couches that defined the hotel, stepped back to see that no light was escaping from its dim display, and then trotted back to Alberto through the darkness, afraid to be caught away from my customary place.

The sudden harsh light of morning found Quintana sitting with his back against a wall, eyes blackened and swollen closed, nose and lips bloodied, and Fong organizing a search. I was among her first targets, and Alberto shortly after me. Brown opened a new round of shouts and accusations, and Fong had to set two of her people to prevent him from assaulting Quintana further. It occurred to me that Brown was making Quintana's argument more effectively than Quintana had.

The sense of Brown's status as our savior and best hope of freedom tarnished quickly in the next hours. I felt the confidence the others had in him faltering like the pressure of a coming storm. If they turned on him, unleashed the years of frustration and anxiety and despair upon his fragile human body, I didn't think the guards would be able to reach him in time. It was an interesting possibility, but also a warning should I manage to put myself in his place.

As soon as it seemed plausible, I took Alberto by the hand and drew him toward the hotel. Hardberger and Navarro were going through the crash couches near it, and I was anxious that they would find our golden apple before I had a chance to taste it. I thought Navarro scowled at me as I made my way toward privacy and the hiding place, but it might only have been my imagination.

Once we were in the hotel and visually cut off, I retrieved the hand terminal.

Now, with light and proximity, I could actually see it: blue-gray casing with an extended keyboard for full scientific notations; a scratch along the right side of the screen that caught and refracted the light of the display, rainbows out of the yellow default image; a logo of the Mars Congressional Republic Navy stamped into the casing and echoed on the screen. I stroked it with my fingertips, feeling serene and untouchable. If church had felt half as good as this, I would have been a religious man.

With a sense of nearly superhuman calm, I opened the data files. Charts and readings appeared before me.

It was the experiment. *My* experiment. Only it also was not. The basic structures were there: the peculiar way the individual molecular engines unfolded; the instantaneous networking that suggested entanglement communication; the beautifully complicated tertiary beta sheeting studded with proteins dense with information and vulnerable to oxidation. I had the sudden, powerful memory of being in the lab on Phoebe seeing the nanoparticles express those sheets for the first time. Krantz had described it as *snowflake castles looking for the nearest blowtorch.*

They were still beautiful, still fragile, but they had defied the blowtorch. They had found ways to express themselves, creating what appeared to be massive constructions implied first in their microscopic structure, like an infinite cascade of fractal design. There were maps of control points that were clearly cellular machinery that had been hijacked and modified, complex layers of pattern-matching mechanisms that stank of human neocortical structures, and something...else.

I was looking at the oak and recognizing the acorn.

I spooled through the information as quickly as I could, taking in the first and last paragraphs of the reports, glancing at the diagrams and data just long enough to take a general sense of them and then moving on. The navigation keys of the hand terminal clicked as I pressed them, like I was crushing tiny beetles. There was clearly a deeper structure that the development of the beta sheets was protecting and promoting. I didn't begin to understand the energetic dynamics of it, but there was, I thought, a privileged group. Something about the logic of the individual particles reminded me of a paper I'd read in Tel Aviv that reexamined sperm. The thesis was that rather than a homogeneous collection of equally competing cells, there were classes of sperm; subspecies that acted as a team to present a chosen cell or class of cells to the ovum.

Alberto said my name, and I was aware of it the way I might have been aware of a candle flame in the noonday sun. It was there, but it had very little impact.

The privileged group could probably be identified by its place within the logical structure of the network, but something about that felt wrong. I paged back through the diagrams. I had the sense there was an asymmetry in the network someplace that I could almost—not quite, but almost—place. It was analogous to something I already knew about, but I didn't know what. I growled and went back to the start. Alberto said my name again, and I looked up too late.

Fong stood over us both, her expression carved from hardwood. I felt a flash of resentment at her interruption and swallowed it quickly. I held out the hand terminal.

"Look what I found," I said.

She took it from me and paused. I could see the desire to punish me in her mouth and the angle of her shoulders. Alberto squirmed beside me and Navarro appeared at Fong's side. I heard Brown yawp with delight. He'd caught sight of his lost treasure. I anticipated Quintana's anger and disappointment, but it didn't matter to me. My goal had never been to help him.

"Quintana's an asshole, but he isn't wrong. He won't solve it," I said, and Fong shook her head as if to say *I don't know what you're talking about*. I smiled tightly. "Brown won't solve it. He won't give them what they're looking for. We may not get another chance."

"That's not how this works," she said.

"I can help," I said. "Tell him to let me help." For a moment, it seemed as if she might reply, but instead she turned away without pressing the issue.

It felt like a victory.

My advisor at Tel Aviv—David Artemis Kuhn—had a beautiful name, a way of wearing a formal jacket just messily enough to say he was in on the joke, and a voice that sounded like the first sip of rum feels: sharp and warm and relaxing. His office smelled of coffee and freshly turned soil. I admired him, I crushed on him, I aspired to be him. If he had told me to quit the university and write poetry, I probably would have.

"Nanoinformatics is perfect for you," he said. "It's deeply interdisciplinary. You can apply it to a career in medical research or computer architecture or microecology. Of all the degree programs we have, this is the one that will keep the most doors open for you. If you're not sure what direction you want your studies to take you…" He paused and tapped his desk three times with the tip of his index finger. "This is the one."

There is nothing so destructive and also so easy to overlook as a bad idea.

A thought experiment from my first course in the program: Take a bar of metal and put a single notch in it. The two lengths thus defined have a relationship that can be expressed as the ratio between them. In theory, therefore, any rational number can be expressed with a single mark on a bar of metal. Using a simple alphabetic code, a mark that calculated to a ratio of .1215225 could be read as 12-15-22-5, or "l-o-v-e." The complete plays of Shakespeare could be written in a single mark, if it were possible to measure accurately enough. Or the machine language expression of the most advanced expert systems, though by then the notch might be small enough that Planck's constant got in the way. How massive amounts of information could be expressed in and retrieved from infinitesimal objects was the driving concern of my college years. I swam in an intellectual sea of qubits and data implication, coding structures and Rényi entropy.

I spent days in the computation labs with their leather couches and ancient ceramic lockers, talking with people from all across the world and beyond. The first Belter I met was a woman from the L5 station who had come down to study crystallography, though since she lived in the consistent spin gravity of that station, she looked more like a Martian than the elongated soldiers who would eventually become my guards. My nights I divided between my dorm room and the bright bars and sober coffeehouses along the edge of the campus.

Slowly, I began to take the sad, traumatized boy who had fled Londrina and a life on basic and build from him a deeper, more serious, more focused man. I styled myself a scientist and wore the thin black vests and sand-colored silk shirts that the biology students had adopted as their fashion. I even joined the student union for scientific outreach, sitting through the long, angry, clove-cigarette-hazed meetings and arguing when people from the more traditional programs complained that my work was closer to philosophy than engineering.

I drank a bit of wine, I smoked a little marijuana, but the drugs that fueled the university were not recreational. Tel Aviv Autonomous University ran on nootropics: nicotine, caffeine, amphetamine, dextroamphetamine, methylphenidate, 2-oxo-pyrrolidine acetamide. Aaron, my roommate, provided both a route for these to reach me and the worldview that justified them.

"We're the bottom," he said, leaning on the arm of our cheap foam-sculpt couch. "You and me and everyone else in this place. If we weren't, we'd have gone to a real school."

"We're at a real school. We're doing good work here," I said. We were eating noodles and black sauce that they sold from a cart that passed down the halls of the dorm house, and the smell of something like olives rose from every mouthful.

"Exactly," Aaron said, stabbing a fork in my direction. "We

are keeping up with the most advanced, best-funded schools any-where. Us, a bunch of basic jump-ups. Our mommies aren't giv-ing multimillion-dollar grants to the school. We aren't skating on discoveries made by some department chair seventy years ago. Do you think they have a nanoinformatics program at the École?"

"Yes," I said, feeling contrary.

"They don't. We do. Because we *have* to be on the cutting edge to survive. We don't have status, we don't have money, we don't have any of the things you need to get a foot in the door with recruiters or unions or grant specialists. So we make our own." With this he took a thin case from his pocket and rattled it. "What the others can't, or won't, or don't feel like they need to do is just necessary for us."

Deep in my chest, a sluggish sense of fairness twitched in its sleep, but I could find no argument against, especially since it seemed as though everyone else in the program agreed. What would make it unfair, I told myself, was if the drugs tilted the playing field. If everyone was using them, then it stayed even.

As my career at the university went on and I came nearer to the knife-edge horizon of graduating, I found myself caring less and less about the fairness of the situation and more and more about my own well-being. Since nanoinformatics was a new program it didn't have its own permanent faculty. Half of the classes on its requirements list were borrowed from other programs, and the professors often hadn't tailored the content to include me. In my culmination-level seminar, all of the other half-dozen students were strict biologists working from a shared curriculum that I had only brushed against. Taking focus drugs in that context seemed like the obvious thing.

In my last year, both Aaron and David Artemis Kuhn left. Aaron graduated early with a job offer for a cutting-edge R&D group so deep, even its name was under nondisclosure. Kuhn left to take a tenure-track position at Nankai University on Luna, heading up their nascent nanoinformatics program. I acquired other friends and professors in my time at Tel Aviv, but I found the absence of those two particularly unmooring, and my use of drugs ramped slowly up. I came to include sedatives in my study rituals, telling myself that they helped me rest and recharge. That I enjoyed the sense of release and mindlessness they brought, I chose to interpret as the measure of the stress I was under.

My graduation ceremony took place in a synagogue with white pillars and arches, beautiful sculpture in gold along the walls, and Hebrew script inlaid around the ceiling. The notes of "Auld Lang Syne" reverberated in the space, the melody taking on a depth and gravity I had never ascribed to it. My body, struggling from the massive nootropic abuse surrounding final examinations compounded by several whisky-and-sodas, punished me with nausea and dizziness. I spent my glorious hour, the pinnacle of my new life, trying not to vomit. I didn't know whether to imagine my mother's spirit viewing me from the afterlife with pride or despair. Afterward, diploma in hand, robes draped from my shoulders, I walked to a public park, sat on a stone bench, and wept, calling my mother's name with an oceanic grief I had avoided for years.

It would be difficult to say which sign of trouble deserved the title "first." When I visited my placement advisor after graduation, I spent an hour explaining to her what my degree entailed and applied to. It left her only slightly better prepared to help me find work. Letters began to arrive—actual physical letters on thin, yellow paper—from the benefits administration office asking whether I would be returning to the basic rolls. My applications to Stravos Group, Beyaz/Siyah, and Unfinished History all brought acknowledgments of receipt, and then nothing.

I laughed it all off for three months. I told myself and my friends that the cutting edge always confused the people who weren't part of it. My advisor's job wasn't to understand me, just to make connections. If she couldn't, other paths existed. I played it as more an inconvenience than a problem, and the prospect of going back on basic as laughable. I had a degree from a recognized university. I had letters of recommendation. The cheap housing, gray-tasting food, recycled clothing, and minimalist medical care of basic marked where I came from, not where I was going. The applications took longer than I'd expected, but I could be patient. I still had six months of supported postgraduate housing, until I had three, and then seven weeks, and then twelve days.

When I could no longer ignore that I would be out of housing allowance before I found employment, my friends had for the most part scattered to new positions of their own. The sense of isolation pressed at the back of my head all through the days and nights. I began growing angry at the slightest provocation.

In practice, the course of study meant to give me the most options had instead left me as the fourth-rank pick for everything behind people who had specialized. And even that was not the worst of my problems. I assumed that after my last exams, my use of nootropics and sedatives would end more or less of its own accord. The need, after all, evaporated. If now and then I used a tab to help me navigate the surprising complexities of my post-graduation world, others did as much with no stigma or ill effect. Without the drugs, my merely normal cognition felt sluggish and unfocused. And the sedatives were only to make my sleep deeper, more restful, more productive.

The penny dropped for me at a café on Yigal Alon Street where I sat under a copper awning with my hand terminal cradled in my palms. Over a cup of tea and a bit of scone, I reviewed my expenses with an eye toward how I could extend my job search without going on basic. The first-pass numbers felt like a kick in the gut. When I redid the math, I found the same thing. In the months since completing my program, my drug use had gone *up*.

I don't know how long I sat there, the waiter coming by now and again to touch my shoulder and ask if I was well. I remember very clearly that there were two young women at the table beside me planning a wedding while I came to grips with the truths I had denied. I'd exchanged Londrina and life on basic for a degree I couldn't use and a rainbow of addictions. I was, if anything, worse off now than when I had spent my days watching my mother fade into death.

I can't say why at that point I didn't fall into despair. Despair was certainly open to me. In practice, I did not. Instead, I made what I called my rescue plan: a list of fifty work positions that, while they fit poorly with my education and ambitions, would suffice to keep me off basic; a consolidated account with what little actual money remained to me; a month's supply of fruit and whole grain foods; a hotel room where I could sleep and pace and weep while I withdrew. I put in my fifty applications all at once, checked in to my exclusive and unlicensed treatment center overlooking an alleyway, and prepared myself for hell.

I did not sleep for the first week. My body ached like I'd been beaten. My eyes dried until my vision grew blurry. I watched my emotions cycle up and down and up again, the wavelength of my illness growing shorter and shorter until I could no longer tell where in the cycle I was. The cravings were like hunger or thirst or overwhelming lust, and I only postponed acting on them by promising myself that if I still wanted so badly when I was done, I would indulge myself to death. I anticipated my eventual overdose like a zealot looking forward to Armageddon.

I have no clear memory of the second week. When I came to myself again in the middle of the third week—ten days still remaining on my rented room—I felt weak and hungry and clear headed in a way I had not realized until then how much I missed. My mind was my own. I could not help but think of my mother and the way her disease blinded her to its own symptoms. I understood her better then. My own addiction functioned in a similar way. In the exhaustion of my recovery, I dreamed of finding doors that had been plastered over that opened to rooms I'd had once and forgotten about, filled with books and scientific instruments that I needed and had been unable to locate. The metaphor wasn't subtle. I swore that I would never compromise my mind that way again, though like all such resolutions, I have since broken it profoundly.

With seven days remaining, I bathed, shaved, and took myself out for a meal of eggs and coffee I could barely afford. My time in the underworld nearly over—so I thought—I had to prepare for my return to the world of the living. If there was nothing waiting for me, that meant turning myself over to benefits administration. I cannot express how terrible that option seemed to me, but I was willing to face it, should it prove necessary. I thought I had moved beyond illusions about myself and what I was capable of enduring. That might even have been true. Remembering what I felt then and feeling it again now are very different things, and one is easier than the other.

I had five messages waiting. Four were from the applications I had sent out, two asking for more information about my qualifications, two scheduling interviews. The last, to my surprise, was Aaron returning to my life. His research-and-development gig had come across something that justified bumping up the budget. There were new positions opening up, including a full nano-informatics team. Later, I would wonder if I saw the changes in him even then. A recording on a terminal can't carry the same weight of nuance as an actual conversation and sociopathy often approaches undetectability, even under the best of circumstances. I hope that I genuinely missed it. If I saw it and chose to edit it out of my perceptions, if the leaping hope in my breast was more important to me than the new-won integrity of my mind, it speaks poorly of me. I would rather be damned as naïve than willfully ignorant.

I responded at once: I would be delighted to talk about work. I told him that, just between the two of us, I'd been in a dry spell, and was even beginning to think that David Artemis Kuhn had led me astray with his professorial charisma and beautiful name. I made a joke of my season in hell, telling him but also not telling him, afraid of what he would think of me. At the time I gave more weight to the opinions of others.

Aaron's response came quickly. He'd spoken to the powers that be, and the project lead wanted to speak with me. He would be reaching out in the next few days. His name, so I could expect it, was Antony Dresden.

The others, even Alberto, didn't really understand what it meant to be research. I do believe that's true. On Thoth Station, we were treated as different—as dangerous—which we were. But their sense of our monstrosity was misplaced. The changes that we went through to become what we became didn't blind us to humanity. Our emotional lives didn't stop. All of us in research suffered the same loves and hopes and jealousies that administration and maintenance and security did. If someone felt flattered or excluded or tired, we saw it just as anyone else might. The difference, and I think it was the only difference, came from not caring anymore.

The confusion rose from metaphors of mental illness. The others thought of research as a collection of borderline autistics, and while there were several who did participate on that spectrum—Owsley in chemical signaling, Arbrecht in modeling—they were not created. They brought their diagnoses to the table with them. The other pigeonhole, sociopathy, was nearer the truth, though I believe there were still some differences.

I remembered caring about people. My mother. Samuel, a boy two years my senior, who was my first lover. Aaron. I remembered caring deeply about whether they were well, whether they suffered, what they thought of me. I remember defining myself by the opinions of people around me. My worth had been determined from without, by how I imagined that I appeared to others. That is what being a social animal is, after all. Emotional and definitional interdependence. I remembered it like remembering that I once knew a song, but not the melody itself.

Quintana broke my nose.

It was midmorning, as we reckoned such things in the room, and Brown, his precious hand terminal clutched to his breast, had been taken away by the guards again. Alberto and I walked, making a slow circuit of the room for the simple pleasure of feeling my body in motion. I had just reached the corner farthest from the hotel when Quintana walked up to us. The benignity of his expression surprised me at first. I expected rage or sorrow or confusion. Alberto recognized something threatening in Quintana's demeanor before I did. He shouted and tried to push me out of the way, but Quintana stepped in close, twisting his body from the waist. His elbow hit the bridge of my nose with a sound like a wine glass being stepped on: sharp and deep at the same time.

I rolled to my side, uncertain how I'd fallen down. My hands guarded my abused face but didn't touch it. Contact made the pain worse. Blood ran down my cheeks and dampened the collar of my jumpsuit. Shouting voices came at me from a great distance that turned out to be about four meters. Alberto and two of Fong's men wrestled Quintana, pushing him back and away from me. Half a dozen other prisoners ran toward us, to help keep the peace or to watch it being broken. Quintana's voice buzzed with rage so badly I couldn't understand what he was calling me or threatening me with. I rose to my knees and looked up. The Belter guards leaning on the windows above us seemed slightly less bored than usual. One, a woman with short red hair and a tattoo across her chin, smiled at me sympathetically and shrugged. I stood, but the throbbing pain brought me to my knees again.

Quintana turned away, followed by Fong herself to make certain he wouldn't circle back. The others watched them go, then Alberto came to my side.

"I told you war would come out of it."

"You're so very smart," I said, the sound of my voice like something from a child's cartoon.

He took my guarding hands and gently guided them away. "Let's survey the damage," he said. And then, "Oh, darling. You poor thing."

They stuffed my nose with two tampons donated by women in security before we reset it. Our Belter guards never made an appearance. The politics of the enormous room were our own to work through, and the Belters took no side. Still, when Brown and his escort did come, no one in the room talked about anything but the violence he'd missed.

The guards didn't allow us mirrors. The expressions of the others gave me the nearest thing to a reflection, and from that I assumed I looked pretty rough. Alberto ripped the sleeve from his jumpsuit and dampened it at the showers. My drying blood grew sticky, adhering my suit and beard to my skin and tugging at me when I moved. I sat with my back to the wall, accepting Alberto's ministrations with as much grace as I could muster. I saw Brown approach Fong, watched them speak. Brown kept shifting his weight from one foot to the other and glancing behind him, as if expecting to be Quintana's next target. I waited, still and patient, afraid that any movement on my part would scare him off. Quintana paced at the far end of the room, muttering to himself with several of Fong's security people and Mellin from imaging. Around me, the narrative of the room changed. With Quintana as the villain, I shifted to being the victim. And as the victim, approachable.

"Fong told me what happened. You look like shit," Brown said, establishing dominance before he had to admit weakness.

"I blame myself," I replied, then paused, making it a joke. "No, actually, I blame Quintana."

Alberto, approaching with a freshly dampened rag, caught sight of us, paused, and angled off to sit by himself. Brown lowered himself to sit beside me. "He's always been an asshole."

I grunted my agreement and waited. Brown shifted, fidgeted. A tightness filled my gut, and the certainty that he would offer me his sympathy and walk away filled my throat. I took hold of his arm as if I could keep him there by force, but spoke calmly. "He's been talking to you a lot?"

"They have," he said. "The Martian officer hasn't been there. It's just the Belter guards."

"What do they say?"

"They ask me what it is."

"And what do you tell them?" I asked. When he didn't respond, I tried again. "What is it?"

"It's an elaboration of the original protomolecule sample. You saw that much, didn't you? Before you gave back the terminal?"

"I did," I said. Candor about that cost me nothing.

"The thing is, they know. I'm sure of it. This isn't a problem they need to solve. It's a test. They want to see if we can solve a puzzle they've already cracked. They don't say it, but I can hear them laughing at me."

That piqued me, but this wasn't the moment to sit with it. Brown's open shell gave me my opportunity, and I drove my knife in to keep him from closing again. "Tell them they need two. Tell them to take both of us, and I'll help."

I saw the spark of greed in his eyes, his moment of bovine cunning. Once I helped him, I would have no way to enforce any agreement, and so his betrayal of me carried no price. I fought to keep my expression innocent. My wounds and my beard helped with that, I think.

"Thank you, Cortázar," he said, and drew the hand terminal from his jumpsuit.

I took it from him gently, forcing myself not to grab at it. Under my fingertips, the files bloomed like roses, measurements and images and analytic summaries opening one after the next like diving into an ocean of data. The surface I had skimmed before lay over an abyss, and I fell joyfully into it. Some of the large-scale structures boasted an organic origin: lipid bilayers, proton pumps, something that might once have been a ribosome now altered almost past recognition. That, I believed, had led Brown astray.

He assumed that a cell membrane would be acting as a cell membrane, rather than considering what cell membranes did and how they might be used to some purpose other than simply creating a boundary between things. They could just as easily provide highways for molecules vulnerable to the partial charge of water molecules. Or any polar solvent. Like the optical illusion of faces and vases, the bilayers could define either the volumes separating them or the web of pathways they created. And these were only massive, macro-scale expressions of the information in the initial particles.

I paged through, going deeper, my mind sailing across seas of inference and assumption. Time did not stop so much as become irrelevant. I forgot that Brown was beside me until he touched my shoulder.

"It's…interesting. Let me see what I can find."

"Just understand," he said. "I'm lead."

"Of course," I said. As if I could have forgotten.

It took me longer than I would have liked, sitting with the data and dredging up what I could remember of the experiments before. Time had eaten some of my memory and likely falsified some as well. The core of it remained, though. And the sense of wonder so deep it sucked my lungs empty from time to time. But slowly, I found a pattern. The thing at the center. What I thought of as the Queen Bee. While a great many of the structures I was looking at were beyond my understanding—beyond, I thought, any human understanding—there were others that did make some sense. Lattices that mimicked the beta sheets and expanded on them. Complex control and pattern-matching systems that were still just recognizable as brain tissues, two-stage pumps adapted from hearts. And at the center, a particle that nothing led to. A particle that both required and provided a massive amount of energy.

When I realized that the physical dimensions of the structure-particle were macroscopic, the knowledge rushed through me like a flood. I was seeing a stabilizing network that could bring subquantum effects up to a classical scale. A signaling device that ignored the speed of light by shrugging off locality, or possibly a stable wormhole. If I wept, I wept quietly. No one could know what I'd found. Especially not Brown.

Not until I had time to make my alternate.

"There's no doubt we're seeing the ruins of Eros," I said.

"Obviously," he said, impatient and rightly so.

"But look at these tertiary structures," I said, pulling up the graphic I'd prepared. "The connection between networks follows the same graph as embryonic profusion."

"It's making…"

"An *egg*," I said.

Brown snatched the hand terminal from me, his eyes jerking back and forth as he compared my graphs. It was a plausible lie, backed by fascinating and evocative correlations that didn't share a shred of cause. It built on his prejudices of biological structures being used for biological uses. I watched his face as he followed along the arguments I'd constructed to mislead him. He had been desperate for a narrative, and now that I'd given him one, it seemed unlikely that he would see anything else. I don't know whether relief or awe set his hands to trembling, only that they trembled.

"This is it," he said. "This is what gets us out of here."

I appreciated his use of the plural, and I didn't for a moment consider it sincere. I clapped him on the shoulder, levered myself up, and left him to convince himself of what he already wanted to believe. The others stood scattered about the room in groups of two and three and four. Whatever they pretended, all attention focused on Brown, and because of him, on me. I reached an open space and considered the observation windows. The Belters looked down on us. On me. Their weirdly large heads, their thin, elongated bodies. Chromosomally, they were as human as I was. What separated each of us—them and me—from the rest of humanity happened at much later stages than the genetic. I caught the eye of a greasy-haired man I recognized as one who had taken Brown to and from his sessions. I lifted my arms in a kind of boast. *I know your secret. I solved your puzzle.*

Brown bonded with the wrong answer. Quintana hadn't so much as been allowed a glimpse of the dataset. All I needed was for the Martian to ask me as well as Brown, and I would be the one they took. The prisoner they exchanged.

If something still nagged at my hindbrain—the guards hadn't come when Quintana stole the terminal, the Martian hadn't been there during Brown's questioning—it had no form, and so I pushed it away. But there was a moment, that hypnagogic shift where the thoughts of the day faded into dream and the guards of rationality fell.

The poisoned thought crept in upon me then, and I went from my half doze to a cold terror in less than a heartbeat.

"It's okay," Alberto said. "It's a nightmare. They're watching him." I looked down at him, my heart beating so violently I thought it might fail. In the shadows, Alberto rolled his eyes and turned his back to me, his head pillowed by his arm. It took me a moment to understand his assumption. He thought I feared Quintana. He was mistaken.

The filthy thought that had slipped into me was this: If the Belters were negotiating a trade of prisoners with Mars then they might well still be enemies. If they were enemies, the Belters would want to give over whatever they had with the least intrinsic value. The Belter guards had questioned Brown twice now, without the Martian present. They might very well be probing not to see whether he had divined the secrets the data held, but to determine that he couldn't.

By trotting out my idiotic egg hypothesis, Brown might prove to our guards that he would be of the least use to their enemies. Or Quintana, by his violence and ham-handed duplicity, might convince them that Mars wouldn't be able to work with such a fragile and volatile ego.

I'd plotted my course assuming that being competent, insightful, and easy to work with would bring reward.

I astonished myself. To have come so far, through so much, and still be so naïve...

"Say I'm developing a veterinary protocol for...I don't know. For horses. Should I start by trying it in pigeons?" Antony Dresden asked. He was a handsome man, and radiated charisma like a fire shedding heat. Protogen's intake facility looked more like a high-end medical clinic than an administrative office. Small, individual rooms with medical bays, autodocs, and a glass wall facing a nurses' station outside able to look in on them all, panopticon style. The company logo and motto—*First. Fastest. Furthest.*—were in green inlay on the walls.

The language in my contract mentioned a properly supervised medical performance regimen, and I assumed this had to do with that, but it still felt odd.

"I'd probably recommend trying it in horses," I said.

"Why?"

"Because that's the animal you're trying to develop a protocol for," I said, my voice turning up at the end of the sentence as if it were a question.

Dresden's smile encouraged me. "The pigeon data wouldn't tell me just as much?"

"No, sir. Pigeons and horses are very different animals. They don't work the same ways."

"I agree. So do you think animal testing is ethical?"

"Of course it is," I said.

"Why?" The sharpness of the word unnerved me. My belly tightened and I found myself plucking at my hands.

"We need to know that drugs and treatments are safe before we start human testing," I said. "The amount of human suffering that animal testing prevents is massive."

"So the ends justify the means?"

"That seems a provocative way to phrase it, but yes."

"Why not for horses?"

I shifted. The wax paper on the examination table crinkled under me. I had the sense that this was a trick, that I was in some kind of danger, but I couldn't imagine any other answer. "I don't understand," I said.

"That's okay," Dresden said. "This is an intake conversation. Purely routine. Do you think a rat is the same as a human being?"

"I think it's often close enough for preliminary data," I said.

"Do you think rats are capable of suffering?"

"I think there is absolutely an ethical obligation to avoid any unnecessary suffering—"

"Not the question. Are they capable of suffering?"

I crossed my arms. "I suppose they are."

"But their suffering doesn't matter as much as ours," Dresden said. "You seem uncomfortable. Did I say something to make you uncomfortable?"

At the nurses' station, a man glanced up, catching my gaze, and then looked away. The autodoc in the wall chimed in a calm tritone. "I don't see the point of the question, sir."

"You will," he said. "Don't worry about it. We're just getting a baseline for some things. Pupil dilation, eye movement, respiration. You're not in any danger. Let me make a suggestion. Just see how you respond to it?"

"All right."

"The idea that animal suffering is less important than human suffering is a religious one. It assumes a special creation, and that we—you and I—are different *in kind* than other animals. We are *morally* separate from rats or horses or chimps, not based on any particular physical difference between us, but just because we claim that we're sacred by our nature and have dominion over them. It's a story we tell that lets us do what we do. Consider the question without that filter, and it looks very different.

"You said there's an ethical obligation to avoid unnecessary suffering. I agree. That's why getting good data is our primary responsibility. Good experimental design, deep datasets, parallel studies whenever they don't interfere. Bad data is just another way of saying needless suffering. And torturing rats to see how humans would respond? It's *terrible* data because rats aren't humans any more than pigeons are horses."

"Wait, so you're...are you saying that skipping animal testing entirely and going straight to human trials is...is *more ethical*?"

"We are the animal we're trying to build a protocol for. It's where we'd get the best data. And better data means less suffering in the long run. More *human* suffering, maybe, but less suffering *overall.* And we wouldn't have to labor under the hypocrisy of understanding evolution and also pretending there's some kind of firewall between us and other mammals. That sounds restful, don't you think?" The autodoc chimed again. Dresden looked at it and smiled. "Great. So tell me only the good things you remember about your mother." At my horrified look, he smiled and waved the comment away. "No, I'm joking. I don't need to know that."

Dresden turned to the glass wall and gestured. A young woman in a lab coat with a stethoscope around her neck like a torc came in and guided me gently back to prone. As she did Dresden leaned against the wall, casual and at ease.

"This is part of our proprietary research regimen," he said. "Performance enhancement strategies. The thing that gives us our edge."

Looking back now, I believe I felt something like fear in that moment. A sense that important decisions were being made that I was only dimly aware of. Dresden's smile and the doctor's nonchalance seemed to belie that feeling, but for a moment I almost demanded that they stop, that they let me leave.

I'm not sure if that memory is true, but fear tends to be the thing I feel and remember most acutely now, so that leads me to believe it is.

Before I could act on my fear, the doctor leaned in close to me. She smelled of lilacs. "You might feel a little odd," she said. "Can you please count backward from twenty?"

I did, the autodoc clicking and shifting on the wall as the numbers grew smaller and smaller. At twelve I stuttered, lost myself. The doctor said something, but I couldn't make sense of her words or find any of my own. Dresden answered her, and the ticking stopped. The doctor smiled at me. She had very kind eyes. Sometime later—a minute, an hour—language came back to me. Dresden was still there.

"The preliminary we're doing here is magnetic. It suppresses some very specific, targeted areas of your brain. Reduces fixity.

Some of our staff finds that it helps them see things they wouldn't have otherwise."

"It feels…"

"I know," he said, tapping his temple. "I did it too."

I sat up. A feeling of almost superhuman clarity washed through me. A calm like the sea after a storm smoothed my muscles. It was better than all the drugs I'd taken at the university—the focus of the nootropics, the euphoria of the sedatives. I remember thinking at the time *Ooh, this could get addictive.* Whatever fear I might have felt no longer seemed important.

"It's nice," I said.

"So tell me," he said. "Is animal testing ethical? Or does it make more sense to skip to human trials?"

I blinked at him, and then I laughed. I remembered the distress I'd felt when he'd asked the same thing just minutes before, but I no longer experienced it. A clarity and calm took that space for its own, and the relief felt joyful, like I'd just heard the punch line to the best joke ever. I couldn't stop giggling. That was the moment I became *research*. I have never regretted it.

Necessity, they say, is the mother of invention, but it is the mother of any number of other things as well: sacrifice and monstrosity and metamorphosis. Necessity is the mother of all necessary things, to coin a tautology. I gave my permission to make the change permanent that afternoon without ever dipping back into my previous cognitive states. I didn't miss or want them. Excitement fizzed in my belly; freedom as I'd never known it sang in my blood. A burden I hadn't known I was carrying vanished, and my mind became sharper, able to reach into places that shame or guilt or neurosis would have kept me from before. I didn't want to be what I had previously been any more than a depressive would long for despair.

And anyway, as Dresden said, we at Protogen weren't concerned with remaking the destiny of rats and pigeons.

I left Earth for the first time when I shipped to Phoebe. All I knew of the planets and dwarf planets and moons that made

the habitable human system—Mars, Ceres, Pallas, Ganymede—
I learned from watching the feeds. The politics of the alliance
between Earth and Mars, the dangers posed by the Outer Planets
Alliance and other Belter resistance groups. The story of man-
kind's torturous reach out into the vast emptiness of the system
formed a complex story that felt as removed from my experience
as the crime dramas and musical comedies that appeared on the
same feeds as the news. Phoebe Station wasn't even among that
number.

An obscure moon of Saturn, it began as a cometary object that
found itself trapped by the gas giant's gravity as it passed by, pre-
sumably from the Kuiper Belt. It stood out from the other moons,
four times as far from the planet as the next nearest. Its retrograde
orbit and the lampblack darkness of its surface gave it a sense of
menace. Phoebe, the ill-omened moon.

The alien weapon.

Tucked within the planetesimal's icy layers, the joint research
group—Protogen and the Martian Naval Scientific Service—had
found tiny reactive particles the size, roughly, of a midrange virus,
but with a design structure and informational depth unlike anything Earth's biosphere had ever imagined. The protomolecule,
we called it, branding it immediately in a territorial move that
irritated the Martian scientists. We ignored their protests as
irrelevant.

Our best guess was that it had been sent from some distance we
couldn't guess at a time when a defined cell membrane stood as
the heights of terrestrial life. The protomolecule appeared to be a
message in a bottle, but one that included its own grammar books
and instruction tutorials, ready to teach whatever aboriginal cells
it found how to become the things it required. We argued whether
something as inert as a spore might be intelligent, at least implic-
itly, but without coming to a conclusion. The first evidence of a
tree of life apart from our own enchanted and confounded us. Me.

The base itself showed its military origins in its bones. The
corridors, hardened to shield us all from the void's vicious

background radiation, were in the colors of the Martian navy. Each hallway bore the identification marks that told installation order, structural specifications, location within the base, and the date on which it needed replacement. The walls sported the same anti-spalling coatings as the ships. The food in the mess tasted of Mars: hot chile peppers, hydroponic fruit, ramen noodles in vacuum-sealed pouches, daily low-g pharmaceuticals. We had no extra space. The rooms I'd had on basic were larger than the cells I lived in there: a rack of bunks four high with a shared head so small that I braced my knees against the opposite wall every time I used the toilet. Of my eighty-five kilograms, I felt a little over three. Exercise took almost a third of the day, the lab a third, eating and sleeping and showering in the tight steel-and-ceramic shower a third.

The Protogen nanoinformatics team there claimed only four seats: Trinh, Quintana, Le, and myself. Mars had a matching number who joined us. The others would join in later, when we shifted to Thoth Station, though by then the Martian contingent would no longer be in play. The rest of the research team wasn't more than fifty, all told. With our counterparts from Mars and the naval support staff, Phoebe Base was a few hundred people on a black snowball so far from Earth that the sun would have been no more than the brightest star if we had ever looked for it.

If I chose a time in my life to return to, a high-water mark, those months on Phoebe would be it. The protomolecule astounded me every day. The depth of information in it, the elegance of its utterly minimal quasi-flagella, the eerie way it self-organized. One day I would convince myself that we were looking at something like a hive of termites, the next a colony of mold spores, the next neurons in a weird distributed brain. I struggled to find analogies, to make what I saw in the scanners fit into what I already knew. Every night, I slipped into my bunk, strapping myself down with wide padded straps to keep from throwing myself out with an unintentional twitch, and thought of what I'd seen and heard, what tricks the protomolecule had performed that day. We were all of us in research quivering with the sense of being just a moment from revelation.

When the news came from Dresden's office of the second- and third-phase plans, I felt like the universe had leaned down and kissed my cheek. The opportunity to see what the protomolecule chose to do with large-scale structures was the best thing I could have imagined. The prospect filled me to the point of spilling over, and then filled me some more.

We killed the Martians in the middle of my work shift. It had all been plotted out, of course. Planned in back channels where our partners wouldn't hear us. When the moment came, I left my desk, moving toward the head, but paused to key in the override sequence. The Martians didn't notice anything. Not right away. And by the time they did, it was too late. We infected them and trapped them in a sealed level 4 containment lab. Watching the initial infection stages work on humans set the course for everything that would come later, but we couldn't afford to let the transformation fully run its course in a location we didn't control. So once we had our early-stage data, we gassed them and then burned the bodies.

When the *Anubis* arrived to retrieve the team and our precious samples, I walked to the dock with an odd wistfulness but also with a sense of anticipation. On the one hand, I'd loved my time there, and I would never again walk through these corridors. On the other, the experiment rising on my personal horizon promised to crack open everything we understood about the universe. I anticipated seeing the fascinating little particles arrange themselves, expressing layers of implicit information like a lotus eternally blooming.

When the ship left, the plume of our fusion drive finished sterilizing the base. The dataset we took from the infected Martians, while interesting and evocative, suffered from a relatively small absolute biomass. Phoebe base was smaller than a city elementary school, and our analyses strongly suggested that the protomolecule went through behavioral phase changes with increased mass as profound as a switch between states of matter.

In the ship burning toward Thoth Station, the team sat in the galley, putting up models to show how the men and women we'd recently shared meals and sometimes bunks with had been infected, disassembled, and repurposed into larger-scale tools to express the protomolecule's same underlying information structure. Trinh maintained that her data scheme outperformed Quintana's and she did so with a ferocity that ended with her stabbing a fork into his thigh and being confined to quarters. There were also rumors of assaults among the other research groups, the natural expression, I thought, of the excitement and stress we had all been under. I was almost certainly projecting, but I couldn't help comparing us to our subject. All of us in research had become exotics, and with time and changing environments, we—like it—would reassemble and reconfigure and become something unpredictable and possibly glorious.

We had almost reached the flip-and-burn at the middle of our transit when it occurred to me that the vast sorrow I had carried with me since the day my mother dropped the glass was gone. I could think of her now without weeping, without wanting to bury myself in activity or anesthetize myself with drugs. I didn't know if it was because I had finished the natural progression of grief, or if the process of becoming *research* had burned the ability to feel that guilt and horror out of me.

Either way, it was a good sign.

I didn't sleep again that night, though occasional slips of dream assaulted me when I slipped into a light doze. In these I searched an empty room for something precious I knew belonged there. In the periods when full wakefulness pinched me, I wrestled with strategies and second guesses. The prohibition against changing a first answer served me well in university, as it had generations of students before. Now and here, the certainty that change offered me my only hope seemed obvious and suspect and obvious again, switching valence sometimes with every breath. The urge to run to Brown and destroy the arguments I'd made before, show him the real truth behind the data on his hand terminal, warred with the fear that doing so condemned me to life and death in the room. I remembered old comedy routines about intellectuals overthinking problems: I know, but he knows I know, but I know he knows I know, and on and on until subtlety iterated itself into the absurd.

Brown suffered none of it. All that morning he walked through the room, smiling and nodding to our fellow prisoners. Quintana sulked in a far corner of the room, sitting by himself and glowering across the emptiness at us. He stayed too far away for me to make out his features, but I imagined him in a permanent scowl. Alberto tried to engage me in conversation, concerned, I think, by my sullenness.

When the doors opened and the guards appeared carrying our morning meals of textured yeast protein in the spun-starch boxes that we ate as dessert, a spike of cold horror split me, and I came to my decision. Brown trotted toward them, beaming. I ran across to him, waving my arms to catch his attention, and coincidentally the guards' and Fong's as well. That my action aided Quintana's plan only became clear later. It wasn't my intention.

"I was wrong," I said plucking Brown's sleeve like a child imploring his father. "It came to me last night. I was wrong."

"No, you weren't," Brown said, his tone impatient. "I went over all of it."

"Not all. There's more. I know more. I can *show* you."

A tall woman with hundreds of tiny black moles dotting her face led the guards. I knew her as I knew all the Belter guards: as a force of nature imposed on us. Still, I'd seen her enough for the familiarity of her face to let me read the curiosity in her. I plucked Brown's sleeve more anxiously, trying to draw him away, out of her earshot. The conviction that the Belters would give the Martian the worst, not the best, of research seemed self-evident now. I feared letting her hear me say something that might suggest I knew the truth. Brown didn't move, so I leaned in closer to him.

"It's not an egg," I hissed. "It's the support frame for a stable nonlocality. Something to pass information. Maybe even mass. It only looks biological because it co-opted biological material."

For the first time, I saw doubt flicker in Brown's eyes. I hoped that truth would be enough to sway his certainty. "Bullshit," he said. I'd done my work too well.

"Do an implicit structure analysis," I said. "Look at the membranes as pathways, not walls. See how the resonances reinforce. The protomolecule *opened* something. It's not an alien, it's a way for the aliens to talk to us. Or to *get* here. Don't trust me. Look at the *data*."

Brown looked deeply into my eyes, as if he could measure my sincerity from my pupils. A voice behind us rose in a weirdly strangled cry, and I turned toward it.

That is the last clear memory I have for a time.

I had never been stabbed before. It wasn't at all what I would have guessed. My recollection is of a sudden impact driving me up and off my feet. Very loud shouting, very far away as multiple voices barked conflicted orders, though to whom I couldn't say. The unmistakable and assaulting noise of gunfire. Lying on the deck, looking up at the empty row of observation windows, convinced that I'd been hit or kicked hard enough to break one of my ribs, then putting my hand to my side and finding it bloody and reaching the conclusion that, no, I'd been shot. Quintana, four meters away, his head and chest mutilated by bullets. I have a vivid image of Fong standing over his body with a pistol in her hand, but I'm almost certain of that memory's falsehood. I can't imagine the Belter guards suffering us to be armed, even if we shared a common enemy.

Other shards of my memory of the attack, though more plausible, have nothing I can attach them to. Alberto with his hands in bloody fists. The Belter guards pressing their bodies over mine, to protect me or subdue me or stanch the bleeding. The smell of gun smoke. The gritty feel of the floor against my cheek and hands. Perhaps normal people take these things and weave them into a coherent narrative, like making sense of a particularly surreal dream. For me, they simply exist. The prospect of a discontinuous cognitive life holds no terror for me, or, I suspect, for anyone in research.

Afterward, I heard the story told: Quintana's battle cry, his rush toward us. According to Navarro, he pushed Brown out of the way in order to reach me. The Belter guards shot Quintana to death, and afterward the mole-speckled woman stood over his body cursing in the incomprehensible argot of her people and shouting into her radio. Brown, they rushed away, out the door and into whatever rooms they used to protect and isolate him from us. The medical team that treated me arrived quickly, but didn't evacuate me. I lay first on the floor and then one of the crash couches. Quintana's improvised knife, a length of steel pried from the base of a couch, inserted just below my ribs on the right, angling up toward my liver. A few more centimeters and my chances of survival would have fallen drastically, but they didn't. I found it difficult to focus on things that might have happened, knowing as I did that they hadn't. But that came later.

At first I slept in a narcotic cloud like a physical memory of university. When I woke, Alberto lay curled beside me, his body feeling oddly cold, though in fact it was my fever that made it seem that way. For two more days, I rested and slept, Belter medics coming both with and between meals to switch out supply packs on the autodoc they had strapped to my arm. When I asked them where Brown was, what was happening with him, they answered with evasions or pretended I hadn't spoken. The only information I gleaned in those terrible days was once, when I demanded to know, weeping, if he'd gone, and one of the medics twitched her head in an almost subliminal *no*. I told myself she'd meant that he was still on the station rather than the equally plausible negatives that she didn't know or she wouldn't answer or I shouldn't ask. Hope survives even stretched to a single molecule's thickness.

The room spoke of nothing but the attack during all the time Brown remained absent, even—perhaps especially—when they spoke of something else. Just before lights-out, Ma and Coombs fought, shouting at each other for the better part of an hour over whether Ma had taken too long a shower. Bhalki, who usually kept to herself, approached Enz, talking tearfully for hours on end, and wound up in the hotel with loud and unpleasant-sounding intercourse. Navarro and Fong put together patrols that, in a population now under three dozen, felt both ridiculous and threatening. All of it was about the attack, though I didn't understand the complexity of it until Alberto held forth on the subject.

"Grief makes people crazy," he said. We were sharing a container of white kibble that looked like malformed rice and tasted like the unholy offspring of a chicken and a mushroom.

"Grief?" I must have sounded outraged at the thought, and in fairness, I was a little. Alberto rolled his eyes and waved the heat of my reply away.

"Not for Quintana. Not for the man, anyway. It's the *idea* of him. We were thirty-five people. Now we're thirty-four. Sure, the one we lost was an asshole. That's not the point. It was the same for Kanter. Every time one of us dies, it will be the same. We are all less in ourselves because we're less together. They aren't mourning him. They're mourning themselves and all the lives they could have had if we weren't stuck in here. Quintana's just a reminder of that."

"For whom the bell tolls? Well, that's a thought. Thirty-six," I said, and Alberto frowned at me. "You said we were thirty-five down to thirty-four, but there were thirty-six of us."

"No one counts Brown anymore," Alberto said. He took a mouthful of kibble using his index and middle fingers as a spoon, then sucked the food between his cheek and his teeth, pulling out the broth before swallowing the greasy remnant. It was the best way to eat Belter kibble. "They would be mourning you, if you'd gone," he said, and turned to me. There were tears in his eyes. "I would be."

I didn't know if he meant gone the way they assumed Brown to be already apart from the group, or dead like Quintana, but I didn't ask for clarification. Perhaps leaving the room by dying out of it or being traded to the Martian were interchangeable for the people left behind. I guessed that was Alberto's point.

We put the rest of the kibble aside and lay together, his weight on my left to keep the wound in my side from hurting. Between my own discomfort, the uncertainty over Brown's status, and—unaccountably to me—Van Ark and Fong weeping loudly through the night, I slept poorly. And in the morning, Brown came back.

When the lights came on and the doors opened, he walked in with the guards. The time he'd spent sequestered had changed him. The others crowded around him, but he extricated himself from them and came to me. The brightness in his eyes reminded me of our best days on Phoebe and Thoth Station. I stood as he approached, and he grabbed my shoulder, pulling me away where the guards and the others couldn't hear us.

"You're *right*," he said. "It took me three days to find the fucker, but you're *right*."

"Did you tell them?"

"I did," he said. "They confirmed. When I get out, I swear to God, I will—"

The shout of the Belter guard interrupted us. The large, gray-haired man led the group today, and he strode toward us with his assault rifle drawn. "Genug la tué! No talking, sabé?"

Brown turned toward the guard. "This is the other nanoinformatics. I need to—" The guard pushed him aside with a gentleness more dismissive than violence.

"You come you," the guard said to me, gesturing with the barrel of his gun. My heart bloomed; my blood turned to light and poured out through the capillaries in my eyes and mouth. I became a thing of fire and brightness. Or that was how it felt.

"Me?" I said, but the guards didn't speak again, only formed a square around me and ushered me away. I looked over my shoulder as the doors closed behind me to see Brown and Alberto standing together watching me in slack-jawed astonishment.

Mourning, I supposed, the lives they could have had. The doors closed on them. Or else on me.

The guards didn't talk to me and I didn't engage with them as they led me through the station corridors. The chamber they delivered me to boasted a laminate bamboo table, four cushioned chairs, and a carafe of what appeared to be iced tea. At the gray man's nod, I took a seat. A few minutes later a woman came in. From the darkness of her hair and the shape of her eyes, I knew her family had been East Asian once. From her body and the slightly enlarged head, I knew they were Belters now.

"Dr. Cortázar," she said. Unlike the others, her accent was as soft as a broadcast feed's talking head. "I'm sorry we haven't spoken before. My name is Michio Pa."

"Pa," I said, assuming from her military bearing that she was not a first-name sort. Her slight smile suggested I'd guessed correctly. The gray man said something in Belter polyglot too fast for me to follow and Pa nodded.

"Am I correct that you've had an opportunity to review the same data as Dr. Brown?"

I folded my hands in my lap, squeezing my knuckles until they hurt. "He let me look at it, yes."

"Were you able to draw any conclusions?"

"I was," I said.

Pa poured out glasses of tea for the both of us and then pulled up a virtual display. I recognized the data structures as I would have a lover's face. "What do you make of it?"

I felt the trembling as if it rose up from the station itself, and not my own body. I drew in a shuddering breath. "Based on the profusion rate data and the internal structures, I believe the latent information within the protomolecule is expressing something similar in function to an egg."

Her smile pitied me. "Walk me through that."

I did, recounting for her all that I'd already said to Brown, back when I'd meant to make him out the fool. I wore my invisible jester's cap well; I capered and grew excited. By the end, I managed to half-convince myself that everything I said was possible. That the gate—I never called it that—might *also* be an egg. The most effective lies, after all, convince the liar.

When I finished, she nodded. "Thank you."

"You can't give them Brown," I said. "He did liaison duty. The real work belonged to us. Send me instead."

"We're considering how to go forward." She rose, and I moved to her, taking her hand.

"If you put me in the room again, he'll kill me."

She paused. "Why do you say that?"

"He's from the research group."

"So are you."

It took me long seconds to put words to something so obvious. "It's what I would do."

After the squalor and close quarters of Phoebe, the spacious, well-lit corridors of Thoth Station felt like distilled luxury. Wide, white halls that curved with a near-organic grace. Team workspaces and individual carrels both. I slept in a private room no larger than a medieval monk's cell, but I shared it with no one. I ate cultured steak as tender and rich as the best that Earth had to offer and drank wine indistinguishable from the real thing. The local climate, free from the temperature inertia carried by Phoebe's eight quadrillion tons of ice, remained balmy and pleasant.

Thoth boasted a research staff larger and better qualified than the universities on Earth or Luna, and the equal of even the best on Mars. The nanoinformatics team grew larger than before, even counting the loss of our Martian naval colleagues. Instead of only Trinh and Le and Quintana, I could now talk through my ideas about the protomolecule with a professional musician turned information engineer named Bouthers and an ancient-looking woman named Althea Ecco, who I didn't realize for almost a week authored half of my textbooks from Tel Aviv. And Lodge, and Kenzi, and Yacobsen, and Al-Farmi, and Brown. We sat up nights in the common rooms, mixing now and then with the other groups: biochemistry, signaling theory, morphology, physical engineering, chemical engineering, logical engineering, and on and on until it seemed like Thoth represented every specialty that cutting-edge research could invent. Like the coffeehouses of Muslim Spain, we created civilization among ourselves. Or at least it felt that way. It might only have been the romance of the times.

Everyone in research had undergone the treatment, which admittedly posed some problems. Singh in computational biology held forth on her theory of the protomolecule as a Guzman-style quantum computer one night over dinner, and when Kibushi used the information without citing her, she snuck into the showers at the gymnasium and beat him to death with a ceramic workbench cap. After that, security kept a closer eye on us all, but they also switched to nonlethal weapons. Singh, while formally reprimanded by Dresden, kept her status on her team. It only tended to confirm what we all already knew: Morality as we had known it no longer applied to us. We had become too important for consequences.

We prepared then and we waited, the tension of every day growing more refined and exquisite. Rumors swirled of the sample going awry and being recovered, of information ops plans put in place to distract any possible regulatory bodies from our work until they also understood the transcendent importance of what we would have accomplished, of our sister research stations on Io and Osiris Station and the smaller projects they were engaged with. None of it mattered. Even the greatest war in human history would have been paltry compared with our work. To bend the protomolecule to our own will, to direct the flow of information now as whatever alien brilliance had done before, opened the concept of humanity beyond anything that even we were capable of imagining. If we managed what we hoped, the sacrifice of Eros Station would unlock literally anything we could imagine.

The prospect of the protomolecule's designers arriving to find humans unprepared for their invasion gave us—or me at any rate—that extra chill of fear. I had no compunctions, no sense of regret. I'd had it burned out of me. But I believe that even if I'd refused the procedure, I would have done precisely as I did. I'm smart enough to know that this is almost certainly not true, but I believe it.

The word came nearly at the end of shift one day: Eros would be online in seventeen hours.

No one slept that night. No one even tried. I ate dinner—chicken fesenjan and jeweled rice—with Trinh and Lodge, the three of us leaning over the tall, slightly wobbly table and talking fast, as if we could will time to pass more quickly. On other nights we would have gone back to our rooms, let ourselves be locked in by security, watched whatever entertainments the heavily censored company feeds provided. That night we went back to the labs and worked a full second shift. We checked all our connection arrays, ran sample sets, prepared. When the data came in, it would be as a broadcast, available everywhere. We only had to listen, and so tracking us through that signal became impossible. The price of this anonymity was high. There would be no rerunning a missed sample, no second chances. The equipment on Eros—both the most important and the most vulnerable—lay beyond our control, so we obsessed over what we could reach.

My station, and the center of my being, had a wall-size screen, a multiple-valence interface, and the most comfortable chair I have ever had. The water tasted of cucumber, citrus, and oxiracetam. The stations for Le, Lodge, and Quintana shared my space, the four of us facing away from each other in a floor plan like the petals of a very simple flower. Eros had a million and a half people in an enclosed environment, seven thousand weather-station-style data collection centers in the public corridors, and Protogen-coded software updates on all the asteroid station's environmental controls, including the air and water recycling systems. Each of us waited for the data to come, hungry for the cells in our databases to begin filling, the patterns we felt certain would be there to emerge.

Every minute lasted two. My sleep-deprived body seemed to vibrate in my chair, as if my blood had found the perfect resonance frequency for the room and would slowly tear it apart. Le sighed and coughed and sighed again until the only things that kept me from attacking her out of raw annoyance were the security guard outside our door and the certainty it would mean missing the beginning of our data stream.

Quintana cheered first, and then Le, and then all of us together, howling with joy that felt sweeter for being so long delayed. The data poured in, filling the cells of our analytic spreadsheets and databases. For those first beautiful hours, I traced the changes on a physical map of Eros Station. The protomolecule activity began at the shelters that we'd converted to incubators, feeding the smart particles with the radiation that seemed to best drive activity. It spread along the transit tunnels, out to the casino levels, the maintenance tunnels, the docks. It eddied through the caves of Eros like a vast breath, the greatest act of transformation in the history of the human race and the tree of life from which it sprang, and I—along with a handful of others—watched it unfold in an awe that approached religious ecstasy.

I want to say that I honored the sacrificed population, that I took a moment in my heart to thank them for the contribution they were all unwittingly making for the future that they left behind. The sort of thing you're trained to say about any lab animals advanced enough to be cute. And maybe I did, but my fascination with the protomolecule and its magic—that isn't too strong a word—overwhelmed any sentimentality I had about our methods.

How long did it take before we understood how badly we'd underestimated the task? In my memory, it is almost instantaneous, but I know that isn't true. Certainly for the first day, two days, three, we must have withheld judgment. So little time afforded us—meaning me—only a very narrow slice of the overall dataset. But too soon, the complexity on Eros outstripped us. The models based on examinations in the lab and the human exposure on Phoebe returned values that seesawed between incomprehensible and trivial. The protomolecule's ability to make use of high-level structures—organs, hands, brains—caught me off guard. The outward aspect of the infection skipped from being explicable in terms of simple cause-and-effect, through the intentional stance, and into a kind of beautiful madness. *What is it doing* to *what does it want* to *what is it doing* again. I kept diving through the dataset, trying one analytical strategy and then another, hoping that somewhere in the numbers and projections I would find it looking back out at me. I didn't sleep. I ate rarely. The others followed suit. Trinh suffered a psychotic break, which proved something of a blessing as it marked the end of her coughing and sighs.

Listening to the voices of Eros—human voices of the subjects preserved even as the flesh had been remade, reconfigured—I came to grips with the truth. Too many simplifying assumptions, too little imagination on our part, and the utter alienness of the protomolecule conspired to overthrow all our best intentions. The behavior of the particles had changed not only in scale but in kind and continued to do so again at increasingly narrow intervals. The sense of watching a countdown grew into a certainty, though to what, I couldn't say.

I should probably have been afraid.

With every new insight in the long, unbroken stretch of consciousness that predates even humanity, a first moment comes. For an hour or a day or a lifetime, something new has come into the world. Recognized or not, it exists in only one mind, secret and special. It is the bone-shaking joy of finding a novel species or a new theory that explains previously troubling data. The sensation can range from something deeper than orgasm to a small, quiet, rapturous voice whispering that everything you'd thought before was wrong.

Someone would have to be brilliant and driven and above all lucky to have even a handful of moments like that in the span of a stellar and celebrated career. I had five or six of them every shift. Each one felt better than love, better than sex, better than drugs.

The few times I slept, I slept through dreams of pattern matching and data analysis and woke to the quivering promise that this time, today, the insight might come that made it all make sense. The line that connected the dots. All the dots. Forever. I lived on the edge of revelation like I could dance in flames and not burn. When the end came, it surprised me.

It found me in my cell, silent in the dark, not awake and not asleep, the bed cradling me in its palm like an acorn. The sharp scent of the air recycler's fresh filters reminded me of rain. The voices I heard—clipped, angry syllables—I ascribed to the combination of listening to Eros for hours on end and the hypnagogic twilight of my mind. When the door opened and the three men from security hauled me out, I could almost have believed it was part of my dream. Seconds later, the alarms shrieked.

I still don't know how the Belters discovered Thoth Station. Some technical failure, some oversight that left the trail that came to us, the inevitable information leakage that comes from working with people. Station security pushed us like cattle, hurrying us down the corridors. I assumed our path ended in evacuation craft. It didn't.

In the labs, they lined us up at our workstations. Fong commanded the group in my room. It was the first time I'd recognized her as anything but another anonymous extension of the lump of biomass and demands that was security. She gestured to our workstations with her nonlethal riot gun. All their weapons were designed for controlling research, not defending the station.

"Purge it," Fong said. "Purge everything."

She might as well have told us to chew our fingers off. Lodge crossed her arms. Quintana spat on the floor. Fear glinted in Fong's eyes, but we defied her. It felt like nobility at the time. Ten minutes later, the Belters broke through. They wore no standard uniform, carried no unified weapons. They shouted and screamed in shattered bits of half a dozen languages. A young man with tattoos on his face led the charge. I watched Fong's eyes as she reached her conclusion and lifted her hands over her head. We did as she did, and the Belters surrounded us, peppering us with questions I couldn't follow and whooping in a violence-drunk delight.

They threw me to the deck and tied my hands behind my back. Two of them carried Le away as she threatened them with extravagant violence. I don't know what happened to her after that. I never saw her again. I lay with my cheek pressed to the floor harder than I thought the low gravity would allow. I watched their boots and listened to the chatter of their voices. At my workstation, an analysis run ended with a chime and waited for attention that would never come.

Less than two meters from me, the new interpretation that might have been the one, that might have cracked open the mystery, waited for my eyes, and I couldn't get to it. In that moment, I understood fully the depth of the abyss before me. I begged to look at the results. I whined, I wept, I cursed. The Belters ignored me.

Hours later, they hauled me to the docks and into a hastily rigged holding cell. A man with a hand terminal and an accent almost too thick to parse demanded my name and identification. When I told him I didn't have a union representative to contact, he asked if I had family. I said no to that too. We burned at something like a third of a g, but without a hand terminal or access to a control panel, I lost track of time quickly. Twice a pair of young men came and beat me, shouting threats to do worse. They stopped only when the larger of the two started weeping and couldn't be consoled.

I recognized the docking maneuvers only by the shifting vectors of the ship. We had arrived at wherever we were going, for however long we were meant to stay there. Guards came, hauled me out, shoved me in a line with others from Thoth. They marched us as prisoners. Or animals. I felt the loss of the experiment like mourning a death, only worse. Because out there, like hell being the absence of God, the experiment was still going on but it had left me behind.

They kept us in an enormous room.

"How could she not know?" Michio Pa asked me. "If she was dropping glasses and things, she had to notice."

"One of the features of the illness is that she wasn't able to be aware of the deficits. It's part of the diagnosis. Awareness is a function of the brain just like vision or motor control or language. It isn't exempt from being broken."

The conference room had a table; soft, indirect lighting; eight chairs built for longer frames than my own; a nonluminous screen displaying Leonardo da Vinci's sketch of a fetus in the womb; two armed guards on either side of the double doors leading to the hall; Michio Pa wearing sharply tailored clothes that mimicked a military uniform without being one; and me. A carafe of fresh water sat in the center of the table, sweating, four squat glasses beside it. Anxiety played little arpeggios on my nerves.

"So the illness made it so she couldn't see what the illness was doing to her?"

"It was harder for me than her, I think," I said. "From outside, I could see what had happened to her. What she'd lost. She caught glimpses now and then, I think, but even those didn't seem to stay with her."

Pa tilted her head. I recognized that she was an attractive woman, though I felt no attraction to her and saw none in her toward me. Something focused her on me, though. If not attraction, fascination maybe. I couldn't imagine why.

"Do you worry about that?"

"No," I said. "They screened me when I was still on basic. I don't have that allele. I won't develop her illness."

"But something else, something that acts the same way..."

"I went through something like it in college. I won't be doing that again," I said and laughed.

Her eyelids fluttered, her mind—I supposed—dancing through a rapid succession of thoughts, each quickly abandoned. She chuffed out a single laugh, then shook her head. I smiled without knowing what I was smiling about. Her hand terminal chimed, and she glanced at it. Her expression cooled.

"I have to see to this," she said. "I'll be right back."

"I'll be right here."

After the guards closed the door behind her, I got up, pacing the room with my hands clasped behind my back. At the Leonardo screen, I stopped and stared. Not at the sketch, but at the reflection of the man looking at it. It had been three days since I'd left the room, and I still struggled to recognize my reflection as my own. I wondered how many people, roughly, went through years without a mirror. Very few, I thought, though I personally knew almost three dozen.

Even with my hair barbered, my scrub-brush beard shaved away, I looked feral. Somewhere during my years in the room, I'd developed jowls. Little sacks of skin puffed under my eyes, a shade darker and bluer than the brown of my cheeks. I had gray hair now, which I'd known intellectually, but seeing it now felt shocking. Quintana's attacks on me had left no marks. Even the knife wound, cared for by the station's medical expert system, would leave no scar. Time had done me immeasurably more damage, as it did with everyone. If I squinted, I could still make out traces of the man I thought of when I pictured myself. But only traces. I wondered how Alberto had been able to bring himself to fuck the tired old man in my reflection. But, I supposed, beggars and choosers.

That I would not return to the room seemed a given now. They had not sent me back there, had given me new clothes, new quarters. Even Brown, during his long interrogations, hadn't been allowed to shave. My naked, white-stubbled chin bore witness to the fact that I'd surpassed him. For the first day, I'd proudly marched out my egg hypothesis for one person, then another, then another, then the first again. Then they gave me a read-only access file that covered the years I had been gone. Two thousand pages, and I read it with the kind of longing and jealousy I imagined of someone following the career of an estranged child. From the uncanny transit of Eros to the surface of Venus to the creation of the ring gate to the discovery and activation of more than a thousand other gates that opened to a thousand empty solar systems, it filled me with wonder and joy and the bone-deep regret that I hadn't been there to see it happen.

I dropped the egg theory and took up my more natural hypothesis of the gate. They thought they'd given me a cheat sheet, a way to pass myself off as better than I was for the Martian. I wasn't concerned with what they thought. If they considered me a fool, it still wouldn't be less than I thought of them. I could only hope that the negotiation between the Belters and Mars went well. My fate was in their hands, as it had been for years now.

The door opened and Michio Pa returned. The Martian was at her side. The same unfortunate skin, the same nut-brown hair. My heart beat with a violence that left me short of breath, and for a long moment I feared that something dire and medical was happening.

"Dr. Cortázar?" the Martian said.

"Yes," I said, rushing toward him too quickly, pushing my hand out before me like the unfounded presumption of intimacy. "Yes, I am. That's me."

The Martian smiled coolly, but he shook my hand. No physical contact had ever been more electric.

"I understand you've made some sense of our ring gates?"

Michio Pa, at his side, nodded as if unconsciously prompting me.

"Not in exhaustive depth," I said. "But I have the broad strokes."

When he replied, it was like a punch in the gut. "Why did you lie to us at first?"

"About?" I asked, trying to buy time.

He smiled, though the expression had no humor. "You had to know that every sound in that holding cell is monitored and recorded."

No. I hadn't known that. Though in hindsight it seemed obvious.

He continued. "You deliberately fed Dr. Brown a false story about your analysis, then at the last minute gave him the correct version. I'd like to understand why."

"I rethought my…" I began, then trailed off when I saw the knowing look in his eye.

"You were gaming him," the Martian said. "Manipulating him to try to secure your position. Incorrectly believing that we would be traded the least valuable prisoner."

The way he said it was not a question, but I found myself nodding anyway.

"The fact that he didn't spot your falsified conclusions in the data," the Martian continued, "is the reason you're here. So, I suppose, your plan failed its way to success."

"Thank you," I replied inanely.

"Be aware that we know exactly what you are, what tactics you favor, and will not tolerate this behavior in the future. The consequences of failing to understand this fact of your future existence would be extreme."

"I understand," I said, and it was the truth. Something in my expression seemed to please him, and he relaxed a little.

"I am developing something of a private task force to examine the data that's coming in from the initial probes that have gone through to the other side of the ring gate. Your experience with the initial discovery puts you in a rare position. I'd like you to join us. It won't be freedom. That was never in the cards. But it won't be here, and it will be work."

"I don't need freedom," I said.

His smile held an echo of sorrow I couldn't parse. I wondered if Alberto would have known what it meant. The Martian clapped my shoulder and a wave of relief lifted me up.

"Come with me, Doctor," he said. "I have some things to show you."

I offered silent thanks to whatever imaginary God was listening and let the Martian lead me to this wide new universe, opening before me.

I did let myself wonder how the room would be without me. Whether Brown would ever understand how I'd outplayed him. Whether Alberto would take another lover. How many years would stretch out before Fong and Navarro gave up hope that I would somehow come back for them all. Questions I did not expect ever to answer, because in the end I didn't actually care.

The Vital Abyss
Author's Note

Oh, so much to talk about with this one.

If there's one real regret in writing The Expanse, it's that we didn't keep the right title for this story. When it was written, it was "The Necessary Abyss." Our editor at the time was adamant that the title wouldn't work, and we needed to change it. We went back and forth and landed on "The Vital Abyss."

We should have stuck to our guns.

Here's the thing. We don't know what a vital abyss is. But a necessary one? That goes back to *Will & Grace*.

You remember *Will & Grace*, right? It was a sitcom with Eric McCormack and Debra Messing. It was also maybe the most widely missed obscure philosophy joke in popular culture. Will and Grace are common first names, but put together like that, they're also one of the central questions of Western philosophy—how much we are self-determined and how much we are controlled by deterministic forces. Agents of our own free will or else predestined cogs whose fates are out of our hands, determined instead by the grace of God. Freedom or necessity. Will or Grace.

Cortázar makes himself a kind of moral zombie in this story. There's a reason that Dresden has the modification made permanent before Cortázar recovers from the temporary version of it. If he had come to, he would have had the capacity to understand what he'd lost. Instead, he becomes someone incapable of moral choice. The way that his mother lost parts of her experience, he loses his ability to judge—and even be interested in—questions of right and wrong. He's beyond good vs. evil and deeply into effective vs. ineffective. It's a very Nietzschean place to be, and so the abyss. And it's the abyss where there can be no moral choice. The Abyss of Grace. The Necessary Abyss.

But the editor didn't like it. So it's Vital. You win some, you lose some.

Paolo Cortázar is named after Paolo Bacigalupi and Julio Cortázar, not because those two writers have much to do with the character but because they're writers whose work we admire. The physical setup of the jail is a reference to *The Enormous Room*, which is an autobiographical novel by E. E. Cummings about his time as a political prisoner in France during the First World War.

And Dresden's thing about biology being an exercise in pretending to be different in kind from animals, while every study proves more and more that we're not, is a large part of why Daniel decided not to keep going as a biologist after he got his bachelor's degree. He's still looking for the hole in that argument.

Strange Dogs

The day after the stick moons appeared, Cara killed a bird.

That wasn't exactly right. There had been stick moons—which her parents called platforms—as long as Cara could remember. At night, they'd glowed with reflected sunlight like burnt orange bones, and in the daytime, they'd been lines of white bent behind the blue. In her books, the moon was always a pale disk or a cookie with a bite taken out, but that was Earth's moon, Luna. Laconia was different.

So it wasn't that they had *appeared* the night before she killed the bird. It was only that they lit up red and blue and gold for the first time ever. Her parents had gotten up from the dinner table and gone out into the yard, staring up into the sky, and she and her little brother, Xan, had followed. Her father stood there slack-jawed, looking up. Her mother had frowned.

The next afternoon, lying in the blue clover by the pond with sunlight warming her skin and making her sleepy, Cara watched the newly glittering stick moons swim through the sky. They were as bright in the daytime sky as stars were against nighttime black. The colors shifted on them, rippling like videos of sea creatures. As if they were a little bit alive. They drifted east to west, high lacy clouds passing underneath them, and Cara at the bottom of the gravity well, looking up into the vastness like it had all been put there for her to appreciate.

The pond was one of her favorite places to be alone. The curve of the forest ran along one side. Thick trees with three or four trunks that rose up into a knot before blooming out in green-black fronds longer than her body and so thickly packed that a few steps under them was like walking into a cave. She could find as much shade from Laconia's bright sun as she wanted, whenever she wanted it. The blue clover beside the water was softer than her bed at home and had a smell like bruised rain when she laid on it. The brook that fed the pond and then flowed back away from it again murmured and burbled in a gentle, random concert with the chirping of the goat-hair frogs. And there were the animals that came there to drink or hunt or lay their eggs. She could lie there for hours, bringing her own lunch and a handheld to read from or draw on or play games on, away from her parents and Xan. Away from the town and the soldiers and Mari Tennanbaum, who was her best friend when they weren't enemies. The township was five thousand people—the biggest city on Laconia—and the pond was Cara's place away from it.

She was halfway through her tenth year, but this was only her third summer. Her mother had explained to her that Laconia moved around its star more slowly than Earth did, and then talked about axial tilt in a way that Cara pretended to understand so they could talk about something else. It didn't matter. Summer was summer and birthdays were birthdays. The two didn't have any more relationship than her nut-bread sandwiches had with her shoes. Not everything had to be connected.

Cara was half asleep when she heard the soft tramp of paws

and the creaking of the underbrush. She thought at first it was just in her imagination, but when she tried to change the sound into music the way she sometimes could when she was dreaming, it didn't respond. She opened eyes she hadn't realized were closed. Bright-blue dots like fireflies fluttered and spun in the air as the first of the doglike things came out of the trees.

Its body was long and low, four legs with joints that were put together just a little wrong—like a drawing by someone who'd only ever had legs described to them. Its jaw seemed too small for its face, and its bulbous brown eyes were set at angles that made it seem apologetic. She'd never seen anything like it before, but that happened fairly often.

"Hey," she said, stretching. "What are you?"

The dog paused.

"It's okay," she said. "I'm friendly. See?" And she waved.

It was hard to be sure with the thing's eyes set the way they were, but she thought it was looking at her. She sat up slowly, trying not to startle it. Nothing on Laconia ate people, but sometimes they could get scared, and her mother always told her that frightened things weren't safe to approach.

The dog looked up, staring at the stick moons for a moment, and then down again at her. She felt a wave of disorientation, like being dizzy but different, and then a twinge of uncertainty. The dog stepped forward, and two more like it came out from the darkness under the trees. Then two more.

On the pond, a sunbird hissed, lifting its leathery wings to make its body look bigger and baring its soft greenish teeth. Its fury-twisted face looked like a cartoon of an old woman, and half a dozen new-hatched babies darted behind her. The first dog turned to look at the momma bird and made three sharp sounds: *ki-ka-ko*. The other four picked up the sound. Momma bird swiveled her head toward each of them, hissing until flecks of saliva foamed at the curves of her mouth. The *ki-ka-ko* cry echoed in a way that didn't match the space around the pond. It made Cara's head ache a little. She levered herself up to her knees, partly out of fear that the dogs might eat sunbirds, and she didn't want to see anything get killed, but mostly because she wanted them to stop making that sound. Her lunch pack and her handheld tumbled to the clover. When she stepped forward, the dogs went quiet and turned their attention toward her, and she had the sense that maybe she was dreaming after all.

She stepped between the dogs and the water's edge. Momma bird hissed again, but it seemed to Cara like the sound came from a great distance. The dogs drifted closer, moving around her like children around a teacher. She knew in a distant way that she should probably be scared. Even if the dogs didn't eat people, they could still attack her for getting between them and their prey. She didn't know why she felt that they wouldn't.

"You can't be here right now," she said.

The lead dog, the one that had come out first, looked past her at the water. Its embarrassed, bulbous eyes shifted back to her.

"Later, maybe," she said. "You can be here later. Right now you have to go. Go on. Shoo."

She pointed at the trees and the darkness underneath them. The dogs went perfectly, eerily still for the space of two long breaths together, then turned and shambled back into the forest on their weirdly built legs.

Cara watched them go with a kind of surprise. It was like shouting at a storm to go away and having the rain stop. Probably the dogs had just decided that dealing with her wasn't worth the trouble. Still, the way it had happened let her feel a little magic. Momma bird was swimming along the side of the pond now, her back to Cara. When the sunbird reached the far edge and turned, she was grunting to herself, the danger of the dogs and the girl equally forgotten. Sunbirds weren't smart—they weren't even particularly nice—but Cara still felt good that she'd kept them from getting eaten.

She tried lying back down on the blue clover, but her lazy half sleep was gone now. She tried closing her eyes, then watching the stick moons and their shimmer of colors, but she could feel in her body that it wasn't coming back. She waited a few minutes to be sure, then sat up with a sigh and gathered up her handheld and her lunch pack. The sun was high overhead, the heat a little bit oppressive now, and it had been a long time since breakfast. She popped open her lunch pack. The sandwich was simple and exactly the way she liked it: two slices of nut bread, each about as thick as her thumb, with a layer of cinnamon and molasses cream cheese between them. Her mother said that honey was better than molasses, but there weren't any bees on Laconia. Cara had only ever seen pictures of them, and based on those, she didn't like honey at all.

She took a bite, chewed, swallowed, took another. The baby sunbirds were jumping out of the water, running on the ground, and then plopping back into the pond, sputtering and angry. Momma bird ignored their little sighs of distress, and before long they stopped trying to get her attention and devoted themselves to swimming and searching for food. Earth birds didn't look much like anything on Laconia, but Cara remembered something about how to treat them. How to share. When Momma bird turned toward her, Cara broke off a tiny bit of nut bread and tossed it out on the water. Momma bird struck at it like it was a threat and swallowed it greedily. Later on, she'd puke up little bits of it to feed her babies. Cara had watched them at the pond for months. She knew how sunbirds worked maybe better than anyone.

So when Momma bird made a noise—a wheeze with a click in the middle of it—Cara knew it was something new. The babies knew too. They gathered around Momma bird, chittering in agitation and slapping the water with their wings. Momma bird didn't seem to notice them. Her head was wobbling on its long, thin neck. Her unfocused eyes seemed fierce and confused.

Cara put down her sandwich, a knot tightening in her chest. Something was wrong. Momma bird spun around in the water, then turned and spun the other way with so much violence that the nearest of her babies overturned.

"Hey," Cara said. "Don't do that. Don't hurt your little ones."

But unlike the dogs, Momma bird didn't even seem to listen to her. She spread her wings, slapped the water twice, and hauled herself up into the air. Cara had the impression of half-closed eyes and a gaping green-toothed mouth, and then Momma bird sped up into the air, paused, and fell. She didn't try to catch herself when she landed—just crashed into the clover.

"Momma bird?" Cara said, stepping closer. Her heart was tripping over itself. "Momma bird? What's the matter?"

The babies were calling out now, one over the other in a wild frenzy. Momma bird lifted her head, trying to find them from their voices, but too disoriented to do more than wave her head around once, twice, and then set it down. Cara reached out, hesitated, then scooped up the bird's warm, soft body. Momma bird hissed once, halfheartedly, and closed her angry black eyes.

Cara ran.

The pathway leading toward home was barely wider than an animal track, but Cara knew it like the hallway outside her room. It only seemed treacherous because she couldn't wipe her tears back, since she needed both her hands to hold Momma bird. She was still three hundred meters from home when the bird shifted in her hands, arched its back, and made a deep coughing sound. After that, it was still. The thick sack-and-earth walls of her house came into sight—red and orange, with the rich-green panels of their solar array on top canted toward the sun—and Cara started shouting for her mother. She wanted to believe there was time. That Momma bird wasn't dead.

She wanted to believe. But she also knew better.

Her house stood out just past the edge of the forest. It had the lumpy snakes-lying-on-top-of-each-other walls that all the first-wave colonial structures had. They curved around the central bulb garden, where they grew food. The windows stood open, screens letting in the air and keeping out the insect analogs. Even the little toolshed, where Dad kept the clippers he used to cut the vinegar weed and the cart to carry the stinking foliage away, had windows in it.

Cara's feet slapped down the stone-paved path, her tears making the house, the sky, the trees blurred and unreal. Xan's voice called out from somewhere nearby, and his friend Santiago answered back. She ignored them. The cool, dry air of the house felt like walking into a different world. Rays of light pressed in from the windows, catching motes of dust. For the first time since the pond, Cara's steps faltered. Her legs burned, and the vast, oceanic sadness and horror stopped up her throat so that when her mother stepped into the room—taller than her father, dark-haired, fixing a necklace of resin and glass around her neck like she was getting ready for a party—all Cara could do was hold up the body of Momma bird. She couldn't even ask for help.

Her mother led her to the kitchen and sat there with her and the dead bird's body while Cara coughed out a version of what had happened between sobs. She knew it was muddled—the bird, the dogs, the babies, the bread—but she just had to get it all out of her and hope that her mother could make sense of it. And then make it make sense to her too.

Xan came in, his eyes wide and scared, and touched her back to comfort her. Her mother smiled him away again. Santiago ghosted into the doorway and out again, curious and trying to seem like he wasn't. Tragedy drew attention.

Eventually, Cara's words ran out and she sat there, feeling empty. Deflated. Defeated. Momma bird's corpse on the table didn't seem to care one way or the other. Death had robbed the bird of her opinions.

"Oh, babygirl," Cara's mother said. "I'm sorry."

"It was me, wasn't it?" Cara said. "I killed her, didn't I?"

"You didn't mean to. It was an accident. That's all."

"But it was in the book," Cara said. "Feeding bread to birds. The lady in the park in the book did that. And they didn't die. They were *fine*."

Her mother took her hand. It was strange, but Cara knew if she'd been just a little younger—Xan's age, even—her mother would have hugged her. But she was getting to be a big girl now, and hugs weren't for big girls. Holding hands was.

"These aren't birds, babygirl. We call them that because they're sort of like birds. But real birds have feathers. And beaks—"

"No bird I've ever seen."

Her mother took a deep breath and smiled through her exhalation. "When life comes up on a planet, evolution forces a bunch of choices. What kinds of proteins it's going to use. How it's going to pass information on from one generation to the next. Life on Earth made those decisions a long time ago, and so everything that comes from Earth has some things in common. The kinds of proteins we use. The ways we get chemical energy out of our foods. The ways our genes work. But other planets made other choices. That's why we can't eat the plants that grow on Laconia. We have to grow them special so they'll be part of our tree of life."

"But the old lady fed bread to the birds," Cara said. Her mother wasn't understanding the problem, and she didn't know how to say it any more clearly. In the books, the old lady had fed bread to the birds, and the birds hadn't died. And Momma bird was dead.

"She was on Earth. Or someplace where Earth's tree of life took over. Laconia doesn't eat the same things we do. And the food that Laconia makes, we can't use."

"That's not true," Cara said. "We drink the water."

Her mother nodded. "Water is very, very simple, though. There aren't choices for living systems to make with water because it's more like a mineral or—"

"Dot!" Her father's voice was like a bark. "We have to go!"

"I'm in the kitchen," her mother said. Footsteps. Cara's father loomed into the doorway, his jaw set, his mouth tight. He'd combed his hair and put on his best shirt. He shifted his gaze from Cara to her mother to Momma bird with an expression that said, *What the hell is this?*

"Cara accidentally poisoned one of the sunbirds," her mother told him, as though he'd actually asked the question aloud.

"Shit," her father said, then grimaced at his own language. "I'm sorry to hear that, kid. That's hard. But, Dot. We have to gather up the kids and get out of here."

Cara scowled. "Where are you going?"

"The soldiers are hosting a party," her mother said. "It's a celebration because the platforms came on." She didn't smile.

"We need to be there," her father said, more to her mother than to Cara. "If they don't see us, they'll wonder why we didn't come."

Cara's mother pointed to her necklace. *I'm getting ready.* Her father shifted his weight from one foot to the other, then back. Cara felt the weight of his anxiety like a hand on her shoulder.

"Do I have to go?"

"No, kid," her father said. "If you want to stay here and hold down the fort, that's fine. It's me and your mom."

"And Xan," her mother said. "Unless you want to be responsible for keeping him out of trouble."

Cara knew that was supposed to be a joke, so she chuckled at it. Not that it felt funny. Her mother squeezed her fingers and then let her go. "I am sorry about the sunbird, babygirl."

"It's okay," Cara said.

"We'll be back before dinner," her father said, then retreated back into the depths of the house. A few breaths later, Cara heard him yelling at Xan and Santiago. The focus of the family spotlight had moved past her. Momma bird was over. She couldn't put her thumb on why that bothered her.

The town was half an hour away, down past a dozen other houses like hers. The older houses all came from the first wave— scientists and researchers like her parents who'd come to Laconia just after the gates opened. The town itself, though, came later, with the soldiers. Even Cara could remember when construction waldoes started laying down the foundations of the barracks and the town square, the military housing and the fusion plant. Most of the soldiers still lived in orbit, but every month, the town grew a little—another building, another street. Xan's friend Santiago was seven years old. He was the child of soldiers, and had their boldness. He often came all the way out to her house by himself so he could play. Someday, her father said, the town would grow out around all their houses. The pond and the forest would be taken down, paved over, rebuilt. The way he said it, it didn't sound like a good thing or a bad one. Just a change, like winter moving into spring.

For now, though, her house was her house and the town was the town, and she could sit at her kitchen table while the others got ready to go someplace else. Momma bird didn't move. The more Cara looked at the bird, the less real it seemed. How could something that clearly dead ever have swum or flown or fed its babies? It was like expecting a rock to sing. The babies would be wondering what had happened by now. Calling for their mother. She wondered if they'd know to go back up to the nest with no one there to show them when.

"Mom?" Cara said as her father herded Xan and Santiago back out the door again. "I need to use the sampling drone."

There was a line that appeared between her mother's brows when she got annoyed, even when she was smiling at the same time. "Babygirl, you know I can't go out right now. Your father and I—"

"I can do it. I just need to help take care of Momma bird's babies. Just for a few days, until they're used to her being gone. I messed things up. I need to fix them."

The line erased itself, her mother's gaze softening. For a moment, Cara thought she was going to say yes.

"No, baby. I'm sorry. The sampling drone's delicate. And if something goes wrong, we can't get a new one."

"But—" Cara gestured to Momma bird.

"When I get back, I'll take it out with you if you still want to," her mother said, even though that probably wasn't true. By the time they got back from the town, Xan would be tired and hyperactive and her parents would just be tired. All anyone would want to do was sleep. A few baby sunbirds didn't really matter much in the big scheme of things.

Santiago's voice came wafting in from outside with a high near-whining note of young, masculine impatience in it. Her mother shifted her weight toward the doorway.

"Okay, Mom," Cara said.

"Thank you, babygirl," her mother said, then walked out. Their voices came, but not distinctly enough for her to make out the words. Xan shouted, Santiago laughed, but from farther away. Another minute, and they were gone. Cara sat alone in the silence of the house.

She walked through the rooms, her hands stuffed deep in her pockets, her scowl so hard it ached a little. She kept trying to find what was wrong. Everything was in place, except that something wasn't. The walls had the same smudges by the doors where their hands had left marks over the months and years. The white flakes at the corners showed where the laminate that held the house in place was getting old. The house had only been designed to last five years, and they'd been in it for eight so far. Her room, with its raised futon, across the hall from Xan's, with his. Her window looking out over the dirt road her family had just walked down. The anger sat under her rib cage, just at her belly, and she couldn't make it go away. It made everything about the house seem crappy and small.

She threw herself onto her futon, staring up at the ceiling and wondering if she was going to cry. But she didn't. She just lay there for a while, feeling bad. And when that got boring, she rolled over and grabbed her books. They were on a thin foil tablet keyed to her. Her parents had loaded it with poems and games and math practice and stories. If they'd been able to get in touch with the networks back on the far side of the gates, they could have updated it. But with the soldiers, that wasn't possible. All the content in it was aimed at a girl younger than Xan, but it was what she had, so she loved it. Or usually she did.

She opened the stories, looking through them for one particular image like she was scratching at a wound. It took a few minutes to find it, but she did. A picture book called *Ashby Allen*

Akerman in Paris, about a little girl back on Earth. The image was in watercolors, gray and blue with little bits of gold at the street-lights. Ashby and her monkey friend, TanTan, were dancing in a park with the high, twisting, beautiful shape of the Daniau Tower behind them. But the thing Cara was looking for was on the side. An old woman, sitting on a bench, throwing bits of bread at birds that her mother called pigeons. That was where the rage came from. An old woman being kind to a bird and nobody was dying. No one was hurt. And it wasn't even exactly a lie, because apparently she could do that on Earth. In Paris. Where she'd never been and didn't have any reason to think she'd ever go. But if all the things in her books were about other places with other rules, then none of them could ever really be about her. It was like going to school one morning and finding out that math worked differently for you, so even if you got the same answer as everyone else, yours was wrong.

So no, it wasn't a lie. It went deeper than that.

She made herself a bowl of bean-and-onion soup, sitting at the counter by herself as she ate. She'd half expected that, as upset as she was, she wouldn't be able to keep the food down. Instead, eating seemed to steady her. The quiet of the house was almost pleasant. Something about blood sugar, probably. That was what her father would have said. Momma bird's skin had started shining, like it was growing a layer of oil or wax. It could stay there on the counter. She thought about taking it back in case the babies would understand that they shouldn't wait. That they were on their own. She hoped they could get back up to the nest. There were things that would eat baby sunbirds if they couldn't get someplace safe.

"Fuck," Cara said to the empty house, then hesitated, shocked by her own daring. Her mother didn't allow profanity, not even her father's, but they weren't here right now. So like she was running a test to see if the rules were still the rules, she said it again. "Fuck."

Nothing happened, because of course no one was watching her. And since no one was watching...

The sampling drone was in a ceramic case next to her mother's futon. The latches were starting to rust at the edges, but they still worked. Just a little scraping feeling when she pulled them open. The drone itself was a complex of vortex thrusters as wide as her thumb connected by a flexible network of articulated sticks able to reconfigure itself into dozens of different shapes. Two dozen attachable sampling waldoes built for everything from cutting stone to drawing blood stood in ranks in the case like soldiers, but Cara only cared about the three grasping ones. And of them, really just the two with pliable silicone grips. She put the waldoes in her pocket, hefted the drone on her hip as if she was carrying a baby, and shoved the case closed again before she headed out to the shed.

Momma bird and the drone fit into her father's cart with plenty of room to spare. She thought about it, then grabbed a little hand spade too. She'd use the drone to put the babies safe in their nest, and then give Momma bird a proper burial. It wasn't enough, but she could do it, so she would.

The sun was starting its long slide down into night. The low mist that came from the east smelled as bright as mint, and the shadows of the trees all had a greenish tint against the reddening light. The cart had one wheel that stuck sometimes, skidding along behind her like a stutter until it broke loose again. Cara put her head down, her mouth set, and marched back toward the pond. The tightness between her shoulder blades felt like resolve.

The forest was mostly hers. Xan played there some, but he liked the other kids more than she did, so he spent more time in town. Her mother and father stayed near the house or working on the community greenhouse—which wasn't really a house or green—to keep the food supplies coming. She knew what the sounds of the forest were, even if she couldn't always figure out what made them. She knew the drape of a hook vine from a straight one, the call of a red clicker from a green one. Most of the things that lived there didn't have names. Laconia was a whole world, and humans had only been on it for about eight years. Even if she gave names to everything she saw every day for the whole rest of her life, most of the species there would stay nameless. It didn't bother her. They just were what they were. Common things got names so that she and her schoolmates and the grown-ups could talk about them. Sunbirds, rope trees, tooth worms, glass snakes, grunchers. Other things, no one talked about, so they didn't need names, and even if she named them, she'd probably just forget.

That wasn't strange, though. All names were like that. A shorthand so people could talk about things. Laconia was only Laconia because they called it that. Before they'd come, it had been nameless. Or if not, the things that had named it were all dead now, so it didn't matter.

She reached the pond, a few bright-gold streaks in the sky where the last of the sun still lit the high clouds. The baby sunbirds were still in the water, peeping in distress at her arrival. The water was dark already, like it had pulled the shadows under the trees into it. The night-feeding animals would come out soon— scratchers and hangman monkeys and glass snakes. She slaved the drone to her handheld. The control panel was more complicated than she was used to, with half a dozen control modes listed down the side that she didn't understand. She was pretty certain she could do everything she needed with only the basic setup. She just needed to get the babies up out of the water and safe into their nest. And maybe take some food up to them. Do the things Momma bird had done. Then she could bury Momma bird, and things would be…not right. But the least wrong she could make them. She took the waldoes out of her pocket and compared them to the babies, squinting in the deepening gloom to see which of them looked like they'd be able to hold on to the little bodies but not hurt them.

"I'm sorry," she said to the pale, round-mouthed birds as she fit the smallest waldo onto the drone. "I'm new at this."

One of the babies caught sight of Momma bird's body in the cart and tried to haul itself out of the water to waddle toward her.

It was as good a place to start as any. Cara sat cross-legged on the clover and started the drone. It whirred as it rose in the air.

The first baby shrieked, hissed, and ran. Cara smiled and shook her head. "It's okay, little one.. It's only me," she cooed. "Everything's going to be all right."

Only it wasn't.

The babies scattered to the edges of the pond and bit at the drone when it came near. When she was able to get a grip on one, it wriggled out a meter and a half above the ground and fell back into the water. Cara didn't want to hurt them, but the light was fading faster now, and she had to get them up to the nest and then bury Momma and still get back home before her parents and Xan. The time pressure made everything harder. She didn't realize she was clenching her teeth until her jaw already hurt. After nearly an hour she'd only gotten three safely back to the nest. Momma bird lay in the cart, sightless eyes reproachful. Cara's hands ached, and the drone's batteries were half drained.

"Come on," she said as one of the last two babies skittered away from the waldo and ran into the brush at the edge of the pond. "Stop it. Just…"

She reached the soft rubber claw down, and the little sunbird struck at it, biting and tearing with its soft teeth. It wrenched its head around and darted back off across the water, leaving little ripples in the dark water, and then stopping to bob on the surface and chew at its wings as if nothing was wrong. Cara brought the drone in to land beside her while she thought. The last two babies were the biggest. Faster than their siblings, and they weren't getting tired the same way. Maybe they were big enough to avoid predators without her. Maybe they didn't need to be in the nest.

One of the babies swam near her, chirped, and shook its fleshy, pale wings. Without the whirring of the drone to run from, it seemed placid, in a disgruntled kind of way. Its black eyes shifted around at the night, taking in the forest and the pond, the cart and Cara with the same disinterest. It was so close.

Cara shifted forward slowly so as not to startle it. The little sunbird huffed to itself, ducked its head under water, and Cara lunged. Cold water soaked into her sleeves and sprayed her face, but the little ball of squirming flesh was locked in her hands, hissing and biting. She stood up, grinning.

"There you are, little one," she said. "Oh, you're a pain, but I've got you safe now."

Except she wasn't quite sure what made sense to do next. She needed both hands to drive the drone and the waldo, but if she put the sunbird down, it would just run off again. The nest was low enough in the tree, she might be able to climb up one handed and reach it in. She stepped backward, looking through the foliage for a pathway that would work.

The crunch under her heel was confusing for a moment, and then horrifying. She yelped, dropped the baby sunbird, and danced back. The drone glittered on the clover, two of the vortex thrusters caved in by her weight. She dropped to her knees and reached out, fingers trembling in the air, caught between needing to put it all back together and being afraid to touch it. The drone was broken. Her mother's drone that they couldn't replace because it came from Earth and now nothing came from Earth. The sense of having done something terrible that she couldn't take back washed over her—the broken body of Momma bird and the drone building on each other.

It was too much. She'd hide the drone, just for now. The case for it was still back at the house, and her mother might not need it again for weeks. Months. If Cara kept it here, where she could work on it. If she could keep it safe until there was light, then maybe it would be all right. She lifted up the drone, felt the limp ceramic clicking against itself, the sharp edges where before there had been smooth round cylinders, and knew that there were shards of it still in the clover. With the instinct of a thief, she carried it away from the edge of the pond. She shoved it under a little bush and dragged dead tree fronds over it, hardly aware that she was sobbing while she did it. It would be okay. Somehow, it would be okay.

It wouldn't.

When she turned back around, the dogs were there.

She hadn't heard them shamble out of the darkness, and they stood there as still as stones. Their five faces looked like an apology for intruding.

"What?" Cara shouted, waving at them with one sopping arm. "What is it?"

The dog in front—the same lead dog from when they'd been there before—squatted down, its muzzle toward her. Its legs seemed to have too many joints in them, folding together primly. She stepped toward the dogs, wanting to hit them or shout at them or something. Anything that would distract her from her misery. She grabbed the shovel up from the cart, holding it like a weapon, but the dogs didn't react. They only seemed embarrassed for her. She stood for three long, shaking breaths, wet and cold and raw as a fresh-pulled scab, then sat down on the cart next to Momma bird's body, hung her head, and wept. The corpse shifted when the cart rocked, its skin glistening with whatever that death wax was.

"I didn't mean to break anything," she said. "I didn't want to break anything. It all just…broke, and I, and I, and I…"

The strange noise began again. *Ki-ka-ko, ki-ka-ko*, but instead of being disorienting, it seemed comforting now. Cara pushed the blade of the shovel into the soft dirt beside the cart and rested her arms on her knees. The dogs came closer. She thought for a moment they were going to console her. She didn't understand what they were really doing until one of them reached its wide muzzle into the cart and took Momma bird's body in its mouth.

"No! Hey! You can't have that! That's not food!" She grabbed at Momma bird's stiff, dead feet, but the dog was already trotting away, the others following it into the dark forest and the mist. "Wait!" Cara shouted, but the *ki-ka-ko, ki-ka-ko* sound faded and then, like flipping a toggle, went silent. Cara stood without remembering when she'd gotten to her feet. The sunset was over, full night fallen and stars scattered across the sky above her. The two baby sunbirds grunted in the pond, little noises of animal distress. Her wrists were cold where her sleeves still dripped. She sank to the ground, lying back on the clover, too wrung out to cry. The sounds of the forest seemed to grow slowly louder around her. A soft knocking call off to her left, answered by two more behind her. A hush of wings. The angry harrumph of the sunbirds that she was still going to have to catch somehow, put into their nest somehow. Feed somehow. Everything was terrible, and she couldn't even stop yet. That made everything worse.

High above, the stick moons wavered and shone, lights rippling along their sides while they did whatever the hell it was they did.

Drunk on her own despair, Cara didn't make the connection between the moons and the dogs. Not until much later, when her brother, Xan, was already dead.

Laconia was only one of thirteen hundred and some new worlds. Her parents, like all the others in the first wave, had been intended as a survey force. Cara's mother had come as a materials engineer, her father as a geologist. She'd come as a baby.

She'd seen pictures on her mother's handheld of herself in the tight-seal diapers, floating in the family cabin of the *Sagan*. The ship was still in orbit—a pale, fast-moving dot when it caught the sun just right—but she didn't remember it at all. Xan had been born a year after they'd all made landfall, and Cara didn't remember that either. Her earliest memory was of sitting in a chair at home, drawing in an art program on her handheld while her mother sang in the next room.

Her second earliest memory was of the soldiers coming.

Her parents didn't talk about that, so Cara had built the story from bits and pieces of overheard conversation. Something had happened on the other side of the gates. The Earth had blown up, maybe. Or Mars had. Maybe Venus, though she didn't think anyone lived there. Whatever happened meant that the scientific expedition that had only been intended to stay for five years was now permanent. The soldiers had come to be the government. They had ships in orbit and the beginnings of cities already being constructed on the planet's surface. They'd made the town. They'd made the rules for how the town worked. They had a plan.

"You've probably noticed," Instructor Hannu, her teacher, said, "that the orbital platforms have been activated."

The schoolroom was the old cafeteria from the first landing. Ten meters by eight, with a vaulted ceiling and reinforcements that let it double as a storm shelter, or would have if there were ever any storms bad enough to shelter from. The inner layer of environmental sealant had started to whiten and flake with age, but the early fears about quarantining themselves from Laconia's ecosphere had gone by the wayside, so no one was in a hurry to repair it. There were no windows, the light entirely from ceramic fixtures set into the walls.

"We've been asked to keep an eye out for anything that changes down here," he went on, "and report it back to the military."

Which, Cara thought, was stupid. Everything changed on Laconia all the time. Telling the soldiers whenever a new plant showed up would be a full-time job. *Was* a full-time job. Was what all of their parents did, or were supposed to do, anyway. She wondered if the windowless room was like being on a spaceship. Months or years without ever once going outside or hearing the rain tapping into puddles or being able to get away from Xan and her parents. Never being alone. Never feeling the sunlight on her face. Nothing changing. Nothing new. It sounded awful.

And then circle meeting was over, and the kids scattered around the room to find their tasks for the morning work period. Cara helped Jason Lu with his phonetic-sounds lesson, because she was older and had already mastered it. Then she spent some time on complex multiplication. And then it was recess, and they all piled out to the meadow and the sunlight. Xan and two of the other younger boys ran across the road to skip rocks across the water-treatment reservoir even though they weren't supposed to. Since his best friend, Santiago, went to school in the military's program,

Xan had to make do with first-wave children for playmates. So did Cara, but it wasn't as much of a burden for her. She didn't have any friends among the soldiers anyway.

That would change when they set up the lower university and everyone went to the same school, first wave and soldiers both. But that wouldn't be for another two years. There was plenty of time for things to happen between now and then.

Mari Tennanbaum and Teresa Ekandjo came and sat with her, and before long, they'd arranged a zombie-tag game with the other older children. The call for second work period seemed to come too soon, but that was the way time worked. Too fast when you weren't paying attention, and then slow as mud when you watched it. Xan wanted her to teach him phonetic sounds, more because she'd helped Jason with it than because he cared about the lesson, but she did it anyway. When she was done, she did some research of her own.

The classroom had access to the observational data that the survey team had collected since they'd arrived on Laconia. Sunbirds were a common enough species that there might be something there—what they ate, how they matured, when they stopped needing to be cared for—that would help her. Because as soon as school was over, Xan headed out to play with Santiago in the town's center. She was free to get her bicycle, the one her father had printed for her at the beginning of summer, and start back to the pond and the babies.

The buildings in the town were of two different types. The old ones, the ones like her house, lumpy and round, built from the soil of Laconia and constrained by printed polymer sheaths, marked the original township. The other kind, solidly efficient metal and formed concrete, came later with the soldiers. The roads were new too, and still being built. She and all the other kids loved riding on the smooth, hard surface, feeling the bumps and uncertainty of the land vanish into a steady low hum that traveled up from the wheels through the handlebars and into her bones. They weren't supposed to ride on the roads because the soldiers sometimes had transports and cars come through, but everyone did it anyway.

The sunlight pressed down, warm against her skin. The air had the soft, musty smell it got when rain was coming, the smell her mother called "moldy coffee grounds." A swarm of smoke gnats rose up, swirling into the sky above her in their weird angular patterns, like writing in an alphabet that no one knew. She almost stopped to watch. The road ended at a barracks and construction yard, soldiers in their crisp blue uniforms watching her as she passed. When she waved, one of them waved back. And then she was on the rough trail again and had to keep both hands on the bars.

The effort of riding and the warmth of the afternoon brought her to a kind of trance, comfortable and mindless. In the moment, her body and the world felt like they were all the same thing. As she got near home, she tried to bring her focus back. There hadn't been a lot of study done on sunbird life cycles in particular, but she'd found some notes from one of the early surveys. They said sunbirds ate a lot of things, but they seemed to like the little gray encrustations on water roots the best. She thought that meant Momma bird would have been diving deep into the pond to crack the little gray things free, and then the babies would gobble them as they came up. So she had to find a way to do the same thing. For a few more weeks at least. Until the babies were old enough to leave and make their own nests.

At home, the doors were open, letting the cool air into the house. She pulled the bicycle up beside the door. Her parents' voices came from inside, raised the way they did when they were having a conversation from different rooms. Her mother's words sounded jagged and stretched, like a wire on the edge of breaking. Cara paused to eavesdrop.

"*We're* bearing the risks. As long as we're here, anything they do can affect us. They don't know what they could wake up."

"I know," her father said. "Look, I'm not saying you're wrong. But we're not in a position to say what those risks are. And… what are the options?"

She knew the rhythm of her parents, how they talked when they knew she and Xan were listening, and how it changed when they thought they were alone. This was alone-grown-up talk.

"I'm not arguing for that," her mother said, and Cara wondered what "that" was. "But look at Ilus."

"Ilus was uncontrolled, though. Admiral Duarte seems pretty certain they can at least influence how it behaves here."

"How did they even get a live sample?" Her mother's voice had gone peevish and frustrated. "Why would you *want* that?"

"You know this better than I do, honey. The protomolecule was a bridge builder, but it also has an interface aspect. And being able to *talk* to other artifacts is..." His words faded as, somewhere inside, he walked back to her mother.

Cara looked at the shed. She was pretty sure there was a tree-core sampler in there she could use to scrape the roots, but it was heavy. It probably made more sense to just roll her sleeves up and use her fingers. Plus which, she didn't want to tear the roots.

She walked out toward the pond, thinking about her school-work. The phonetics lesson. Part of the background had been about how babies learn the phonemes by listening to their parents even before there are any words involved. The way different places use sound—the difference between a particular diphthong on Ceres and the same one in the North American Shared Interest Zone or Korea or on Titan or Medina Station—was something babies mastered even before they knew that they knew it.

She'd read something once about a man back on Earth who'd tried to figure out how to speak with octopi by raising his baby children with octopi, hoping that the human children would grow up bilingual in octopus and English. It had sounded crazy at the time, but who knew? The way the phoneme thing worked, maybe it made sense after all. Only she was pretty sure no one spoke octopus, so it probably hadn't ended well...

She walked down the path, her steps following the little scrapes that the cart's wheels had made. The pond water was going to be cold. She could already imagine how it was going to feel pushing her arm down into it. She wondered if the babies would still be in the nest. They might be old enough to get themselves down and into the water, and she couldn't decide if that would be a good thing or a bad one.

The smell of coming weather was getting thicker, but the only clouds were light, scudding veils over the sun, not much more than a lighter shade of blue. The breeze was hardly enough to stir the fronds of the trees; they made light tapping sounds when they touched, like dry raindrops. She wondered if anyone had ever studied the little gray things on the water roots to see what they were. Probably they hadn't. Laconia had too many things on it, and there were only so many people there. It would be lifetimes before everything on the planet got discovered and understood. If that ever even happened. She'd had a history-of-science lesson the year before that traced how long it had taken people back on Earth to understand the ecosphere there, and there had been billions of people on Earth for thousands of years. Laconia had a few thousand people for less than a decade.

At the pond, the babies were on the water, splashing pale leathery wings and piping to each other. That was good. They were independent enough to look after themselves that much anyway. With the drone broken, she'd still have to carry them up to the nest. She didn't like thinking about the drone, though.

"Okay, little ones," she said. "Let's see if I can get you some food, okay?"

She knelt at the water's edge, the wet of the mud seeping through the knees of her pants. Deep in the water, she could just make out the pale roots. They looked deeper in than she'd remembered. She was going to wind up soaking her shirt, but she started rolling up her sleeves anyway.

Momma bird hissed.

Cara fell back, scrambling on feet and elbows, as Momma bird swam out of the scrub at the pond's edge. The bird bared her greenish teeth. The tiny wrinkled face deformed in rage as she rushed forward, wings spread. The babies on the pond's surface gathered behind her, clicking in distress. Cara stared, and Momma bird coughed, spat, and turned away. For a moment, Cara tried to make this into some other bird that had happened upon the orphans and taken over the care of them.

But things were wrong. The bird's skin had the same waxy, dead look it had gotten on her counter. The black eyes didn't quite focus the way a normal bird would. There were sunbirds all across the town. Cara had seen dozens, and none of them had the awkward movements this one did. None of them had the weird stillness between its movements or the hesitation like every muscle had to be reminded how to work. Cara pulled herself up the bank, dragging her heels across the blue clover. Momma bird ignored her, paddled to the center of the pond—paused, still as a statue—and dove down. The babies circled, excited, until she bobbed back up. All their little mouths struck at the water, spat out whatever they didn't filter out as food, and then struck again.

Cara's throat felt thick. Her breath came in snatches and gasps, like someone had turned off the planet's air supply, and her heart felt like something that had blundered into her rib cage by accident and was frantic for a way back out.

"Really?" she asked.

Nothing answered. She pulled her legs up under her, not realizing until she'd done it that she was taking what her teacher called prayer position. She tried to be still, as if moving might pop the moment like a soap bubble. Momma bird dove again, reemerged. The babies fed, as calm and pleased as if nothing had ever gone wrong. Momma bird went motionless, then moved again.

Cara's shock began to fade, her heart to resume its usual beat, and a slow, wide grin pulled at her lips. She wrapped her arms around herself in a hug and watched silently as the mother who had been dead now protected and fed and stayed with her children again. Some deep, animal relief turned her bones to water and left her empty of everything but gratitude and wonder.

Something shifted in the darkness under the trees. The dogs

stepped into the light, walking toward her with slow, careful steps. The bulbous eyes apologetic.

"Was this you?" Cara breathed. "Did you do this?"

The dogs didn't answer. They only folded their complex legs and rested for a moment, looking toward Cara. She leaned over, stretched out a hand, and pet the closest one on the top of its head, where the ears would have been if it had been the kind of dog they had on Earth. Its skin was hot to the touch, soft with hard underneath, like velvet laid over steel. It made a gentle humming sound, and then all of them rose up together and turned back toward the trees. Cara stood up and walked after them, not sure what she wanted except that there was a sudden urgency in her heart. They couldn't leave. Not yet.

"Wait," she said. And the dogs stopped. They waited. "Can you...can you help me?"

They turned toward her again, their movements eerily synchronized. In the distance, something trilled and buzzed and trilled again.

"You fixed Momma bird," she said, nodding toward the pond. "Can you fix other things too?"

The dogs didn't move, but they didn't turn away either. Cara held up a finger in a don't-go-away gesture, and moved off to the bushes. The sampling drone was just where she'd left it. Something small had scattered the shattered bits a little, but they were all still there, as far as she could tell. She lifted up the broken machine, its limp, deactivated limbs clacking against each other. The shards she plucked up into her palm.

The dogs watched, motionless. Their constant embarrassed expression now seemed to offer some sympathy, as if feeling her shame at having broken the drone. One of the dogs came forward, and she thought it was the lead from before, though she couldn't be sure. She knelt and held out the drone. She expected the eerie *ki-ka-ko* noise again, but the dog only opened its mouth a little. What she'd taken for teeth, she saw, were really just little nubs, like the gripping surface on a wheel made for off-road travel. It had no tongue. There was no throat at the back of its mouth. It made her think of the dinosaur puppet Xan used to love. It leaned forward, taking the drone in its jaws. The little machine hung limp.

A second dog stepped forward, tapping Cara's hand with one wide paw. Cara opened her shard-filled hand. The dog leaned forward, wrapping its mouth around her palm. Something in the touch tingled like a mild electrical shock or the first contact of a caustic chemical. The dog's mouth rippled against her skin, sweeping the shards away. She kept her hand flat until all the bits and pieces were gone and the dog leaned back. Her hand was clean apart from a brief scent of disinfectant, gone almost before she noticed it.

"Thank you," she said as the dog stepped carefully into the darkness under the trees. The one with the drone in its grip turned back to look at her, as if it was embarrassed by her gratitude but felt obligated to acknowledge it. Then they were gone. She listened to the receding footsteps. They went silent more quickly than she'd expected.

She sat quietly, arms wrapped around her legs, and watched the weird miracle of the dead-but-not-dead sunbird until she felt like she'd given the moment all of the honor and respect it deserved.

Like someone rising from a pew, she stood, peace in her heart, and headed back home. As she walked, she imagined telling her parents about the dogs, about Momma bird. But that would mean telling them about the drone too. After it was fixed, she'd tell them. And anyway, it was still too sweet having it just for herself.

"I don't know," her mother said. "I don't feel comfortable with it."

Xan's eyes got large. His mouth gaped like she'd just said the worst, most unexpected thing he'd ever heard. "*Mom*!"

It was Sunday, and the walk into town for church was warm, the air thick and sticky. A soft midnight rain had left the track muddy and slick, so Cara kept to the edge where moss and clover made a kind of carpet. The tiny green-black leaves made wet sounds under her feet, but didn't soak her shoes.

"You have responsibilities at home," her mother said, and Xan lifted his hands in exasperation and disbelief, like he was a half-sized copy of their father. Cara had seen the same gesture a thousand times.

"I already told Santiago I'd help him," Xan said. "He's *expecting* me."

"Have you finished all your chores?"

"Yes," Xan said. Cara knew it wasn't true. Her mother did too. That was what made the conversation so interesting.

"Fine," she said. "But be home before dark."

Xan nodded. More to himself, Cara thought, than to their mother. A little victory of persistence over truth. After services, Xan could go off and play with his friends instead of being home the way he was supposed to. Probably she should have been angry at how unfair it was that her brother got to bend the rules and she didn't, but she liked it better when the house and the forest were hers. Maybe her parents did too. It wasn't really such a bad outcome if everyone was tacitly happy with it.

Cara's father walked a dozen meters ahead with Jan Poole, the agricultural specialist. Jan's house was on the way to town, and the older man joined them for the walk in to church each week. Or anyway, he did now that they went in for services.

Before the soldiers came, Cara remembered church being a much more optional thing. There had been months when Sunday morning hadn't meant anything more strenuous than sleeping in and making breakfast for all of them to eat in their pajamas. Cara still wasn't sure why the arrival of the soldiers and their ships had changed that. It wasn't as though the soldiers made people come. Most of the men and women who'd come down from the ships to live on the planet didn't come to church, and those that did weren't any different from the science teams. When she'd asked, her mother had made an argument about needing to be part of the community that hadn't made any sense. It all came down to: this was the way they did things now. And so they did them. Cara didn't like it but didn't hate it either, and the walk could be nice enough. She already knew—the same way she knew she'd get her period or that she'd move into her own house—that someday she'd push back against the weekly routine. But someday wasn't yet.

Services were held in the same space as school, only with the tables taken out and benches made from local wood analogs hauled into rows for people to sit on. Who gave the sermon varied week by week. Most times, it was someone from the original science teams, but a couple of times one of the soldiers' ministers had taken a turn. It didn't really matter to Cara. Apart from the timbre of their voices, the speeches all sounded pretty much the same. Mostly she let her mind wander and watched the backs of the heads of all the people in front of her. The people from town and the soldiers who'd come to the surface all sitting together but apart, like words in a sentence with the spaces between them.

It wasn't the same for the kids. Xan and little Santiago Singh played together all the time. Maggie Crowther was widely rumored to have kissed Muhammed Serengay. It wasn't that the kids didn't recognize the division so much as that it didn't matter to them. The more soldiers came down the well, the more normal it was to have them there. If that worried her parents, it was only because they were used to it being a different way. For Cara and Xan and all the others in their cohort, it had always been like this. It was their normal.

After the sermon, they trickled out into the street. Some families left immediately, but others stood around in little clumps, talking the way the adults did after church.

The results of the new xenobotany run looked promising and *The soldiers are breaking ground on a new barracks* and *Daffyd Keller's house needs repair again, and he's thinking of taking the soldiers up on their offer of new accommodations in town.* Speculation on the water-purification project and the weather cycles data and the platforms or stick moons or whatever people wanted to call them. And always the question—sometimes spoken, but often not—*Have you heard anything from Earth?* The answer to that was always no, but people asked anyway. Church was all about rituals. Standing with the sunlight pressing against her face trying not to be impatient was as much a part of the day as the sermon.

After what seemed like hours and hadn't been more than half of one, Xan and Santiago ran off with a pack of the other children. Stephen DeCaamp finished his conversation with her parents and wandered off toward his own home. The church crowd scattered, and Cara got to follow her parents back to their house. The road was flat, but the prospect of going back to the pond, of seeing the dogs again, made it feel like she was walking downhill.

"More," her mother said when they were out of earshot of the others. Her tone of voice told Cara it was part of a conversation that was already in progress. One she hadn't been part of. Her father's sigh confirmed that.

"We knew that would happen," he said. "You can't expect them to live in orbit forever. Being in a gravity well will be good for them."

"Not sure what it will be for us."

Her father shrugged and glanced toward Cara, not to include her but to postpone the conversation until she wasn't around. Her mother smiled thinly, but she let it drop. "Why don't you ever go play with the other children?" she asked instead.

"I do when I want to," Cara said.

"Must be nice," her mother replied with a chuckle, but didn't go farther than that.

As soon as they were home, Cara changed out of her good clothes, grabbed a lunch of toasted grains and dried fruit, and ran out the back. She took a jacket, but not because she'd get cold. She figured that if the dogs brought the drone back, she'd be able to wrap it up and sneak it back into the house that way. Then she could put it in her mother's case later, when no one was watching. A drone had to be easier to fix than a sunbird, after all.

At the pond, Momma bird was sitting at the edge of the water, unmoving and wax-skinned. The tiny, angry black eyes focused on nothing in particular. The babies hissed and spat and chased each other around the pond, diving sometimes, or flapped their pale leathery wings. Cara sat a little way off and ate, watching them. The dogs might not come back today. They might never come back. Maybe they ate drones. Or maybe sunbirds rose from the dead on their own. That was the thing about Laconia: with so much that no one knew, anything was possible.

After a while, she folded the jacket into a pillow, got out her handheld, and read part of a book about a lost boy looking for his family in the overwhelming press of people in the North American Shared Interest Zone. She tried to imagine what it would be like, walking down a single street with a thousand other people on it. It seemed like it was probably an exaggeration.

The afternoon heat drew a line of sweat down her back. A chittering flock of four-legged insectlike things roiled through the sky like a funnel cloud before diving onto the water, covering the pond in a layer of shining blue-and-green brighter than gemstones for five or six minutes before rising again at the same instant and shooting away into the trees. Cara hadn't seen them before. She wondered if they were a migrant species, or something local that hadn't crossed her path before. Or maybe this was the kind of thing she was supposed to tell Instructor Hannu about.

That seemed weird, though. What was there to say except *I saw something I haven't seen before*? As if that wasn't always true. It would be a strange day when that *didn't* happen.

She did feel a little guilty not saying anything about the dogs, though. Something that took dead animals and made them not-dead would be the sort of thing the soldiers wanted to know about. Would want to capture and study. She wondered if the dogs would want to be captured and studied. She thought not, and they'd already done more for her than the soldiers ever had.

The sun slid westward. The fronds of the trees clattered in the breeze like someone dropping a handful of sticks forever. The anticipation and excitement of the morning mellowed and soured with every hour that the dogs didn't come back. The shadows all lost their edges as thin, high clouds caught the sunlight and softened it. A flash of red and yellow from the stick moons faded and flared and faded again. Artifacts of whatever long-dead species had built the gates.

She watched the lights flutter and stream like a kite caught in some different, gentle wind. Or a bioluminescent creature like they had on Earth. Something alive, only not alive. Like Momma bird. She wondered if maybe the stick moons were like that too. Something in between. And maybe the dogs…

Something moved in the darkness under the trees, and she sat up. The dogs came out, ambling toward her gracefully on their oddly jointed legs. Cara scrambled to her feet, stepping toward the dogs that weren't dogs. Or if they were, they were what Laconia meant by the word.

The big, apologetic eyes fixed on her, and she grabbed her own hands. She didn't know why, but she felt like she should wave or bow or do something to show them that she was glad they were there.

"Hi," she said. "I didn't think you'd come."

The dogs came around her, making a semicircle with her at the center. The drone hung from the mouth of one at the back, vortex thrusters powered down and clicking against each other like fingernails.

"Were you able…?" Cara said. Then, "Did you fix it?"

The dog with the drone came forward, lifting its head toward her. She took the drone, and the dog let it go. It was her mother's drone, there was no question about that. And the section she'd shattered was intact, but it looked different. The shards and splinters of its carapace were there, but a lattice of silver-white made a tracework where the breaks had been. Like a scar that marked a healed wound. There was no way her mother would fail to notice that. But it wouldn't matter, as long as it worked. She put the drone down on the clover, slaved it to her handheld. The thrusters hummed. The drone rose into the air, solid and balanced as ever. Cara felt the grin in her cheeks.

"This is perfect," she said. "This is everything. Thank you so much."

The dogs looked embarrassed. She powered down the drone and wrapped it carefully in her jacket as they turned and walked back into the dimness under the trees. She wondered where they went when they weren't at the pond. If there was some cave they slept in or a pod where they curled up at night. She had a hard time picturing that. And it wasn't as if they had real mouths to eat with. Maybe they all went to some kind of alien power jack and filled up whatever they used as batteries.

"Thank you," she shouted again into the shadows. She stood, holding the drone to her chest like it was a baby. "If there's anything I can do for you..."

She didn't finish the sentence.

She walked back home quickly, her steps quickened by the prospect of being home, of sneaking the drone into her room unseen. She'd have to be clever to get it back into its case without her parents knowing she'd taken it. There were two ways into the house—the front that faced the road to town, and the back by the garden and the shed. The question was which would be most likely to get her past her family's watchful eyes and safely into her room. It was getting close to dinnertime, so the front would probably be best, since at least one of them would be in the kitchen. Or she could stow the drone in the shed under the cart and wait until everyone was asleep. That probably made more sense...

She knew something was wrong the moment she stepped in the back door. The air *felt* different, like the moment before a storm. Soft voices she didn't recognize came from the living room. She walked toward them with a sense of entering a nightmare.

Her father was sitting on a chair; his face had literally turned gray. A uniformed soldier stood beside him, head bowed, and

Santiago Singh was behind them, looking away. The boy's eyes were puffy and red from crying. No one turned to her. It was like she was invisible.

Her mother walked in from the front door, footsteps hard and percussive. Her mouth was tight and her eyes as hard as rage. She gazed toward Cara without seeming to see her.

"Mom?" Cara said, and her voice seemed to come from a long way away. "What's wrong?"

It was one of those things. An accident. If any of a thousand details had been just a little different, no one would have even noticed it. The soldier who'd been driving the transport had indulged in a couple beers with his lunch, so his reaction times were just that much delayed. Xan and Santiago and the other boys had decided to play football instead of tag, so there was a ball that could take a wild kick. Xan had been nearest the road, so he'd been the one to run out to retrieve it. The whole thing was over before anyone understood it had begun. Like that, her little brother was dead, and the drone and Momma bird and the dogs didn't seem important anymore.

Cara sat while the soldier explained it all. Santiago Singh stood at attention, weeping as he retold all he'd seen like the good little soldier he was. Her father lurched out of the room at some point. Her mother dropped her favorite serving bowl, the fragments scattering across the floor. They were like moments out of a dream, connected because they were about the same thing, more or less. But she couldn't have said which happened first. Which one led to the others. Xan was dead, and it shattered time for her. It broke everything.

Admiral Duarte sent his condolences. This was a lapse of discipline that should never have happened. The admiral had already ordered the drunk soldier's execution. Cara's family would be put first on the list for a place in the new housing facilities, and Cara would be guaranteed a place in the academy when it opened. The admiral understood that nothing could compensate for their loss, but the soldiers would do what they could. With the family's permission, the admiral would like to attend the wake. Someone had said, *Of course,* but Cara didn't know if it had been her mother or her father. She might even have said it herself.

The town didn't have a mortuary. In the years they'd been on Laconia, there hadn't been more than a handful of deaths, and none of them had been a child. Not until now. No one seemed to know what to do or how to go about it. Cara had never been to a funeral before. She didn't know what to expect.

They brought Xan home that afternoon, and his body had already been cleaned. Someone had found or made a burial gown for him, white cloth from his throat down to his bare feet. They put him in the front between the door and road on a table. His eyes were closed, his hands folded on his belly. Cara stood at his side, looking down at him and trying to feel. Everything in her seemed to have gone numb.

To her, Xan looked like he was sleeping. Then he looked like he wasn't really Xan, but only a statue of him. A piece of art. Cara found she could flip her brain between seeing him one way and then the other, like he'd become an optical illusion. Her brother, but only asleep. Something not alive, but also not her brother. Back again. Anything except the two together: Never both *Xan* and *dead.*

People from town came. Edmund Otero. Janet Li. The Stover family, with Julianne Stover carrying her new baby on one hip. They brought food. A couple of times, they tried singing hymns, but the songs died out before they could really take root. At one point, Mari Tennanbaum seemed to well up out of the crowd and grab Cara in an awkward hug, like Cara was supposed to be comforting her instead of the other way around. Then Mari faded back into the swirl of bodies and hushed conversation. Cara went back to looking at her brother's corpse.

There was something. Not a bruise really, but where a bruise would have been if Xan's blood hadn't stopped where it was. A discoloration on his head. Cara couldn't get the idea out of her mind that this was where Death had touched him.

She didn't see the soldiers arrive so much as hear it. A change in the voices around her. When she thought to look up, Admiral Duarte was there, silhouetted by the light spilling out of their doorway as he talked to her parents. It was the first time she'd seen him in person and he wasn't as tall as she expected. A centimeter or two shorter than her father. His uniform was perfectly tailored. His pockmarked cheeks made him look older than he probably was.

He was talking to her parents when she saw him, his head bent forward like he was putting all his attention into listening to them. It was a little bit like having a Greek god or a character out of history show up. It wasn't the only unreal thing about the evening, but it was one among others.

Her mother said something she couldn't hear, and the admiral nodded and touched her arm as he replied. He shook her father's hand, neither man smiling. When he walked in her direction, she thought it was to see Xan. To view the body, if that was the phrase. She was surprised when he stopped in front of her.

"Cara?" The way her name sat in his mouth, it was like he was making sure he had the right person and also talking to someone that was his equal. His eyes were soft brown. She could see the sorrow in them. "My name is Winston."

"I know," she said like she was accepting an apology. Letting him off the hook.

He shifted to look at Xan. They were silent for a few seconds. He sighed. "I wish I could make this better. I've lost people I love before. It was very hard."

"Why?" she asked, and her voice was sharper than she'd expected. It wasn't a fair thing to ask. She wasn't even sure quite what she meant by it other than who the hell was he to come to her brother's funeral and talk about his own pain. Winston took the question in, pursing his lips like he was sucking on it. Tasting it.

"Because I hate feeling powerless," he said. "I hate being reminded that the universe is so much bigger than I am. And that I can't always protect people." He shifted to look at her directly again. Like he actually cared about her reaction to this explanation. She understood why the soldiers would follow him. Why they all loved him.

"Would you undo it," she asked, "if you could? If you could bring him back?"

Maybe he heard something in the question. Maybe it was only that he was listening to her so deeply. He paused, thought. "I believe that I would, yes. I need your family to be well. To be part of what I'm doing here."

"Taking over Laconia?"

"And everything that comes after that. I want to keep people safe. Not just here but everywhere. The people on Laconia, not just the ones who came with me but all of us, are my best chance to do that. And yes, if I could save your brother, I would. For him, and for your parents, and for you. If I could wave a magic wand and go back in time to keep him off that road? I would do it."

"You killed the soldier who killed him. Didn't you need him too?"

"Not as much as I needed you and your family to know that your brother mattered to me. I'm the government here. I imposed that. I didn't ask your permission first. That puts some obligations on me. It means I have to show sincerity and respect for our rules, even when that requires doing something I might not want to do. I don't have the right to compromise."

"I think I understand that."

"We have to be one people," he said. He sounded sad. "There's no room for tribes on Laconia. That's how they do it back in Sol system. Earth and Mars and the Belt. That's what we're here to outgrow."

"Everything is different here," Cara said, and the admiral nodded as though she'd understood him perfectly, then touched her shoulder and walked away.

Behind her, someone was weeping softly. She didn't turn to see who. For the first time since she'd come home, she felt almost clearheaded. When she put her hand on Xan's foot the same way she used to when she woke him up, his body was cold.

"It's going to be okay," she said. "I know how to fix this."

Her parents were in the kitchen with Mari Tennanbaum, each of them with a squat glass of wine. Usually her father would be making jokes about it being vintage fifteen minutes ago, but now he didn't seem to notice it was in his hand. The missing joke made her sad, because it meant he was sad.

"What happens to him tonight?" Cara asked.

Mari blinked and reared back a centimeter as if Cara had shouted something rude. Her father didn't react at all, just turned the fixed, polite smile a degree more toward her. Her mother was the one to answer.

"This isn't the time—"

"I know the funeral's tomorrow," Cara said, "but it's not like there's a place in town that he can stay in until then. Can he be here? It's the last night he can, so he should stay here. With us."

Her voice was louder and shriller than she'd intended. Mari Tennanbaum wasn't looking at her, but other people were. Her mother's eyes were as dead as Momma bird's.

"Sure," her mother said. "If it's important to you, he can stay here until the funeral. That would…that would be nice. To have him here."

Then her mother started crying and didn't stop. Her father put down his wine, still with the same smile, and led her away. For a moment, Cara expected Xan to rush in and ask what was wrong with Mom, and then she remembered again. She went back out to stand guard over the body. To make sure that if anyone came and tried to take him away, she'd be there to tell them her mom said not to.

The memorial ended late, people staying until the darkness felt like it had always been there. Like daytime was some other planet.

She was still standing beside Xan when Admiral Duarte and the soldiers left, and when Stephen DeCaamp and Janet Li came to move Xan's body inside. Probably nothing in the local system would mistake him for food, but they brought him in anyway, still on the table. They left him between the dining area and the kitchen, dressed in his funeral whites. It was like something out of a dream.

Her parents saw everyone out, said their last farewells, and closed the door. None of them spoke, and Cara went to the wash-room and pretended to prepare for bed. Brushed teeth, washed face, changed into a nightgown. She kissed her mother on the cheek and went to her bedroom. She left the door open just a crack, though, so the latch wouldn't make noise when she opened it. Then, as quietly as she could, she took the nightgown back off and pulled on work clothes. She tucked her handheld into her sock drawer. If they checked, it would look like she was in her room. She crawled into bed and pulled the covers up to her neck so if her parents did come in, she'd look normal. The trick, she thought, would be waiting until they went to bed without falling asleep herself.

In the darkness, she bit her lip, chewing the soft flesh so the pain would keep her awake. She counted backward from five hundred, one number with each breath, and then counted back up to five hundred again. She was just shifting the blanket aside to get up when she heard the back door open and her parents' voices drift in. She froze, listened.

The strangest thing was how normal they sounded. How much grief sounded like regular life.

"I'll get that cleaned up later," her father said.

"It's fine. I don't care."

"I know, but I'll clean it up anyway."

The ghost of a laugh, gone almost before it started. She could imagine her mother leaning against the counter the way she always did, except that Xan was dead. So maybe they acted differ-ent. It seemed like everything ought to have changed.

"I can't believe this is happening," her mother said. "It's just not...plausible?"

"Yeah. I keep feeling like I just had a little seizure or something. Like I was having some kind of hallucination, and now I'm back. Or I'm asleep again. I don't know. I can't...I don't feel like he's gone."

Cara felt a little smile tugging at her mouth. For a second, she was tempted to run out and tell them. To have them help. Then they could all do it together.

"I don't want to be here anymore," her mother said. "We weren't supposed to be here anymore. Not us. Not—" Her voice thickened and stopped, like the words had gotten too gooey to get out. Her father was making noises. Like little cooing sounds Cara might have heard from paper bugs. She shifted a little, thinking that maybe she could peek through the crack in her door. See what they were doing. The tightness in her gut was the seconds of nighttime slipping away, and she had to find the dogs.

"He should have been back in Paris," her mother said. "He should have been with his cousins, not on this fucking nightmare of a planet."

"I know," her father said.

"I *hate* it here. I want to go home."

"I know, Dot. I want to go home too."

Cara felt the words like a punch. Home? They wanted to go home? They *were* home. *This* was home. What they meant was Earth, where she'd never been, where she didn't belong. Where Xan didn't belong.

She must have made a noise, because her mother called out in her tear-thickened voice. "Babygirl?"

Cara froze, then inched back toward her bed. She couldn't be found now. Not dressed like this.

"Babygirl?" her mother said again, and Cara jumped back into the bed, hauled the blanket up to her neck, and turned her face to the wall. If they saw her face, they'd know she was only pretending to sleep...

Her door opened. She fought to keep her breath slow and deep. What would she say if they touched her? Should she pretend to wake up? What did she look like when she was just waking up? She didn't know.

"I love you, babygirl," her mother whispered, and the door closed, the latch clicking home. Cara let out a long, stuttering breath. Her pulse was going fast enough for two people, which struck her as funny, because it was sort of true. Her heartbeat and Xan's too. For a while at least.

Her parents' voices were less clear now, but she heard the door to their bedroom close. She waited, counted to five hundred and down again, waited some more. No more noises. No more voices.

The latch was louder than she wanted it to be, no matter how gently she opened it. It felt like it was echoing in the empty house, but she'd spent too much time waiting already. She walked carefully, rolling her weight from carefully placed heel to her toe. Xan lay still on his table. She opened the back door, stepped out to the shed. When she pulled the cart out, she was almost surprised to see that the sampling drone was still in the shed. It seemed like an artifact from some other life, like it had been hidden there for years and not hours. Funny how time worked like that. She ran her fingertips over the repaired shell with its new veins.

Xan's body was heavier than she expected. She'd carried him before sometimes, but he'd always been helping her, at least a little. He wasn't stiff anymore, and she staggered a little getting him through the back doorway. It got easier when she stopped trying to carry him less like a boy and more like a sack of soil. When she dropped him into the cart, his head hit the side with a thump.

"Sorry," she whispered as if he had felt anything. "But really, this is your fault. When this is done, you're going to have to do my chores for me from now on."

Xan's eyes had opened a little. Tiny wet slits hidden behind his eyelashes, catching the starlight. His arms had folded under him when she put him down, twisted and bent at angles that made her own shoulder ache to look at. There wasn't time to make him comfortable, though. She fumbled with the cart's handle and started down the path, then paused and snuck back into the house. She pulled a bag of fruit and some rice bars out of the pantry, and a bottle of filtered water from the refrigerator. She tucked them beside her brother's corpse, took up the cart handle, and started out.

Night on Earth was bright. That's what they said. Their moon shone like a kind of second, crappy sun. Cities were big enough to drown out the stars with their extra glow. She'd seen pictures of it all, but that wasn't what it had been like for her. On Laconia, day was bright and night was dark. The wide, smeary glow of the galactic disk was the brightest thing in the sky, and she could only navigate by it roughly. Enough to know which direction she was going. Two stick moons floated against the stars, shimmering and shifting, swimming toward each other in the darkness above the sky.

Cara put her head down and pulled. She'd been down this path so many times at so many times of day and in such different weathers that her body knew the way even when she couldn't exactly see it. She knew the sound of the grass and the water, the places where the breeze changed shape, the smell of broken soil and the pattering of bug honey on the lower fronds of the trees. She could have made the trip with her eyes closed, and with the darkness, she very nearly did.

At the pond, a rock deer lifted its head at her approach, its scales shifting and reflecting starlight like a little slice of sky that had come down for a drink. It was too dark to see its eyes.

"Shoo," Cara said, and the animal turned and launched itself into the darkness, tramping through the underbrush and then running away faster than a soldier's truck, even though there were no roads. Cara stopped. A film of sweat covered her forehead, and her armpits felt swampy. She was here, though. She'd made it.

"Hello?" she shouted. "Are you there?"

The darkness didn't answer back. Even the night animals and bugs went quiet, like they were listening with her. Now that she was here, the plan that had seemed so simple was showing its holes. For her to take Xan to the dogs, the dogs had to be there. If they weren't...

"Hello?" Her voice sounded thin, even to her. Stretched and desperate. "Please, are you there?"

She parked the cart in the soft ground at the water's edge and stepped toward the trees. The already black night grew darker. There wasn't even starlight here. Only an absence, like looking straight into the pupil of an eye as big as the world. She put her arms out, fingertips waving for the fronds and scrub that she knew were there but couldn't see. Her eyes ached from trying to see anything. Her ears rang with the silence.

"Please? I need help."

Nothing answered. Despair she hadn't known she was fighting washed into her. If the dogs weren't there, then Xan was gone. And gone forever. And he couldn't be. Grief shifted in her belly, shook her legs and hands. The dogs had been there for Momma bird. They couldn't leave her brother dead, and just save a fucking sunbird.

Her parents would wake up. They'd see the body was gone, and her with it. They'd be angry, and what would she tell them? What would she say to make them understand that the rules they knew weren't her rules, that Xan didn't have to be dead? They'd stop her. She balled her hands into tight, aching fists. She couldn't let them stop her.

"Hey!" she shouted. And then again, loud enough for the air to scrape at her throat. "*Hey*! I need you! I need *help*! It's *important*!"

The silence was absolute.

And then it wasn't.

She couldn't tell how far away it was. With nothing to see, sound could deceive her, but somewhere ahead of her, a hiss and crackle of scrub being pushed aside. The rock deer maybe. Or a shambler. Or any of the thousands of uncategorized animals of Laconia that were still waiting to be named.

Or the dogs.

Uncertainty came over her in a wave. It was too big and too strange. Like she'd waved at the sun and it had waved back. Maybe this had been a bad idea, but it was too late now. She steeled herself to face whatever came from the black. The tramping drew nearer, louder. It multiplied and spread. They were coming.

Something touched her hand. A gentle pressure that tingled like a mild electric shock.

Cara dropped to her knees and threw her arms around the dog, hugging the strange, too-solid flesh close to her. It was warm against her cheek, and rough. It smelled like cardamom and soil. It went still, like it wasn't sure what to do with her affection and joy, and it stayed still until she released it.

"Over here," she said, stumbling back to the pond. She gestured in the darkness. And maybe the dogs could see her, because they followed. Starlight glimmered in their bulging eyes.

Xan's funeral whites glowed in the darkness, a paler shadow. The dogs gathered around him, and it was like watching what was left of Xan dissolve. Darkness consuming darkness.

"He's my brother," Cara said. "A truck hit him. It killed him, like with Momma bird. But I need him back. And you brought her back, so you can bring him back too, can't you? I mean you can, can't you?"

She was babbling, and the dogs didn't respond. Mostly blind, she stepped in close, her hands on their backs. The dogs were still and quiet as statues. And then one began making its *ki-ka-ko* call, and the others picked it up until it felt like a choir around her. Until her head spun with it. She sank to her knees to keep from losing her balance. In the sky, the stick moons glittered green and white and blue. The stars looked warmer than their lights.

Xan bobbed up to the surface of the darkness. The dogs were

carrying him, one under him bearing his weight on its back. Others holding his arms and legs to steady him as they walked.

"You can, can't you? You can fix him?"

The dogs didn't answer. Xan floated out to the trees, and then behind them. And then there was only the sound of the dogs walking. Then not even that.

Cara sat by the water, hugging her knees. Slowly, the natural sounds of the night came back: the trill of insects, the trill of birds. A high, fluting call from something a long way off, and an answering call from even farther. The stillness cooled her, but not badly. All she had to do now was wait.

Voices woke her. They were calling her name, and she couldn't remember where she was. It wasn't her bed or her room or her house, because there was a dawn-stained sky overhead. Her clothes were wet with dew.

"Cara!"

She was on the edge of calling back, when the last forgetfulness of sleep slid off her mind. She clamped a hand over her mouth as if her arm didn't trust her throat to stay quiet. She scrambled to her feet. Momma bird and the little ones were already on the pond. The dead, black eyes didn't take Cara in. The cart squatted where she'd left it. She snatched the little bag of food out of it, took two steps toward the voices, and then two away. Her mind felt like it was buzzing.

If she told them now, they'd call the soldiers. They'd come and they'd track down the dogs. She didn't think they'd wait for Xan to come back, and he had to come back. But there were only so many paths. They'd find her at the pond, and soon. She'd have to say something, wouldn't she? And what if they didn't let her come back?

She felt like she was still struggling with the dilemma even as she trotted out toward the forest, and the darkness under the fronds. She pushed through the underbrush, twigs and the stick-hard fingers of the scrub sliding off her. A rough break in the plants showed where the animal path led away to the south, and she followed it.

She'd never gone past the pond before. There were probably surveys of the land somewhere. Or maybe not. A decade was a long time to live somewhere, but a planet was larger than the best intentions. She might be going places humans had never been before. Or no one except for Xan, anyway.

The voices grew more distant, but still clear. Her legs ached, but the work of moving fought back the cold. The voices went silent. She thought maybe they'd given up looking for her, but when they started again, there were more. Voices she recognized. Instructor Hannu, Stephen DeCaamp. Mari Tennanbaum.

Her father.

"Babygirl!" he cried. His voice sounded raw. Like he was hurting himself by shouting. "Babygirl, if you're out there, we're right *here*! Baby!"

She wanted to go back to him, to tell him everything was all right. That she was and that Xan was too. Tears rose up in her eyes, blurring the world.

"Sorry," she said softly, pushing forward. "I'm so sorry."

She didn't stop until the sound of the voices was gone. The search would keep going, though. There would be drones. There would be thermal scanning. If the soldiers helped, there would be visuals taken from orbit. She stayed under the canopy of fronds. There were plenty of large animals in the forest. It wouldn't be easy to tell which heat came from them and which came from her. At least she hoped it wouldn't.

The sun tracked through the sky, changing the angle of the few, thin dapples that pushed down into the permanent twilight of the forest. Cara felt herself getting tired. She'd have to rest. She'd have to eat. And at some point she'd have to find her way back to the pond. She had to be there when the dogs came back with Xan. After that, everything would be better.

She found a place where a long brown stone pushed up out of

the land. It was too round to be a real bench, and whatever the blue moss was growing on, it felt slick and oily. She sat there anyway. The fruit and rice tasted better than it ever had at home, and the water was sweet. She hadn't realized how dry her throat had become until she drank. Her muscles twitched with fatigue. It wasn't a bad feeling.

The forest around her was hushed, but not silent. Little things the size of her thumb ticked at her from the trees. They had big wet eyes and tiny mandibles that looked like they were frozen in permanent comic alarm. A bird fluttered by on wide leathery wings, landed on a frond across the way from her, and muttered to itself like a bored child in school. The soft breeze smelled like burnt coffee and fresh grass and rubbing alcohol. An insect buzzed past on bright wings that left a little rainbow afterimage on her eyes.

A sense of peace crept over her, and it felt like the world had sat beside her, opened its own lunch bag, and was just being with her. Everything about the little space was beautiful and calm and rich with a million things that no one had ever seen before. And every place was like this. A whole planet and a solar system beyond it. There would be caves somewhere, with fishlike things living in the waters. There would be ocean coves with tide pools filled with living systems that weren't animals and weren't plants. That didn't have names or an idea of names. She tried to imagine what it would be like going back to Earth, where everything was already known and there weren't any miracles left. It seemed sad.

She pinched the last grain of rice between her fingertips and dropped it on her tongue. She didn't know if the adults were still searching for her. She didn't know how long it would take the dogs to bring back Xan. She'd have to go back home eventually for fresh water and food. But just then, just for that moment, she could let herself feel at peace.

She pushed the empty water bottle back in her pocket, folded the empty bag and shoved it in too. She didn't want to hurry for fear of hearing her name called in a familiar voice. She couldn't stay for fear of missing the dogs. There wasn't a perfect answer, but she didn't need a perfect one. Good enough was good enough.

Making her way home was harder than leaving had been, which made some sense to her. Going away from a point, there were any number of paths, and all of them were right. Going back to the point, most paths were wrong. The rock-deer trail wasn't as clear, now that she was walking back along it. Branches and turns she hadn't noticed on the way out confused her now. And as the sunlight changed its angle and warmth, the colors under the forest canopy changed. Twice, she backtracked to a place she was almost sure was part of the right way and tried again, making other decisions.

The sunlight had started to shift into gray and orange, the air to grow cool, when she came around a stand of trees and the dogs were scattered there, legs tucked primly beneath their bodies. Their embarrassed, apologetic eyes shifted toward her as she came forward. Excitement or fear or both raced through Cara's body like an electrical shock. And then Xan sat up, his head turning toward her.

He was changed, that was obvious. He was still wearing his funeral whites, but a long black stain ran from his left shoulder down to his belly. His skin had a grayness where the red of blood should have been. His eyes had gone pure black. When he moved, it had the same utter stillness broken by considered action as Momma bird, like every muscle that fired had been thought about for a fraction of a second first. But his hair still stood out in all directions the way it did when he'd just gotten up in the morning. His mouth was the same gentle curve that he'd inherited from their dad.

"Xan?" she whispered.

He was still as stone for a moment, then he shifted his head. "I feel weird," he said, and his voice was his own.

Her grin was so wide it hurt her face. She rushed the last meter between them and hugged him, lifting him up in her arms. For a moment, it was like lifting the dead weight of his corpse. Then his arms were around her too, his head against her neck.

"I was scared," he said. "There was something wrong. And someone was talking to me, only they weren't talking to me."

"There was an accident," Cara said. "You got hurt. Really hurt. *Killed*-hurt."

A hesitation. "Oh," Xan said. She stepped back, but she kept hold of his hand. She didn't want to let go of him. He blinked. "I feel pretty good for killed."

"I brought you to the dogs. They fix things."

"Like me," Xan said. And then, "There's something wrong with how things look."

"I guess they had to change you some," she said. The nearest dog shifted and looked away, as if chagrined by the limits of their powers. Cara shook her head. "It's okay. This is wonderful. Thank you."

"There are things I didn't see before," Xan said. The words sounded faint. Like he was speaking them from farther off than right here in front of her. "There are other things here. I don't know what they are."

Cara tugged on his hand, pulling him along with her the way she used to sometimes before.

"Come on. It's getting late. We should get home."

"What does it mean to be in a substrate?"

"I don't know," Cara said, tugging him again. "Let's go ask Mom. If I can figure out how to get there from here." She turned to the nearest dog and bowed. She didn't know why that seemed like the thing to do, but it did. "Thank you so much for bringing my brother back to us. If there's anything I can do to help you, just let me know and I'll do it. Really."

The dog made a chirping noise, and then they all rose as one, walking away through the forest on their strangely jointed legs. She half expected them to start their *ki-ka-ko* song, but they didn't. They only faded into the forest again, as if it was the place where they most belonged. Cara started out for what she was pretty sure was the south, and Xan followed along behind, his cool gray hand still in hers.

She didn't find the pond, but a break in the trees opened up on the road to her house. The charcoal sky of twilight glittered with stars and the stick moons. At least now she knew where she was and how to get where she wanted to be. She just hoped no one would see them along the way. She wanted her parents to be the first to see what she'd accomplished.

A soft breeze came from the north and set the fronds of the trees clacking against each other. They walked the same way they came home from school every day, all of it familiar even through the changes. Cara was already imagining a bowl of barley soup and her bed and waking up in the morning to the amazement and wonder of the town. Xan asked how he'd died, and she spent the walk telling the story of his death, his funeral, everyone who'd come, how she'd made sure his body had stayed there for her to steal. He listened more intensely than he ever had before and hardly interrupted at all.

"The head of the soldiers really came to see me?" Xan asked when she was done.

"He did."

"Do you think he'll want to see us again now that I'm back? I don't want to get them in trouble."

Them. He meant the dogs. Cara felt a moment's unease. The soldiers would want to know about the dogs, about Momma bird and the drone and Xan. Especially with the dogs showing up after the stick moons came alive. She'd have to talk to her parents about what to tell the soldiers and how to tell it to them.

She thought of Winston. The way he listened. *I need your family to be well.*

"The admiral understands," she said. "He knows that Laconia's not like other places."

Xan thought about that a beat too long, then nodded more to himself than to her.

The house glowed from every window. Every light in every room had to be burning. It wasn't like her parents to run the power down like that. And they were there too, framed in the window like it was the screen of her handheld. Her mother standing in the kitchen, hands on the counter. Her father sitting at the table. They looked as tired as Cara felt. She wondered if they'd been searching for her all day. If there were still people out there looking.

Xan stopped, staring at the house with his newly black eyes. His face was all stunned amazement, as if he was seeing it all for the first time. In a way, he was. Cara squeezed his fingers gently. He didn't follow her right away when she walked toward the front door. Cara stopped and waved him forward.

"It's going to be okay," she said.

When she opened the door, her mother startled as if Cara had fired a gun, then rushed at her and grabbed her by the arms hard enough to hurt.

"What did you do?" her mother growled through rage-bared teeth. "What the *fuck* did you do?"

And then she pulled Cara close in a hug so tight, it felt like drowning. Her mother's sobs shook them both. Cara put her arms around her mother and found she was crying a little too. Guilt and joy and the echoing sorrow of Xan's death and the triumph of his return all washed together in the moment, and she held on to her mother's body like she hadn't since she was a baby.

"It's okay, Momma," she said through her tears. "It's all okay now."

Her father said her mother's name. *Dot.* One low syllable, but with alarm in it louder than a shout.

Xan stood just outside the open door in the space where he wasn't exactly in the darkness or in the light. His funeral whites carried so much dirt and stain they were like camouflage. His bare feet were filthy. The angle of his eyebrows over his black wet eyes reminded Cara of the dogs—uncertain, embarrassed, apologetic. He stepped through the doorway into the house and went still. Then, in a flicker, lifted his hands toward them all like a baby reaching for an embrace. His fingernails were dirty. The grayness of his skin made his face seem smudged even where it wasn't.

Cara felt her mother gasp, a sharp, sudden inhalation that she didn't breathe out. Her arms went stiff around Cara, grabbing her in so much it hurt. Xan tried a smile. His gaze clicked from Cara to their father to their mother and back to Cara, as fast as an insect leg twitching. He spread his fingers wider, took another step forward.

"It's okay," Cara said. "I got him back."

Her mother yanked her back, grabbing Cara up and away with a violence that hurt her neck. Cara was back behind the counter, her feet off the floor, her mother's arms pressing the air out of her almost before she realized they were moving. Her father pushed them both behind him. She didn't understand why he had a knife in his hand.

"Gary?" her mother said. "What the fuck is that?"

"I see it," her father said. "It's real."

Cara couldn't speak. She didn't have the air. She wriggled against her mother's grip. She had to explain, to tell them what was going on. This wasn't how it was supposed to happen.

"I want a hug too," Xan said.

Xan took another awkward step forward, still and then the flicker of motion, then still again. Her father yelled, a deep, ragged sound too big for the man she knew. He lunged toward Xan, knife shining in his fist, and terror flooded Cara's blood. She kicked at her mother hard, and felt the blow connect. The grip around her released a little.

"Stop it!" Cara screamed. "What are you doing?"

Xan blocked the knife with his hand, the gray skin opening and black blood pouring from his palm. Xan's eyes went wide with shock. Her father barreled forward, still shouting wordlessly. He grabbed Xan's funeral whites and lifted the little boy off the floor. Cara pushed against her mother's neck hard, and stumbled to the floor. Her mother was keening now, a high, tight sound of panic.

Her father had the pantry door open. He threw Xan into it and slammed the door shut, still yelling. There were words in it now. He was shouting, *Leave my family alone.*

"What is the *matter* with you?" Cara shouted. She punched her father's back and then froze. She'd never hit him before. She'd never hit anyone before. He didn't even notice. He grabbed one of the kitchen stools and used it to jam the pantry door closed. Xan banged against the door harder than Cara would have thought he could. Her mother yelped and started cursing fast and low, almost under her breath. It sounded like praying.

Tears were streaming down Cara's cheeks, but she wasn't sad. All she felt was a powerful, growing outrage.

"I brought him back!" she yelled. "He was dead and I took him to the dogs, and they *fixed* him!"

"Dogs?" her father said. "What dogs?"

"The dogs that came after the stick moons turned on," Cara said. There was so much they didn't understand, and the words were like trying to drink through too thin a straw. The meaning wouldn't all fit. "They fixed Momma bird and the drone and they fixed Xan because I asked them to, and he's back. I brought him *back* and you *hurt* him!"

She heard her mother somewhere behind her, talking into her handheld. *I need the military liaison. It's an emergency.* Cara's outrage and impatience felt like venom in her blood. She pushed at the stool, trying to get the pantry door open again. Her father grabbed her shoulders, pulled her close until his face was the whole world.

"That's not your brother," her father said, biting off each word. "That's. Not. Xan."

"It is."

"The dead don't come back," her father said.

"They do *here*," Cara said.

"His eyes," he said, shaking her as he spoke. "The way he moves. That's not a human, babygirl. That's something else wearing my little boy's skin."

"So *what*?" Cara said. "He knows everything Xan knows. He loves everything Xan loves. That *makes* him Xan. How can you do this to him just because he's not perfect!"

Her mother's voice came, hard as stone. "They're sending a force from town."

"The soldiers?" Cara said, pulling away from her father's grip. "You called the *soldiers* on him? You *hate* the soldiers!"

She grabbed at the stool again, but her mother lifted her from behind, hauled her feet off the floor and carried her back toward her room. Xan was calling from the pantry, his voice muted and rough with tears and confusion. Cara tried to twist back toward him. Tried to reach for him.

Her mother pushed her into her room and blocked the door with her body. When she looked down at Cara, her expression was blank and hard. "It's going to be all right," her mother said. "But you have to stay here until I get this under control."

A rush of thoughts fought for Cara's voice—*It was under control* and *Why are you making this a bad thing?* and *You let Daddy cut Xan*—and left her sputtering and incoherent. The door closed. Cara balled her hands, screamed, and pounded the wall. Her parents' voices came from the house in clipped, hard syllables that she couldn't make out. She sat on the edge of her futon, bent double, and put her head in her tingling hands. Her blood felt bright with rage, but she had to think.

The soldiers were coming. Her parents were going to let them take Xan away. *Make* them take Xan away. They'd say the dogs were bad. Dangerous. They might hurt them.

All because it didn't work like this on *Earth*.

The room was filled with her things. Her clothes—clean and folded in the dresser and worn and scattered on the floor by the hamper. The picture over her bed of dinosaurs running from a man in a big pink hat. The picture she'd made when she was seven from Laconian grass and paste, with Instructor Hannu's note—*Good work!*—beside it. The tablet with her book on it. She scooped it up, turned it on. It was still open to the page of

Ashby Allen Akerman in Paris. The old woman feeding bread to the birds. She put her fingertips on the picture. It wasn't a real woman. It wasn't even a real painting. It was just the idea of an idea. It didn't have anything to do with her life, and she didn't lose anything by letting it go.

She closed the book and opened the recording function. She felt the time slipping past, but she took a long look around the room all the same. Her whole life was here, written in little notes and objects that added up to a story that only she would understand.

Or else no one would.

The window was easy to open, but the screen was harder to rip than she'd expected. Once she'd gotten a hole big enough for a couple of fingers, it got easier to pull it apart, but it still hurt her fingertips. A little puff of dust came off the fibers when she ripped the hole big enough that she could squeeze through it. The empty water bottle slipped out of her pocket as she climbed out, clattering onto the paving outside her window. She didn't go back for it. She ran across the road to where the underbrush started getting thick. High clouds interrupted the stars in streaks, as if giant claws had ripped strips out of the sky.

The light in the house and the darkness of the world let her see her mother and father in the main room perfectly. Her father had a length of metal as long as his arm held in both hands like a club. He was crying, but he didn't wipe the tears away. He wouldn't put the weapon down long enough for that. Her mother stood at the door, ready to usher the soldiers in when they came. It would be soon. Town wasn't far away when you had military-transport vehicles.

Cara started the tablet recording. She took a deep, slow breath, waited fifteen seconds, and screamed.

"Momma!"

Her mother's head came up sharply as she looked out into the darkness of the night. Cara tapped the playback and loop, threw the volume to max, and then flung the tablet as hard as she could into the brush. Her mother came out the front door, scanning but blind from the light. From the brush, Cara's voice came again. *Momma!*

"Cara?" her mother said. "Where are you?"

Her father came to the door. She heard him say, "What is it?"

Cara started running. She heard her own voice again, behind her, and her mother screaming for her. And her father now too. She didn't have much time. She looped around the back of the house and in the back door, opening it carefully to keep from making noise. Both her parents had gone out the front to find her. To save her. Their voices reminded her of the search party that she'd avoided. All the ways they wanted to help her, but never asked how she wanted to be helped.

She kicked the stool away and hauled open the pantry door. Xan was kneeling in the darkness, his legs folded under him just like the dogs. Wet tracks of tears marked his cheeks. His black eyes took her in. She held out her hand.

"Come on," she said. "We have to warn the dogs."

The front door stood open. Across the road, the brush crackled and hushed as her parents crashed through it, calling her name. They sounded frightened. Cara felt sorry for them, but they'd made their choices. She'd made hers. Xan took her hand with his uninjured one, and she hauled him up.

Then they were running out the back, into the night, toward the dogs, wherever they were. Xan matched her stride for stride, never letting go of her hand. Her parents' voices faded behind her. She didn't know if they'd found her tablet or if she'd just gotten far enough away that the sound wouldn't reach her.

It didn't matter.

Xan laughed, and the sound was just like the joy he'd had playing a game with his friends. She felt herself smiling. The feeling of freedom lifted her up. Even with the knowledge of the soldiers following behind her. Even with the grief just starting in her heart that she'd never go home. The night was hers, and Laconia was hers, and that was joyous.

Her legs burned and she felt light-headed from hunger. She hadn't had anything to eat since the fruit and rice in the forest. And there wouldn't be anything for her out in the world. All the plants that Laconia grew were indigestible for her at best. Poison at worst. The sunbirds, the blue clover, the grunchers, the glass snakes, everything alive knew, at a chemical level, that she wasn't one of them. But that didn't matter either.

The worst that could happen was she'd die.

The dogs would fix her.

Strange Dogs
Author's Note

This one is often read as a horror story. That's fair. It is one. But it's another story too. It just depends on which generation you're identifying with.

The other story that's like this is *Romeo and Juliet*. They usually trot that one out in high school. When you read (or watch) the play at about the same age and level of maturity as Romeo and Juliet, and the story is about two lovers who catch a series of bad breaks. They wind up dead because the world around them is just a little too fucked up for their more tender emotions to have a place in it. And that's a perfectly legitimate reading. Hell, it's the one that the play steers us toward.

But read it again when you're old enough to play Capulet or Montague, and it feels very different. What Romeo and Juliet experience as the only world they know is the one Montague and

Capulet made. From the old-guy seats, the tragedy is watching the fight you started and then failed to end go on until it kills your kids. And that's worse, because you're still there to suffer the loss after they're gone. Your failure to fix things takes the people you love the most, and it's your fault. That's *Romeo and Juliet* for middle-aged guys.

From the perspective of the parents, "Strange Dogs" is a horror story and a tragedy. Xan dies and comes back changed. And then they lose Cara to the same fate because they can't get her to see the situation through their eyes. They can't make her understand why they see this unexpected resurrection as a bad thing.

From Cara and Xan's perspective? It's an immigrant story.

They've come to a new place, and their parents are still living in the old country that exists in their minds. The children's books are all about birds Cara and Xan have never seen and rules they've never lived by. Their home—their real home—is the place they're growing up. On Laconia, it turns out dead doesn't always mean dead. Sometimes it just means changed. And for them, that's okay because it's just the way the world they've grown up in works. But because Mom and Dad can't shed the old ways, the old rules, they can't see it.

We know a lot of second-generation immigrant families that suffer this break between an old world that the parents know and the culture their kids belong to.

For parents, that's always going to have the potential to be horror.

Auberon

The old man leaned back in his chair, ran his tongue over his teeth, then lit a fresh cigar. His left arm was a titanium and carbon-fiber prosthetic grafted deep into the bones of his shoulder, but his natural right arm was just as intimidating: scarred and pocked by decades of violence and abuse. His hair was a fluffy white fringe that cupped the back of his skull, and he wore a thin mustache like it was a joke he was in on.

"All right. So we'll get a new governor who answers to a different boss," he said. "It happens. Everyone's playing by the rules, and then something rolls through and changes them all. Things get scrambled for a while until everyone figures the new rules out."

His second went by Agnete because it wasn't her name. She didn't roll her eyes. She was used to the old man getting poetic, especially when he was thinking something through. The fingers of his metal arm shifted unconsciously, the wrist curling in on itself the way the real one had, back in the day.

The office wasn't really an office at all. At the old man's level, business could be done anywhere, and he liked the little bar on the Zilver Straat plaza with its wide-bladed ceiling fan and the smells of salt and sulfur coming off the bay. He claimed it reminded him of the kinds of holes and corners he'd grown up in, back on Earth. Some days, people came to meet him there. Occasionally, he'd go out and sit with people in other parts of the city. Someone powerful needed a loan and couldn't get one. Someone needed a supply of agricultural chemicals or drugs, pornography or off-book sex workers, untraceable security teams or zero-day code exploits, then sooner or later they came to the old man.

"The thing is," he said, "you only have so long to figure out the new rules. That's what kills you. You've got to look at the situation like you're just coming into it, because you are. And sure, maybe it's got the same street and the same people. That doesn't mean it's the same place. All the things you just take for granted about how it works are up for grabs again, and—"

"Permission?"

He scowled, but he nodded her on.

"Boss," she said, "we didn't just get a new governor. We got *conquered*."

The old man grunted dismissively. He didn't like being interrupted. Agnete nodded toward the wallscreen behind the bar. The newsfeed from Sol had the secretary-general of Earth, the speaker for the Martian parliament, and the president of the Transport Union—the most powerful people among all the scattered human billions—being humiliated and brought to heel by the new order like the burghers of some half-razed medieval town. The combined fleet was in tatters. The void cities broken or occupied. Pallas Station was reduced to pebbles and hot gas. Medina, at the heart of the gate network, taken over by the half-alien ships that had boiled out of Laconia system. The whole human orthodoxy overturned in what felt like a moment. High Consul Winston

Duarte had named himself ruler of all humanity and had killed enough people to make it true. Emperor of the galaxy.

"This time is different," she said.

The old man spat smoke and grunted again.

The gate network had opened more than thirteen hundred solar systems to humanity, almost all of them with one or two or three planets in the Goldilocks zone. Under hundreds of suns, evolution had improvised new answers to the overwhelming question, *What is life?* With carbon and nitrogen, hydrogen and sunlight and time, the possibilities weren't limitless, but they were mind-boggling. The DNA and asymmetric chirality of organic life on Earth and its Sol system colonies turned out to be idiosyncratic in a wide and creative universe. Even animals shaped by the same selective pressures to look similar to Terran life—the grass trees of Bara Gaon, the humpbacked pigeons of Nova Brasil, the skin-fish of New Eden—only needed a glimpse under a microscope to show they were as different from their Terran counterparts as a bull from a bicycle.

A human being could eat all day and still starve to death in the great garden of Sigurtá, surrounded by bright fruits and soft vegetables, trees heavy with fat birds and rivers filled from bank to bank with things that almost passed for trout.

The forest of life was varied and exotic, and the trees there didn't get along with each other. Or most of them didn't anyway.

At first glance, Auberon system didn't seem exceptional. Three modest gas giants, none of them larger than Saturn. A single wet, life-bearing planet with a large but unexceptional moon. There were no alien artifacts the way there had been in Newhome and Corazón Sagrado. No weirdly pure ore profiles like on Ilus or Persephone. Just a scattered handful of planets, a couple of asteroid belts, and a star burning its slow way toward a billion-year-distant collapse. Among the hundreds of systems to which humanity was heir, it could have been anyplace.

But it was now the most important human system outside of Earth, Laconia, and maybe Bara Gaon Complex. Only a few decades into its settlement, and it already boasted a dozen cities, each of them in the middle of built-up rural areas like the floral disc in the center of a daisy. There were six dwarf planets with mining and refining developments big enough to have permanent civilian populations growing around them. There was a transfer station built to accommodate the trade between it and the other, less fortunate colony worlds. It was the second most developed human settlement in the universe, and on track to keep growing for centuries. And the thing that made its first settlers the winners of history's land-rush lottery was that, apart from competing for sunlight, the biosphere of Auberon barely interacted with the plants and animals of Earth.

There was a famous image of an Earth apple tree and an Auberon-native tree, their roots intertwined as if each were acting as soil for the other. That mutual biochemical shrug made open-air farming possible on Auberon. Contamination by local organisms tended not to mean more than a mild case of gas. And because it was the most habitable of the new planets by orders of magnitude, it was developed. Because it was developed, it was influential. Because it was influential, it was wealthy. And because it was wealthy, it was corrupt.

And now, it was Biryar Rittenaur's problem.

A woman's face appeared on his handheld. She had a prominent chin, long white hair in tight curls, and a high forehead...Biryar tapped his fingers against his thigh. He should know this one. A face like a spade. A spade is a garden shovel. Shovel...

"Michelle Cheval," he said. "President of the Agricultural and Food Production Workers Union."

The handheld shifted to a young man's face. Pleasant, neutral, with a mole at the side of his mouth that reminded Biryar of a cartoon rabbit. That was the image he'd built—cartoon rabbit with a basketball. He knew it was the right image, but he couldn't make the jump to why he'd chosen it.

"Damn it," he said, and tapped the man's profile. His name was Augustin Balecheck. He was the deputy minister in charge of planetary transportation security. Mona leaned over his chair, resting her chin on Biryar's shoulder.

"What was this one?" she asked. He could smell the almonds on his wife's breath and feel the shifting of her jaw against his as she chewed. It was the third year of their marriage, and he had never stopped loving the smell of her skin close to his.

"A rabbit basketball player," he said. "The mole was like a rabbit whisker. Balecheck like 'ball check.' Also traveling is a foul in basketball, and he's planetary transportation."

Her sigh meant she was thinking. She pointed a thin, graceful finger at Deputy Minister Balecheck's mole. "He got that because the guy he was deep-throating had paving tar on his scrotum."

Biryar coughed out something close to a laugh.

"That man's cheek is a ball check," she said, "and the paving tar will remind you of the road system."

"Good lord. Are you always this obscene, Dr. Rittenaur? I'm not going to shake the man's hand while I imagine him having sex."

"If you don't like it, erase it from your memory and go back to the cartoon rabbit thing," she said.

"I don't think I'll be able to now."

She tapped her forehead with the tip of her finger, and she grinned. "Which is my point. It works better if you commit to the process," she said. Then she kissed his ear.

Biryar had two hundred and eighteen individuals and fifty-three organizations to commit to memory. More than any literal cartography, it was the map of the territory he was going to have to travel as the first Laconian governor of Auberon.

He hadn't been surprised when Duarte had chosen him. He'd worked for the empire since he was old enough to enter government service, excelled in his coursework, taken every initiative to rise among his peers. He had done his thesis on High Consul Duarte's early philosophical works and their relationship to examinations of grand strategy throughout human history. Auberon hadn't been a specific ambition of his, but a posting of importance to the empire had been. Medina or Bara Gaon or Sol, a position in the High Consul's cabinet or teaching at the university on Laconia would have served his hopes as well.

The reason, he knew, that he was in the cramped military cabin en route to a governor's mansion was Mona. Her small, round face and wide, dark eyes made her seem younger than she was and somehow elfin, but his wife was the best soils scientist of her generation. While he had been writing an academic love letter to the most powerful man in the empire, she had been mapping out paths to bring the thousand different biospheres into accord, to engineer everywhere what Auberon had happened onto by chance.

Before she'd taken a single step under Auberon's sun or drawn a breath of its air, Mona understood the richness of its dirt, and the potential that rested there. Her post would be at the Xi-Tamyan Agricultural Concern in the capital city of Barradan, where the governor's office would be. Their skills and backgrounds were perfectly suited for the post. He could only hope that the millions of inhabitants of Auberon saw that too.

He switched to the next image. A hard-faced woman with dark-brown eyes. He didn't need a mnemonic device for her. Suyet Klinger was the Auberon representative of the Association of Worlds, and one of the only people he would be ruling over that he'd actually met. He tapped to move to the next image but the screen shifted on its own and a scheduled request took its place. He let a breath out between his teeth and rose from his crash couch. Mona popped another almond into her mouth and watched him walk the few steps to the cabin door.

"I'll be back," he said. She nodded, and didn't speak.

They were already in their braking burn, the floor of the *Notus* pushing up against them at almost half a g. It was a short walk to the meeting room where the head of his security, newly assigned from Medina Station and picked up on the way through the gate hub, was waiting for him. The relief Biryar felt at putting aside the memorization work was evidence that greater discipline was called for. He made a mental note to go back to it as soon as the meeting was done. Not because he wanted to, but because he didn't. And it was his duty.

Major Overstreet was a thickly muscled man with pale skin and bright-blue eyes that left him seeming eerily corpse-like. He'd served with honor and distinction most recently under Colonel Tanaka and then Governor Singh of Medina Station. And when Medina had faced its crisis, Major Overstreet had stepped in to prevent atrocities being carried out in the name of the empire. He was a hero, and to be honored. But when Biryar sat across from him, the back of his neck itched a little and felt the shadow of the guillotine.

"Governor Rittenaur," Overstreet said, rising to his feet and saluting. "Thank you for your time."

"Of course, Major. Thank you for your work." Their usual pleasantries. There was neither warmth nor animosity behind them. They were two people entirely defined by their formal relationship: fellow cogs in the machine to which they were committed. It was comfortable.

"I've reviewed the report from the Association of Worlds," Overstreet said. "There are some decisions that need to be made about your accommodations, and it would be useful to me to have some guidelines about your risk tolerance."

"What are we looking at?"

Overstreet pulled up a report and sent it to the wallscreen. The format was familiar. Biryar had been reading and interpreting security reports for years, and usually for places he'd never physically been. He took in the slopes of Barradan's hills and the curve of its roads from a scattering of lines. The compounds that had been offered to him were marked in Laconian blue. He touched the northernmost.

"This has the fewest angles of approach," Biryar said. "That's a fence?"

"Decorative fence on a half-meter wall. Easy to reinforce. But it's also the farthest from the Xi-Tamyan campus, here," Overstreet said, indicating the far side of the city. "Which means the most exposure in transit for Dr. Rittenaur."

Biryar leaned forward, considering the other options for his new home in this new light. "What about this one?"

"Open grounds—like most places in Barradan—and approachable from three directions. But we can build a wall, the structures are defensible, and it would minimize daily transit exposure."

The potential for separatist violence had been proven on Medina and in a handful of the colony worlds. The enemies of Laconia and the High Consul were out there, and some would be on Auberon. In Barradan. Some would pass him in the streets, and he might not know them.

And they would pass Mona as well.

"The one closest to Xi-Tamyan will do," he said, and as soon as he said it, he felt a rightness in the choice. "And there's no need to build any walls. Let's not establish our new administration by hiding in our shell like a turtle. Personnel and active security show more engagement and openness."

"Yes, Governor," Overstreet said with a bland smile as he collapsed the reports.

The real protection wouldn't be walls and fences. It would be the narrative of power. The *Tempest* in Sol system was a massive deterrent, even though it was very far away. The *Notus* was smaller, but close by, and Auberon system didn't have the military power to deny it.

"There will be a reception after we arrive," Overstreet said. "I'm coordinating with the local authorities."

"If you are satisfied with the security arrangements, please move forward," Biryar said, agreeing. "I trust your judgment."

It occurred to Biryar then that he'd just chosen the home he might spend the rest of his life in based wholly on its abstract qualities, without knowing the color of the walls or the shapes of the windows. If he had, it wouldn't have changed anything.

The *Notus* was rated for atmosphere, so there was no reason to dock at the lunar station. There was a landing complex just east of the city designed to withstand the ship's drive plume until they switched to maneuvering thrusters and settled to the ground. With the turbulence of atmospheric passage and the vibration of the drive gone, there was nothing to drown out the soft ticking of the hull plates as they cooled. Biryar let the crash couch hold him up. The gravity of his new home planet pulled him gently into its cool blue gel.

He had imagined this moment a thousand times. His arrival at his new post, and the heroic, grave impression he wanted to give to the people who were now under his control. It was important that they should see him as something near the platonic ideal of a wise governor—stern, merciful, wise. And he also wanted them to recognize his loyalty to the High Consul and Laconia, as a model for them. As an example to be followed.

Now that the occasion was actually upon him, he was mostly aware of just how badly he needed to visit the head.

He heard his cabin door open, and then the soft padding of feet on the deck. Mona smiled down at him. She had her formal dress folded over her arm, ready to be put on. It was high-waisted and high-collared with layers of lace in Laconian blue. She was dressing for this moment not in her role as soil scientist but as the spouse of a governor. Her eyes betrayed only a little of her tiredness and anxiety. To anyone who didn't know her, not even that.

"Ready?" she asked.

Are you ready to take control of a planet? Are you ready to command the lives of millions of people and forge the most valuable planet in the greater human sphere into a tool that will, in time, feed trillions of people under a thousand different suns? He told himself that the flutter he felt in his stomach was excitement. Not fear. Never dismay.

If she had been anyone else in all of humanity, he would have said *Yes, I am.* But it was Mona, and so his true feelings were safe.

"I don't know."

She kissed him, and the softness of her lips and the strength of them were a comfort and a promise. He felt his body starting to react to her and stepped back. Distracted and aroused was no way to start his tenure as governor. The millimeter lift of her eyebrows meant she understood everything he hadn't said.

"I'm just going over to my cabin to change," she said.

"That sounds wise."

She took his hand, squeezed it. "We're going to be fine," she said.

Less than an hour later, he walked down the gantry and stepped for the first time onto the planet. *His* planet.

From sunrise to sunset lasted a little over four standard hours on Auberon, with cycles of light and darkness changing only slightly with the seasons. By local convention, day was two cycles of light and one of darkness, night the reverse. Noontime on Auberon was always dark, and midnight was bright. It was midmorning, but it looked like sunset. Red clouds high above them, and huge sessile organisms like trees or massive fungi lifted red streamers as if all the world were touched by fire.

The small group that had been invited to greet him was by definition the most honored citizens of Auberon. The order in which he acknowledged them was important. The formality with which he held himself, whether he smiled or didn't when he shook their hands. Everything mattered deeply, because what High Consul Duarte was to the empire, Biryar Rittenaur was to Auberon. Beginning now.

The streets of Barradan were narrower than the broad boulevards of Laconia, with buildings that crowded the pavement. Brick the gray-green color of the local clay. The lights all glowed with the full spectrum of sunlight to say that this darkness was daytime, and would become dimmer and warmer when consensus night came. Security forces with rifles and riot gear kept his path clear as he moved through the maze of intersections. If someone had planned the city, they'd done it with the aesthetics of an earthbound ghetto. More likely, Barradan had bloomed with no intention beyond satisfying the needs of the moment.

Biryar traveled in an open car, the wind of his passage stirring his hair. Something smelled foul. Like a sewer that had failed. Mona wrinkled her nose at it too.

"Indole," she said. She saw the blankness of his response. "Technically 2,3-benzopyrrole. Just a couple carbon rings and some nitrogen. The local biome really likes it. Nothing to worry about."

"It smells like…"

"Shit. Yes, it does," Mona said. "The soils team tells me we'll get used to it in a couple days."

"Well. Elements are elements, and there's only so many things you can make with them, I suppose," he said. "Some smell better than others."

The compound was lit for noon when they pulled in. The house was shaped like a horseshoe, with pink stucco walls and polished metal sconces every few meters. Local insect analogs swarmed around the brightness. The courtyard in the center was paved in plates of carbon-silicate lace engineered to shine blue as a beetle's carapace. Starlight seemed to swim in its depths, reflections of the galactic disk overhead. The capital city of his planet didn't yet generate enough light pollution to drown the sky. The stars were the only things that reminded him of Laconia.

His personal staff stood at attention beside the building's wide central doors. Laconian guards and local administrators, all in formal dress, all waiting for Major Overstreet's inspection before they met their new master.

He was home now. For better or worse, this was his place in the universe, and might be for the rest of his career. Mona's sigh was barely audible, and he thought there was regret in it until she spoke.

"It's beautiful," she said.

The reception began a few hours later. The sun was directly overhead in the second of the day's two brightnesses, and Biryar kept reflexively thinking of it as midday. He was impressed by the heat of the sunlight and the humidity of the air. Either the sewer stench had gone down with the rising sun or he was already growing used to it.

There were easily a hundred guests at the reception. Many of them were on the lists he'd committed to memory, but there were some others: a thin-faced woman with her hair in an elaborate plait, an older man with a thin mustache and a prosthetic arm, an agender person with a pinstriped linen suit and the studied respectability of a banker. Today was Auberon's first glimpse of what Laconian rule would mean, and the people—city, planet, and system—were driven by their uncertainty and their fear. It was Biryar's duty to project calm and strength, the implacable authority of the new regime, and its geniality and benignity to those who gave it their undivided loyalty.

He'd intended to wear a jacket, but he gave up the idea. He was happy to see that the guests had also chosen lighter shirts and soft, airy blouses. Mona's blue lace looked almost heavy by comparison, but she wore it with grace. She moved through the party as assured and confident as if they had lived in these rooms for years, not hours. She laughed easily and listened intently as she spoke to the man with the prosthetic arm. He felt the twinge of jealousy in his breast as a mixture of admiration, love, and exhaustion.

As he moved among the guests, he found himself orbiting her. Touching her arm as they passed, laying claim to her the same way he was laying claim to the world. The glitter of amusement in her eyes, invisible to anyone but him, meant she saw what he was doing, and that she forgave him his weakness. Or that she enjoyed the power she had over him. They were two ways to say the same thing.

The first sign of trouble seemed so trivial that he didn't see its significance at all at the time. They were in a side garden where the local plants pushed their ruddy way up from a lawn of grass. A fig tree from Earth had spread its limbs above a small carved-stone table. The fruit was ripe to splitting, and added a sweetness to the foul air.

Mona was sitting across from a woman maybe twenty years older than either of them. The woman's graying hair was starting to escape an austere bun, and her cheeks were flushed from one drink too many. When he saw Mona's frown, Biryar stepped lightly over, ready to act as his wife's savior. He found he had misread the situation.

"We were so close," the older woman said. "Six more months, and we could have cracked it. I swear to fucking God."

Mona shook her head in sympathetic outrage. The older woman looked up at Biryar, a flash of annoyance at his interruption melting into embarrassment when she recognized him.

Mona took his hand. "Dear, this is Dr. Carmichael. I told you about her work on amino acid array translation."

Biryar smiled and nodded as his mind churned. Carmichael. What was array translation? He'd known this one…He found it. "Coaxing the local biology into growing something that can nourish us."

Carmichael nodded a little too strongly. A lock of her hair escaped unnoticed and fanned out behind her head as if she were on the float. When she spoke, her voice was reedy, caught in the uncertain space between anger and whining. "My funding was reallocated. They just took it away. I wouldn't pay the bribes, and so they said I was difficult to work with!"

"That sounds distressing," Biryar said, putting sympathy in his tone while keeping it out of his word choice.

"It was," Carmichael said, nodding. Tears brightened her eyes. "It was really distressing. That's exactly the word."

Biryar nodded back, mirroring her.

"I will absolutely look into this," Mona said.

"Thank you, Dr. Rittenaur," Carmichael said, still nodding. "We were so close. I can show you the data."

Biryar smiled down at Mona. "If that could wait until another time, there's someone I'd like you to meet, dear."

"Of course," Mona said, rising. She and Carmichael exchanged farewells, and Biryar steered her away into the house without any clear idea where he was going except out of the older woman's sight.

"It's early to be taking sides in local disputes, don't you think?" he said as they walked.

Mona looked at him. She was tired too. Overstimulated and out of her element just as much as he was. When she spoke, she snapped.

"Her work is exactly what Auberon should be focused on. If she got sidelined because she wouldn't pay a bribe—"

"Corruption is a problem here. We knew that, and we'll address it. Maybe this is an example, or maybe she just has a story that makes her feel better. Either way, please don't commit us to anything on the first day." It came out harder than he'd meant it. Worse, it came out patronizing.

Mona's smile was warm and inauthentic, intended for onlookers and not for him. She squeezed his arm gently, bowed her head, and disengaged. He felt a little stab of distress. They should have put off the reception until they were both more rested. This was the kind of fight they only had when they were tired or hungry. They'd finish it in private if they had to. He didn't think it would amount to more than that.

Still, he regretted it.

The reception carried on through the remaining two hours of daylight and into the second sunset of the day. The light grew redder, and the crowd of people began to thin. Biryar went over his mental list of people he thought it was important to acknowledge. Arran Glust-Hart, the forensic accountant with the Association of Worlds. Nayad Li, the director of planetary logistics. Devi Ortiz, the minister of education. A dozen more. As the evening drew to its close, the irrational fear of introducing himself twice to the same person started to grow. He hadn't accomplished everything he'd hoped with the reception, but he knew himself well enough to recognize the point of diminishing returns. He remembered one of the High Consul's sayings: Overdoing is also falling short. Better to have a good night end well than push for perfect and undo what had been achieved.

He'd woken on a ship under burn. He would sleep at the bottom of a gravity well. The thought was enough to make his limbs feel heavy. A glass of whiskey, maybe. A boiled egg with some pepper and salt. And sleep.

He didn't notice quite how he found himself in the little drawing room that looked out over the courtyard. It was a cozy space with a tall, thin window and chairs made of some thick, fibrous wood strung with raw silk. The floor was made with the same green-gray bricks he'd seen on the drive in. A knotwork carpet commanded the center of the room. The older man with the prosthetic arm stood at the window, looking east toward where the sky was just fading from black to charcoal with the coming of the nighttime dawn, which put the hour near ten o'clock.

Biryar was certain the man hadn't been in his briefings list. The arm—titanium fused to his living flesh—would have been hard to forget. But even without that, the face was striking. The man's skin was pale and papery without seeming frail. Only well lived-in. A line of fluffy white hair ran from ear to nape to ear, leaving a wide, smooth scalp. A thin, white mustache. He wore tight black trousers and a pale shirt with an open collar. An unlit cigar was clamped in his lips. The one-armed man turned and nodded to Biryar as if he'd been expected.

"Turd of a planet," he said. "It's home, though. I remember the first time I came down. I thought I was gonna puke, it smelled so bad." He lifted his cigar between a thumb and finger. "It's when I started with these. Just to kill off my sense of smell. But I do love it now."

"I'm looking forward to making it my home too," Biryar said. "I don't believe we've been introduced."

"Makes me think of the Raj," the one-armed man said, as if he hadn't heard Biryar. "That was a weird thing, wasn't it? Dinky-ass little Britain using maybe a hundred thousand people to keep their boots on three hundred million necks? You can have the best guns ever, and those odds still suck. No, I do not envy you. Not even a little bit."

Biryar's smile went slightly tighter. Something about the moment felt off. "I think your understanding of history leaves something to be desired."

The man turned, pale eyebrows lifted. He shrugged his real shoulder. "Maybe that part. There's other bits of history I know better. You ever hear the question 'Silver or lead?'"

Biryar shook his head. "I don't believe so. What's your name? Who are you with?"

"My friends call me Erich," the one-armed man said, grinning. His teeth were the color of old ivory. "So anyway, there was this thing way back when. They used to have these huge recreational drug companies. Totally illegal. And when someone new would come into town or get elected or whatever, the question was: silver or lead? *Plata o plomo.* Does the new sheriff in town take a bribe or a bullet? Hell of a slogan. It's simple, you know? Boils everything down. You have to admire that."

Biryar's exhaustion fell away. His heart began to tap at his ribs, but he didn't feel panicked. His mind was cold and sharp, and he was suddenly very present. "Are you threatening me?"

"What? Jesus, no. We're just a couple guys talking history." The old man took something from his pocket. At first Biryar thought he was going to light his cigar, but instead the old man placed the little device on the windowsill with a percussive tap. He stepped back from it. A small black shape, curved along one side.

Biryar gestured to it with his chin, asking the question without speaking.

"It's a token for the local exchange network," the one-armed man said. "It's tied to a private, anonymized account with about fifteen thousand new-francs in it. That's enough to buy even someone like you a little privacy."

"For what?"

The man spread his hands. "Whatever. I don't judge."

Biryar stepped carefully to the window and picked up the token. The resin looked like smoky glass. Obsidian. The old man smiled until Biryar dropped it to the floor, put his heel on it, and ground it against the brick. The one-armed man's eyes narrowed. The facade of good humor was gone, and Biryar knew he was facing a predator.

"Are you sure about that?" the old man asked.

"Don't make me raise my voice. This is my house. And there are a lot of armed people in the compound right now," Biryar said.

The man smiled. "There are. And some of them are probably pretty loyal to you. Others, maybe not as much. You a gambling man?"

In the window, the night's single, swift dawn was already breaking. Blue sky and high, scudding clouds. The two men stood still as stone for three long breaths, then the old man turned to the door and walked out. Biryar felt the shout swelling in his chest. He didn't let it out.

He was shaking. Trembling. He picked up the token. The resin was cloudy with scratches now, but he didn't know whether he'd managed to break whatever mechanism it contained. He told himself that he would not leave the room until he could gather himself again into the man he was supposed to be. He wouldn't rush out into the reception looking panicked. But then he thought of Mona earlier in the night, listening intently to the one-armed man, and he couldn't wait any longer.

The one-armed man had vanished. Mona, sitting on a wide sofa with a gin and tonic in her hand, saw him and put her drink down. He hoped it was only the intimacy of their marriage that let her see his distress. When she came to him, he kissed her ear and whispered.

"Find our guards. The ones from the *Notus*, not the locals. Stay with them."

She pulled back, smiling like a mask. She spoke without moving her lips. "Are we in danger?"

"I don't know," he said. "I'll find out."

With Mona warned, he could move to offense. He summoned Major Overstreet to his private office. Sitting at the wide wooden table where he'd never sat before felt like being in a mousetrap.

Overstreet stepped into the room and stood at attention. The only sign of fatigue was a slight darkness in the skin under his eyes. "Sir?"

Biryar kept himself calm, or as calm as he could. When he got to the old man's threat, Overstreet became almost eerily still. When the full report was given, he put the token on the desk. Overstreet picked it up, considered it, and placed it back down. Biryar leaned forward in his chair. He hadn't said anything yet that the old man wouldn't have known from being present when it happened. That was about to change.

"How certain are you that our conversation here is private?" Biryar asked.

Overstreet hesitated. Then, "An hour ago, I would have said I was certain, sir."

"Now?"

"I'm less certain."

The silence had weight. "I think it would be very unfortunate to leave the compound so soon after arriving. I will visit the *Notus* in the morning to finish clearing the diplomatic documents. We can have a conversation there."

"I will have Laconian guards stationed to assure your safety."

"And Dr. Rittenaur's."

"Yes, sir. And I will begin an investigation as to who this individual was at once, and who allowed him on the property."

"Thank you," Biryar said. "This has to be our first priority now."

"Agreed, sir. I'll have a preliminary report ready before you reach the *Notus*. And..." Overstreet pressed his lips together and looked away.

"What's bothering you, Major?"

"This was either an egregious failure on the part of the local forces or an outright subversion of security protocols. Either way, there will have to be consequences. Before I begin an investigation, it would be good to have some sense of how you would prefer to escalate this. Should that be needed."

It was a measure of how much the encounter had shaken him that Biryar hadn't considered this already. On Laconia, a breach of this magnitude would mean someone was executed at the least, and more likely sent to the Pens as a test subject. But on Laconia, a breach like this would never have happened. The first decision of his career would be whether to execute someone and very possibly alienate the planet he'd come to preside over. And the decision was complicated by what had happened with Governor Singh on Medina.

"We both understand the dangers of overreach," Biryar said, speaking the words gently, as if they were sharp. "If the offending party is a native of Auberon, arrest them and turn them over to the local authorities. The processing of their case will need to be thoroughly and completely monitored. We will respect the laws here to the degree that we safely can. I won't escalate until Auberon's legal system has the chance to do this well."

"And if the issue began with us?"

Biryar smiled. That was easier. "If a Laconian is responsible for breaking protocol and putting our administration at risk, either now or in the future, we will execute them publicly. Laconian standards are absolute."

"Understood, sir," Overstreet said, as if Biryar hadn't simply restated a policy that traced back over thousands of light-years to the desk of High Consul Winston Duarte himself. Overstreet hesitated, then: "One thing, sir? Until this is addressed, I'd be more comfortable if you carried a sidearm."

Biryar shook his head. "It will be seen as a sign of fear. I trust your security force to make it unnecessary."

"I appreciate your confidence, but I'm asking you to do it anyway," Overstreet said. "The man was in your house."

Biryar sighed, then nodded his agreement. Overstreet left.

Mona was sitting on the edge of the bed when he reached her.

Worry etched lines around her mouth. Probably around his as well.

"What happened?" she said. "Is there a problem?"

"The criminal element of Auberon is concerned by our arrival. As they should be," he said. "There was a threat. We're looking into it."

She pulled her knees up, hugging them to her chest, and looked out toward the windows. She looked lost and small. She was right to feel that way. They were one ship full of people to command a system of millions.

Thick shutters were closed against the brightness of the too-fast sun and the heat and stench of the consensus midnight. A line of brightness showed the seam where they met. Biryar sat beside her. A dozen things came to mind that he might say to her. *This is our duty* or *Some pushback had to be expected* or *We will destroy them.*

He kissed her shoulder. "I won't let anyone hurt us."

Agnete scratched her chin to make it seem more like she was thinking and less like she was struggling to keep her temper. The old man sat at the breakfast bar. His bathrobe was a gray that could have been any other color before it faded. His fake arm was going through its diagnostic reboot, shivering and twitching. The old man did it every day even though the documentation said it was a once-a-month thing. The speed and violence of the reboot sequence made her think of insects.

When her outrage had subsided enough that she could be polite, she said, "That was a move, boss. Not sure I would have done that."

"It was a risk," he said, dismissively.

But whatever his tone, he wasn't at the Zilver Straat bar. Just the fact that he'd started moving his meeting places said he was taking the situation seriously. She didn't know whether she felt worse because of the new level of threat or better because he knew it was a problem. Even if he wouldn't say it out loud.

They were sitting in an apartment over a noodle bar. It wasn't quite a bolt-hole, although the old man had a few of those around the city and around the planet, and probably some she didn't know about. The light of afternoon dawn slanted in the clerestory windows, tracking down the far wall quickly enough to follow it if she was patient. She wasn't.

The old man poured ouzo over ice with his real arm, the liquor going cloudy as it filled the glass.

"This new governor's going to fuck us up now, isn't he?" she asked.

The old man didn't answer at once. His fake arm was almost done with its reboot. He used it to pick up the glass, and it seemed all right. Steady. He sipped his drink. "He's going to have to try. That's his job. It's still our home pitch, though."

"How hard is this going to be?" she asked. Her irritation was already fading, and her mind was turning toward what needed to happen next. Planning for violence. When the old man spoke, his tone was lighter than she'd expected.

"I don't know. He's a tight-ass, this one. I mean, it seems like these Laconians all are. Not a big surprise. You take a bunch of Martian Congressional Republic fanatics and interbreed them for a few decades, it's not going to tend toward a greater mental flexibility. I've got a few ears in place. We'll see how he reacts."

"Electronic?"

"Nope. Just people who like gossip and drinking. They'll do." The old man ran a metal finger around the rim of his glass, his mouth pulled into something that was almost a smile. "This guy. He's...*hungry*. I just don't know what for yet."

"Does it matter?"

He drank down the rest of the ouzo in a gulp. "Of course it matters. Hungry pays our bills."

"No, I mean, why do we care what he wants or needs when we're going to kill him? Sure, maybe he'd look the other way if we got him a lot of exotic talcum powder and a bottle of whiskey, but that's not going to matter much when he's dead."

The old man shook his head slowly. "I'm not killing him. Not yet anyway. We start knocking off governors, maybe we get a little time to breathe before the next guy comes, but the next guy's going to be even more of a shithead. Better if I figure this guy out."

"Permission?" Agnete said.

The old man waved his metal hand in a slow circle, inviting her to speak her mind.

"You already made the call," she said. "He joins up by taking the bribe, or he turns it down and we kill him. He turned it down, so now we kill him. Those are the rules."

The old man scratched at his hairy, white chest. Outside the window, a local pigeon—six compound eyes and bat wings covered with feathery cilia—landed, chittered, and flew off again. The old man smiled after it as if the interruption had broken his train of thought. When he spoke, she knew it hadn't, and that the conversation was over.

"The rules," he said, "are what I say they are."

Mona Rittenaur's office was on the top floor of the northwest corner of the Xi-Tamyan building. It was twice as large as her cabin on the *Notus* had been, with intelligent glass from floor to ceiling that not only adjusted the level of light as Auberon's sun sped across its wide blue sky, but corrected the color to give the landscape below her a sense of greater constancy. She knew from her briefing that the illusion was supposed to make the transition to Auberon's unfamiliar daily cycle easier, but after the first few days, she disabled the feature. She wanted to see the world around her as it was.

"Dr. Rittenaur?" a woman's voice said from the doorway, and then, belatedly, a soft knock. "You wanted to see me?"

Veronica Dietz was her liaison with the workgroups. Mona had been coming to the office for a week now, and apart from being the living symbol of how anxious Xi-Tamyan Agricultural

Concern was to have a solid relationship with the new Laconian government, her role in the research had been nebulous.

She was ready to define it.

"Yes," Mona said, "I heard about some research on amino acid array translation. I'd like to see the records on that."

"I don't think it's a live workgroup," Veronica said. "We had some preliminary work a few years back, but the powers that be thought the microbiota compatibility work had more potential."

"I understand," Mona said with a smile. "Just bring me what you have on array translation. It doesn't need to be complete."

"You got it. Anything else?"

"Not for now," Mona said, and Veronica vanished back behind the door.

Dr. Carmichael's tipsy, weeping voice had stuck with Mona since the reception. Biryar was focused on the incident, the threat, whatever euphemism he and Overstreet were using for it. The criminals and terrorists who saw Laconia as something that could or ought to be resisted. That they'd made a threat on the same day the *Notus* arrived bothered her, but she couldn't do anything about it directly. This, she could.

The records appeared on her system a few minutes later with a tagged note from Veronica offering to bring in some tea and one of the apple pastries from the break room. Mona thanked her in text but turned the offer down. Veronica's job required that she be solicitous and friendly, but it didn't cost Mona anything to treat her nicely.

The records of Dr. Carmichael's work were preliminary, as Mona expected. They also weren't quite as impressive as she'd been led to believe. There was good, solid work in it, though. If it had been done on Laconia, Carmichael would have had more tools for the experiments. And she might still, if Mona pushed to have her transferred back home. It tickled her a little, the prospect of swooping in and rescuing a languishing career just because she could.

The microbiota compatibility workgroup that had been funded

instead was headed by a broad-faced man with brown eyes and hair as thin as mist: Dr. Grover Balakrishnan, previously from Ganymede, one of the oldest and most respected agricultural centers in Sol system. His plan was essentially harnessing evolutionary pressure to develop soils that supported both Sol and Auberon trees of life. Start a few hundred samples of mixed microbes, then part out the most successful ones. Iterate a few dozen times, and let selective pressure do the work.

It was sloppy. And, to her eyes, less likely to get replicable results than Dr. Carmichael's work. That didn't mean that there had really been a conspiracy to quash the array translation project. It might just have been a bad decision. She went back to look at the funding committee reports. It took her most of the morning and well into the midday darkness before she found the smoking gun.

Deep in the patent payment agreement that covered any products derived from the microbiota compatibility studies, a new name appeared. Only it wasn't really new at all.

V. Dietz.

Veronica.

Mona went through all of the present workgroups, and again and again, all through the studies, it appeared. Whatever discoveries Xi-Tamyan made in their facilities on Auberon, Veronica Dietz was contractually entitled to a cut. Each one was small, but taken together, they would be enough to make her fantastically wealthy. People had been murdered for much less money than her liaison made in a month. And that was before her salary.

Mona went through again, this time looking for the justification for the payments. Some service that Veronica did for the researchers that made the payments make sense. There was nothing apart from the inescapable conclusion that if anyone was going to make anything, Veronica Dietz got a slice.

When her system chimed, she flinched. Veronica's voice came from the speaker, as friendly and casual as ever. It was only the intensity with which Mona listened that made it seem fake as a carnival mask.

"Hey, Dr. Rittenaur. I'm heading down to the commissary. Do you want me to get you anything?"

The steadiness of Mona's voice surprised her. She would have thought that something would make it tremble: surprise, fear, anger. But she only said, "No, I'm fine," and let the connection drop.

Biryar had only ever been to two executions. The first time, he had been a child, and Laconia had still been more wilderness than civilization. One of the soldiers who had come with the first fleet had been careless in his driving. Maybe even intoxicated, it was hard to remember the details now. A boy from the original scientific expedition had been struck and killed. Duarte himself had overseen the punishment, and attendance at the death had been mandatory.

Before they killed the man, Duarte had explained that discipline was critical for them all. They were a small force in a single system, with no influx of immigration to draw from. It had seemed a strange argument at the time. If people were so rare and precious, killing one seemed wasteful.

Later he understood that the preciousness was what made the sacrifice profound. The soldier had died quickly, and while it didn't undo the man's crime, it showed the members of the civilian scientific expedition that Duarte and his followers valued their lives and the lives of their children. If the driver had lived, bringing the two populations together would have been difficult or impossible.

The second time, it had been a young construction worker in the capital who used the wrong proportions when mixing concrete for the foundations of one of the buildings. No one had died, but the error, if it hadn't been found, could have led to hundreds of deaths when the structure collapsed. Duarte had held a ceremony—again mandatory—so that everyone could understand the severity of the problem and the sorrow with which the young woman was being sent to the Pens. Biryar hadn't watched her die, but he still remembered her tear-streaked face as she made her apology to the community.

Laconia had always been the few and the pure against the many and the corrupt. Like the Spartans from whom they took their name, Laconians were severe within their group, both to forge the iron discipline that had led them to victory and to demonstrate to others the sincerity of their beliefs.

It was hard, but it was necessary.

Now the Laconians present in the courtyard stood at attention, representing the empire and its uncompromising resolve. Biryar had his place of honor at the front of the assembly.

"I apologize," the prisoner said, "for the shame I brought on my companions. And for the wrong I have done to my commander and the High Consul."

The sunlight hurt Biryar's eyes, and a thin film of sweat stuck his shirt to his back. The pistol felt heavy, the holster like someone constantly tapping his hip for attention. There were more locals in attendance than he'd expected. Some were employees of the local newsfeeds, but many of them had come as sightseers and tourists drawn by the spectacle of punishment the way they would be to a sporting event.

The prisoner, an ensign assigned to logistics and supply, had given a pharmaceutical printer and two boxes of reagents from the *Notus*'s medical supplies to a local criminal to produce untaxed recreational drugs. The local buyer was in an Auberon-administered prison and faced two years' confinement if she was convicted. The trial was apparently a lengthy process. The Laconian side of the theft would be dead before Biryar ate dinner.

The prisoner hung his head. A guard led him up the steps to the little platform. The prisoner knelt. Biryar's nose had grown mostly insensible to the sewer smell of Auberon, but a particularly strong whiff of it came on the breeze. It felt like a comment. Tradition, such as it was, allowed anyone higher in the chain of command to give the order, but symbolically, Biryar knew it had to be him. The prisoner's commanding officer, a woman Biryar had known peripherally for almost a decade, stood on the platform with a sidearm at the ready.

Biryar stepped forward to the sound of a single, dry drum, met her gaze, and nodded. He half expected tears to glisten in her eyes, but her expression was blank. After a moment, she nodded in return, pivoted, and fired a single round into the back of the prisoner's head. The sound was weirdly flat. The drum stopped, and a medic came out to certify the death.

And it was over. Biryar turned to the cameras of the local newsfeeds, careful to present his better profile. The crowd looked shocked. That was good. State violence was meant to be shocking. It was done to prove a point, and it would have been a pity for the sacrifice not to have its effect. He paused long enough to be sure that they'd all gotten a good image of him for the feeds, then turned toward the Laconian contingent. He wanted to go back to his office, get a cold gin and tonic, and close his eyes until his head stopped aching.

Most of the people in Laconian blue had come with him on the *Notus*, but Suyet Klinger, the local representative of the Association of Worlds, and her staff had also chosen clothes that echoed Biryar's uniform. Blue almost the right shade and tailored in a similar cut. Not Laconian uniforms, but something that rhymed with them. Her face, as he stepped to her, was grave.

"I'm very sorry, sir," she said. "I'm sure that was very difficult for you."

He knew what he was supposed to say. *Discipline is the policy of the High Consul.* It should have been easy, but the words that came to his mind were *Why are you sure?*

Klinger knew nothing about him but what she'd been told by Laconia. She would have been just as solicitous to anyone who had come in his position. And if someone else had been in her role, he would have treated them the same way he did her. They weren't people to each other. They were roles. This was etiquette, and the inauthenticity of the situation oppressed him.

He nodded to her. "Discipline is the policy of the High Consul," he said, and she averted her gaze in respect. The forms were there to be followed.

He moved through the grim crowd, acknowledging each of them and being acknowledged. Form. It was all just keeping form. The shadows shifted around them as the sun raced for the horizon and left him feeling like he'd been there for hours, but there were more nods to exchange, more words to mouth. The dead man was hauled away to the recyclers, and the medics retreated.

It was strange and in a way unfair that the local thief would live and might even go free. Being Laconian meant being held to a higher standard, and so transgression against that standard required a higher response, but it still bothered him. Or at least it did for the moment. If he could get some rest and a decent meal, it might not. The faces in the group began to blend together, one following another following another until he didn't know or care who he was speaking to.

He came to a man he hadn't met in person before, with brown hair, a serious expression, and a mole on his cheek like a dot of paving tar. Biryar almost pulled away, shocked by the sudden visceral image of how the fleck of tar had gotten there, and then felt amused and even strangely pleased.

"Deputy Balecheck," Biryar said. "Good to finally meet you."

Balecheck's eyes widened a fraction. The surprise at being recognized melted quickly into a smile as they shook hands, and then Biryar moved on. From the other man's point of view, it had been a gratifying moment that showed his importance to the new governor. Functionally, it was an example of building the kind of good relations with the local authority that would cement Laconian rule on Auberon. It was also a smutty joke with his wife, but that was a fact Biryar would keep entirely private. At least until he was alone with Mona.

It works better when you commit to the process, she'd said. He had to commit to the process of governing Auberon, even the parts that he found difficult. Especially to those parts.

A car waited for him at the edge of the courtyard, ready to take him back to his offices. When he ducked into it, Major Overstreet followed and sat across from him. His pale, bald face shone with sweat.

"How are you doing, sir?"

"Fine," Biryar said. "A bit of a headache."

"The stutter," Overstreet said.

"The what?"

The car pulled away, and cool air, as fresh as if it came from the *Notus*'s recyclers, touched his face and filled his nose. He noticed the absence of Auberon's stench and dreaded the end of the ride when he'd step back into it. It made more sense to keep exposing himself to the foul air. Breaks from it like this could only prolong his acclimation.

"They call it the stutter, sir. It's common among new arrivals. The four-hour cycles don't sync well with normal circadian cues. Irritability, headache. Some people get vertigo after about a month that clears in a few days. It's just our brains learning the new environment."

"Good to know," Biryar said. "Is it bothering you?"

"Yes, sir, it is," Overstreet said. "I'm looking forward to it being over."

The growing twilight in the streets was the real one. The end of the day and the beginning of evening. If he did it right, Biryar hoped to be asleep before the nighttime dawn. If he could just sleep through and give his body the impression of a full twelve hours of darkness...The longing for rest surprised him. Maybe he was more tired than he knew.

"What progress have you made on that other investigation?" Biryar asked.

"The man with the metal arm," Overstreet said, making the words like the heading on a report. Neither a question nor a statement, but a tag that identified the content to follow. "He is a known figure in the local criminal demimonde. He goes by several names, but he has no entry in the law enforcement systems.

He has no accounts on the exchanges, though given the token he tried to bribe you with, it's safe to assume he has significant access to untraceable funds."

"Where did he come from?"

"There aren't any records of his arrival in the databases."

"So he grew out of the dirt?" Biryar said, more sharply than he'd meant to.

Overstreet shrugged. "I'm moving forward with the assumption that the local databases are at least inaccurate and more likely suffering ongoing compromises."

Biryar leaned back in the seat. A group of young men were playing football in the street, and the security detail was yelling at them to move off and let the cars through. Biryar watched them. Long-limbed, lanky young men. Maybe Belters. Maybe just adolescents. Any of them could be a separatist terrorist. All of them could be. For a moment, it felt like madness to be on the planetary surface at all. There was no safety here. There couldn't be.

"He's not a criminal mastermind," Overstreet said as the car started forward again. "He's just got a head start. We will track him down."

"Don't turn this one over to the local police. He should be our guest until we can fully understand how he got past our security arrangements."

"I understand," Overstreet said. "No formal arrest, then?"

"Once he's helped with our security review, we can revisit the issue," Biryar said. And then, a moment later, "He was talking with my *wife*."

"Yes, sir. I understand."

The compound was well guarded now. Laconian marines in powered armor stood like sentries at the approaches and on the roofs. He lost something by having them there. Duarte's rule through him should have been inevitable and confident. A standing guard made him seem concerned, and concern made him look weak, but he couldn't bring himself to dismiss them or release them to other duty.

As he stepped into the private rooms, he unbuttoned his collar. In the time since they'd arrived, Biryar had made some changes to the governor's compound. He hadn't brought many things from their old home on Laconia, but what there was had pride of place. The picture of Mona receiving her Laconian distinguished service award, framed on the front wall where the light caught it. The clay sculpture she'd given him as a wedding gift. A calligraphic print of one of High Consul Duarte's sayings—*Effort in Discipline. Effortless in Virtue*—in gold leaf.

Everything else in the rooms was foreign. The fluted wall sconces with different spectrums of light for daytime darkness and night. The grain of the false wood paneling, made from the treelike organisms of Auberon to mimic the trees of Earth. Neither one was his home. It felt like the room itself was telling him that he didn't belong. Like it was pushing him away. He was sure that, with time, the sensation would pass.

He stretched. The knot between his shoulders appeared to be there permanently now, like the grit in his eyelids. The door behind him opened with a click, and Mona's footsteps—as familiar and unmistakable as her voice—followed. He looked over at her, and his heart sank to his gut.

"What's wrong?" he asked.

She dropped into a cushioned chair and shook her head. A small, tight, unconscious gesture he'd seen before. Anger, then. Well, better that than fear. He went to sit near her, but didn't touch her. Her rage didn't respond well to physical comfort.

"This place is rotten," she said. "Xi-Tamyan has a scam going on in it that has profoundly compromised its research priorities for years. *Years.* Maybe since they came here."

"Tell me," Biryar said.

She did. Not only the way her liaison had added herself to the patent agreements, but that she was married to the union comptroller, that she had gotten the placement in Mona's office over several other more qualified applicants, that her reported income didn't remotely match the payments made to her. With every sentence, Mona's voice grew harder, the outrage rising the more she thought about it. Biryar listened, leaning forward with his hands clasped and his gaze on her. Every new detail felt like a weight on his chest. Corruption layered on corruption layered on corruption until it seemed like there was more disease than health.

"And," Mona said, reaching her crescendo, "either management and the union didn't know, in which case they're incompetent, or they did, and they're complicit."

Biryar lowered his head, letting it all settle. Mona's gaze was fixed on nothing, her head shaking a fraction of a centimeter back and forth, like she was scolding someone in her imagination. She probably was.

There was a soft knock at the door. One of the housekeepers hoping to sweep or change their bedding. Biryar told them to come back later and got a muttered apology in return. Mona hadn't even noticed. He risked taking her hand.

"That is disappointing," he said.

"We have to *fix* it," she said. "This can't be permitted. This scam has cost *years*. Veronica has to be arrested and removed. The union has to be investigated and purged. I don't know how deep this goes."

"I will bring this to the attention of the local magistrates," Biryar said. "We'll address it."

"Magistrates? No, we need to go now and arrest her. Ourselves. She's undermining the most important colony world that there is. You're the governor."

"I understand that. I do. But if what she's done is illegal under Auberon's law, then it's a matter for the local courts. If I step in, I have to step very carefully."

Mona drew back her hand. The weight in Biryar's gut grew heavier, the knot in his back ached. He pressed his lips thin, and went on.

"I am building on fear and hope," he said. "Fear of the *Tempest* and the *Typhoon*, and hope that they won't come. Our best path is to be seen as all-powerful but benevolent. Even indulgent. When we have a larger fleet, more experience, loyalty among the local police and military forces? Then we can enforce our ways here. We're still in our first days. I have to be careful not to overreach."

Disappointment changed the shape of Mona's eyes. It softened her mouth. He felt the apology at the back of his throat, but it would have sounded like he was sorry for not giving her what she wanted, and he would mean he was sorry that the situation was what it was.

"If the payments to her don't really go to her..." Mona said. "What if her income report is accurate? She could be part of a crime syndicate. That man who was here? With the arm? She could be working for him."

"And I will have our people look into that. If she is, we'll take action."

"We should be taking action anyway," Mona said. "I'm Laconia's eyes on the most significant agricultural research that there is. You're the governor of the planet. If we aren't doing something, why are we here?"

"Please lower your voice."

"Don't patronize me, Biryar. It's a real question."

"We're staying alive, Mona," he snapped. "We are picking our fights, we're identifying the most immediate threats and addressing them, and we are doing everything possible to give the impression that we could bring overwhelming power to bear and merely choose not to."

"Because that isn't true," Mona said.

"It will be. Given time to establish ourselves, we can dominate any system, but we can't dominate all of them at once. So this is how we govern. We are present, we exert influence, we exercise power when we have to, and we graciously allow self-rule until another option exists for us."

"Self-rule?" Mona said, and her voice could cut skin. "Duarte sent us here so we could see the situation firsthand. And *react* to it. How is the two of us doing nothing self-rule?"

"Self-rule for them," Biryar said. "Not for us."

The old man sat on a metal barstool at the edge of the warehouse. Dust floated in the beam of light from holes near the roofline where ratdoves—which were neither rats nor doves—had chewed their way through to shelter. Agnete stood beside him, shifting her weight from one foot to the other, a pistol in her hand. The old man was watching and rewatching video from the official government newsfeed. The poor asshole kneeling on the platform, mouthing some words, then the governor nodding like an old Roman emperor giving the thumbs-down, and the executioner putting a bullet through the prisoner's skull. Every time the gun fired, the old man laughed. It wasn't mirth. It was derision.

"This man," the old man said, tapping the frozen image of Governor Rittenaur, "is fucking hilarious."

"He just killed one of his own men to make a point," Agnete said.

"Right? You know who does that shit? Theater majors," he said. Then, seeing her expression, he put the hand terminal in his pocket. "It's easy to execute your own. Someone that follows your orders, they're easy to kill. This 'We hold ourselves to an exacting standard' thing? I've seen it before. It's showy, because who does that shit? But it's easy."

"I don't know, boss. It made an impression," she said. In the distance, the whine of an electric motor and the clash of the steel fence rolling open. The old man heard it and rose from his stool.

"Well, it shouldn't have," he said, walking toward the loading dock. "We're sure they were fighting? Him and his wife?"

Agnete shrugged. She didn't like the way the boss thought about two things at once. It made her feel like he wasn't concentrating on the business at hand.

"They were yelling at each other," she said. "Your friend in housekeeping couldn't make out all of what they were saying."

"Interesting. Our guy didn't want money, so maybe he's not

greedy. But if he and the sweetheart aren't getting along, maybe there's an itch we can scratch there."

"Honeypot?"

"There's a reason the classics are classic."

"I'm on it," Agnete said. "But after we're done here."

The loading dock door hummed for a second, warming up, then clattered as it rose. Dust and translucent scales came down into the light. The truck was old and rusting. The logo of a grain hauling company that had gone bankrupt four years earlier still peeled on its side. The back of the truck opened and four men came out. All of them carried guns.

The old man sniffed, cleared his throat, sneezed.

"Bless you," one of the four men said. The leader.

"Thanks," the old man said. The new men waited, motionless. Agnete tightened her grip on the gun, but didn't raise it. For a long breath, no one moved.

"If this is the delivery," the old man said, "maybe you could deliver it. If it's something else..."

Bless You shook his head. "It's the delivery, but the price has gone up."

"Disappointing," the old man said, but amiably. "How much?"

"Doubled."

"Nope," the old man said. "Too greedy. Try again."

Bless You raised his gun and the old man's titanium arm moved too quickly for the eye to follow. The deafening report of the gunshot almost drowned out the metallic sound of the bullet impact. The thugs were quiet, as if they'd been stunned by their own violence.

"Boss?" Agnete said.

The old man had his real hand pressed to his chest, pain in his features. His false arm reached out before him and opened its closed fist. The bullet dropped to the warehouse floor with a sharp tick.

"You boys," the old man said, enunciating each word clearly, "just fucked all the way up."

"Hey, Erich," Bless You started to say, fear in his voice. An apology? Whatever it was, he never got to finish.

High in the rafters, the turret emplacement had heard the old man give the go phrase. The warehouse went bright with the stutter of its muzzle flash. The four men fell together. The staccato roar of the gun echoed through the warehouse space and then faded, leaving only a high-pitched whine in Agnete's ears.

"You all right?" she asked. Her voice sounded faint and distant. She opened and closed her jaw a few times to make the ringing in her head go away.

"Yeah, yeah," the old man said. "I just hate it when the arm does that. Feels like the fucking thing's about to rip loose every time."

"One of these days, it will." She walked to where the men were writhing in the guano and dust on the warehouse floor. Fléchette rounds had ripped bright red holes in their skin. The electrical smell of the shock rounds mixed with charred skin like roasting pig.

This was how the old man worked. Everyone had been looking at Agnete and her pistol, thinking she was the muscle. It had made them overconfident.

"You see," the old man said, not to the fallen thug but to Agnete, "this is the difference. A buy goes bad, and I need to send a message that that's not okay. I could go the Laconian way, right? Kill *you* and send these fuckers home. Would that make any sense?"

"I guess not," she said.

"Grandstanding," the old man said, his false hand wrapping fingers around Bless You's throat. "It's immature, is what it is."

Bless You tried to say something. Before he could, the old man used him to send a message.

Self-rule for them. Not for us.

Mona knew enough about psychology to put her feelings in context. As Veronica sat across the table from Mona, shifting the display between the reports, breaking down the datasets into digestible summaries and giving an overview of where the labs stood with the active experiments, Mona knew intellectually that the woman's voice wasn't really all that grating. Veronica's habit of interrupting herself and never quite getting back to the first sentence wasn't all that rare a quirk. Her haircut didn't really make her look like she was wearing a "respectable administrator" costume. Those were all artifacts of Mona's own state of mind.

The knowledge didn't help.

"We're expecting to see some data from the photosynthesis study at North Field by the end of the week," Veronica said. "The preliminary report is, as you can tell, looking pretty good."

She had to know, Mona thought. There was no way that the tension and antipathy were going under Veronica's radar. The smile was just the same as it had always been, the solicitous manner, the ready facts and reports. The woman had to know that Mona loathed her, but there was no sign of it. So either Mona was very good at hiding her emotions or Veronica was.

"What about the microbiota compatibility studies?" Mona asked.

Veronica shook her head as she spoke. "Those aren't in North Field. Balakrishnan's workgroup is all in the old facility. I mean, nothing's really old around here, right? We've only been on the planet for a couple decades."

You're changing the subject, Mona thought. Making Veronica Dietz uncomfortable was one of the few real pleasures in her day.

"When do we expect results from Balakrishnan's study?" she asked.

"I think the next assay starts in about a month, but I'm not a hundred percent on that," Veronica said. "I can check if you want."

And tell me whatever is most convenient for you, Mona thought. If Balakrishnan's results needed to be a failure to keep Veronica's skimming unnoticed, Mona had no doubt that the study would mysteriously fail. Just the way Dr. Carmichael's array translation study had become less promising when this woman—this snake, this parasite—didn't get a piece of it.

"Take a look for me," Mona said, standing up. "We can go over it in...five?"

"All right," Veronica said, as if the request were perfectly reasonable. Prepare a report in the time it takes to brew a cup of tea. Mona waited as Veronica walked out—she wouldn't leave the woman in her office alone—and then locked the office door behind her and headed right along the pale-green hall and then right again into the commissary.

She poured herself a cup of green tea and picked up a sugar cookie from the dessert table before sitting down alone at a table by the window. Tall white clouds rose on the horizon, glowing gold and red in the sunlight. She scowled at them. Someone had cracked the window open, and the breeze actually smelled fresh. She'd become so desensitized to the local environment that the fecal smell of the planet's biology didn't even register to her anymore.

The situation with Veronica was becoming a problem, and not just because Veronica was a problem. Mona was meant to be reporting back to Laconia. There was a whole team of soil researchers and agricultural biologists waiting for her to share the insights of Xi-Tamyan and Auberon. There had even been queries from Dr. Cortázar, which was one step short of attention from Winston Duarte himself. She should have had a preliminary report ready to go, outlining the state of play not only for research here but across the colony worlds that Auberon partnered with. Instead, she had notes on a criminal conspiracy, and a solemn injunction from Biryar that she should leave any action to the same regulatory bodies that had let it happen in the first place. The frustration was a restless energy in her spine. It was keeping her from focusing on her work. She had to get past it.

She couldn't get past it.

She kept remembering Dr. Carmichael at the reception her first night on Auberon. Her own excitement she'd felt when she heard about the array translation, the possibilities that a comprehensive mapping plan would give, not just here but across all the colony systems. And the disbelief that anyone would intentionally undermine something with so much potential. It had been so recent, and yet that past version of herself already seemed so naive. Auberon was changing her, and she wasn't sure she liked what it was changing her into.

She finished her cookie in a bite, gulped down the last of her tea, and headed back to her office. Not that she wanted to be there. Just that the commissary was annoying her now too. Or rather that she was still annoyed, and nothing she'd found gave her any respite.

Veronica hadn't returned with the report. Mona sat at her desk, looking sourly out her window. Same world, different view. Barradan spread out to her right: streets and houses and domes. The local wilderness was on her left, exotic and untamed and almost unimaginable in its diversity and richness and strangeness. This should have been everything she'd hoped for. All the pieces were there.

Self-rule for them, her husband said in her memory. *Not for us.* But…

Something shifted in the back of her mind. The thought came to her fully formed, like she had already planned everything and had only been waiting for the right moment to be conscious of it.

Point one: Either the administration of Xi-Tamyan was aware of Veronica's scheme or their eyes were so thoroughly off the ball that it had been permitted by default. Two: as the spouse of the governor, she was more valuable to Xi-Tamyan than Veronica Dietz would ever be. Three: What was good for the goose might very well be quite excellent for the gander.

She turned to her desk, a frown etching itself into her forehead almost hard enough to ache. She pulled up the financial records and tried to reallocate funds, just to make sure she couldn't. That was fine. Her breathing was shallow and fast, but when she made the connection request, her voice sounded calm.

"Dr. Rittenaur?" an older man said from the screen. He had thin, gray hair and a little beard that didn't disguise his double chin. "How can I help you?"

"I'm having trouble with accounting. I need to allocate funds for a Laconian state project, but it gives me an error code."

The man with the double chin looked chagrined. "I'm not… I'm not sure that…"

"It should be under Special Projects with the code for the Laconian science directorate? What would that be?"

"I don't think we have a code set up for that, ma'am."

"We'll have to find something temporary, then. There is something for cooperative governmental programs, isn't there? We can use that for now."

"I…um…I guess you could," the man said.

"Not perfect, but…" She shrugged and laughed. "If you clear the access problem, I'll take care of it that way."

She smiled patiently. She'd done nothing wrong. Not yet. If he pushed back, everything could be explained away. But she was the face of Laconia at Xi-Tamyan. And Laconia had just destroyed the largest navy in history and conquered the human race. She let the silence stretch. The man's face flushed a shade darker as he decided whether he was going to tell her she couldn't.

He tapped something into his console. "There you go, ma'am," he said. "It gives you any more trouble, just let me know."

Mona's smile widened by just a few millimeters. "Thank you," she said, and dropped the connection.

After that it was easy. She copied Dr. Carmichael's old funding structure and put it in a new branch under joint governmental projects, updated the contact information so that any issues or questions routed directly to her. She was expecting the funding level to refer back to some pool of money, but it was just a text field. She could put in any value she liked, and the money was summoned from nothing. She put in the value that Veronica's unspecified *powers that be* had refused. Then she doubled it, and closed the file.

Just like that, she'd funded the project that should have been going for months. She'd wait for a few days. Make sure that no red flags came up, and then she'd tell Dr. Carmichael to start renting lab space and equipment.

She sat back in her chair, folded her hands, and let out a long, satisfied sigh. There was a warmth in her chest, spreading slowly out toward her limbs like she'd just had a shot of gin. Her back relaxed, her heart felt like she was dropping from orbit for the first time. Pleasure and risk. On impulse, she kicked her shoes off and ran her bare feet through the office carpet, feeling the texture of it against her skin.

The soft knock came, and Veronica stepped in. "Sorry that took a little longer than I'd thought. Interruptions all the time. You know how it is."

"Yes, I do," Mona said.

Biryar didn't know what changed in Mona, only that something had, and he was glad of it. He saw it in small things. She slept more deeply now, and woke without being prodded. She ate better, and explored more of the local foods—fish and onion and a spicy red sauce the locals called sarkansmirch. He'd sampled it himself, but found a metallic aftertaste he didn't care for. She was laughing more than she had, and there was an ease in the way she held herself.

Her work with Xi-Tamyan might have been part of it. She had started sending reports out to the researchers on Laconia, and the responses from home had been positive and encouraging. She'd begun negotiations for Laconia to get full datasets directly from the company and integrate some of its high-level researchers into the staff on Laconia proper. It was part of Duarte's long-term plan that coming to the capital should be a reward. A mark of favor. The soft power of culture and status would do more to stabilize Laconia's central position in the grand human project than any number of warships. It was good that Mona's position let her advance that.

Biryar's own job wasn't going quite as smoothly.

He hadn't found the trick yet of sleeping through the Auberon nights. Most nights, he woke as the midnight sun fell, lying awake in their bed for half of the dark hours until morning. He'd considered talking to the physician about it. If it continued, he might. The local food also unsettled him, and he found himself eating the same diet he had on the *Notus*: mushroom curries and yeast-based cheeses. Even those didn't quite taste the way they should. He might not register the stink of the planet as often these days, but it had affected his senses all the same. And the pervasive sensation of unease, as vague as it was profound, wasn't helped by Overstreet's security briefings.

In the weeks since Laconia had officially taken over governance of the system, Overstreet had uncovered a dozen examples of embezzlement, theft, extortion, and financial misconduct just in the mechanisms of government that Biryar had inherited from the former head of state. Only two had involved Laconians. One had been the execution in the square, the other had killed himself when Overstreet's military police had come to arrest him. Everyone else had been turned over to local authorities, but Overstreet suspected that the judicial system was as flawed as the executive government. As the security audit broadened to the major businesses—the Transport Union, Xi-Tamyan, Oesterling Biotics, and half a dozen more—Biryar expected more rot to come to light.

The only good news Overstreet had to offer was the disappearance of the one-armed man. He hadn't appeared in any monitored public spaces. He hadn't shown up in any financial scans. If it hadn't been for the footage from the reception, he might only have been an unpleasant dream. Overstreet's analysis was that a local criminal had tried to come on strong, overplayed his hand, and fled when he understood the magnitude of his miscalculation.

The reports coming in from other systems showed that the separatists were still very much at work. The governor of Nova Catalunya, a man Biryar had trained with, had died in a shuttle accident that was being investigated for sabotage. Governor Song, on Medina Station, found another discrepancy in the station map that hid a service corridor, abandoned now, that the terrorists had used as they planned their missions. Drive plumes had been sighted in half a dozen systems that couldn't be tracked back to known ships.

The ghosts of unrest were everywhere. The separatists couldn't stand in an open battle with Laconia, but they could resist in small ways, and those small ways could have body counts too. He didn't bring his worries to Mona. Better that one of them should sleep well. If it felt a little strange not to tell her everything, at least the cause was noble. He still felt the urge now and then to unburden himself to her. He didn't have anyone else.

Instead, he tried to keep his attention on his own duties: playing kingmaker in local politics until Laconia was so established and unquestionable that he could play king. He found himself crafting the role of Governor Rittenaur as if he were acting a part in a play. He had come to notice when his own impulses were different from what Governor Rittenaur's would be, and then bury his own judgment to give space to the requirement of his office. He was a professional impersonator of himself. It required, among other things, a close relationship with the local newsfeeds.

"I understand that the *Notus* is slated to leave Auberon," Lara Kasten said. She was a host for one of the popular public newsfeeds. Not a reporter, but a warm, approachable interviewer whose greatest strength was the intensity with which she could listen.

"It's already burning for the ring gate," he said. "It will still be weeks before it leaves the system, but yes. It's on its way."

"That's got to feel a little odd."

His office, decorated in the local style, had casual chairs set beside a window that looked out over a garden of Earth plants. This was the fifth interview he'd granted her. It was important that the local population know him. Normalize his presence. Lara's approach to their conversations suited his needs.

"Not really," Biryar said, looking out at the red sunset of late morning. Clouds on the eastern horizon already turning from gold to gray. "The *Notus* is a valuable resource, and needed elsewhere. We have a great deal of work to do here, but Auberon doesn't need a warship. We're a very safe system. The situation is quite stable, and with the loyalty and cooperation of the authorities, I expect it will stay that way."

Lara smiled and leaned forward to pick up a glass of iced tea. She took it with sugar. He knew that from the last time they'd talked. Previously, she'd worn a high-collared white blouse, but today she had one in Laconian blue with a scoop. Instead of returning the glass to the side table, she leaned forward and put it by her feet. He was careful not to notice the tops of her breasts as she did it.

"But it was your way home, wasn't it?" she said. "Even if you never intended to use it. You spent your whole life on Laconia?"

"I did. But Auberon is my home now."

"What's that like for you?" she asked, and he thought there was a real curiosity in the question. He saw himself for a moment through her eyes. The proverbial stranger in a strange land, given power and responsibility and asked to be strong for his nation and the people over whom he ruled.

"I'm happy to be here. I am. Auberon is a beautiful planet and an important part of the empire."

He nodded to himself, silently approving his own answer. That was the right thing to say, and the right way to say it. Turn the question back to the system itself. Not him, but them. Good that when the locals look at him, they see themselves reflected.

He waited for the next question, but Lara was quiet. The sky darkened, and the first stars came out. The little moon, halfway to full, glimmered. She tilted her head, the straight, honey-colored hair hiding one eye, an impish smile on her lips. Biryar felt himself smiling back, and he chuckled when he spoke.

"What?"

"You're happy to be here? That's all? You're the most important man in this system. There are literally millions of people looking up to you. You're on a planet you didn't set foot on until it *belonged* to you. It must be...hard? Intoxicating? What is it like for you, Biryar?"

He shook his head. The breeze from the window was warm against his cheek. Lara's eyes were locked on his. He found that he wanted to tell her. He wanted to spread out all the ways that being Governor Rittenaur of Auberon system was different from what he'd expected, even after his training. The displacement of being so far from everything he'd known, the unease of knowing that there were people who hated him, not for himself but what he stood for.

That wasn't what his duty required of him.

"I can't imagine anyone's terribly interested in that," he said, and his voice sounded almost melancholy in his ears. That was odd. He recentered himself and said, "I am really very happy to be here."

Lara's smile faded. The last red light of sunset caught the curve of her throat, and Biryar felt the impulse to turn the office lights on. He also felt the impulse to leave them off. He didn't move. Her expression wasn't impish now. He remembered the time in their third interview when she'd told him about her brother's death, how sorrowful she'd been. How strong in her grief. Of all the people on this stinking world, he felt closer to Lara than to anyone that hadn't come on the *Notus* with him. She knew him.

She leaned forward again, this time reaching not for her drink but her handheld. She held it up for him to see. The recording marked second after silent second. She turned it off and set it back down.

"What is this like for you?" she said.

He was silent for a moment, uncertain whether he was going to answer. However much he wanted to.

"It's..." Biryar was surprised to find a thickness in his throat. "It's difficult. Sometimes."

She nodded, acknowledgment and encouragement in the same single motion. Biryar leaned toward her, his elbows on his knees, his hands clasped.

"I am trained for my duties as thoroughly as anyone could be. But knowing something intellectually or from simulations…it isn't the same."

"You feel alone," Lara said.

"I do, in a way," Biryar said. "This is off the record, of course."

Her smile was in shadows now, but he could make it out. "Just between us," she said, and traced an X over her chest. "Cross my heart."

He felt something shift, deep in his gut. Like a relaxation of a fist held clenched so long that the letting go ached. He drew in a breath, held it, and as he exhaled, he sank. "It's overwhelming. Not always, but sometimes. I feel like a splinter, and Auberon is festering around me. Isolating me. Trying to push me out."

Her voice was soft, but not pitying. He couldn't have stood it if she pitied him. "That's terrible, Biryar."

"It is. And I don't know what to do about it."

For a moment, the only sounds were the ticking of the walls as they cooled in the darkness and the murmur of midday traffic in the distant streets. Lara shifted, and he found himself very aware of her presence. Her physicality and solidity. Her hand touched his, and it felt like a rope to a drowning man. She moved close to him, and he had the weird impression that she was reaching for the pistol at his side, that she was going to take it from him to make some demonstration of a larger point. It was only when her lips touched his that his mind exploded in cold alarm.

He stood up, backing away in the darkness of the room. "I'm sorry. No, no. I'm very sorry. I didn't…This is not…"

He found his desk, pulled up his controls, and turned on the lights. The office flooded with the bright blue-yellow of the daytime. Lara knelt in the space between their chairs, looking up at him in surprise. Biryar wiped his hands on the sides of his jacket. His tongue felt like it wasn't responding the way it should. Like he was having a stroke.

"This is…" He shook his head. "We should…we should finish

the interview. This was very nice. I'm glad to have your friendship. Yes. We should finish the interview."

He pressed his lips shut to make himself stop talking. He sounded like an idiot. Lara rose to her feet. She wasn't blushing as much as he was.

"Biryar, I'm sorry," she said. "It's just—"

"No. It's fine. Everything is fine. There won't be any repercussions."

Lara eased herself back into her chair, plucked her blouse straight. Biryar stepped closer, but didn't take his seat. His blood was still electric. What if someone had seen them? What was he going to say to Mona, because he had to tell Mona. It would be a betrayal not to. He swallowed.

"I didn't mean to spook you," Lara said.

"I'm not spooked," he said. He meant to follow it up with *I'm married*, but what came out was different. "I'm Laconian."

Lara quirked a smile, and he thought there was regret in it. She took her handheld, her finger hovering just above the button to start the recording again. Her eyes were asking if he was certain, but he was himself again. Or no. He was Governor Rittenaur. That was better. She tapped the button, and the seconds began counting up again. Biryar put his hands on the back of his chair, pressing into it like it was a podium. He thought back to where the conversation had been.

"I'm really very happy to be here," he said. "Auberon is a fascinating planet with a great future before it. I hope that my service here will help it come into its rightful place as one of humanity's great centers of science and culture. And I know the High Consul has the same ambitions for it."

He nodded sharply, more to himself than to her. That was the right answer. That was what he was supposed to say. Who he was supposed to be.

Lara tilted her head. "Do you want to sit down?"

The yacht was a small one, and the old man didn't like it much. In all the time Agnete had been with him, he had only used it three or four times that she knew of. He'd grown up in a coastal city, but she didn't have the impression there had been a lot of yachts involved. The fact that he was in it now meant he was running out of places to be that he was certain the local security forces weren't watching.

He sat with his arms out at his sides. Two days of stubble competed with his thin mustache. The sun was overhead, the light glimmering off the water and his false arm. He was smoking a cigar as thick as his thumb and as long as his finger. The city rose up at the horizon like a mirage.

The woman sitting across from them had gone by KarKara when they'd first met her. It was Lara now, which suited her better.

"I swear to God, I had him."

"We shouldn't have rushed you," the old man said.

"I didn't rush. I had him. We had rapport. We had shared jokes. He was into me."

"And then?"

Lara opened her hands. "Then the moment came, and he backpedaled. I don't know. Clearly he and his wife have a monogamy agreement, and he's taking it seriously. Maybe that's a Laconian thing."

"Did he say that?"

"No, it's a guess," Lara said. "He was babbling by the end. Lots of words, but none of them meant anything."

"What do you think of him?"

She considered. Agnete could see from the way the woman held her hands that Lara almost liked the mark. There was nothing like being told *no* to make someone attractive.

"That man needs something," Lara said, "and he needs it bad. But it's not what I was offering."

The old man blew out a cloud of white smoke and watched the wind shred it. "That's what I think too. Is he maybe into guys?"

"That's not it," Lara said. "I've met maybe one person in twenty who claims to be monogamous and actually is. I think this guy is really into his wife."

The old man muttered something obscene. Then, "I don't get it. He's not looking for money. He's not looking for kink. What is it with this guy?"

Lara said, "I think he's looking for a way out."

"Of what?"

"His own skin."

"Well *I'm* looking for a way not to take that literally, but this fucker does make it hard." He looked out over the water. Something large and pale passed under them, but didn't break the surface. The old man sighed. "Maybe we should just kill him."

Agnete said, "Why were they fighting?"

He shifted his head to look at her. Agnete met his gaze without flinching. "He and his wife were fighting about something. And then they stopped. Maybe there's something in that?"

The old man weighed the idea while he took another puff on his cigar. His eyes shifted up to the sky, but he wasn't looking at anything. Or not anything that was there.

"He have any friends?"

Lara shook her head. "None that he ever talked about. He doesn't do relationships with people. Just responsibilities to them."

"So just the wife, then, as far as you know. Sex and friendship. That's a tough knot to unwind."

"I think he really loves her," she said. Again the little twitch of regret. They were going to have to be careful how they used her, moving forward. She was going to talk herself into falling in love with Rittenaur if they took their eyes off her.

The old man made a deep, soft sound. Like satisfaction. The yacht bobbed on the waves. "I forget, you know? I just forget."

"What, boss?"

"How complicated people are. How many kinds of hunger we're working with."

"Not following you."

The old man shrugged, and the fake arm almost matched the real one. The movement was still just a little asymmetrical. It made him seem jaunty.

"There was a guy I knew back in Sol system used to say that money was like sex. You thought it would fix everything until you got a lot of it. Because that's what we all reach for. Anything we need, anything we want, anything that's grinding us down, we can get high or rich or laid and make it better. Only if that was true, people would eventually get enough drugs or money or sex and be happy."

"We'd be out of jobs," Agnete said.

"But Rittenaur..." The old man went on like she hadn't spoken. "This guy lives his whole life in this culture where it's about..."

"Duty," Lara said.

"So," Agnete said, "the way a normal person tries to get out of the hole by putting a needle in their arm or fucking a pretty body or working a hundred hours a week, he tries to get out by being a good man." She said the words slowly to see if they sounded true.

"Only it doesn't work for him any better than that other shit does for the rest of us," the old man said. Then, a moment later, "Look at the wife. If he loves her as much as Lara thinks, she's the weak spot."

"What am I looking for?" Agnete asked.

"Whatever's there. Every addict has to hit bottom," the old man said. "Maybe we can help him with that."

"I'll see what I can do," Agnete said.

"I know it didn't exactly work, but..." Lara hesitated, afraid to ask. "Our thing?"

She was asking about the debt her attempted seduction was going to pay off.

"How much did you owe us?" he asked.

"You know exactly how much," Lara replied.

"Yeah, yeah, it's off the books now," the old man said. "But stay out of my casinos. You're very bad at poker."

Business concluded, they watched the sun speed across the sky and dive for the horizon. The water was turning golden as they angled back for shore. The old man made them all steaks on the little range, the meat decanted fresh from the growth disk.

When they got back to civilization, Agnete put her resources into the wife and Xi-Tamyan Agricultural Concern, where she had offices. She wasn't looking for something in particular—an affair, an illegal drug habit, a second life. Anything.

Even so, it took her days to find it.

Biryar didn't know what he had expected from Mona when he told her. Anger, perhaps. A sense of betrayal. A rupture in their marriage at least, an estrangement at worst. He had laid out all that had happened: the interviews, the connection that had been cultivated during them, and—with his heart in his throat—the kiss. Mona sat across the breakfast table from him, listening to every detail. Only at the end, when he outlined all the precautions he was putting in place to see that it never happened again, did a line of concern draw itself on her forehead.

"She just stole a kiss?" Mona asked. "That's all?"

"But I allowed myself to permit a sense of…of intimacy that made it possible," Biryar said. His eggs had grown cold and thick while he spoke. "This was my fault. It will never happen again."

She'd taken his hand then, and when she spoke there was a seriousness in her voice so studied and careful that he suspected there was amusement behind it. "Thank you for treating me with respect. I mean that. But I'm not angry with you at all. Don't beat yourself up over this, all right?"

He kissed her fingers, and the subject had never come up again. He went back to his duties with the relief of having dodged a bullet. He policed himself more harshly, wary of any other transgression. Biryar the man wasn't to be trusted. There was only room for Governor Rittenaur, so he tightened his control and pushed out anything besides duty and decorum. It was the only way.

He attended meetings with Suyet Klinger of the Association of Worlds and approved the trade agreements for the Transport Union. He stood witness at another execution when Overstreet discovered a Laconian guard who had been extorting sexual favors from a local man. He made his reports to the political officer back on Laconia and received guidance that tracked back to Winston Duarte himself.

That he couldn't sleep, that his food tasted strange and left his stomach upset, that the sunlight began to give him headaches, that he sometimes had the weird oppressive sense of drowning at the bottom of an ocean of air, that was only his acclimation going slowly. A few more weeks, and he would be fine, he was sure of it.

He was able to maintain the illusion that everything was under control until the day the one-armed man reappeared.

The conference was in Carlisle. It was the third-largest city on the planet, and fewer than a million people lived in it and the area around it. It was in a higher clime than Barradan and in the northern hemisphere where the seasonal shift made the air cold and the daylight periods slightly briefer. The trees were similar to the ones in Barradan, but with the cold weather, they had shriveled, wrinkled, and gone limp. The dark trunks bent toward the stony ground. The reception and Biryar's speech had been planned for a courtyard in the center of the mayoral complex, but a storm changed direction as Biryar's transport left Barradan, and a cold and bitter rain was pelting down from low clouds when he arrived. As his liaison rushed him from his transport and into the mayoral complex, Biryar sniffed the air, hoping to find some hint of the minty smell of wet Laconian soil. Rain on Auberon smelled like nothing. Or it smelled like an open sewer, and he couldn't tell any longer. One or the other.

The liaison apologized his way down the wide, pale hallway. The change in the weather had come with no warning. They hadn't thought they would need to shift to the secondary venue—a public theater just across from the complex—until the last moment. It would only take them a little time to have it ready and the audience of local business and government leaders taken there. Biryar swallowed his annoyance and made himself as gracious as he imagined Duarte would have been in his place.

The waiting area belonged to the mayor herself, part of her private apartment. If he would make himself at home and be comfortable...

In fairness, the waiting room was pleasant enough. A wide glass window looked out over a vast, wild landscape. Rough, toothlike mountains rose above the city, halfway lost in the gray of the storm. The rain that struck the window froze there for a moment, then melted and dripped down. When the clouds finally cleared, the landscape would be encased in ice. Ice like a second skin. Ice like a shroud.

His speech was on the importance of maintaining robust trade with the other systems and Laconia's commitment to keeping the economy of Auberon strong. He knew it by heart. Instead of reviewing it again, he sat on the little couch and looked out at the weather. The door opened behind him, and a man in a crisp white jacket and matching gloves came in carrying a tray with a thermos of coffee, two cups, and a plate of pastries.

"Put them on the table here," Biryar said. "I can serve myself."

"You know, Governor," the old man said as he placed the thermos and cups on the table at Biryar's side, "I have got to give it to your security people. I've been trying to see you for a while now, and they've got your place buttoned up tighter than a horsefly's asshole."

The old man smiled. Even before Biryar registered the glint of metal between the man's cuff and his glove, he remembered the thin mustache.

He's come to kill me, Biryar thought, and a thrill ran through him. He felt the weight of the sidearm on his hip, even as he sensed that a gun probably wasn't going to help. He knew enough killers to know that he wasn't one, and that the man facing him was. He nodded solemnly.

"I was wondering if I'd see you again. You've been hard to find as well."

The one-armed man sat down across from him and spoke as he

plucked off his gloves. "Well, I was worried that we'd gotten off on the wrong foot. That's my fault. I come on a little strong sometimes. You want some coffee?"

"Cream, please," Biryar said. His heart was tapping against his ribs like it was desperate for his attention. He let his hand casually drift toward his hip.

The one-armed man's voice was harder. "If you pull that gun, it'll mean we're having the worst version of this conversation. Honest to Pete, you'll wish you hadn't. No sweetener?"

"No," Biryar said. He let his hand drop to the sofa, near his holster but motionless. It was dangerous to move forward, but he wasn't going to give up ground either. He imagined pulling the gun and firing. How quickly could he do that? How long could it take? The rest of his life, maybe. "Just cream."

"Good choice. I like it black myself. The older I get, the more bitter shit suits me. You ever feel like that?"

"Sometimes," Biryar said.

The man held out a coffee cup on a saucer, and Biryar nodded toward the table. He wouldn't take it. The old man was holding it with his prosthetic hand. How fast was the mechanism? What weapons were concealed in it? It was like watching a snake that he knew was venomous, and wondering how long a bite would take to stop his breath.

"What can I do for you?" Biryar said, trying desperately to make the words sound casual. As if he were in control. "Or are you here to make good on your threat?"

"Nah, we're past that. But I am here on business, as it were," the man said, putting the coffee cup down on the table. "I have something for you. Kind of a peace offering."

"I didn't know peace was an option between us. I was hoping to have you tried, sentenced, and executed." The provocation struck home. The man smoothed his mustache. Biryar knew he shouldn't have said it, but the fear was shifting in him. Turning to something like courage. Or anger. Or a mad, dark, rushing hope that Biryar didn't wholly understand.

"I get that. But let me ask you something. Hypothetically, there's someone in your organization. Laconian, not one of ours. Let's say they're making up projects in your name, using them to falsify work orders. Fudging the budget. That's a problem for you, right?"

"You know the answer to that."

"I do. But I'd like to hear you say it just the same. If it's not a problem."

The one-armed man looked distracted by the conversation. A few centimeters would put his hand on the pistol. The angle made it awkward to draw. Biryar shifted his weight a little to make it easier, and the one-armed man shook his head like he was reading his mind.

"Misappropriation of Laconian funds is at best larceny, at worst treason," Biryar said. "One is a prison sentence. The other is death."

"What about a governor's pardon? You can do that, right?"

"No Laconian is above the law," Biryar said. "That is what discipline means."

"That's what I thought," the old man said. His eyes locked on Biryar's as he drew a handheld from his pocket. "For what it's worth, I am sorry about this."

He held it out. Biryar's gaze flickered down to it, and then back up, ready for the attack. It took a few seconds for what he'd seen to register. Mona Rittenaur. Almost against his will, his eyes drifted back down. The old man kept holding it out, and this time Biryar took it.

The financial records were marked as Xi-Tamyan, and the spreadsheet listed Mona's name. And monetary amounts. Budget levels and outflows. There were other names, and one rang a bell. Carmichael. The woman whose research had been unfairly canceled. The one they'd fought over. The one-armed man forgotten, he shifted through the files. Mona's name was highlighted. And the words *cooperative government programs*. If programs like that existed, he would have known about them. He would have had to approve them. He hadn't.

The storm had grown worse, the wind so terrible, it was shaking the building itself, making the walls shudder, only it wasn't any louder. And the beige surface of the coffee was smooth and still. Something else was shaking. Biryar put down the handheld.

"What do you want from me?"

"Nothing," the man said. "I'm just letting you know that one of your own stepped a little off the path."

"Blackmail?"

"For blackmail, you need an ask. I don't want anything from you. I have this information. I'm giving it to you. That's all. I'm being the good guy here."

And now it was his duty to tell what he'd learned to Major Overstreet. And it would be Overstreet's duty to arrest Mona. Biryar would have to recuse himself, so they'd send her back to Laconia for trial. His Mona. The woman whose fingers he kissed in the morning. He tried to imagine what it would feel like to see her sent to the Pens. It was like trying to imagine being dead.

Or he could hide the information, make her scrub away all sign of it. Cancel the projects. Erase the financial trail that led to her. Then, when Overstreet found them, they would die together. His sternum ached like he'd been punched there. Everything under it was hollow. He could hardly draw a breath.

It was perfect. Even if he could pull his pistol and shoot the one-armed man dead, there was still a bullet coming for him. Worse, it was coming for Mona, and there was no way to stop it. He couldn't even die to protect her. He tried to move, but he was made from clay. He saw sympathy in the other man's eyes.

"Truth is, if Xi-Tamyan found out about this, they'd probably praise her initiative and give her a raise. Those guys just do business that way. But she's one of yours, so..."

"Discipline," Biryar said. There was no way out. The end of his world had come. There was nothing to do but welcome it.

It wasn't a thought, it wasn't considered. Like water moving down, it was simply the way things worked. The way they had to be. Natural. Biryar drew the pistol, lifted it to his head, and pulled the trigger. The old man's eyes barely had time to widen.

His false arm, though, had a mind of its own, and it was faster than either of theirs. Before the trigger came back a full millimeter, the gun wrenched away. The old man cried out, clutching his real hand to his chest. The metal hand held Biryar's pistol, its barrel visibly bent.

"Jesus *fuck*, but I hate it when it does that," the old man said. Then, with heat, "Fuck is *wrong* with you, kid?"

Biryar didn't answer. He wasn't there. Governor Rittenaur, the voice and face of Winston Duarte, didn't make sense here, and without him, Biryar was like a vine whose trellis had collapsed. He had no form. No structure. He couldn't even die.

The one-armed man put the ruined pistol on the table, picked up Biryar's cup of coffee, and sipped from it.

"Okay. I get it."

"I can't lose her," Biryar said. "I can't stay with her, and I can't lose her. What else is there to do?"

"They really do a fucking job on you people, don't they?" the one-armed man said. Then after a long moment, he sighed. "Listen to me. I didn't lose my arm in a fight or anything. I was born wrong. Something about not enough blood flow. Stunted development. Whatever. It was like a skinny little baby arm. Mostly I just kind of curled it up against my chest here and forgot about it. I did fine. It was nothing big. I kept meaning to get it seen to, you know? Take it off and regrow it from gel? But one thing and another, I just never seemed to get around to it. You know what I mean? People would give me shit, and I'd laugh and say how, yeah, it would be a good idea. But I didn't do it. Then maybe fifteen years ago…"

He raised his metal hand, rotating it in the light.

"This," the old man said. "It's fucking badass. Basically a built-in waldo with virtual intelligence and pattern matching. It's not networked, so it's unhackable. And it's strong as shit. Bends steel. Stops bullets. You know what else it does? Plays piano. No shit. I can't, but it can."

"It's very nice," Biryar said.

"You're young yet. I'm not. There's this thing when you get older where you have to make a choice. Everyone does. You have to decide whether you care more about being your best self or your real one. If you're more loyal to who you ought to be or who you really are. You know what I'm talking about?"

Biryar nodded. He was weeping.

"Yeah," the old man said. "I thought you might. I'm going to tell you a secret. I've never told anyone this, not my girlfriends, not my closest allies. No one. You listening to me?"

Biryar nodded again.

"I miss my real fucking arm," the old man said. "I liked it better when I was me."

Biryar sobbed, and it sounded like a cough.

"I don't want anything from you, Governor. But I would ask you this. Looking at where you are now, and the choices you've got? Is there anything you maybe want from me?"

The wind howled, threw a handful of hail at the window. Biryar barely heard it.

"You can't make this go away," he said. "Overstreet will find it. He'll know."

"He will," the old man said. "You know. If."

They were quiet. Biryar felt something happening in him. Something he both didn't recognize and also knew as well as the sound of his own voice. "Could you have done it? Could you have killed me?"

"Yeah," the old man said. "Half a dozen times. Easy. But it would have been a risk. I don't get to pick your replacement, right? Thing about this Overstreet fella? He's not on his home pitch. If something happened to him, maybe it'd be a good idea to put together some locals to take over the security jobs. People who know the lay of the land. How things work here."

"If something happened to him?"

"Yeah. If," the old man said. And then, "Do you want it to?"

Biryar breathed *yes*.

The one-armed man relaxed and stood up. He put on his gloves again, looked out at the sleet and rain and hail. The half-hidden mountains. "This isn't just you."

"What?"

"Don't feel bad, because it ain't just you," the one-armed man said with a lopsided shrug. "There are, what, a couple hundred decent-sized colony worlds with shiny new Laconian governors on them? And this thing has or is going to happen on every single one. It's the basic problem with religion, be it Jesus or Vishnu or God Emperors. Ideological purity never survives contact with the enemy."

"I don't—" Biryar started.

"Yeah, you do," the one-armed man said, then stepped out and closed the door behind him.

Biryar sat for a moment, waiting for the guilt and horror to come, for his conscience to overwhelm him. Half a planet away, Major Overstreet was probably just waking up. There was time to call him. To warn him. Mona was waking up too, in their bed. Biryar took a long breath and let it out through his teeth. He felt something deep and profound, but he didn't know what he felt. It was too big to judge.

The liaison came in, and Biryar tucked the handheld in his pocket. The liaison's eyes widened at the pistol, but Biryar pretended not to notice that it was there. They walked together across a covered bridge and into the theater where his audience was waiting.

Mona felt the hair on the back of her neck go up the moment she stepped into her house and found Veronica Dietz waiting in the parlor. It had been a long day that followed a restless night. Biryar had been in Carlisle, and she never slept as well when he wasn't on the other half of the bed. She'd wanted nothing more than to come home, take off her shoes, drink some wine, and relax. Finding Veronica lying in wait was like feeling a snake move in her pillowcase.

"Veronica," she said, feigning pleasure.

"Yes, ma'am," Veronica said, and then stopped. It was like she was waiting for Mona to say something. The moment stretched.

"I wasn't expecting to see you here," Mona said, carefully.

Veronica blinked, confused. "Oh," she said. "I had a request from the governor's office. I thought…that is I assumed that you—"

"I'm sorry," Biryar said, coming into the room. "That was me." He took Mona's hand, squeezed it gently, and kissed her fingers. "I missed you."

"I'm glad you're back," Mona said. Something was wrong. Or if not wrong, at least very different. She didn't understand what was happening, except that Biryar was ushering them both to sofas and motioning them to sit. "How was Carlisle?"

"Fine. It was fine. I had some time to think, and I wanted you both here."

Mona felt a stab of fear, but she took a seat. Veronica lowered herself into a chair. "What's this about, dear?" Mona asked.

"It's important that Auberon and Laconia be very much coordinated. In the sciences," Biryar said. There was something very odd about the way he spoke. He seemed looser. Calmer. Maybe a little melancholy. That might have been more alarming than Veronica's presence. "So I've taken the liberty of requesting a placement at the science directorate in the capitol. And I've recommended Ms. Dietz for the position. Transport will be entirely taken care of. Your housing will be in the university complex with some of the best minds in the empire. Xi-Tamyan has already been informed."

Veronica's mouth was open. Her face was pale. Mona felt like she'd been spun too long on a swing. She didn't understand what Biryar was thinking. And then she did.

"Her living expenses…" Mona said.

"All overseen by Laconia," Biryar said. "*Everything* will be overseen by Laconia."

"I can't do that," Veronica said, and her voice was tight. "That's very kind of you. That's...But I have so much here that I can't really—"

Biryar raised a hand, and his voice went quiet. Quiet, but not soft. "Ms. Dietz, it is critical to the success of this colony that you understand what Laconian culture and discipline are, just as we learn what it is to be from Auberon. You will accept this position, and you will take the honor seriously. We will be treating you as one of our own."

Veronica seemed to be having a little trouble breathing. Mona felt something equal parts joy and vindictiveness brighten her heart. She thought she saw Biryar glance at her, a smile ghosting on his lips, but it was gone before she could be certain. His handheld chimed, and he looked at it before refusing the connection. When he looked back up, he was somber. He stood and drew Veronica to standing.

"This position could change your life," he said.

"I don't know what to say," she said.

"You're welcome," Biryar said, and escorted her to the door. "Please don't mention it. I hope you won't think I'm rude, but—"

"No," she said. "No, of course."

"Good," he said, and closed the door behind her. When they were alone, he seemed to sag into his bones, all his muscles gone slack. He turned back to her and smiled sheepishly. Mona shook her head.

"Are you all right?"

"Yes. No. I don't know. I feel like I'm smiling more often," Biryar said as he came back and sat beside her. He rested his head on her shoulder the way he had when they were first courting. It made him seem younger. "Next time, let me approve it. It's safer that way."

She was about to say *Approve what?* but the question would have been a lie. He knew, and she knew that he did. Instead, she said, "I will."

His handheld chimed again. She caught a glimpse of it as he silenced it. The red band of a high security alert. An emergency. He took her hand, lacing his fingers in among hers.

"Who's that from?" she asked.

"Overstreet's office," Biryar said. "I'll get back to them. It's nothing that won't wait a few minutes."

She shifted to look him in the eyes. He was serene. He was grieving. He was himself in a way she hadn't seen in months.

"What happened?" she whispered.

She felt him shrug. She watched him look into her. "I've committed to the process," he said.

The handheld chimed again.

Auberon
Author's Note

This is the story that came out of order. It was supposed to be published after *Persepolis Rising* and before *Tiamat's Wrath*, but things got a little out of sync.

One of the joys of the project has always been how we were able to play around with genre. Science fiction is great that way. There's not a particular story at the root of it the way there is with other genres. A romance, either the people are going to hate each other at the beginning and fall in love by the end or love each other at the beginning and die, depending on whether it's in the shadow of *Pride and Prejudice* or *Romeo and Juliet*. A mystery, generally someone's going to be killed and someone's going to find out why. Science fiction can be anything from a rigorous speculative adventure like Andy Weir's *The Martian*, to a semi-hallucinatory philosophical allegory by Philip K. Dick, to a locked-room mystery on a spaceship. There's room for all of it.

"Auberon" was our crime story, and it was an answer, in a way, to Santiago Singh's fate in *Persepolis Rising*. Biryar Rittenaur is Singh's path not taken. He came to Auberon with the best intentions, and the corruption of the place overcame his idealism. But in doing that, it also gave him a little space to love something more than the state or the party. For a crime story, it winds up being pretty humane.

It was also a treat for us to see Erich again. One of the questions we often get about him is why, in a world with regrowth gel, he still had a malformed arm. This was our answer.

And years after writing this, with literally hundreds of thousands of words between drafting this story and writing these notes, we can still remember Balecheck's name and that fucking mole. It really does work if you commit to the process.

The Sins of Our Fathers

The monsters came at night.

First came their calls: distant and eerie. Their wide, fluting voices echoed down the valley, complicated as a symphony and mindless as a cricket swarm. The deepest of them sang in a range below human hearing: subsonic tremors that the people in the township felt more than heard.

Then the night scopes showed movement. It could start as far as twenty klicks away, or as near as two. The science team still hadn't figured out what they did during the daylight hours or during the long, empty days when they seemed to disappear, but the feeling that they rose up from the planet's flesh with the darkness made the approach feel almost supernatural. Like the town had offended some nameless local god by coming here. It was only a mystery, though. They'd figure it out eventually. If they survived.

After the movement, assuming the monsters kept to their same pattern, their chorus would go on until the little retrograde moon started rising in the west. Then it would stop. Then they would come.

"They'll aim for the breach," Leward said, pointing with his chin. The perimeter wall was constructed out of prefabricated plates of carbon-silicate lace scavenged from ship hulls. The braces were titanium and compression-resistant ceramic. The place where the monster had come through last time looked like God had come down and pressed against the wall with His thumb. Ten meters of shattered plate and bent brace they'd shored up with local trees and scrap.

"Might aim for the breach, might not," Jandro said, with a slow shrug. He was the head of construction and maintenance, and a bear of a man. "What you think, Nagata?"

Filip shrugged. His mouth was dry, but he tried to keep the fear out of his voice. "Wall didn't slow them down much even when it was intact."

Jandro grinned and Leward scowled.

The town was the second largest on the planet Jannah, at four hundred and thirty-six people. It had been named Emerling-Voss Permanent Settlement Beta, but everyone called it Beta. And with the ring gate to anywhere else broken, that meant Beta was its name from now on. Without the gates, the corporate headquarters of Emerling-Voss was just shy of twenty-three light-years away. Alpha settlement, with more than a thousand people, was seven and a half thousand klicks to the south. With no orbital shuttles or reliable ground vehicles, it might as well be seven million. And Alpha had gone silent when the ring gates shut down. Whether it was just a radio malfunction or something larger was an open question, and the residents of Beta had more immediate problems.

There were two dozen people drawn from different work-groups all along the north wall. Leward was in charge there. Another group was along the east, with lookouts and runners at the west and south in case something unexpected happened. In case the monsters changed the direction they'd traveled up to now. Filip considered the faces of the others stationed below the wall, finding signs in each of them of the same fear he felt. Almost each of them. Jandro and the four men from the maintenance team seemed relaxed and at ease. Filip wondered what drugs they'd taken.

Leward hefted his torch: a titanium rod with a solid, waxy mat of the local mosslike organism on a spike at one end. When he spoke, it was loud enough for everyone to hear. "When they come—*if* they come—we deflect them. Don't go at them straight on. Just turn them gently aside so they don't get to the walls. We aren't fighting them. We're just herding." He nodded while he said it, like he was agreeing with himself. It made him seem uncertain.

"Should just shoot them," Jandro said. It was a joke. Everyone knew the town had run out of rifle cartridges and the reagents they'd need to print fresh ones.

"We keep them outside the walls," Leward said. "But if they get in anyway? Get out of the way." He pointed up and to the south at the fabrication lab, the only two-story building in Beta. "The engineering team has a magnetic slug thrower set up. We don't get between it and the target."

"Maybe they won't even come this time," one of the others said. As if in answer, the uncanny chorus swelled. The overtones rang through each other like a ship drive finding a hull's harmonic. Filip shifted his weight from foot to foot and hefted his torch. Everything was too heavy here. He'd spent most of his life on ships, and the float or one third g were his natural state. When he accepted the job to join Mose and Diecisiete at Beta, he'd expected three years down the well at most. Now, it looked more like a lifetime. And a lifetime that might not last until dawn.

Leward's hand terminal chimed, and the team lead accepted the connection. Evelyn Albert's voice came loud enough that Filip could make out every word. "Get your people in place. We have movement half a klick out. North by northeast."

"Understood," Leward said, and dropped the connection. He

stared out at all of them like an actor who'd just forgotten the St. Crispin's Day speech. "Get ready."

They moved toward the wall, and then through the access gate to the strip of cleared land outside it. The night sky was bright with stars and the wide disk of the Milky Way. With the autumn sun gone behind the horizon, the air cooled quickly, with a scent like mint and toilet cleanser. The atmosphere of Jannah smelled nothing like Earth, the Earthers at Beta said. Take away the mint, and Filip thought it smelled a bit like a freshly scrubbed ship.

None of that changed the fact that Filip and the torch bearers walking at his side were the invaders here, and he'd have argued for leaving again if there were a ship that could take them and any-place to go. Instead, the walls, the darkness, and the rising howls of monsters outside.

He tried to hear a difference in the chorus. He imagined the huge beasts hauling themselves up out of the dark soil like the ancient dead coming up from their graves. It seemed like the kind of thing that would have to change how they sang, but he couldn't be sure. He took his place outside the wall. To his right, a couple of women from the medical team. To his left, a young man named Kofi with the long bones and just-too-large head that said he was another Belter like Filip.

"Hell of a thing," Kofi said.

"Hell of a thing," Filip agreed.

In the west, a dim light glowed at the top of the mountain ridge like a pale fire was burning there. It brightened, and resolved into a crescent, smaller than Filip's thumbnail. It looked to him like inverted horns.

All through the wide valley, the choir of alien voices stopped. Filip felt his heart start to labor. His head swam a little. The sud-den silence made the valley feel as vast as space, but darker. The fear crept up the back of Filip's throat, and his hands gripping the torch ached.

"Steady," he said under his breath. "Steady, coyo. Bist bien. Bist alles bien." But it wasn't true. Everything was profoundly not fine. Leward paced behind them, breath fluttering like the edge of panic. Then from the darkness, a steady, heavy tramping that grew louder.

"Time to dance," Jandro said. A flare of orange fire sprang up to Filip's right. Jandro holding his lit torch.

"Not yet, not yet," Leward said, but Jandro's team had already started lighting all of their torches, and the approaching footsteps were so loud, Filip had to agree. The others along the line set fire to the moss, and Filip did too. The Belter beside him was struggling with the igniter, so Filip leaned his own fire close until the flames spread. The cleared space was a bright monochrome orange. Smoke stung Filip's eyes and throat.

The first of them loomed up out of the darkness.

It stood higher than a building, at least any of the buildings on Beta. It moved with weirdly articulated shoulders and hips that seemed to ripple with every step like there was a vastly complicated mechanism under the rough skin. Its head was little more than a knob, set low between its shoulders, comically flat. The eyes were black: two at the front and two on the sides, and its mouth curved up like an obscene, toothless grin. It lumbered forward, into the light, seeming not to notice the line of flame and primates in front of it.

"Not straight on!" Leward shouted. "Turn it! Make it turn!"

The line to Filip's right surged forward, shouting and waving their torches. To his left, they hung back. In the center, he could go either way. The monster took a slow step, then paused as Jandro and his crew rushed at it from the side screaming obscenities and threats. The monster's grin seemed to widen, and it trudged forward, the ground shaking under each step. Filip lifted his own torch and rushed in. The monster's smile was an accident of its physiology and evolution, but it still felt like the great beast was pleased to see them. Or amused. Filip pressed himself in among the men, shouting and reaching up to thrust fire at the thing's dark eyes.

The monster made a deep fluting groan, and its next step angled away to the right, if only a little bit. A few degrees.

"Hold the line!" Leward shouted over the roar of the torch bearers. Over Filip's own shout of victory. "It's not over. Keep turning it!"

Filip pressed closer, waving the flame above him. Other bodies were with him, a mob of frightened mammals with the first glimmer of victory. It felt better than being drunk. Someone—maybe Filip, maybe not—touched the beast's skin with the fire, and it shifted again. The shouting redoubled. There were more people in the crowd now, and the monster strode forward, its pace hardly changing, but its path bent until it was walking parallel to the town wall. Leward was yanking them back one at a time. *Let it go. It turned away, just keep it going forward until it clears the corner.* But there was a kind of bloodlust. They'd made the thing that had frightened them before now bend to their will, and it was intoxicating. A knot of people pushed toward it, drawn like a tide by the gravitational pull of power. Here was the enemy, and their victory over it. Even if the victory was just changing the direction it was walking. They waved the same fires, but now from spite and in triumph.

The monster smiled its fixed smile and lumbered forward, along the wall to the corner where Leward and two of his people made a barrier and stopped the mob. The monster shifted its weirdly flat head, groaned a vast, shuddering groan, and turned back to its original heading like it was following a star.

They shouted as it moved off into the wildlands to the northwest of the town. Jandro picked up a rock in his off hand and threw it at the monster's wide retreating back, and the others laughed and howled. Their torches were starting to gutter.

"Regroup!" Leward said, waving them back toward their posts. "Everyone grab new torches! This isn't over. We have to be ready."

Filip trotted back to his place and handed off the failing torch to a young woman in a science team jumpsuit. As she ran back into the town to refresh the oily moss fire cap, someone shouted. If there were words in it, they didn't matter. Filip couldn't make them out, but he knew what they meant.

A second monster loomed out of the darkness. Its head was a little higher up on its shoulders, its skin a little more green. Filip shouted and tried to light his fresh torch, but the beast had already come closer. Every step made the earth shake the way dinosaurs and elephants were supposed to have. Like a nightmare.

"Line up!" Leward shouted. "Form the line!"

But it was too late. The people who had kept their torches burning and held their ground were clumped at the eastern end of the wall. The mob like Filip and Jandro and the others were just lighting up new ones on the west. A gap of darkness between the fires was guiding the monster straight toward the thing they'd sworn to protect. Filip waved his torch at the lidless black eyes, but the flame was weak and pale. The monster moved forward and hunched its forelegs. When it rose it was less like a jump than a weird unfurling of flesh, and it crashed down onto the wall with a sound louder than thunder.

Somewhere nearby, Leward was shouting, "We have a breach. We have a breach. We have a breach." The same phrase over and over like the disaster had turned him into a siren. The monster slid into the darkness of the town, and the sounds of destruction echoed back. Filip's mind jumped ahead, trying to think what they were losing. The medical center. The science barracks. The dry storage.

"Get back to the line," Leward shouted, waving a torch in each hand. "Back to the line! Let the slug thrower take that one."

"I don't hear it." That was Jandro. There was soot on his face, and his arm was red like it had been burned. Filip didn't know how that had happened.

"Form up!" Leward said.

"He's right," Filip said. "The slug thrower's not firing."

"I don't know about that. It's not my job."

In the dark of the town, someone screamed.

"Fuck," Jandro said, then held out his hand toward Filip. "Nagata. Gimme your torch."

Filip shifted it, dropping the handle into Jandro's wide palm.

The chief of maintenance put the burning moss on the ground, scraping it off with his boot like the flames were dog shit. The spike where the mat had been was five inches long, set at ninety degrees from the main shaft. Jandro banged the spike against the ground once, testing it.

"Form up!" Leward shouted.

"Fuck yourself," Jandro said, like he was suggesting what kind of sandwich would go with Leward's coffee. The big man turned toward the new gap in the wall and started off at a long, loping run.

"I'll get him back," Filip said, but it was more that he didn't have a torch now, and there was a monster loose in the town. He had to do something.

The darkness and the destruction made the town unfamiliar. A wall lay across the pathway, peeled off its building. The wraith-thin body of Arkady Jones sat, back against a water recycler and head resting on their knees. The lights were off to keep anything from drawing the monsters in. It seemed like a fantasy protection now. If you can't see them, they can't see you. Filip's heart tapped fast against his chest, reminding him that it hadn't been built for this. That he was a Belter down the well. That he was old.

Ahead, a huge shadow moved against the darkness. Filip went toward it, not knowing what he meant to do when he got there. Only that was the problem, and it had to be solved. In the starlight and the faintness of the moon, all he could see was the wide, shifting back. The twin tails, wider than both his legs together. The monster seemed to twitch, like it had stumbled to the left. When it roared, it roared in pain.

A spotlight went on at the top of the fabrication lab where the slug thrower was supposed to be. It tracked the monster as it shifted and stumbled toward the open ground of the town plaza. At first, Filip didn't understand what he was seeing. Jandro was on the thing's back, hunched down with his body pressed against it and one free hand banging the unlit torch against its head. The spike was dark and bright at the same time. Wet with blood. Filip paused.

Of all the places in the town, the plaza was the one with the least to destroy. The least that they couldn't rebuild or replace. Even so, he had to convince himself that Jandro had steered the monster, ridden it where he'd wanted it to go. Watching the huge man whip the titanium spike into the smiling monster's side, Filip felt something like awe.

Human voices floated down from the top of the fabrication lab, and a fast, loud rattle cut through the chaos. A line of wounds drew themselves along the monster's flank, and it writhed in pain.

"Stop shooting!" Filip shouted. "You'll hit him!"

But Jandro had already jumped free. The monster shifted and turned, confused by the light and by the new pain. The blood that sheeted down its side and poured from its eye and cheek was as red as anything Filip had seen. As red as a human's blood. Another shaking rattle, with better grouping now, a new wound opening on the beast like the slug thrower was a mining drill coring through its side. The monster raised its head and tried to sing again, but the sound that came out was choked and strained. It took another step forward, shifted, stepped back, and folded itself gently onto the bare dirt of the plaza like it was stopping to take a nap. The eyes didn't close, but they went dull.

Filip ran to Jandro, more than half expecting to find him dead. Instead, he was on his knees, swatting clouds of dust off his pant legs and grinning.

"You okay?" Filip asked. "You need a medic."

"I'm fine," Jandro said.

"You could have been killed, coyo."

Jandro's grin widened, and he shrugged. The monster seemed to breathe out, some last trace of life escaping the corpse. Even dead, it was huge. Jandro bent down, grabbed the bloody pole, and tossed it back to Filip. "Thanks for the borrow, yeah? Let's go show these pinche fuckers who's boss."

Jannah system was—had been—one of more than thirteen hundred connected to Sol and Laconia by the gate network. It had a middle-aged star and two planets in the goldilocks zone, four gas giants strung out into the stars with clouds of moons around them like little solar systems all their own, and a thin, disappointing asteroid belt. In the gold rush years, half a dozen different entities had put claims to the two life-sustaining worlds until a disagreement over agricultural assay rights had escalated into a brief and mutually annihilating nuclear war, and the Transport Union had been forced to step in. For the better part of a decade, the system had been fourth or sixth or tenth priority for the corporate lawyers and union administrators, rights adjudication always moving forward without ever quite resolving.

Then the Laconian Empire had rolled through, smashed through the red tape with the iron fist of imperial fiat, and Emerling-Voss Minerals and Financial Holding dusted off its blueprints.

It was more than possible that somewhere in those plans, there had been a little square with a double line hashing one side that had meant temporary barracks. Or, more likely, general-purpose room. Now, it was two-and-a-half-meter walls of prefabricated metal with yellow chips in the blue sealant and a patina that made them look dirty no matter how much Filip scrubbed them. The ceiling had the same kind of full-spectrum worklights as the cabin on his last ship, the *Rhymer*. And inside the building's only room, two canvas cots. One was his. The other belonged to Mose, his supervisor. Diecisiete, the third of their three-person team, was in Alpha if she was anywhere.

"Wake up," Mose said.

Filip turned on his cot and moaned.

"Wake up."

"Can't wake up," Filip said. "I died. Dead men don't wake up."

"You didn't die."

"Then why do I hurt so much?"

"Because you didn't die," Mose said with a long, wheezing laugh. "Dead men don't hurt. That's being alive."

"Could be in hell," Filip said. By now, sleep had retreated, and all that was left was the ache and sense of fear.

"Could be," Mose said, but the laughter was less now. Filip rolled onto his side, and Mose put a plate on the cloth by his shoulder. Textured protein and the last of their pepper sauce. With the state he was in, it even smelled good. He rose to sitting and took a spoonful. Mose stood, folding his wide arms.

"Now you're done sleeping the day away, there's work to do."

"Be right there," Filip replied, as if his work contract was still what it had been. As if the *Rhymer* was coming back to drop off the new crew and take them back up the well and out to the stars. It was a little piece of theater they played out between the two of them. Mose played at being the good boss, Filip played at being the diligent underling. He could hear in the way Mose talked that the act was wearing thin. It was wearing thin for everyone.

Between them, Alpha and Beta were the whole human population of the planet, and the majority of the people in the system. There was, Filip had heard, a prospector's ship on one of the watery moons of the second gas giant. If that was true, whoever they were needed to get their asses back down to the planet as quickly as they could and then find a way to land. With the gate gone, the human population that mattered—that had any meaningful effect on any of them for the rest of their lives—had gone from tens of billions to under two thousand. Maybe less. If they weren't careful, maybe a lot less.

Filip finished his breakfast, scraping out the last bits of nutritional yeast and mushroom with his fingernail. The voices of the others filtered in from outside. And behind that, the clanging of a mallet on steel. He went to check his hand terminal, but it had broken a week before and there weren't any replacement parts. The fabrication lab could have built some, but the supply of reagents wasn't deep, and he didn't need a hand terminal anymore. He could just walk outside and look up to know the time of day. Or consult with the weariness in his back to know how much rest he still needed.

Of the seven worlds Filip had set foot on—all of them light

gravity, two of them too heavy for him anyway—Jannah had the most changeable skies. Some days it was an indigo so dark he could see the brightest stars at midday. Others, like today, it was a pale olive from horizon to horizon. The breeze was cool and musky, like one of the old water treatment plants on Ceres. The damage to the town was different in the daylight. Better because he could see it and not just let his imagination tell him how bad it was. Worse because he couldn't tell himself they'd gotten off light.

The monster had stumbled through a storage building and the machine shop where the science team worked on their small fleet of prospecting drones. Both of the buildings were flattened. If it had kept on the path it started, it would have gone through all the barracks, and they'd have been digging graves for half the town. Instead, the corpse lay in the plaza, its flesh cut open, swarmed by the local carrion insects and biologists. Leward paced among them, gesturing excitedly with his wide, blood-streaked hands. Filip scanned the crowds until he found Mose coordinating a salvage crew at the dead machine shop. Kofi was there too, and a broad-faced woman whose name was Aliya or Adaliya. Something like that. With the *Rhymer* gone, it probably made sense to pay more attention to things like that now. Filip slid over, hands in his pockets, and looked over the mess. Kofi noticed him and lifted a hand in greeting.

"Could have gone better," Filip said, gesturing to the ruin with his chin.

"Could have gone worse too," Mose said. "We lost some of the fine-work machines, but if we pull this up careful enough, I bet we can reuse almost all of it."

"I'll see if the welding rig's free," Maybe-Aliya said, and strode off. The patch on the back of her jumpsuit said she was maintenance. One of Jandro's crew. Filip looked back at the dead monster and the men and women around it. The ones who were working by talking a lot.

"I see it too," Kofi said.

"Yeah," Filip said. "What can you do, though."

It was natural enough. The scientists and administrators were doing science and administration. The mechanics and workers were working with machines. Filip found a length of conduit and used it to scratch the itch between his shoulder blades. Up between the light olive sun and them, something huge and distant unfolded wide, curving wings and cast them all into shadow for a second.

Mose spat on the ground. "Slug thrower got the fucker, yeah?"

Filip considered the dead monster. The autopsy had peeled it down to bright pink bone and pale flesh. It looked only a little smaller than it had in the darkness. Its flat face still had the permanent smile, like it knew a joke the primates that had killed it didn't understand.

"Took a while."

"Misfired the first time," Mose said. "That's what I was fixing before I came here. They had to ground out the main capacitor and bring the whole thing back up from battery. Overengineered and slapped together at the same time." He spat again.

"Why we been using old-fashioned explosive propellant guns since forever," Filip said. "They're like sharks. We found a perfect design for killing the shit out of some coyo that needs it, why change?"

"Yeah, we used to have spaceships too."

Spaceships and gun cartridges, both relics of their past.

"Coyo in chemistry group says we can get saltpeter from the local guano. Seems like we should try."

"We do this first," Mose said with his supervisor voice.

A woman broke off from the flock of administrators and scientists. She was smaller than Filip, with light brown skin and a mane of tight-curled hair that was auburn where it wasn't gray. She'd done his intake interview when he and Mose had arrived from Alpha. Her last name was a mouthful of Russian that sounded like a puppy falling down stairs, so everyone called her Nami Veh.

"Moses. Filip." She nodded to each of them as she said their names. She had a gift for making it feel like they were friends, and knowing everyone by name was part of it. "We're calling a town meeting tomorrow after dinner."

"Yeah?" Filip said.

"It's to talk about everything we know so far about…" She looked back at the dead monster. "About those. And planning for what we do next. It's important that everyone come."

"We're not really part of all this," Mose said, shaking his head. "Me and Filipito? We're subcontractors, not permanent here."

Filip didn't know if Mose was fucking with her, or if that was really still how he thought of himself. Of them. At a guess, Mose wasn't a hundred percent sure either. Nami Veh's smile was ready and real.

"It matters for everyone, so we want everyone to be part of it."

Mose shrugged. "Okay. We can try. Not like we're going to be out at the dance hall."

Nami Veh laughed like it had been funny, put her hand on Mose's shoulder, and moved off to some maintenance group workers who were resetting a water purifier the monster had knocked down. When she was out of earshot, Mose chuckled.

"I guess she can call 'town meetings' now. Think we can all do that? Go tell the science leads that there's a thing they have to come to? Think we can all decide there's something on the schedule, or is that just them?"

Kofi smiled, but his eyes made him look angry. "Typical, yeah? No problem inners can't solve with more fucking meetings."

"We don't go," Mose said, then turned to point at Filip particularly. "That's the rule. If extra meetings aren't cleared by the union, we don't go. You give these bastards a millimeter, they'll take a klick."

"The union? Are you kidding?" Filip asked, and then regretted it.

Mose's face went dark and his chin jutted forward. "You listen to me. You and me, we're *union*. That's the way it is. All this other shit doesn't change anything unless we let it. And we are not going to fucking let it. *Never.* You understand?"

Kofi looked away, embarrassed. Mose wasn't insane, but here he was shouting about getting something cleared by the union offices, as if that could happen. As if the way things used to be had anything to do with how they were now. If he'd dropped his pants and started dancing with his ass out, it would have been just as connected to their current reality.

Grief made people weird.

At the corpse, Leward was talking animatedly to a half dozen of the science team. Nami Veh was already halfway around the plaza, organizing whatever it was she was organizing. And Mose was staring at Filip with the kind of aggressive silence that could turn into a fight if he let it. Mose was ten years younger than he was, and when he looked at Filip, he just saw an old Belter technician with white in his beard and hair. He didn't see Filip as a threat, and Filip had put a lot of effort into keeping it like that.

"I hear you," Filip said, carefully. "We should probably get this thing salvaged, yeah?"

Mose hoisted up his chin a degree more. Filip imagined slamming the conduit in his hands into Mose's face. The look of surprise the man would give him before he dropped. Instead, he let his own gaze fall, looking more submissive than he felt. It seemed to satisfy Mose.

"Where the hell is Adiyah?" Mose muttered, and stalked off, ready to vent at her. Filip dropped the conduit he'd been holding and started to pace off the ruins of the machine shop. Kofi fell in beside him. After a few seconds, the younger Belter spoke.

"Mose, he's…"

"Yeah," Filip agreed. "Lot of people shook. Strange times, que?"

"Strange times." And then a moment later, "Are you really going to sit out this town meeting because of the union?"

"No."

Forty years could be a long time. Or it could be hardly any time at all. Most often, it was both of those at once. Filip had taken this form of his name as a boy. The older he got, the more distance he had from his childhood, the stranger it became to him. Fifteen was the age when most people were taking their first contracts. He'd been leading terrorist raids that got people he knew and cared about killed. Watching his mother throw herself out an airlock without a vac suit. Helping his father commit genocide. Filip Inaros, he'd been then.

And he'd fallen from grace and renamed himself Nagata. He could remember when all the sins of his childhood had felt like glorious virtue, but he couldn't get the feeling itself back. And then his father died, and the systems of law and commerce remade themselves, and he was just another face among billions. No one knew that he'd left before that final battle. The records of his desertion had been lost with the Free Navy. He was dead, and so he was free to move on with his life. That was the theory anyway. The practice was more complex.

He'd been angry, and he hadn't understood why, not for years. Even saying it aloud—*My father was a terrible man, and I helped him do terrible things*—didn't carry the weight of it. He failed out of his first apprenticeship from having too many panic attacks. And the Filip Nagata name was a thin shield. If anyone looked too closely into him, they'd see past the paint. So he took other names, other pasts. Oskar Daksan. Tyr Saint. Angél Morella. Somehow, though, he always gravitated back to Filip Nagata. His past was like a wound that wouldn't heal. Or a poison.

Other people, they put together lives that followed from one thing to the next. Instead, he'd spent his life dodging justice that might not even have been looking for him except in his head. That had been enough to break him. At thirty-one years old, he had been Tyr Saint for a year and a half, an unofficial part of a group marriage on a Transport Union colony ship, and in line for the chief mechanic's place when she retired. For no reason he could fathom, he'd woken up one morning with an abyss of fear opening under him. He'd murdered billions. He'd seen his own friends die. They, whoever "they" were, would come for him. He'd dropped his identity at the next port and vanished, starting over again from nothing. Never letting anything build.

He took the work nobody wanted. Low pay, high risk, long contract. He signed onto the ships where people didn't talk about their pasts. He avoided any conversation about Marco Inaros or the Free Navy or the bombardment of Earth. And if anything ever went right for him, if he ever seemed in danger of gaining something he might be able to keep, he ran.

Once, he'd tried reading about the experience of child soldiers and the paths they'd taken through the trauma of their adult lives. Before he'd even finished the first half of the book, he'd descended into panic so deep that the ship medic had put him on antiseizure medications. He'd never tried again.

Forty years could go fast that way. They could feel like a thousand.

The *Rhymer* was the latest in a long string. Filip Nagata had never dropped out long enough to lose his place in the union, but his work history had long and inexplicable gaps in it. There were a million work histories like it. Mental illness. Addiction. Religious or romantic fixation. Families made and left behind. There were a thousand reasons for moth-eaten careers like his. And there were slots on a ship like the *Rhymer* for people like him. The ship's full name was *Thomas the Rhymer*, and it was owned by a trade organization out of Bara Gaon that catered to new and struggling colonies. For the first few years, he'd been on strictly as crew as they carried workgroups through half a dozen gates, dropped off people and equipment or picked them up again to transfer off to other ships, other systems. When Laconia rolled through, the *Rhymer* and her sister ships had gone from working for the Transport Union to the Association of Worlds without missing a beat. It didn't matter who was in power, they wanted someone doing the shit work that the *Rhymer* made possible.

Filip had been happy there, or at least not unhappy. He'd have kept his slot if two things hadn't happened. First, the XO had taken an inexplicable dislike to him. And second, the junior technician in Mose's workgroup had a heart attack three weeks after they'd passed through Jannah gate. The company needed a replacement, and pulling from the *Rhymer*'s crew meant not having to spend the extra transit time. Filip needed off the ship at least until the XO calmed down or shifted his paranoia elsewhere, and the gravity of the little planet was light enough that Filip could stand it without risking circulatory collapse.

It had seemed like a good choice for everyone, and him most of all.

He and Mose and Diecisiete had delivered a solar power array to Alpha and spent a few months setting it up, troubleshooting it, and helping the locals work out the bugs. Diecisiete had stayed in Alpha to track down a power drop, while Filip and Mose rode a supply shuttle to Beta and started the whole damn thing again. Filip could still picture the shuttle leaving them there, heading back to the relative metropolis of Alpha. There was a strange calm that had come from being at the edge of civilization. Or maybe just past the edge.

The news of the rest of the systems, the attack on Laconia, the loss of Medina Station, the eerie losses of consciousness that turned off minds everywhere, including Jannah, were all things that had happened during his time in Alpha. And the other, stranger thing. The timeless stretch when all minds had smeared together like oil paints being mixed by a gigantic, uncaring thumb had come when he and Mose had reached Beta. Filip's memory of that period was spotty and odd. Like he was trying to recall the details of a dream too big to fit in his finite skull.

When they'd all come back to themselves, the gate was dead. The *Rhymer* was still weeks from its scheduled passage back, and both the ring and the ship were now gone forever. Someone on the astronomy team had spotted the ring falling sunward into a new long elliptical orbit, shoved out of its former place at the edge of the solar system by some unknown, godlike hand. No one on Jannah knew why. They never would. All the problems they had now, all the ones they ever would have, they'd have to work through here.

Alone.

The sky darkened fast. A scattering of high, thin clouds clustered in the north took the red of the sunset and turned it into gold leaf. The monster's corpse had been dragged off the plaza, but the place it had lain was black with blood. A cloud of local insects buzzed around the stain and ignored the people.

The damage to the town was real, but the salvage and repair effort had left it less wounded. What had been the machine shop had become piles of salvage, squared away and ready for reuse. The new breach in the wall was shored up enough to keep the wildlife out. Just because the monsters could walk through it didn't mean that the other animals were welcome. The town kitchen had given out bowls of riced tofu and black sauce, some of the last of their supply, and Filip was finishing his now. The bowl was made of hardened and vacuum-formed vat-grown kelp. He'd eat that too, when the tofu was gone. Every calorie and vitamin was so precious now, that someone on the science team had suggested using calories as the basis of a new currency.

At the edge of the plaza, Jandro and his crew were sitting together, laughing and talking louder than anyone else. They had what looked like beer. Since Jandro had ridden the monster down, he'd been treated like a hero and a badass. Which, Filip figured, was fair enough. If the price of beer was hauling himself up on a monster's back while the bolt thrower on the fabrication lab shot holes in it, water was fine for him.

Mose wasn't there. Probably he was back at the room, making his point about union rules to himself. Kofi was, along with a handful of other Belters, sitting not far from Jandro and his crew. The scientists and administrators were sitting in clumps of their own, except for Nami Veh, who circulated from group to group to group, talking to everyone, touching shoulders and arms, smiling like she was running for office.

As the early-evening sun continued to drop, the golden clouds flared and faded to gray. Filip took a bite of the bowl. It was crisp and layered and salty, like baklava without the sweetness. He chewed and watched Nami Veh approach.

"Filip," she said. "Long day. Thank you for coming. I really appreciate everyone showing up."

"Mose won't be here. But he doesn't mean anything by it. He's just working some things through, you know?"

Her smile dimmed a little. "I think we all are."

"Yeah," Filip said.

She looked for some way to touch him without it seeming awkward, didn't find one, and moved on. The relief he felt as she walked away surprised him. He didn't dislike her. Her kindness seemed a little too consistent to be real, sure, but it wasn't her that bothered him. It was talking. That bothered him because he was trying to listen. And he was listening for the monsters, singing.

So far, they were silent.

At the front of the plaza, Leward hauled out a little metal bench and a holographic projector. From where Filip sat, he could see the science lead's lips moving. Practicing. There were probably four hundred people in the plaza. Almost everyone. Filip shifted. His leg was falling asleep.

Leward stepped up awkwardly, holding his palms out to ask for quiet. Or to demand it.

"Everybody?" he said, and while it was inflected like a question, it wasn't one. "Everybody? Thank you all for coming here tonight. I know we've all been through a lot, and I wanted to start by saying how much I appreciate everything all of you have done."

The sunset was dimming fast. It was hard to make out the expressions of people across the plaza, but Filip thought he saw Nami Veh shake her head just a little.

"We've learned a lot. We know a lot more than we did before, and it's really going to help." He nodded as he spoke. Someone to

Filip's right muttered something. Someone else laughed. Leward's smile widened. "Beta's site was selected based on a slate of criteria. Water availability. Shelter from major weather patterns. So on."

He took out his hand terminal, tapped it, and the projector came to life. A topographical map of the valley sprang into slightly fuzzy existence, with a red ball the size of a fist where the town was. Filip leaned forward, considering the shape of the hills.

"All the reasons this is an attractive site for us?" Leward said. He was getting his rhythm. He sounded like a university lecturer. "They also make it attractive for the locals. We knew that. Bio-sample diversity was a plus for us. But we didn't know about the size of some of the local fauna, or that we were setting down roots pretty much exactly in its migratory path."

One of the communications team stood up, raising her hand. "So the monsters aren't attacking us? We're just...in their way?"

"Turns out we built our houses in their hallway. But that makes a solution pretty straightforward." Leward flexed his wide hands and tapped his hand terminal again. The red ball that was Beta was joined by a green one halfway up a nearby slope. "One of the tertiary sites that we didn't pick is close enough that we can relocate even without the shuttle."

Filip felt himself sink. He glanced around at the town. The structures for more than four hundred people to work and live. The recyclers, the reactor, the power grid. It was all designed to travel in the hold of a colony ship: easy to take apart, easy to put together. *Easy* meaning *maybe not impossible*. He thought of the conduit that he and Mose had put in place, the wire and vacuum channeling they'd laid down. Relocation would go faster if the whole town was focused on the task, but the prospect left him weary all the same.

It wasn't until someone else interrupted that he noticed that Leward had kept talking. Jandro was standing in the middle of the holographic display, gesturing between the two versions of

Beta. The real and the imagined. Filip had missed whatever the start of his comment had been.

"I mean that's got to be half a klick up, yeah?"

"That's true," Leward said, "but the carts were all built with a full g in mind. They're pretty robust for this kind of short-distance travel, and there are game trails that the local animals have made that we can appropriate."

Jandro looked around at the crowd. The stars had come out above them to compete with the worklights and the backscatter of the display. Jandro shook his head slowly, crossed his arms. "This is a bad plan, boss."

"We've run the numbers," Leward said. "The whole move won't take more than five days, start to finish." That sounded optimistic to Filip, and probably to many of the others sitting under the stars. He'd probably picked a low number to make the whole thing sound feasible. But it was so overly optimistic that it made everything else Leward had said seem a little more suspect.

Nami Veh stepped up to the bench, smiling and holding out her hand to Leward like she was doing him a favor by helping him down. He hesitated for a moment, then let her take his place.

"Can you share more of what you're thinking, Alejandro?" Nami Veh said. "This is a big decision, and we don't have a lot of time to make it. Anyone who has thoughts about this, it's important that we hear from you. That's what this meeting is for."

When Jandro spoke, his voice had less of a buzz in it. "Here's the thing. We're talking about taking down everything. All of it. And then putting it back up. Every time we do that, we risk breaking something. It's just wear and tear, yeah? And that's if these big fuckers don't come while we're in the middle of the shift. Look at how much it would take to move, and instead we put that work into making what we already have a harder target. Dig some trenches. Put some spikes in 'em. Get that slug thrower tested out better. Get the chem lab to cook us up some gunpowder. Some bombs, maybe. These big fuckers bleed. They die. We can teach them not to fuck with us."

"Fortification is less effort at first, but it's also a commitment to permanent upkeep," Leward said. "Relocation, we do once and then we can get back to our routine."

"Unless there's something at the new site we don't know about like we didn't here."

"These are interesting questions," Nami Veh said.

Jon Lee, one of the recycler techs, stood up, and Nami pointed to him. "What about water availability? We chose this spot for reasons. What would we be giving up if we went?"

"I can speak to that," a younger woman in a research team jacket said. "The tertiary site is on a creek that feeds down into the valley. We'd be seeing a reduction in overall flow compared to the river, but it's still more than we need in the near term."

"Even with the recyclers?"

"Recyclers, hydroponics, cooling. Even some secondary energy production for when the reactor runs out of fuel pellets. The new site's enough for all of it."

Filip listened and watched but didn't take a turn standing up. He'd spent a lot of his life trying not to get noticed, and there were more than enough opinions to go around.

About half of it, it seemed to him, was really about the monsters and their migration paths. The rest was about fear. Fear of the monsters. Fear of what had happened with the gate and what it meant for them. Fear of losing what little they still had left. Filip understood, because he felt it too.

It was close to midnight when Nami Veh called a halt to the proceedings, told everyone to go get some sleep and think about what they'd heard. They'd take a vote in the morning. Filip joined the line at the latrine, then went back to his cot without changing clothes. Mose was watching something on his hand terminal that had a man in a bright red suit getting into a floridly choreographed gun battle in what was supposed to be Ceres Station but looked more like a cave network on Callisto. It occurred to Filip that the entertainment feeds saved on the local system were the only ones they'd ever have. Unless the data went corrupt. Then they wouldn't have the man in the red suit either.

"You went to the meeting," Mose said coolly as Filip curled under his blanket.

"I did."

"I told you not to."

"I know you did."

"You went anyway."

"Yeah."

Filip waited to see where Mose took it from here. He didn't think he'd push the issue, but times were odd. Things came out sideways sometimes. He almost thought the other man had gone back to his feed or turned over to try to sleep when he spoke. "I'm not going to bullshit you, Nagata. I'm going to have to report that. If I don't and the union finds out, that's my balls in a sling."

"Okay."

"Okay," Mose echoed. And then, "I can maybe make it better if you report in, though. Like you were there to keep an eye on these assholes. What happened?"

"Everyone debated about whether to move the town out of the way or dig in and try fighting the monsters off. The science teams like moving. The technical staff lean toward punching it out. There's going to be a vote at breakfast."

"Shit," Mose said. "Well, I guess we'll see what the plan is tomorrow."

Filip rolled onto his back, looking up at the featureless gray of the ceiling. He thought of Leward's map, and the crowd sitting close to Jandro. The black mark where the monster's blood stained the earth. He remembered his mother saying *The only right you have with anyone in this life is the right to walk away.* He thought about his father's need to frame everything as an epic struggle between himself and the universe. He pictured Nami Veh's calm, sweet voice, and Jandro's angry growl, and knew which way the vote would go.

"Stay and fight has some good points, but it doesn't have the votes. We're going to move the town."

"You sure about that?"

"I am," Filip said.

When morning came, he was right. And he wasn't.

After the vote, Leward and six of the civil engineering and administrative workgroups, Nami Veh among them, headed out to review the new site and the paths they could use to reach it. The rest of the town got to work. Filip and Mose, Beta's only local experts on the power grid, took two hours isolating lines and preparing the pocket reactor for shutdown. When they'd gone as far as they could, Mose went to help with the medical bay equipment and Filip headed over to where half a dozen of the long-timers were breaking down the food production units.

It was a simple enough setup. In the depth of space, a ship's galley could use water and energy to cultivate textured fungus that, with the right compounds and spices, the system could use to mimic a wide range of foods, some with better fidelity than others. In Beta, they had fifty separate meter-long cylinder units mounted in steel racks. The power regulation on them could be tricky. The capacitor design was kind of shitty, and more than one untrained person had died from misunderstanding the caution warnings on the little red box, so Filip took that part of the job himself.

If half of the cylinders went down, the town would still have enough to eat. The fabrication lab could probably keep these in replacement spare parts for six years. It sounded like a long time, until Filip started thinking about what they'd need in year seven. Then it seemed very soon.

The person overseeing the breakdown was named Jackson. Thin as a Belter, but with a Laconian accent. They were a contractor just like him and Mose, but with a different company. Jackson's plan was to break down half the units, install them at the new site, and then come back for the rest.

"If we can get a pinche cart to carry them on," they said with a scowl. "Can someone go find a cart?"

One of the others, a younger man named Cameron, jogged off looking for Jandro and his maintenance crew. Filip shifted the power couples off the unit he'd been working on, but before he could start on the next, Jackson put a hand on his shoulder and shook their head. They had wide lips and a narrow nose that Filip might have found attractive in other circumstances. The barely restrained annoyance Jackson gave off any time they looked at him reassured him his interest was irrelevant anyway.

"No point if we can't get them on carts," Jackson said. "You can strap one of these fuckers on your back okay, but you better really fucking want it."

Filip chuckled and went to clean his hands. All around the settlement, people were at work breaking down what they had. He'd only been there a couple months. There had been people living in Beta for much longer than him. Still, it felt a little like seeing an old ship getting scrapped. There was a loss to it.

He found Mose sitting outside the medical bay. One of the walls had been unhitched and the guts of the bay left open to the breeze. Filip shrugged his question.

"Need some tie-downs," Mose said. "I get the feeling people weren't expecting to take the place down and haul it halfway up a mountain."

"We'll figure it out," Filip said.

"Diecisiete's going to laugh about this when she gets here," Mose said. "Those fuckers at Alpha better get their radio back up, or when the shuttle comes, they're going to piss themselves. Whole place just..." Mose whistled between his teeth and swept one flat hand like he was erasing the town.

Filip sat. The ground was a little damp. It smelled like potting soil and citrus and the ever-present note of toilet cleanser.

Mose chuckled to himself. "Yeah, Diecisiete's gonna laugh." And then, softly, "When we're done here, I'm taking us back to

Alpha. Whole team. That's an established colony. This penny-ante bullshit? It's no way to live. Alpha's better."

Filip nodded. There was a pleading tone in Mose's voice. He recognized it. It was the same sound people had when a ship went unexpectedly dark. The universe wasn't kind. There were millions of things that could go wrong. Every now and then, a ship hit a micro-meteor or had some cascade failure they couldn't catch in time. Every now and then, a colony or station got surprised by an accident. Sometimes, apparently, ring gates went dead. Whole civilizations, billions of people wide, pared down to a few hundred between one day and the next. Look at it that way, and Mose wasn't having a psychological breakdown. He was just thinking things through out loud. Catching up to a universe that had changed faster than he could and didn't give a fuck if anyone kept up or not.

"She'll laugh," Filip agreed. Down near the food pods, Cameron was back and talking animatedly to Jackson. Filip couldn't tell what he was saying, but he kept pointing north and shaking his head. Filip scratched his neck even though it didn't itch.

"Hey," he said. "I'll be right back."

"Whatever," Mose replied. "Where the fuck am I going to go?"

Filip went toward the north end of the settlement. Three other teams were busy breaking down structures and piling up supplies. Beta was packing to move, but no one was moving yet. Even where crates and spools were ready to load, they weren't loaded. The protective wall was broken in two places now where the monsters had lumbered through it. Filip walked slowly, looking for whatever Jackson and Cameron had been talking about. He heard it before he saw it: voices raised outside the wall. It wasn't anger or laughter, but loud all the same. The shouts of people coordinating with each other. Work voices. Filip lifted himself over a low spot in the broken wall.

The carts were there. Past the wall, he could hear their motors whirring and straining, and the whine made him wonder what they'd do when the bearings wore out. For now, they all seemed fine, lumbering along or parked. Great loads of dark soil were heaped up in two of them. The yellow metal was streaked with mud. The workers that crewed them were streaked with mud too. They carried shovels. And from one end of the town almost halfway to the other, a deep gouge ran through the earth, three meters wide and a meter deep, the displaced earth piled in a berm between the hole and the town wall. The smell of fresh-turned soil was thick and weirdly astringent.

Filip strolled toward the workers, his hands in his pockets. They were all maintenance and construction. Jandro's crews. One woman saw him and nodded sharply, as much a challenge as a greeting. Filip smiled and nodded back.

"Nagata."

Jandro, lumbering up beside him, was a mess. Mud caked his legs to the middle of his thighs and smeared his arms and chest. When he grinned, Filip noticed that one of his eyeteeth was chipped. He hadn't seen that before. He found himself very aware of the physical size of the man. The strength, the sense of ease, and a deep maleness that wasn't a threat unless it was.

"Jandro," Filip said. And when Jandro only grunted in reply, "Lot of work."

"Yeah. Figure about four passes. So about twice this wide and twice this deep. Build up the hill on the side. I figure we use the mud and some of that shit that looks like grass. Make bricks. Lace plating doesn't stop these fuckers, but make a hill steep enough, they'll get tired and go around, same as anyone."

Jandro shrugged like he was commenting on all he'd just said and leaned a little forward, waiting. Filip wasn't sure that he wanted to be the one who said the next thing, but he was the one who was there. "The plan was that we move the town, though, yeah?"

"That's a bad plan. Better that we do this."

They were quiet for a moment, looking out over the growing ditch. The maintenance crew working and shouting. Filip wondered what would happen if he made it into a confrontation.

He thought of Mose saying *We're subcontractors*. That wasn't exactly right, but he wasn't the one who'd called the town meeting or held the vote. Nobody had elected him to be in charge of anything.

Jandro shifted his weight again, stretched his shoulders. His smile was friendly enough, but it was friendly with an edge. Like milk that was just starting to go bad.

"Well," Filip said with a nod, then turned to amble back into town. A few others passed him, heading the other way. The news, getting out. He kept his eyes down as he walked. His jaw ached.

Mose and Kofi were at the medical bay, sitting on ceramic crates with their backs against one of the walls that hadn't been taken down. As Filip came close, Mose lifted his hands, asking a question without saying what it was.

"Mining, though," Kofi said, continuing the conversation they were already having. "There's a lot we can do as long as we've got power. The fuel pellets run out, and then what? No hydroponics. The yeast vats stop working."

"Kofi's decided we're all gonna die because he's out of cigarettes."

"It's not just that, it's everything. The guns are out of cartridges. Med center's out of bone density drugs. Security's down to half a dozen tasers. You think those big fuckers are going to give a shit about tasers? And the fabrication lab can't just print new parts out of nothing. The printers aren't magic. They need metal and industrial clay. Carbon. And even if we get everything where we don't starve to death...Shit, we're gonna need to make babies."

"Oh, for fuck's sake."

"No, serious! We don't have any kids here. Youngest person in Beta's probably twenty-something. We're all going to be dead of old age and no one to keep things going if we don't."

"Good thing there's no kids. You'd be scaring the shit out of them," Mose said, and spat like it was punctuation. "How about we don't start freaking out about our legacy until Alpha gets their radio working and we hear from that survey mission? Anyway, what we need now is some fucking carts. I'm not strapping this shit to my back and walking it halfway up a mountain. I don't care if we are under four tenths."

"Don't wait underwater," Filip said.

Mose scowled. "What's that mean?"

Filip shook his head and left it at that.

Over the next few hours, the town slowed to a halt. The teams that had been focused on taking the structures apart paused. The piles of supplies stopped getting bigger. Conversations were quiet and tense, people stood with their heads close together. The expectation of action, of business, of having the hours filled to the top with things that needed to be done and done fast gave way to a half-nauseating torpor. Outside the town, the maintenance crew shouted a little too much and laughed a little too loud.

The afternoon was slipping into early evening when Leward and the others came back. Filip watched from a distance, the same as everybody else, as Evelyn Albert and Nami Veh headed north past the wall. The tightness in Filip's chest made him feel like he was a child again, waiting for something bad to happen. He checked the power feed to the magnetic bolt thrower on top of the fabrication lab. It gave him something to do, and he couldn't bring himself to stay still.

He wasn't there when Leward and Jandro faced off, but he heard about it. Leward had shouted himself red in the face about how Jandro was defying the will of the town and breaking the plan. They'd lost a day because of him, and the carts had *better be* cleaned and ready to start the evacuation in the morning. According to Kofi, Jandro had listened and been calm while Leward poked him in the chest and yelled in his face. Then he'd said that Leward's plan was a bad plan, and that Jandro wasn't going to let the town do something that could get them all killed just to save Leward's feelings. Then he'd tousled the science lead's hair and walked away. Just like that. Like a big brother messing with his little sibling.

"You should have seen it," Kofi said, awe in his voice. "You should have been there."

"No," Filip said. His stomach felt like someone had punched it. "I'm fine here."

They were sitting on a bench with legs made from spools of optical wire and a seat of a local tree analog with veins of green and blue lacing through pale woodlike flesh. Filip, Kofi, and Mose. With their backs against the medical center wall, they could see the plaza. The dark stain had almost vanished, and Filip wondered idly what had happened to the blood. Around the town, other little groups were huddled together like they were. The uneasy sense of conflict was like smoke in the wind, an invisible maybe-threat that everyone felt and no one could see.

"Leward's an asshole," Mose said.

"Is," Kofi agreed. "But he's the boss asshole. Or used to be, I guess. Now, I don't know."

Filip knew how this would have gone before. There would have been a message sent out at the speed of light, tightbeam lasers hitting relays one after another out to the ring gate and back to an administrator at Emerling-Voss, then a conversation with the union rep, then authorization for the company to sanction Jandro and his team. Loss of pay. Loss of union benefits. A berth back out, maybe. Maybe on the *Rhymer*. Maybe on one like her. Part of Filip was still expecting it to play out that way. It wouldn't, though. Leward had made a plan, had gotten people to agree, and he'd failed. There was no corporation or union behind him. There was no process now. Just power.

"You're not eating," Mose said, and Filip realized the man had still been talking to him.

"Not that hungry."

"This is crap," Mose said, lifting his bowl. "Did we run out of sauce?"

"Yeah," Kofi said. "Plain is what we get from now on. Barrett over in the chemistry group is looking at what we can harvest from the local organisms that won't taste like shit or kill us. We'll have something in a few weeks, probably."

"I'm not eating alien shit," Mose said. "Are you crazy? None of this stuff's made with the same chemistry we are."

"There's some overlap. And salt's salt, no matter where you go. I'm just hoping we can find something that tastes like pepper. Or cumin."

"We'll get resupplied from Alpha when the radio comes back up," Mose said. "I can eat shit until then."

"If there's still an Alpha," Kofi said. "They've been down for a long time. And if they didn't eat all their stuff while we were eating ours. Not like they're getting resupplied." He lifted his bowl like he was displaying an exhibit. "This shit is all the shit there is."

Mose's cheeks darkened and his lips went thin. "You know what? Fuck you."

He stood up, shoulders high around his neck, and stalked off muttering. Kofi watched him leave with surprise in his eyes. "What's with him?"

"All of it, I guess," Filip said. "Our ship. Our team in Alpha. The gate. It's a lot, you know."

Kofi nodded. "I forget how new you two are around here. Beta was just supposed to be a stop for you."

"It was."

Kofi took another scoop of the yeast protein in his bowl and nodded toward Filip. "You should eat. It's not good, but none of this gets better by starving."

Filip made a scoop of his first and middle fingers. The mush was bland and viscous. His gut was too tight, but he swallowed it anyway, pleased not to gag. "What do you remember?"

"Que?"

"About the thing before the gate went away."

Kofi nodded. There was only one *thing* before the gate went away. "I don't know. It's hard to bring it back now. I was here working on...I think the water feed. And then, I was other people. Or no one. And I was huge. What about you?"

"It's like a dream, you know? How when it's over, you don't remember? Like whatever it was doesn't fit in your head. I was in this dream…"

"And you woke up in a fucking nightmare."

Filip laughed, and Kofi laughed with him. "Fuck, you know? It's just…Mose is weird. I get that. But I keep thinking the *Rhymer*'s coming. Or that Diecisiete's finishing up in Alpha and coming here. Or I'll go there. Or…Our next contract was in Tridevi system. Five-workgroup contract putting a power grid up for a city of half a million people. We were going to be hauling teams in and out for four years, and we were just doing the backbone. I keep thinking about how that'll be, like it was still going to happen. Half a million people. And now, there's four hundred."

"All those others are still out there."

"Are they? I don't know that. Maybe everyone else everywhere else got snuffed out like candles, and we're the only ones left. How would we know?"

"There's Alpha."

"Maybe."

"There's the survey team."

"You know what I mean."

"Yeah," Kofi said.

Across the plaza, Eric Tannhauser, a short blond man with skin so pale you could see the veins in his forehead, was talking to Mina Njoku. He was shaking his head and pointing an angry finger up in the tall woman's face. Nami Veh appeared at his side, and Tannhauser turned his wrath, whatever it was, on her. Filip tried to take another bite of his food but couldn't bring himself to do it.

"You think they'll call another vote?" he asked.

Kofi shrugged. "If they do, I'll bet you half a week's wages that Jandro wins it. You should have seen him. Leward spitting like a wet cat, and Jandro letting it all wash past him like it was nothing. Anyway, doesn't matter what the vote was. We're staying here. Holding our ground."

"Maybe we won't have to. Maybe those things already moved past us. Moved on."

"Or maybe they're growing wings and getting ready to breathe fire. Who knows on this planet?" Kofi took a last scoop of his meal, then held the empty bowl up like an exhibit. "I am going to get mighty fucking tired of this."

Mose didn't come back to the cots after dinner. Filip lay on his back, one arm behind his head like a pillow, and waited for sleep that wouldn't come. Every time he started to drift, some tiny noise would pour adrenaline into his bloodstream and snap him awake again. He wasn't even certain what he was anxious about. There were so many options.

When he didn't sleep, he thought about Jandro. He imagined the confrontation with Leward, building versions of it from Kofi's description. Putting himself into it. The knot in his stomach kept getting tighter. Jandro smiling his wide, sharp threat of a smile. The man was a hero. He'd ridden one of those monsters. He'd saved the town, maybe, when he'd steered it into the plaza and within range of the slug thrower. He didn't remember who'd said it, but when he'd been much younger, someone had told him that saving money for an economic collapse was a bad plan. Who knew what scrip would matter and what would just be a number in an account no one cared about? The things that would last were bullets and liquor, not cash. When the apocalypse came, bullets and liquor would be the only currency that mattered. They weren't wrong. Beta could have used a lot more of both.

But that half-remembered giver of wisdom wasn't talking about Beta. They'd been talking about the bombardment of Earth. They'd been talking about the billions of people Filip had killed. Filip and his father. He wondered if Mose was out somewhere in the town right now, finding whoever had been smart enough to set up a distilling pot. They'd be the richest person in Beta soon, whoever did that. Until someone else made some bullets and took it from them.

"Fuck," he said to the darkness, and hauled himself up. His

jumpsuit was filthy. He'd take it to the river tomorrow and let some of the dirt wash out of it, but tonight it was slick and sticky, and he felt dirty putting it on. Outside, the night sky was a riot of stars, and the astringent stink of the broken ground north of town was thicker. He didn't know why that was, and probably no one else did either. He stuck his hands in his pockets, put his head down, and walked.

If the monsters were coming tonight, they'd have started singing earlier. He'd be out north of the town with a torch in his hand. With Jandro and Leward and all the others. It was a fucked-up thing to feel nostalgic about. But at least they'd all still be on the same side.

Maybe, they would be. Maybe now it was different. He wondered, if Jandro went to risk his life for the town again, whether Leward would try to stop him the way he had last time. It was harder to picture.

The breeze was cool against his cheeks, and the light gravity wasn't enough to make his joints ache. Here and there in the town, lights glowed, and the local insects drawn by them made little humming clouds. He heard a few voices, but they weren't raised in anger. They were just people talking. Some of them laughing. A couple having some kind of sex, he was pretty sure. Human sounds. It was bigger than a ship, but not so much that he couldn't get back some of the feeling of walking decks. He could almost imagine that Beta was an old colony ship, burning through the long darkness. He could make sense of it that way. The planet was just a weirdly designed ship, spinning through the same vacuum he'd grown up in. The people of the town were crew and passengers, their fates locked together by the ship's recyclers and the thrust of the drive. The problems and dangers they faced might express differently. There weren't great, strange, smiling monsters lumbering through space. But there were micro-meteors and the unforgiving vacuum always trying to get in.

The mission was the same: Keep the food supply going. Keep the water drinkable. Don't boil in your own waste heat. Survive. That was always the job. Survive.

By the time he'd made it all the way back around, the knot in his stomach was looser. The fatigue of the day had come out from under the tension and fear. He could imagine sleep.

Mose was on his cot, snoring gently. Filip stripped down to his undershirt in the darkness and crawled into his own. Mose muttered something once but settled back down to sleep without making sense. Filip's body felt like it was growing heavier, the cot rising up from below like the ground had started a faster burn. Leward and Jandro, Nami Veh and smiling monsters were all still there, floating through his thoughts like echoes from another deck. He could ignore them. Let them go. When he closed his eyes, it felt comfortable to let them stay that way. Even the little pang of hunger wasn't enough to keep him awake.

Filip slept, and for the first time in more than a decade, he dreamed about his father.

"We found them."

"Who?" Jackson said.

"The big fuckers. The monsters," Cameron said. He was practically hopping up and down with excitement.

Jackson made eye contact with Filip in a way that meant *Can you keep the work going while I deal with this?* Filip wiped the sweat off his forehead and nodded in a way that meant he could.

Jackson stood with a grunt. The food production unit they'd started taking apart yesterday, they were putting back together today. The racks that had been emptied of cylinders were almost half full now, and half of the remounts had power. It was slower putting together than it had been taking apart. Filip felt like that was true for a lot of things.

"So what are you talking about?" Jackson asked.

"Muhammed Klein? Fat Muhammed, not the one with the bent nose? He put chemical sensors on the survey drones. The reason we couldn't track them before is that there's another species that follows them. Little bird-things that eat the grubs and stuff that the big fuckers churn up. It's like they're sweeping away the tracks. Only the tracks are outgassing trace ammonia where they dig down to hibernate or whatever. So we found them."

Filip took one of the capacitors, a flat red box a little larger than his hand, and triple-checked the charge status before he fit it into the base of a cylinder. His attention was on Cameron. The big bastards' tracks were giving off trace ammonia. Like a freshly scrubbed toilet. Filip realized they'd had an early-warning system all along.

Jackson spat on the ground. "Where are they?"

"Everywhere. North of here. South of here. All over the valley."

Filip and Jackson shared a look. "I can't finish it all, but I can get it to a good stopping place," Filip said. "I mean if you want to go see about working on the defenses."

"Better should," Jackson said.

"Yeah."

Jackson smoothed their hands on the fronts of their thighs like they were wiping the palms clean, then walked off with Cameron toward the science labs. Filip hoisted the next cylinder into place, steadying it with one hand while he fixed the bolts to hold it. It was a little unwieldy without another pair of hands to help, but it wasn't bad. At a full g, it would have been impossible.

All around the town, people were doing similar work. The false start at moving left everything half broken down. Or half put together. Depended on how you looked at it. The sky had taken on an almost emerald green. To the west, pure white clouds billowed up so high, they seemed like they'd reach orbit. Filip didn't like looking at them. He'd gotten to where living without the safety of a ship didn't panic him, but something about the cloud banks made the scale of planetary life harder to ignore. It was odd, the way that living in an emptiness infinitely vaster than the distance between him and even the tallest cloud could feel comfortable if there was a thin bubble of metal around him. Something about the perspective, probably. The universe was always vast, if he thought about it. The trick was not to see more of it than he could stand at any given moment. And picking the right part to look at.

He put the last bolt in place, checked that everything was stable, and grabbed up another capacitor. This one was still holding charge, so he set it to a safe-ground cycle and sat back for the minutes-long wait. He heard Leward before he saw him.

"Put that back. That isn't yours!"

Filip leaned forward to get a better look. They were coming from the east side of town, moving in the aisle between the buildings where months of habit had stripped away the plants and left packed dirt behind. Not dignified enough to call a street, but where one would be, given time. Two men in maintenance crew uniforms were pulling a handcart. It was a low thing, with wheels broader than they were deep, like a yellow steel pallet on rollers. The science lead was behind them, chin high, and lifting his knees with every step like he was marching. He looked angry, which Filip had seen before. But he also looked ridiculous, which was new. It wasn't him, not really. It was the grinning and snickering of the maintenance crew.

"You stop!" Leward shouted. "We have need of that! You can't just take it."

The taller of the maintenance crew pair leaned over and said something to the shorter one too quietly for Filip to hear. The shorter one chuckled. It wasn't a kind sound. Around the other buildings, a few people paused to look. Leward made a strangled sound and darted forward. He grabbed the back end of the cart and tried to yank it back. The cart bucked, and the two maintenance men stopped smiling. They let the cart's lead drop to the ground and turned. The smaller one put his arms out at his sides, widening him.

"What the fuck are you doing, coyo?" he asked, and Filip felt a little thrill of fear. He knew that tone. He knew what it meant, even if Leward didn't.

"This," Leward said, stabbing a finger at the handcart, "is the property of the bioscience lab. It is not construction equipment.

You can't just come in and take whatever you want whenever you want it!"

The taller one feigned sadness. When he spoke, his voice was a high, mocking singsong. "Ooh! It's not construction equipment! Oh no! So sad. So *angry*." Then he grinned and stepped forward, speaking in a regular, low voice. "It's what we say it is."

"Take it back now," Leward said, but he quavered. He was starting to understand what was going on.

"Or else what?" the shorter one said.

"What are you talking about?"

"I said, '*Or else what?*' What are you going to do when we don't, eh?"

Leward glanced around, saw the eyes on them. Filip felt his humiliation like they were passing through a resonance frequency. Like they were back in the dream together. Like it was his own. Leward stepped forward, reaching for the cart again, ready to take it back himself. The tall one put both hands on Leward's chest and shoved. In the light gravity, the fall took a few seconds, Leward's legs flailing as he went down. When he landed, it still knocked the breath out of him. The shorter one laughed and stepped forward, his hands in fists.

"Hey!" Filip shouted. One syllable, but hard. Sharp. It brought the two maintenance men around. *Well, fuck*, Filip thought as he stood up. It was too late to think about whether he wanted to be in this. He already was. And as he walked across toward the two men, he didn't actually regret it.

The taller one made a show of looking Filip up and down. "You a friend of this one's?"

"I don't know him," Filip said. "I'm just a subcontractor."

"So what are we talking about, subcontractor?"

Behind them, Leward was coming to his feet. There was finally some real fear in his eyes. Late, but better now than never. Filip considered the two men. They were younger than he was. They'd grown up in gravity wells, he could tell from their builds. In a fight, they'd kick his ass. The smart thing was to back down. He wasn't feeling smart.

All around them, work had stopped. The violence against Leward was shocking, maybe, but with everything going on, they had to expect it. The new guy standing up was unexpected. If he weren't doing it, he'd be keeping a weather eye on it too.

"Just want to know how you're going to be when I come take your tools without asking," Filip said. In the back of his mind, Mose said, *We're union.* It was ridiculous, but what else did he have? "Jandro's pissed at him, that's not my problem. I don't care who likes who. I'm just here getting the work done. But you need something, union has rules about how you get it. This isn't that."

"Union?" the short one said, tilting his head.

For a moment, Filip was sure the man was going to come for him. That there was about to be violence between them. He wasn't scared. He wanted it. He had a visceral memory of being a child, barely in his adolescence, leading a raid on Martian shipyards. Watching soldiers die, the enemy and his own. He remembered that joy. More than that, he felt it again, just a little. The short one must have seen something change in him because he looked confused for a moment and took a half step back.

"He's right, Alyn," Jackson said, appearing at his elbow. "You know better than this."

The taller one shrugged theatrically. Alyn, apparently. Filip really needed to start learning these names. "Whatever, Jacks."

"Whatever your whatever," Jackson said. "It's a worksite. Not a playground. Get the fuck back to work."

When the maintenance men turned back to the cart, Leward was gone. No one mentioned him. They just took the cart by the lead and pulled it off to the north. Filip watched them go.

"Well, you got balls, Nagata," Jackson said when they were out of earshot. "I'll give you that. You want some free advice, don't get in the middle of this."

"I hear you," Filip said. "Cover for me for a little, okay?"

"You've got something to do?"

"Yeah," he said. Then, "Don't let Cameron—"

"We'll wait for you on the power hookups. I'm not stupid," Jackson said. "Just…be careful."

He hadn't been in Nami Veh's office since he and Mose had arrived on the shuttle. They'd done their project intake there, affirming all the corporate boilerplate they always affirmed, getting their bunk assignments and the review of local legal policy. He hadn't paid much attention.

It was the same space. Just green and gray prefabricated walls with a little window and a light metal desk. All the small details he noticed now had probably been there before. The picture of a man with dark hair and a thin beard in a silver frame on her desk. The little vase with local flowers in the corner. The discreet silver cross on the wall. He hadn't picked Nami Veh as pious, but it didn't surprise him.

The woman herself was the same. He had an image in his mind of what she looked like, but as he talked, as he watched her for signs of how she was hearing him, she didn't really match the picture. He thought of her as professionally, blandly attractive, with the gentle eyes and hard smile of someone whose job it was to say things were all right even when they were not. But she actually had a much more expressive face, with a webwork of wrinkles at the corners of her mouth and eyes that seemed equally at ease with both sorrow and laughter. Her hair was auburn and touched with gray, but it had more warmth to it than he remembered. He suddenly found himself wanting her to like him.

"Sit," she said, gesturing to a rickety stool in front of her desk.

He did, and spread his hands in an old Belter gesture of passing on a task. "You're administration here. I don't know what needs to happen, but I'm not the one to do it."

He half expected her to say *What am I supposed to do?* And it would have been a good question. To her credit, she leaned forward, elbows on the desk, and pursed her lips.

"Did they hurt him?"

"I don't know," Filip said. "You'd have to ask him. They knocked him down."

"And Alejandro wasn't there."

"They were his people. There's a way people get sometimes, and if it sets in, you can't get it back. It's like..."

"Contempt," Nami Veh said, and her voice had none of its usual pleasantness. There was exhaustion in its place. And maybe a kind of mordant humor. "It's contempt."

"It's a problem. Somebody has to do something about it."

"And that somebody is me," she said ruefully. "Thank you, Filip. I may need your help again. But I hear you, and I will take this seriously."

"Is that going to be enough?"

She frowned her question.

"I mean," Filip said, "does Jandro still listen to you? You used to have pull, but you had the company behind you then. I had the union. We had... Now, is he going to listen?"

"We'll make it work," she said with enough conviction that he could almost convince himself she had answered the question.

"You don't understand what he is," Filip said, trying to keep the frustration out of his voice.

To his surprise, Nami Veh didn't brush him off. Whatever she was seeing on his face made her frown and settle back in her chair. "Tell me, Filip."

"Men like him—" he started, then stopped. "My father was like that. Strong. Certain. People loved him, and wanted him to love them. They wanted to have even a tiny piece of his confidence, if they could. It made them do terrible things so that he would notice them."

"Like what?" she asked.

Filip didn't answer. He suddenly found he couldn't meet her eyes. She nodded and smiled, then pointed at the cross hanging on the wall.

"My mother was a saint," she said. Filip couldn't tell if that was sarcastic or not. "When she died here a few years ago, I think a lot of the people at this colony were surprised that the sun didn't go out."

"Sorry I never met her."

"You say that now," Nami said with a laugh, "but having any-one care that much and try that hard to save you from yourself can be fucking exhausting."

"Do I get to pick? Because—"

"Look," Nami said. "I don't need to hear all the ways your father made life harder for you, and I'm not going to explain how living with Saint Anna broke a few things for me. We have no reason to compete, you and I. The only point is that our parents can lay burdens on us, all without meaning to, that we'll have to carry around for the rest of our lives and there's nothing we can do about that. But you and I still get to decide how we carry those burdens."

She reached across the table and took his hand. Hers was warm and dry. Her smile was both sad and comforting at the same time. It made Filip want to scream at her.

"That's all well and good, but this Jandro problem isn't going away," Filip said, and yanked his hand away, needing to break the shared intimacy of the moment and finding himself almost happy to see her smile disappear.

"I know," she replied.

Filip jumped up off the stool and bulled his way out the door, slamming his shoulder into the frame as he went. Once he was back out of her office and into the town, things felt different. He couldn't tell whether the others were watching him, seeing the junior power tech in a new light, or if he only imagined that they were. His chest felt tight, like he was just a little too far from his ship with not enough air in his tank. He found himself bouncing up with each step, pushing too hard against the ground.

Mose was waiting for him by the food cylinders, arms crossed. The clouds in the west had come much closer, and the smell of rain was in the air. Jackson and Cameron weren't there, but their toolboxes were, like Mose had asked them to leave for a little bit. Filip put his back against the steel racks and shoved his hands in his pockets.

"The fuck are you doing, Nagata?" Mose's voice was soft, but there was a buzz in it. Anger. Maybe fear. "Are you getting us involved with these people's problems? Is that what you're up to?"

"We're going to be here. At least for a while, maybe for longer than that. Their problems don't stop with them."

"That's bullshit."

"It isn't," Filip said, and Mose took a step back like the words had been a slap. "I know men like Jandro. People are scared and they're hurting, yeah? And some big man comes along, and he seems confident. He looks sure of himself. All the things that are eating at your heart, they aren't eating at his. And yeah, he gets a team. Everyone falls in line behind him, and bad things happen. The worst things."

Mose cleared his throat, but Filip kept going before he could speak. "We're at the start of something here. We can't let it slide. If it's okay now, it's okay forever. You plug a leak when it's small, or you suffer when it's big."

"And you think you're going to fix it?"

"I saw a problem, I took it to administration. But these are not the kind of people who know what to do with this."

"What kind are they, then?" Mose asked.

"Gentle," Filip said. "They're gentle."

"So maybe it's not your job to find the toughest son of a bitch in this place and make an enemy out of him?"

"That's how it works, Mose. No one stands up, and no one stands up."

"I don't know what the fuck personal shit you're working through," Mose said. "I don't much care. I'm telling you as your supervisor we stay out of local drama. We're putting in time here until we can get back to Alpha and Diecisiete."

"And when I tell you to fuck off? When I tell you your rules don't matter anymore, and I do what I want, then what, Mose? When I'm like Jandro, what do you do? How do you stop me? Because we both know there's no union behind you anymore, and don't fucking mistake me for one of the gentle locals, coyo."

Mose's scowl dug lines into his cheeks.

"You're out of line, Nagata," he said, pointing a finger at the center of Filip's chest. "You're way the fuck out of line."

But then he walked away. What else was he going to do? Filip turned back to the cylinders. He needed to get them mounted and the walls back up before the storm came.

Filip walked through the downpour. The rain floated down, moving slowly enough in the fractional gravity for the drops to join each other and become a heavy, unforgiving mist punctuated by water balloons. Somewhere behind the cloud cover, the sun was setting. He could only tell by the world growing slowly darker around him.

The plaza wasn't empty. Several of the buildings had walls that swung up and out, making awnings where people could sit with the weather without being in it. Little pools of light, like pictures of street carts on planets Filip had never stood on. He passed the place where the monster had been unmade. Even close up, there was no sign of the blood, but he thought he caught a whiff of something strange, like overheated iron.

By the time he reached the administration building, he was soaked. He knocked on the door, and Nami Veh called him in. In the hours since he'd been there, the metal desk had been taken out and more chairs had been brought in and put in a little circle. It looked like a very small support group meeting.

Leward sat with his back to the door. Jandro, across from him, sat with his legs spread and his arms out, resting on the backs of chairs to either side of him. Nami Veh was the professional version of herself again, smiling and gracious. Filip was surprised to realize he was sorry to see that.

"Hey, Nagata," Jandro said.

"Oye, Jandro," Filip said, then turned his attention to Nami Veh. "You wanted me?"

"And thank you for being here," she said, motioning him into one of the empty chairs. "There were some questions about what exactly happened today? I was hoping you could help us with what you remember."

Jandro turned a half smile to the space about halfway between Filip and Leward. Leward crossed his arms tight across his chest.

"Okay," Filip said. "Sure."

He told the story again. Leward, the cart, the push. Jackson coming to back him up. He didn't look at any of them while he spoke, but he didn't put his head down either. Just focused on a spot on the wall. When he was done he shrugged.

"Well," Nami Veh said. "That doesn't sound exactly like your experience, Leward?"

"It was an assault," the science lead said. "Does it matter how many times they hit me? I was *assaulted*."

"Maybe you were, maybe you weren't," Jandro said. "You ever been in a fight, Nagata?"

Filip felt a surge of something cold. The hum of the rain seemed to go a little quieter. "What are you asking?"

"You ever been in a fight? Ever seen someone really trying to hurt someone else? You see a few guys messing around. It gets a little physical. If you haven't been in a real fight, maybe you get mixed up. See some things that aren't really there."

Filip said, "I've been in a fight," but he said it softly, and Nami Veh was talking over him. "Regardless, it's clear a line was crossed. And we all know who was involved, so the question for us now is how we move forward. Jandro, these were your crew. They need to make this right."

Filip saw the amusement in Jandro's eyes and the corner of his mouth. "Yeah, okay. I'll make sure they come apologize. You bet."

"And return the cart," Nami Veh said.

"If he needs the cart, he can have the cart."

"And Leward?" Nami Veh said, turning to the science lead. "I think it would be good for the community if you and some of the science team could help with building the defenses."

The cold feeling in Filip's chest shifted, swelled. "What about the vote?" Three sets of eyes turned to him. "We voted to move the town. What about the vote?"

"Yes," Leward said, waving a wide hand toward Filip. "Exactly."

"We're past that now," Nami Veh said. "Leward? For the community."

"We'll give you the easy jobs," Jandro said. "It'll be fun."

Leward pressed his lips together, thin and bloodless, then stood without speaking and walked out. Jandro chuckled as the door closed. He'd won, and he knew it. Filip knew it too.

"You need to keep your crew in line," Nami Veh said, somewhere to Filip's right. It seemed like she was a long distance away. "We desperately need everyone in the community working together."

"They will," Jandro said. "As long as we're working on the right things, they absolutely will."

Filip rose, made himself nod to both of them, and walked out. There was something wrong with him, but he didn't know what it was. It felt a little like nausea, a little like vertigo. It wasn't either one, though. This was something different, but though he didn't have a name for it, he knew it. He had felt this before.

In the plaza, fewer of the buildings had their awnings up. The rain was getting colder and lighter. Filip listened for the song of the monsters behind it, but the white noise of the rain hid anything. If there was trouble coming, someone would have to warn them. And if there wasn't trouble tonight, there would be soon. Every night of peace made the next night more dangerous. Filip thought that felt familiar too.

At the room, Mose was sitting on his cot. His jumpsuit was unzipped to the navel, and his eyes were red and bleary. Even without the smell of alcohol, Filip would have known he'd been drinking. Mose had finally found the still that some enterprising future rich person had set up. Filip sat on his own cot, his back against the wall. His clothes were wet, and rain seeped out of his hair and down his neck. He let it.

"You need a towel, Nagata," Mose said, and then when Filip didn't answer, he pulled a steel bottle out of his pocket. He reached over and put it on the cot by Filip's leg. "One of the biochemists is making gin. I mean, it's not real gin, but it's close. It's good. No tonic water, but it's got the right…" He shook his head, searching for a word he couldn't find. "It's good."

"Thanks," Filip said, but it sounded like someone else's voice.

Mose laced his fingers together, then looked down at his hands like they were a puzzle he was trying to solve. "I, ah, wanted to apologize. I keep it to myself, you know, but this whole thing? It's been…It's made me less good than I used to be, you know? Less professional."

"It's okay."

"Denial. That's what they call it, yeah? It's just…I can't…" He started to wheeze. It could have been laughing or crying or just the man starting to hyperventilate. Filip waited, watching Mose's knuckles go pale where he was squeezing the blood out of them. After a while, the wheezing stopped. "Nobody's coming. No ships. No shuttle. The gate's gone. Whatever happened at Alpha, they'd have gotten the radio back up by now. We're all there is. This shit-ass little squat of a town is all that's left."

It was true. It had been true for a while. It was still strange to hear Mose say it out loud, admitting the secret they both already knew. "It makes things more important," Filip said.

"If I think about it too much, I can't do anything. I'm taking off a fastening clip, and I think what if I break it? We're never going to get another one. What if I fuck it up, and it turns out we need it later on? For this to work, a million things have to go right. For it to fall apart, just one of them has to go wrong."

Filip opened the bottle and took a drink. It wasn't anything like gin, but it wasn't bad. He wiped the mouth of the bottle on his sleeve and passed it over. Mose unlaced his hands to take it. Where he'd squeezed, there were marks in his skin. Filip watched his throat work as he drank. He wasn't leaving much.

"One thing," Mose said. "One thing wrong, and we all die. We're all there is, and we all die. And no one even knows."

"Could be worse."

Mose's gaze swam slowly upward until it found him. Outside, the rain had stopped and some of the local insects had started calling to each other with a sound like an air compressor going bad. Filip looked at him, and when he spoke, he felt like the cold in him was talking.

"What scares me, Mose. It isn't fucking it up and dying. What if we fuck up, but we don't die. What if we fuck it all up and live? We're at the end of something, sure. Maybe we're at the beginning of something too. Maybe we make a whole new world. A whole new planet like Earth used to be. Hundreds of generations. Billions of people, that all start here. And we fuck it up for them."

"I don't understand."

"What if we just go on like people always have? The same bullshit. Give the same bullies and liars power like we did before. Cut all the same corners. Put up with all the same hypocrites. Make everything here into more of the shit that got us here. That seems worse. For me? That's worse."

"I just want you to know I'm sorry for how I've been," Mose said. He seemed confused by this new direction the conversation had taken. "I try to hold it together, but it all comes out anyway."

"Everyone's like that right now," Filip said. "I'm sorry for how I've been too. For all of it."

Mose started crying then. Not the wheezing, but slow, racking sobs. Filip went and sat beside him, one wet arm around Mose's shoulder, and held him while the sorrow crested and fell away. He let Mose slide down onto the cot, pulled a blanket over the man, who was asleep almost at once. Filip rescued the liquor, put the lid back on, and left it on his own pillow like it was sleeping there.

He made one stop on the way to the maintenance barracks.

Jandro and his crew had two of the little prefab buildings near the western edge of the town. One was standard sleeping quarters with bunks stacked four high against the walls. The other had a few utility cots like Mose and Filip used and a lot of supply lockers. A little group was gathered outside the sleeping quarters in the light of half a dozen torches. Filip recognized the long metal shafts with spikes at the ends from the last time the monsters had come. The mat of oily moss burning at the end seemed like an improvement over what they'd had, though. The flame, longer-lived.

He counted ten people, most of them men, in the flickering light. Jandro, in a chair leaning back on two legs, had his back against the building. He was at the center like a king or a celebrity. Filip stepped into the light, and the conversation and laughter went silent. One of the people was Kofi, but the Belter didn't acknowledge him. Fair enough. Filip didn't know what he would have done if their places had been switched. Or, really, he did, and so he could forgive Kofi for his youth and cowardice. He also saw the two men who'd taken Leward's cart. Their expressions were blank as snakes.

Jandro tilted his head. "Nagata," he said. "You're up past your bedtime, yeah?"

One of the others snickered, but Filip plastered on a little grin, like he was in on the joke. Like the little humiliations were shit he was willing to eat. He knew how to do that. One of the few useful lessons his father had taught him. "Guess so. I had some things on my mind."

"Yeah?" Jandro let his chair come slowly down. Filip averted his eyes, showing his submission. The coldness in his chest was rage.

"About what she was saying," Filip said. "Nami Veh. Community, you know? The good of the community."

"I remember that part," Jandro said.

"I thought I should clear the air."

"You didn't do anything to cross me. Maybe Alyn and Yuri got a little annoyed, though."

Filip looked over to the two from the cart. "Hey, Alyn. Hey, Yuri."

"Hey, subcontractor," Yuri said. Jandro made a disapproving grunt, and Yuri looked away. Chastised.

"I just wanted to say—" Filip meant to apologize, but the coldness in his chest wouldn't let him say those words. The lie of it was too big to fit through his throat. "I just wanted things to be right. I want things to be better than they were."

The two glanced at Jandro, unconsciously seeking for what reaction they should have. It was all so familiar, Filip could almost see Cyn and Karal, Wings and Chuchu and Andrew. The ghosts of the war he'd fought and lost. The dead he'd turned his back to.

"Your boss tell you to come?" Jandro asked.

"Mose? No. I'm just…following my conscience. And, hey. Something else. Something to help, yeah?"

He took the little red box out of his pocket, sliding off the protective rubber sleeve as he did it. He held it out, careful not to touch the case and the power port at the same time. It was wider than his hand, but just by a little. Jandro frowned and pointed his chin at it. *What is that?*

"You remember how the slug thrower failed that night the monsters came? They had to cycle the capacitor."

"That's true," Kofi said. "I heard him talking about it."

"Okay," Jandro said, but there was interest in his eyes. Now they were talking about when he'd been a hero. They were talking about killing. He liked that.

Filip held up the box with a grin. "This, though? *This* is a capacitor from the yeast tanks. Take a look."

He tossed it gently, like he was passing a beer to a friend. Jandro caught it, turned it over. "I don't know about this power grid shit, Nagata."

"Open the back plate," Filip said. "You'll see what I'm talking about."

Jandro steadied the box on his knee and pressed against the back plate with a palm. "What does this thing do?"

The discharge was as loud as a gunshot and as bright as lightning. Jandro drifted to the side, collapsing slowly in the light gravity. His thigh had popped open like an overcooked sausage, and his eyes were empty.

"It kills monsters," Filip said, but no one was listening to him. They were all shouting and jumping to their feet. Filip turned and walked into the darkness. Jandro's crew were so shocked and confused that he made it almost thirty meters before they caught him.

The improvised cell was dark and cold. He lay on the bare floor. Everything hurt. He was pretty sure that at least one of his ribs was cracked, and his left wrist was swollen badly. Whatever other damage the beating left, he'd have to wait to discover. For now, it was enough just to hurt.

He knew that day came from a little fault in a weld about a third of the way up the wall. A pinpoint of light that started fainter than the smallest star and grew slowly brighter until a tiny shaft of light pushed through. A pale dot no bigger than his thumbnail began its slow track across the floor. He watched it. The air tasted like dust.

Outside, there were occasionally voices. He recognized a few. Kofi. Mose. Nami Veh shouting in a way that wasn't her usual style at all. He wondered if she was holding off a lynch mob. It seemed plausible.

The shaft of light came closer and closer to the wall, and then faded as the sun came overhead. Filip became aware of a growing thirst, but there wasn't any water, so he tried to sleep instead. The most he could manage was a half doze disturbed by his aches. He'd lost all sense of time when the sound of a bolt being thrown roused him.

The door opened, light spilling in around Nami Veh's silhouette. Filip tried to sit up, but his back had stiffened so badly that it took three tries.

The administration woman sat across from him. In the spill light from the next room, she looked both tired and resolute. An angel, come to pass sentence or grant absolution.

"Well, it took eighteen hours," she said after a long pause, "but we lost him. You are now officially a murderer. What? Is that funny?"

"I don't mean to laugh," Filip said. "There's some context that makes that...I didn't mean to laugh."

"What were you thinking?" The angel was gone. The façade of gentleness and kindness and professionalism was gone. It was almost like meeting her for the first time. The weary anger in the words was like the back of his own head, given voice.

"That it had to be done," he said. "And no one else was going to do it."

"It didn't have to be done."

"I've known men like Jandro. He showed you what he was. He showed all of us what he was. And he got away with it. There's no law with a man like that. The town voted, but he was more important. And you bent. You failed. You let him do what he wanted, and there was never going to be a path back for him. When someone like that wins? He'd never stop pushing."

"And so you decided that deserved a death sentence? You're seeing the irony here, right?"

"There's a difference," Filip said. "You're going to punish me. I'm going to answer for what I did."

Nami Veh shook her head. "Oh, Jesus."

"This is how it's supposed to go. You do something wrong, and you're supposed to pay for it. Supposed to suffer. That's what keeps the Jandros from taking over everything all the time, just because they can."

"So that's your plan? Make yourself a martyr on the cross of the law? Am I supposed to thank you for that?"

"You don't understand what men like him are."

"Of course I do," Nami Veh said. "Alejandro was a bully and narcissist. And more than a little sadistic too. And he was physically strong. And he was charismatic. And he was brave. He'd throw himself into danger without a second thought. Leward? He's one of the smartest people I've ever met, and he's a snob. He can't ask you to pass him a fork without rubbing someone the wrong way. Adiyah will work double shifts and never complain for the rest of her life if you let her, and she'll stir up romantic drama every chance she gets. Moses is a solid worker and emotional wreck. Merton is one of the most lovely, empathetic, kind-hearted people I've ever met, and he's already got a still set up in the biolab because he's an alcoholic. We're all like this. This is what humans are."

"Jandro was different," Filip said.

"And you," she said, leaning over and putting her hand on his ankle. "You are a very experienced technician, with an irreplaceable wealth of knowledge and experience. You're also desperate to be punished for something, and I don't know why."

"He would have taken over. You'd have lost control to him."

"Maybe."

"If I have to die for saving you from that, it's all right."

Nami Veh's laugh was low and earthy and rueful. "Oh no. As my sainted mother would say, no easy way out for you. I've failed at a lot of things, but I won't be the one who gives this settlement capital punishment. Can you walk?"

"Can I get some water first?"

Walking hurt badly when they started. His whole body was stiff, and when they got outside, he could see the bruising more clearly. All the others in the town lined the little almost-streets. Mose was there, looking dour. A clot of people in maintenance crew uniforms, standing together with hatred in their eyes. They didn't follow, but they watched him pass. Filip tried to keep his back straight, to carry himself with some dignity. Nami Veh walked with him, ready to steady him if he needed it. He made a point not to.

Yesterday's rain had left the ground slick with mud, but the sky was wide and clear now. Cloudless. Filip found himself expecting the crowd to do something. Cheer him or vent their rage. They stayed quiet, watching him go.

By the time they reached the wall at the edge of town, his joints were starting to loosen. His wrist had angry, shooting pains when he tried to turn it, but that was the worst. He didn't complain. Nami Veh walked out the access gate between the plates that had once been the hull of a ship.

The southern valley rolled out before them. It was easy, staying inside the town, to forget how wide the valley was, and how full. Things that looked not entirely unlike trees rose along the banks of the river below them. A pack of long-legged animals somewhere between deer and huge spiders made their way to the west, following some trail he couldn't see or else making their own. A pile of equipment lay in a circle where human boots had crushed the ground cover. Nami Veh walked to it and stopped.

"That's an emergency blanket you can use for shelter," she said, pointing to a tiny silver packet. "That's a micro-solar array. It'll power the yeast cylinder there. Moses said that the carbon fixation chamber is only good for about two years at best, so you should find something local that provides sugar if you can. Hopefully the device can make it nontoxic for you, but be careful eating new things."

"Exile?"

"It's the compromise I could make," she said. "The maintenance team wanted you dead, no surprise. I think Leward would have given you a public stipend and housing. It was between incarcerating you in town or... This takes up fewer resources. It's the best I could do."

"It's probably more than I deserve."

"If anyone from maintenance sees you here in the next five years, they'll probably just kill you, and I won't be able to stop them. I think most of the rest of the town wouldn't, but there are some that would, and you won't know which is which. After that, if you're still alive, you can come petition to be let back in. If we've survived that long."

He looked at the equipment. It was heavy, but it wasn't unworkable. There were straps on the yeast cylinder, and a mounting for the solar array. He could wear it on his back and trickle power into the food supply, as long as he didn't walk in the shade. A bottle for water, and if he stayed by the river, he'd have enough. Unless some native microorganism slipped through the filter and decided he was a good environment to set up shop in his bloodstream.

"All right," he said. "Thank you. I'll go."

"Do you have a plan?"

"No," he said. "Maybe I'll try for Alpha. It's a long way, but there could be supplies there. Maybe people. If not, I can find out what happened to them."

"If you figure out why the choice you made to kill Jandro was wrong, come back to us, okay? I'll do everything I can to make sure you have a place here."

Filip picked up the emergency blanket. It was very light, and small enough to put in a pocket. "Thank you, but I don't deserve any mercy."

"Of course you don't. That's why they call it mercy. If you deserve it, they call it justice." She put her hand on his arm the way she always did with people. It seemed more genuine to him now. "I'm going to do everything I can to keep these people alive. I'm going to compromise and bend and be adulterated and impure and imperfect. And there's going to be a time not too long from now that I'm really going to wish you were here. Just like I'm really going to wish Alejandro was."

Filip was silent, but she nodded like he'd spoken.

"That's the mystery, and that was your clue," she said, stepping back. "Try to figure it out."

He watched her as she walked back to the wall, and then past it. Once she had vanished, he got to the task of loading up his kit. It was like a little, scattered ship. The blanket was his environmental controls. The cylinder was his food recycler. The planet, vast around him, was his air recycler. There was a logic to survival that didn't change, no matter which vastness he was traveling through. And the regret was there too, the way it always had been.

He walked south, keeping far enough from the river that the land wasn't damp. It was less than an hour before the valley curved and Emerling-Voss Permanent Settlement Beta passed out of sight. The sun tracked to the west, reddening, and Filip found what seemed like a good spot to make the first camp of his new life. The yeast output was less than he'd hoped, but the carbon fixation chamber looked clean. He found a creek and filtered the water before he drank it.

At sunset, the stars came out. The great smear of the galactic disk. The universe that humankind had once been heir to and then lost, now just a light show and a promise. Or a hope.

In the distance, the monsters began to sing.

The Sins of Our Fathers
Author's Note

What's the opposite of an overture? A summation, maybe? Naomi never knew that her son didn't die along with the rest of the Free Navy, and people kept expecting him to show back up in the novels, but that wasn't the story we were telling with him. The real end to his story with Naomi was a passage in *Babylon's Ashes*. Naomi is talking to Holden about the video pieces he'd made hoping to humanize the Belt for the inner planets and, in answer, the inner planets for the Belt. This passage goes like this:

> "I don't know that those mattered," Jim said. "Did they do anything?"
>
> "You don't get to know that," Naomi said. "They did or they didn't. You didn't put them out so that someone

would send you a message about how important and influential you are. You tried to change some minds. Inspire some actions. Even if it didn't work, it was a good thing to try. And maybe it did. Maybe those saved someone, and if they did, that's more important than making sure you get to know about it."

On one hand, she's talking about just what she seems to be talking about. On the other, she's also us, talking about Filip and the end of their relationship. She saved him from his father, and that she never knew is less important than the fact that she did. Doing the right thing has to be enough in itself. It's not about getting the pat on the head.

But this is the end. The last story in the cycle, and there he was. One loose thread. And you're not Naomi, so maybe you wanted to know how it turned out for him. And also, of course, for Nami Volovodov, who we last saw heading out to the colonies with her moms.

And the end isn't really entirely the end. One of the central arguments we've made with these stories is that, when you look at history, you see the same kind of people doing the same stupid, selfish, delusional, gorgeous, kind, astonishing things that we do today. And we'll keep doing the same, as long as the species survives. Technical knowledge advances. The organism stays the same.

And, to quote Nami from her younger days: We're spending our whole lives together, so we need to be really gentle.

Acknowledgments

We often talk about collaboration, but we haven't specifically mentioned the collaboration between writer and editor. Without a few people on the editorial side, this volume would not exist. John Joseph Adams asked for the very first Expanse short story we ever wrote, so everything in here is sort of his fault. And Jonathan Strahan bought another one of these stories and encouraged us to keep making them. Along the way, all our editors at Orbit have contributed to one or more of the stories in this volume. A heartfelt thanks to them all.

And as always, this series and all that came with it would not exist without the hard work and dedication of Danny Baror and Heather Baror-Shapiro, and the whole brilliant crew at Orbit, including (but by no means limited to) Bradley Englert (and his predecessors Darren Nash, DongWon Song, Will Hinton, and Tom Bouman), Tim Holman, Anne Clarke, Ellen Wright, Alex

Lencicki, and Lauren Panepinto. Special thanks are also due Carrie Vaughn for her services as a beta reader, and the gang from Sakeriver: Tom, Sake Mike, Non-Sake Mike, Jim-me, Porter, Scott, Raja, Jeff, Mark, Dan, Joe, and Erik Slaine, who got the ball rolling.

And, as always, none of this would have happened without the support and company of Jayné, Kat, and Scarlet. We lost time with them in order to do this, and it wouldn't have been worth doing if they hadn't been there for us when we got back.